Dear Target Guest,

A few weeks ago I was giving a talk in the splendid medieval town of Durham, in Britain. The subject was the wonders of the Italian Renaissance and using fiction to bring it alive. As I finished, a young American woman came up to me and said—these were her actual words—"Would you mind if I gave you a hug?" How could anyone refuse such a request? As we broke apart she started to tell me how, as a lost and unhappy fifteen-year-old in Montana, she had read *The Birth of Venus*, and the story of Alessandra Cecchi, with her passion, her awkwardness, and her determination, had helped light a fire in her, not just for her own life, but also for the richness of history. Now, ten years later, she is a student at Durham's prestigious university, studying for her master's in history. The fire is clearly still burning.

That autumn meeting in a chilly lecture theater was as powerful for me as it was for her, not least because it brought back memories of my own lost teenage years, when I found solace and inspiration in a novel about the past (in my case, Margaret Irwin's *Young Bess*), which started a fascination with history that has never left me. But her words also took me back to the moment when the idea for *The Birth of Venus* was born.

I was on holiday with my daughters (ages ten and thirteen at the time) in Florence, standing in the middle of a piazza, waxing loud and lyrical about the city we were about to explore and about the power of that cultural revolution known as the Renaissance. Not surprisingly, their reaction was a mix of "Boooriiing" and "Oh! Do we have to, Mum?" (An impassioned mother is a serious embarrassment for any child.) But it was only as we set off in search of the first masterpiece, with the promise of the best ice cream in the city to follow, that I started to appreciate the scale of the job I had in front of me. Not because the city wasn't dripping in beauty, but because every work of art we were going to see had been commissioned, designed, built, or painted by a man. Looking at my vivacious, obstreperous daughters, I found myself thinking: So, did women have a Renaissance? What would it have been like to be talented, young, and female in this city five hundred years ago? It was in that moment that the idea of Alessandra Cecchi was born.

Of course I was not the only one to have asked that question, and the deeper I dug into libraries, archives, and the work of dozens of historians, the richer and more nuanced the picture became. But that driving force of young Alessandra never left me, and—in a way I will probably never quite understand—viewing 1490s Florence through the lens of her passionate, frustrated curiosity seems to have enabled me to capture some of the volcanic cultural and political energy of one of the most brutal, yet most beautiful, moments of European history.

Not long after I got back from that encounter in Durham I opened an email from my publishers telling me that Target had picked *The Birth of Venus*, the first book ever in its book club, to be the first of its celebratory legacy titles, and that it was going to be reissued. The news started me doing some math. Ten years ago was just when that young woman in Montana had been reading *The Birth of Venus*, almost certainly through the Target club, as its aim had been to bring new books to new audiences. What perfect serendipity.

As I sit writing this, I am already looking forward to the moment, a decade from now, when I find myself—by then almost as old as the history I write about!—meeting more vibrant young women (and men; it *has* happened) who, through fiction, have found a way into that most glorious secret garden of all: the past.

Sincerely,

Sarah Dunant

PRAISE FOR *THE BIRTH OF VENUS*

"Smart and engaging... The pages are filled not only with long and lovingly detailed descriptions of works of art, but also with vivid images.... Dunant does a remarkable job evoking Florence."

—*The Washington Post Book World*

"Sarah Dunant credibly re-creates a past world and evokes a young woman's passion for its art.... The plot is full of twists.... The biggest surprise for a reader of latter-day fiction is a heroine who, rather than wither under the constraints of patriarchal society, manages to thrive within it."

—*The Wall Street Journal*

"A broad mural bursting with color, passion and intrigue... Sixteenth-century Florence may have been long ago and far away, but as Dunant adroitly demonstrates, its political and religious turmoil... have eerie parallels in the present day."

—*People*

"Alessandra Cecchi begins her recollections in the year 1492.... Her city is the center of an explosion of artistic enterprise.... Historically, this is a fascinating moment.... Alessandra narrates her life story with an eye to the telling detail."

—*The New York Times Book Review*

"Dunant has given us a story of sacrifice and betrayal, set during Florence's captivity under the fanatic Savonarola. She writes like a painter, and thinks like a philosopher: juxtapositioning the humane against the animal, hope against fanaticism, creativity against destruction."

—Amanda Foreman, author of *Georgiana: Duchess of Devonshire*

"A beautiful serpent of a novel, seductive and dangerous... full of wise guile, the most brilliant novel yet from a writer of powerful historical imagination and wicked literary gifts."

—Simon Schama

THE BIRTH OF VENUS

RANDOM HOUSE

NEW YORK

THE
BIRTH
OF
VENUS

A Novel

SARAH
DUNANT

2015 Target Book Club Edition

Published in the United States by Random House, an imprint and division of Random House LLC, a Penguin Random House Company, New York.

RANDOM HOUSE and the HOUSE colophon are registered trademarks of Random House LLC. RANDOM HOUSE READER'S CIRCLE & Design is a registered trademark of Random House LLC.

Originally published in hardcover in the United Kingdom by Little, Brown, an imprint of the Little, Brown Book Group in 2003, and in hardcover and in slightly different form in trade paperback in the United States by Random House, an imprint and division of Random House LLC in 2004.

Library of Congress Cataloging-in-Publication Data

Dunant, Sarah.
The birth of Venus: a novel / Sarah Dunant.
p.   cm.
Includes bibliographical references.
ISBN 978-0-8041-7635-4
1. Florence (Italy)—History—1421–1737—Fiction.
2. Savanarola, Girolamo, 1452–1498—Fiction. 3. Arranged marriage—Fiction. 4. Women painters—Fiction.
5. Married women—Fiction. 6. Teenage girls—Fiction.
7. Painters—Fiction.   I. Title

PR6054.U45756B58   2004
823'.914—dc21   2003046932

Printed in the United States of America on acid-free paper

www.randomhousereaderscircle.com

Book design by J. K. Lambert

TO

MY MOTHER,

ESTELLE,

AND

MY DAUGHTERS,

ZOE

AND

GEORGIA

N O ONE HAD SEEN HER NAKED UNTIL HER DEATH. IT WAS A rule of the order that the Sisters should not look on human flesh, neither their own nor anyone else's. A considerable amount of thought had gone into the drafting of this observance. Under the billowing folds of their habits each nun wore a long cotton shift, a garment they kept on always, even when they washed, so that it acted as a screen and partial drying cloth as well as a night shift. This shift they changed once a month (more in summer when the stagnant Tuscan air bathed them in sweat), and there were careful instructions as to correct procedure: how they should keep their eyes firmly fixed on the crucifix above their bed as they disrobed. If any did let their gaze stray downward, the sin was a matter for the confessional and therefore not for history.

There was a rumor that when Sister Lucrezia had first entered cloisters she had brought with her a certain vanity along with her vocation (her dowry to the church, it was said, included a lavishly decorated marriage chest filled with books and paintings fit for the attentions of the Sumptuary Police). But that was a time when the sisterhood had been prone to such accidents of abuse and luxury, and since the reforming of the convent the rules were stricter. None of the present inhabitants could remember that far back, save for the Reverend Mother, who had become a bride of Christ around the same time as Lucrezia but had long since turned her back on such worldliness. As for Sister Lucrezia herself, she never spoke of her past. In fact, in the last few years she had spoken very little at all. That she was pious there was no doubt. And as her bones stooped and glued together with age, so her piety and modesty had fused. In some ways it was natural. Even if she had been tempted to vanity, what surface could she have found to reflect herself in? The cloisters held no mirrors, the windows no glass; even the fishpond in the gardens had been designed with a fountain at its center sending out an endless shower of rain to prevent any possible narcissism in the water's surface. Of course, even in the purest of orders some infringement is inevitable, and there had been times when a few of the more sophisticated novitiates had been caught surreptitiously considering their own portrait miniaturized in the pupils of their elders' eyes. But more often than not this faded as the image of Our Lord loomed larger.

Sister Lucrezia seemed not to have looked directly at anyone for some years. Instead, she had spent increasing time at devotion in her cell, her eyes filming over with age and the love of God. As she became more ill, so she had been absolved from manual labor, and while others were working she could be found sitting in the gardens or in the herb plot, which she had sometimes tended. The week before her death she had been spotted there by the young novitiate Sister Carmilla, who had been alarmed by coming upon the elderly nun sitting not on the bench but stretched out upon the bare ground, her body under the habit distended by the tumor's growth, her headdress cast aside, and her face tilted up to the late-afternoon rays of the sun. Such an undressing was a flagrant breach of regulations, but by then the disease had eaten so deep inside, and her pain was so evident, that the Reverend Mother could not bring herself to discipline her. Later, after the authorities had left and the body had finally been taken away, Carmilla would spread the echoing gossip of that encounter along the refectory table, telling how the nun's unruly hair, freed from her wimple, had blazed out like a gray halo around her head, and how her face had been lit up with happiness—only the smile playing upon her lips had been one more of triumph than of beatification.

That last week of her life, as the pain flowed in ever deeper waves, dragging her away in its undertow, the corridor outside her cell began to smell of death: a fetid aroma as if her flesh were already rotting away. The tumor had grown so tender by then that she could no longer sit up for its size. They brought in church physicians, even a doctor from Florence (flesh could be exposed in the cause of the alleviation of suffering), but she had refused them all and shared her agony with no one.

The lump remained not only covered but hidden away. The summer was upon them by then, and the convent simmered by day and sweltered by night, but still she lay under the blanket fully clothed. No one knew how long the disease had been eating into her flesh. The volume of their habit was designed to hide any hint of shape or female curve. Five years before, in the greatest scandal to hit the nunnery since the bad old days, a fourteen-year-old novitiate from Siena had concealed nine months of growth so successfully that she was only found out when the kitchen Sister came upon traces of the afterbirth in the corner of the wine cellar and, fearing it was the entrails of some half-devoured animal, nosed around till she found the tiny bloated body weighted down by a bag of flour in a vat of Communion wine. Of the girl herself there was no sign.

When questioned after she had first fainted during Matins a month earlier, Sister Lucrezia confessed that the lump in her left breast had been there for some time, its malignant energy pulsing against her skin like a small volcano. But right from the start she was adamant that there was nothing to be done for it. After a meeting with the Reverend Mother, which caused the latter to be late for Vespers, the matter was not referred to again. Death was, after all, a temporary staging post in a longer journey and one that in a house of God was as much to be welcomed as feared.

In the last hours she grew crazy with pain and fever. The strongest herb concoctions gave her no release. Where she had first borne her suffering with fortitude, now she could be heard howling through the night like an animal, a desperate sound that frightened awake the younger nuns in the cells close by. Along with the howling came sporadic words, yelled out in staccato bursts or whispered like lines from a frenzied prayer: Latin, Greek, and Tuscan all stuck together in a thick verbal glue.

She was finally taken by God one morning as another suffocating day was dawning. The priest who had come to deliver last rites had gone and she was alone with one of the nursing Sisters, who recounted how, at the moment the soul departed, Lucrezia's face had miraculously changed, the lines etched by pain melting away, leaving the skin smooth, almost translucent: an echo of the tender young nun who had first arrived at the convent doors some thirty years before.

The death was formally announced at Matins. Because of the heat (the temperature over the last few days had turned the butter liquid in the kitchen), it was thought necessary to inter the corpse with the day. It was the custom of the convent to give any departing Sister the dignity of a clean body as well as a spotless soul and to clothe her in a bright new habit: a wedding dress for the bride finally united with the Godhead husband. This ritual was performed by Sister Magdalena, who ran the pharmacy and administered the medicines (given special dispensation to witness flesh for this most divine of occasions) aided by a younger nun, Sister Maria, who would eventually take on the job herself. Together they would wash and dress the body, then lay it out in the chapel, where it would remain for a day while the rest of the convent paid its respects. But on this occasion their services were not required. Sister Lucrezia, it appeared, had made a special request before she died, asking that her body be left untouched, in the habit in which she had served her Lord for all these years. It was, to say the least, unusual—there was talk among the sisters as to whether it might qualify as disobedience—but the Reverend Mother had sanctioned it and it would have gone unquestioned had it not been for the news, also received that morning, of an outbreak of plague in the village nearby.

The convent was separated from the hamlet of Loro Ciufenna by a strenuous horse ride, though the pestilence matched the speed of any horse's hooves. The first sign had apparently appeared three days before when a young farmer's boy had been stricken with a fever and an eruption of boils that had spread all over his body, growing immediately full of pus and fury. He died two days later, by which time his younger brother and the baker nearby were infected. It was learned that the boy had been at the convent the week before, delivering flour and vegetables. The suggestion was that the Devil's illness had come from there and the Sister who had now died was its carrier. While the Reverend Mother had no time for ignorant gossip and could work out the logistics of infection rates as fast as the next woman, it was her business to keep on good terms with the village, on which the convent depended for many things, and it was an undeniable fact that Sister Lucrezia had died in fever as well as pain. If she had been a carrier, it was a widely held belief that the pestilence would live on in her clothes, only to escape through the earth later and contaminate again. Having lost eight Sisters to an outbreak some years before, the Reverend Mother, mindful not only of her establishment's reputation but also her duty to her flock, regretfully overrode Lucrezia's last wish and ordered that her garments be removed and burned and the corpse disinfected before being consigned immediately to holy ground.

Sister Lucrezia's body lay stretched out on the bed. The delay meant that the rigidity of death was already infecting her limbs. The two Sisters worked nervously fast, wearing pruning gloves from the orchard, the only protection the convent could offer against contamination. They unpinned the wimple and pulled the material away from the neck. The dead nun's hair was flat with sweat though her face remained peachy serene, a reminder of that afternoon in the herb garden. They unfastened the habit at the shoulders and cut it open down the front, peeling away the material, crusted with the sweat of suffering. They were especially careful of the area around the tumor, where the habit and then the shift underneath had fused fast to the skin. During her illness this part of her body had been so painful that Sisters passing in the cloister had stepped away from her in case they might brush against her and cause her to cry out. It was strange to find her so silent now as they ungraciously tugged at the half-soaked mound of cloth and flesh, the size of a small melon and pulpy to the touch. It didn't come easily. In the end Sister Magdalena, who had a strength in her bony fingers belying her years, gave a hefty yank and the material ripped off the body, bringing with it what felt like the whole growth itself.

The old nun let out a gasp as the mass of fat tissue came away in her gloved hand. Looking back down at the body, her sense of wonder increased. Where the tumor had been the surface of the skin was healed: no wound, no blood or pus, no discharge at all. Sister Lucrezia's fatal malignancy had left her body unscathed. This was surely a miracle. And had it not been for the unbearable stench in the small cell they might have fallen to their knees there and then in recognition of God's magnanimity. But the fact was that the smell seemed to grow stronger with the tumor released. So it was that they turned their attention to the malignancy itself.

Freed from the body, it sat in the Sister's hand, a sack of distended growth, oozing black liquid out of one side like rotting offal, as if the good Sister's very insides had somehow leaked their way out of her body into the tumor. Magdalena stifled a low moan. The sack slipped through her fingers and splatted onto the stones beneath, bursting apart on impact and sending a shower of liquid and gore across the floor. Inside the mess they could make out shapes now: black coils and gobbets of blood, intestines, organs—offal indeed. Though it was many years since the older nun had worked in the kitchen, she had seen enough dissected carcasses to know the difference between human and animal remains.

The reverend Sister Lucrezia had died not, it seemed, from a tumor but from a self-applied bladder of pig's entrails.

The revelation would have been shocking enough without what came next. It was Maria who spotted it: the silver streak on the corpse's skin curving up over the edge of the shoulder, growing gradually thicker over the collarbone until it disappeared underneath what remained of the undershirt. This time the younger nun took the initiative, cutting open the shift and tearing it in a single rip until the corpse was revealed naked on the bed.

At first they could make no sense of what was before their eyes. Lucrezia's exposed flesh was white, like the marble skin of the Madonna in the side altar of the chapel. The body was old, the stomach and breasts slackened by age, but with little excess fat, which meant it had retained enough of its figure for the image to have kept its proportions. As the painted line thickened at the collarbone it gained more shape and substance, rounding itself out from a tail into the body of a snake, silver-green in color and so lifelike that by the time it had slid its way over the breast you might swear you could see the movement of its muscles rippling under the skin. Close to the right nipple it curled itself around the darkened areola before sliding down the breast and plunging across the stomach. Then, as it dipped toward her groin, the shape flattened out in readiness for the serpent's head.

Age had defoliated what would once have been a thicket of pubic hair into a straggle of wiry curls, so that what would have been invisible save to the most insistent seeker was now made plain. At the point where the snake's body became its head, instead of the reptilian skull was the softer, rounder shape of a man's face: the head thrown back, the eyes closed as if in rapture, and the tongue, snake-long still, darting out from his mouth downward toward the opening of Sister Lucrezia's sex.

THE TESTAMENT OF
SISTER LUCREZIA

Santa Vitella's Convent,
Loro Ciufenna,
August 1528

PART I

One

LOOKING BACK NOW, I SEE IT MORE AS AN ACT OF PRIDE than kindness that my father brought the young painter back with him from the North that spring. The chapel in our palazzo had recently been completed, and for some months he had been searching for the right pair of hands to execute the altar frescoes. It wasn't as if Florence didn't have artists enough of her own. The city was filled with the smell of paint and the scratch of ink on the contracts. There were times when you couldn't walk the streets for fear of falling into some pit or mire left by constant building. Anyone and everyone who had the money was eager to celebrate God and the Republic by creating opportunities for art. What I hear described even now as a golden age was then simply the fashion of the day. But I was young then and, like so many others, dazzled by the feast.

The churches were the best. God was in the very plaster smeared across the walls in readiness for the frescoes: stories of the Gospels made flesh for anyone with eyes to see. And those who looked saw something else as well. Our Lord may have lived and died in Galilee, but his life was re-created in the city of Florence. The Angel Gabriel brought God's message to Mary under the arches of a Brunelleschian loggia, the Three Kings led processions through the Tuscan countryside, and Christ's miracles unfolded within our city walls, the sinners and the sick in Florentine dress and the crowds of witnesses dotted with public faces: a host of thick-chinned, big-nosed dignitaries staring down from the frescoes onto their real-life counterparts in the front pews.

I was almost ten years old when Domenico Ghirlandaio completed his frescoes for the Tornabuoni family in the central chapel of Santa Maria Novella. I remember it well, because my mother told me to. "You should remember this moment, Alessandra," she said. "These paintings will bring great glory to our city." And all those who saw them thought that they would.

My father's fortune was rising out of the steam of the dyeing vats in the back streets of Santa Croce then. The smell of cochineal still brings back memories of him coming home from the warehouse, the dust of crushed insects from foreign places embedded deep in his clothes. By the time the painter came to live with us in 1492—I remember the date because Lorenzo de' Medici died that spring—the Florentine appetite for flamboyant cloth had made us rich. Our newly completed palazzo was in the east of the city, between the great Cathedral of Santa Maria del Fiore and the church of Sant' Ambrogio. It rose four stories high around two inner courtyards, with its own small walled garden and space for my father's business on the ground floor. Our coat of arms adorned the outside walls, and while my mother's good taste curbed much of the exuberance that attends new money, we all knew it was only a matter of time before we too would be sitting for our own Gospel portraits, albeit private ones.

The night the painter arrived is sharp as an etching in my memory. It is winter, and the stone balustrades have a coating of frost as my sister and I collide on the stairs in our night shifts, hanging over the edge to watch the horses arrive in the main courtyard. It's late and the house has been asleep, but my father's homecoming is reason for celebration, not simply for his safe return but because, amid the panniers of samples, there is always special cloth for the family. Plautilla is already beside herself with anticipation, but then she is betrothed and thinking only of her dowry. My brothers, on the other hand, are noticeable by their absence. For all our family's good name and fine cloth, Tomaso and Luca live more like feral cats than citizens, sleeping by day and hunting by night. Our house slave Erila, the font of all gossip, says they are the reason that good women should never be seen in the streets after dark. Nevertheless, when my father finds they are gone there will be trouble.

But not yet. For now we are all caught in the wonder of the moment. Firebrands light the air as the grooms calm the horses, their snorting breath steaming into the freezing air. Father is already dismounted, his face streaked with grime, a smile as round as a cupola as he waves upward to us and then turns to my mother as she comes down the stairs to greet him, her red velvet robe tied fast across her chest and her hair free and flowing down her back like a golden river. There is noise and light and the sweet sense of safety everywhere, but not shared by everyone. Astride the last horse sits a lanky young man, his cape wrapped like a bolt of cloth around him, the cold and travel fatigue tipping him dangerously forward in the saddle.

I remember as the groom approached him to take the reins he awoke with a start, his hands clutching them back as if fearful of attack, and my father had to go to him to calm him. I was too full of my own self then to realize how strange it must have been for him. I had not heard yet how different the North was, how the damp and the watery sun changed everything, from the light in the air to the light in one's soul. Of course I did not know he was a painter then. For me he was just another servant. But my father treated him with care right from the beginning: speaking to him in quiet tones, seeing him off his horse, and picking out a separate room off the back courtyard as his living quarters.

Later, as my father unpacks the Flemish tapestry for my

mother and snaps open the bolts of milk-white embroidered lawn for us ("The women of Rennes go blind early in the service of my daughters' beauty"), he tells us how he found him, an orphan brought up in a monastery on the edge of the northern sea where the water threatens the land. How his talent with a pen overwhelmed any sense of religious vocation, so the monks had apprenticed him to a master, and when he returned, in gratitude, he painted not simply his own cell but the cells of all the other monks. These paintings so impressed my father that he decided then and there to offer him the job of glorifying our chapel. Though I should add that while he knew his cloth my father was no great connoisseur of art, and I suspect his decision was as much dictated by money, for he always had a good eye for a bargain. As for the painter? Well, as my father put it, there were no more cells for him to paint, and the fame of Florence as the new Rome or Athens of our age would no doubt have spurred him on to see it for himself.

And so it was that the painter came to live at our house.

Next morning we went to Santissima Annunziata to give thanks for my father's safe homecoming. The church is next to the Ospedale degli Innocenti, the foundling hospital where young women place their bastard babies on the wheel for the nuns to care for. As we pass I imagine the cries of the infants as the wheel in the wall turns inward forever, but my father says we are a city of great charity and there are places in the wild North where you find babies amid the rubbish or floating like flotsam down the river.

We sit together in the central pews. Above our heads hang great model ships donated by those who have survived shipwrecks. My father was in one once, though he was not rich enough at the time to command a memorial in church, and on this last voyage he suffered only common seasickness. He and my mother sit ramrod straight and you can feel their minds on God's munificence. We children are less holy. Plautilla is still flighty with the thought of her gifts, while Tomaso and Luca look like they would prefer to be in bed, though my father's disapproval keeps them alert.

When we return, the house smells of feast-day food—the sweetness of roast meat and spiced gravies curling down the stairs from the upper kitchen to the courtyard below. We eat as afternoon fades into evening. First we thank God; then we stuff ourselves: boiled capon, roast pheasant, trout, and fresh pastas followed by saffron pudding and egg custards with burned sugar coating. Everyone is on their best behavior. Even Luca holds his fork properly, though you can see his fingers itch to pick up the bread and trawl it through the sauce.

Already I am beside myself with excitement at the thought of our new houseguest. Flemish painters are much admired in Florence for their precision and their sweet spirituality. "So he will paint us all, Father? We will have to sit for him, yes?"

"Indeed. That is partly why he is come. I am trusting he will make us a glorious memento of your sister's wedding."

"In which case he'll paint me first!" Plautilla is so pleased that she spits milk pudding on the tablecloth. "Then Tomaso as eldest, then Luca, and then Alessandra. Goodness, Alessandra, you will be grown even taller by then."

Luca looks up from his plate and grins with his mouth full as if this is the wittiest joke he has ever heard. But I am fresh from church and filled with God's charity to all my family. "Still. He had better not take too long. I heard that one of the daughters-in-law of the Tornabuoni family was dead from childbirth by the time Ghirlandaio unveiled her in the fresco."

"No fear of that with you. You'd have to get a husband first." Next to me Tomaso's insult is so mumbled only I can hear it.

"What is that you say, Tomaso?" My mother's voice is quiet but sharp.

He puts on his most cherubic expression. "I said, 'I have a dreadful thirst.' Pass the wine flagon, dear sister."

"Of course, brother." I pick it up, but as it moves toward him it slips out of my hands and the falling liquid splatters his new tunic.

"Ah, Mama!" he explodes. "She did that on purpose!"

"I did not!"

"She—"

"Children, children. Our father is tired and you are both too loud."

The word *children* does its work on Tomaso and he falls sullenly silent. In the space that follows, the sound of Luca's open-mouth chewing becomes enormous. My mother stirs impatiently in her seat. Our manners tax her profoundly. Just as in the city's menagerie the lion tamer uses a whip to control behavior, my mother has perfected the Look. She uses it now on Luca, though he is so engrossed in the pleasure of his food that today it takes a kick under the table from me to gain his attention. We are her life's work, her children, and there is still so much more to be done with us.

"Still," I say, when it feels as if we may talk again, "I cannot wait to meet him. Oh, he must be most grateful to you, Father, for bringing him here. As we all are. It will be our honor and duty as a Christian family to care for him and make him feel at home in our great city."

My father frowns and exchanges a quick glance with my mother. He has been away a long time and has no doubt forgotten how much his younger daughter must say whatever comes into her mind. "I think he is quite capable of caring for himself, Alessandra," he says firmly.

I read the warning, but there is too much at stake to stop me now. I take a breath. "I have heard it said that Lorenzo the Magnificent thinks so much of the artist Botticelli that he has him eat at his table."

There is a small glittering silence. This time the Look stills me. I drop my eyes and concentrate on my plate again. Next to me I feel Tomaso's smirk of triumph.

Yet it is true enough. Sandro Botticelli does sit at the table of Lorenzo de' Medici. And the sculptor Donatello used to walk the city in a scarlet robe given in honor of his contribution to the

Republic by Cosimo, Lorenzo's grandfather. My mother has often told me how as a young girl she would see him, saluted by all, people making way for him—though that might have been as much to do with his bad temper as his talent. But the sad fact is that though Florence is rife with painters I have never met one. While our family is not as strict as some, the chances of an unmarried daughter finding herself in the company of men of any description, let alone artisans, are severely limited. Of course that has not stopped me from meeting them in my mind. Everyone knows there are places in the city where workshops of art exist. The great Lorenzo himself has founded such a one and filled its rooms and gardens with sculpture and paintings from his own classical collection. I imagine a building full of light, the smell of colors like a simmering stew, the space as endless as the artists' imaginations.

My own drawings up till now have been silverpoint, laboriously scratched into boxwood, or black chalk on paper when I can find it. Most I have destroyed as unworthy and the best are hidden well away (it was made clear to me early that my sister's cross-stitching would gain more praise than any of my sketches). So I have no idea whether I can paint or not. I am like Icarus without wings. But the desire to fly was very strong in me. I think I was always looking for a Daedalus.

I WAS YOUNG THEN, AS YOU KNOW: FOURTEEN THAT SAME SPRING. The most preliminary study of mathematics would reveal that I had been conceived in the heat of the summer, an inauspicious time for the beginning of a child. During her pregnancy, when the city was in turmoil during the Pazzi conspiracy, there was a rumor that my mother had seen bloodlust and violence in the streets. I once overheard a servant suggesting that my willfulness might be the result of that transgression. Or it could have been the wet nurse they sent me to. Tomaso, who is always rigorous with the truth when it contains spite, told me she had later been arraigned for prostitution, so who knows what humors and lusts I suckled at her breasts? Though Erila says it is only his jealousy speaking, his way of paying me back for a thousand slights inflicted in the classroom.

Whatever the reasons, I was a singular child, more suited to study and argument than duty. My sister, who was sixteen months older and had begun to bleed the year before, was promised to a man of good family, and there had even been talk of a similarly illustrious liaison for me (as our fortune rose so did my father's marriage expectations), despite my emerging intractability.

In the weeks following the painter's arrival my mother was eagle-eyed on my behalf, keeping me closeted in study or helping with Plautilla's wedding wardrobe. But then she was called away to Fiesole to her sister, who was so torn apart by the birth of an oversize baby that she was in need of female counsel. She went, leaving strict instructions that I should go about my studies and do exactly what my tutors and my elder sister told me. I of course agreed that I would.

I ALREADY KNEW WHERE TO FIND HIM. LIKE A BAD REPUBLIC, OUR house praises virtue publicly but rewards vice privately and gossip could always be had at a price, though in this case my Erila gave it for free.

"The talk is that there isn't any. Nobody knows anything. He keeps his own company, eats in his room, and speaks to no one. Though Maria says she's seen him pacing the courtyard in the middle of the night."

It is afternoon. Erila has unpinned my hair and drawn the curtains in readiness for my rest and is about to leave when she turns and looks at me directly. "We both know it is forbidden for you to visit him, yes?"

I nod, my eyes on the carved wood of the bedstead: a rose with as many petals as my small lies. There is a pause in which I would like to think she looks upon my disobedience sympathetically. "I shall be back to wake you in two hours. Rest well."

I wait till the sunshine has stilled the house, then slide down the stairs and into the back courtyard. The heat is already clinging to the stones and his door is open, presumably to let in what little breeze there might be. I move silently across the baked courtyard and slip inside.

The interior is gloomy, the shafts of daylight spinning dust particles in the air. It is a dreary little room with just a table and chair and a series of pails in one corner and a connecting door to a smaller inner chamber ajar. I push it open farther. The darkness is profound and my ears work before my eyes. His breathing is long and even. He is lying on a pallet by the wall, his hand flung out over strewn papers. The only other men I have seen sleeping are my brothers, and their snores are harsh. The very gentleness of this breath disturbs me. My stomach grows tight with the sound, making me feel like the intruder I am, and I pull the door closed behind me.

In contrast the outer room is brighter now. Above the desk are a series of tattered papers: drawings of the chapel taken from the builders' plans, torn and grimy with masonry marks. To the side hangs a wooden crucifix, crudely carved but striking, with Christ's body hanging so heavily off the cross that you can feel the weight of his flesh hanging from his nails. Beneath it are some sketches, but as I pick them up the opposite wall catches my eye. There is something drawn there, directly onto the flaking plaster: two figures, half realized, to the left a willowy Angel, feathered wings light as smoke billowing out behind him, and opposite a Madonna, her body unnaturally tall and slender, floating ghostly free, her feet lifted high off the ground. I move closer to get a better look. The floor is thick with the ends of candles stuck in puddles of melted wax. Does he sleep through the day and work at night? It might explain Mary's attenuated figure, her body lengthening in the flicker of the candlelight. But he has had enough light to enliven her face. Her looks are northern, her hair pulled fiercely back to show a wide forehead, so that her head reminds me of a perfectly shaped pale egg. She is staring wide-eyed at the Angel, and I can feel a fluttering excitement in her, like a child who has been given some great gift and cannot quite comprehend its good fortune. While perhaps she ought not to be so forward with God's messenger, there is such joy in her attention that it is almost contagious. It makes me think of a sketch I am working up on my own Annunciation and brings a flush of shame to my face at its clumsiness.

The noise is more like a growl than any words. He must have risen from his bed silently, because as I whirl around he is standing in the doorway. What do I remember of this moment? His body is long and lanky, his undershirt crumpled and torn. His face is broad under a tangle of long dark hair, and he is taller than I remember from that first night and somehow wilder. He is still half asleep, and his body has the tang of dried sweat about it. I am used to living in a house of rose- and orange-flower scented air; he smells of the street. I really think until that moment I had believed that artists somehow came directly from God and therefore had more of the spirit and less of man about them.

The shock of his physicality sluices any remaining courage out of me. He stands blinking in the light, then suddenly lurches himself toward me, wrenching the papers out of my hand.

"How dare you?" I yelp, as he shoves me to the side. "I am the daughter of your patron, Paolo Cecchi!"

He doesn't seem to hear. He rushes to the table, grabbing the remaining sketches, all the time muttering in a low voice, *"Noli tangere...noli tangere."* Of course. There is one fact my father forgot to tell us. Our painter has grown up amid Latin-speaking monks, and while his eyes might work here his ears do not.

"I didn't touch anything," I bark back in terror. "I was simply looking. And if you are to be accepted here, you will have to learn to talk in our language. Latin is the tongue of priests and scholars, not painters."

My retort, or maybe it is the force of my fluent Latin, silences him. He stands frozen, his body shaking. It is hard to know which one of us was more scared at that moment. I would have fled had it not been for the fact that across the courtyard I spot my mother's bed servant coming out from the storeroom. While I have allies in the servants' quarters I also have enemies, and Angelica's loyalties have long since proved to lie elsewhere. If I am discovered now there would be no telling what outrage it would cause in the house.

"Be assured I never harmed your drawings," I say hurriedly, anxious to avoid another outburst. "I am interested in the chapel. I simply came to see how your designs were progressing."

He mutters something again. I wait for him to repeat it. It takes a long time. Finally he raises his eyes to look at me, and as I stare at him I become aware for the first time of how young he is—older than I am, yes, but surely not by many years—and how white and sallow his skin. Of course I know that foreign lands breed foreign colors. My own Erila is burned black by the desert sands of North Africa from where she came, and in those days you could find any number of shades in the markets of the city, so much was Florence a honeypot for trade and commerce. But this whiteness is different, having about it the feel of damp stone and sunless skies. A single day under the Florentine sun would surely shrivel and burn his delicate surface.

When he finally speaks he has stopped shaking, but the effort has cost him. "I paint in God's service," he says, with the air of a novitiate delivering a litany he has been taught but not fully understood, "and it is forbidden for me to talk with women."

"Really," I say, stung by the snub. "That might explain why you have so little idea of how to paint them." I cast a glance toward the elongated Madonna on the wall.

Even in the gloom I can feel how the words hurt him. For a moment I think he might attack me again, or break his own rules and answer me back, but instead he turns on his heel and, clutching the papers to his chest, stumbles back into the inner room, the door slamming closed behind him.

"Your rudeness is as bad as your ignorance, sir," I call after him, to cover my confusion. "I don't know what you have learned in the North, but here in Florence our artists are taught to celebrate the human body as an echo of the perfection of God. You would do well to study the city's art before you risk scribbling on its walls."

And in a flurry of self-righteousness I stride from the room into the sunlight, not knowing if my voice has penetrated through the door.

Two

"SEVEN, EIGHT, TURN, STEP—NO . . . NO, NO. . . . ALESSAN-dra . . . no. you are not listening to the beat inside the music."

I hate my dancing teacher. He is small and vicious, like a rat, and he walks as if he has something held between his knees, though it is fair to say that on the floor he is better at playing the woman than I am, his steps perfect, his hands as expressive as butterflies.

My humiliation would be bad enough even without the fact that, in the lessons leading up to her wedding, Plautilla and I are joined by Tomaso and Luca. There is a large repertoire to get through and we need them as partners or one of us will have to play the man, and while I am the taller I am also the one with three feet and most in need of tutoring. Fortunately, Luca is as clumsy as I am.

"And Luca, you do not help by simply standing there. You must take her hand and guide her around you."

"I can't. Her fingers are covered in ink. Anyway, she's too tall for me." He wails, as if it were a fault of my own making.

It appears I have grown again. If not in fact, then in my

brother's imagination. And he must bring it to everyone's attention so we can all laugh about how ungainly it makes me on the
dance floor.

"That is not true. I am exactly the same size as I was last week."

"Luca's right." Tomaso is never at a loss for words if he can use
them as darts toward me. "She has grown. It is like trying to dance
with a giraffe." Luca's snort of laughter spurs him on. "Really.
Even the eyes are alike. Look—deep pools of black with eyelashes as thick as box hedges."

And though it is shocking it is also funny, so that even the
dancing teacher, who is paid to be civil with us all, finds it hard
not to laugh. If it were not about myself I would laugh too,
because it is clever, what he says about my eyes. We had all seen
the giraffe, of course. It had been the most exotic animal our city
possessed, a gift from the sultan of somewhere or other to the
great Lorenzo. It lived with the lions in the menagerie behind the
Piazza della Signoria but was paraded out on feast days, when it
was taken to the city's nunneries so that devout women married
to God could see the wonder of His hand in nature. Our street
was on the way to the convents in the east of the city, and more
than once we had stood at the first-floor window and watched its
giddy progress, its stilty legs faltering over the cobbles. And I
must say its eyes were indeed a little like my own: deep and dark,
too big for its face, and fringed by a box hedge of lashes. Though
I am not yet so strange or so tall that the comparison is fair.

There was a time when such an insult might have made me
cry, but as I have grown older my skin has become tougher.
Dancing is one of many things I should be good at and am not,
unlike my sister. Plautilla can move across the floor like water
and sing a stave of music like a songbird, while I, who can trans-
late both Latin and Greek faster than she or my brothers can read
it, have clubfeet on the dance floor and a voice like a crow.
Though I swear if I were to paint the scale I could do it in a flash:
shining gold leaf for the top notes, falling through ochers and
reds into hot purple and deepest blue.

But today I am saved from further torment. As the dancing teacher starts humming the opening notes, the vibrations in his little nose sounding like a cross between a Jew's harp and an angry bee, there is a thunder of knocking on the downstairs main doors and then a flurry of voices, and old Ludovica puffs her way into the room, grinning.

"My lady Plautilla, it's here. The marriage *cassone* has arrived. You and your sister Alessandra are called to your mother's room immediately."

And now my giraffe legs take me out faster than Plautilla's gazelle ones. There are some compensations to beanpole height.

IT IS ALL CHAOS AND CONFUSION. THE WOMAN AT THE FRONT OF the crowd is toppling over, a hand flung out wildly in front as if to steady herself. She is half undressed, her undershirt diaphanous around bare legs, her left foot naked on the stone ground. In contrast, the man beside her is fully clothed. He has a particularly fine leg and a richly embroidered brocade jerkin; if you look carefully you can spot pearls shimmering in the cloth. His face is close to hers, his arms clasped hard around her waist, the fingers knotted together to catch her falling weight better. While there is violence in the pose, there is also a grace, as if they too might be dancing. To the right a group of women, nobly dressed, are huddled together. Some of the men have already infiltrated this group; one has his hand on a woman's dress, another his lips so close to hers that they are surely kissing. I recognize one of my father's gold-veined fabrics in her skirt and fashionably slit sleeves and go back to the girl at the front. She is far too pretty to be Plautilla (he wouldn't have dared to undress her, surely?) but her loose hair is fairer than the others, a transformation of color the like of which my sister would gladly die for. Maybe the man is supposed to be Maurizio, in which case the portrait is a blatant piece of flattery to his leg.

For a while none of us say anything.

"It is an impressive work." My mother's voice, when it finally comes, is quiet but brooks no disagreement. "Your father will be pleased. It brings honor to our family."

"Oh, it's magnificent," Plautilla twitters, happily by her side.

I am not so sure. I find the whole thing somewhat vulgar. To begin with, the marriage chest is too large, more like a sarcophagus. While the paintings themselves are of some delicacy, the stucco and ornamentation is so elaborate—there is no inch of space that isn't covered in gold leaf—it takes away from the pleasure of the art. I was surprised that my mother was so deceived, though I later came to realize that her eye was a subtle thing, as much trained to read the nuance of status as of aesthetics.

"It makes me wonder if we should have employed Bartolommeo di Giovanni for the chapel. He is much more experienced," she mused.

"And much more expensive," I said. "Father would be lucky to see the altar finished in his lifetime. I hear he barely completed this chest on time. And most of it is painted by his apprentices."

"Alessandra!" my sister squeaked.

"Oh, use your eyes, Plautilla. Look how many of the women are in exactly the same pose. It's obvious they're using them for figure practice."

Though I have later thought Plautilla did well to put up with me during our childhood, at the time anything and everything she said seemed so trivial or stupid it was only natural to goad her. And equally natural that she would rise to it.

"How could you! How could you say that? Ah! But even if it were true, I can't imagine anyone noticing it but you. Mama is right; it is very fine. Certainly I like it much better than if it had been the story of Nastagio degli Onesti. I hate the way the dogs hunt her down. But these women are most handsome. And their dresses are perfect. The girl in the front is quite striking, don't you think, Mama? I've heard that in every marriage chest that Bartolommeo does, there is always one figure that is based on the bride. I think it's most affecting how she seems to be almost dancing."

"Except she's not dancing. She's being violated."

"I know that well enough, Alessandra. But if you remember the story of the Sabine women, they were invited for a feast, which then turned into a violation, which they accepted with resignation. That *is* the purpose of the painting. Out of womanly sacrifice the city of Rome was born."

I think of replying but catch my mother's eye. Even in private she will only tolerate a certain level of spatting. "Whatever the subject, I think we can agree that he has done a splendid job. For all the family. Yes, even you, Alessandra. I am surprised you have not yet found your own likeness in the painting."

I stared back at the chest. "*My* likeness? Where do you see me here?"

"The girl at the side, standing apart, engaged in such earnest conversation with the young man. I wonder how well her talk of philosophy is keeping his mind on higher things," she said evenly.

I bowed my head to acknowledge the hit. My sister stared on at the painting, oblivious.

"So. We are decided." My mother's voice again, clear and firm. "It is a noble piece. We must hope and pray your father's protégé serves the family half so well."

"How is the painter doing, Mama?" I said, after a while. "No one has seen him since he came."

She glanced at me sharply, and I thought of her maidservant in the courtyard. Surely not. The encounter had taken place weeks before. If she had seen me I would have known about it before now. "I think it has not been easy for him. The city is raucous after the silence of his abbey. He has suffered from the fever. But he is recovered now and asked to be given leave to study some of the city's churches and chapels before he continues with his designs."

I dropped my eyes in case she should notice the spark of interest. "He could always come with us to service," I said, as if it mattered not a jot to me. "He would get a better view of certain frescoes from our position."

Unlike some families who frequented only one church for worship, we had been known to spread our favors around town. This afforded my father the opportunity to see how much of Florence was wearing his latest fabrics and allowed my mother to enjoy the art as well as compare the preaching—though I doubt either of them would have admitted to it.

"Alessandra, you know very well that would not be fitting. I have arranged for him to make his own way."

The conversation having moved on from her wedding, Plautilla had lost interest and was sitting on the bed, running her hands over the rainbow colors of fabric, pulling them across her chest or lap to see their effect.

"Oh, oh...it must be this blue for the overdress. It must be. Wouldn't you agree, Mama?"

We turned to Plautilla, both of us in our own way equally grateful for the interruption. It was indeed an extraordinary blue, shot through with what looked like metallic lights. Though a little paler, it reminded me of the ultramarine that painters use for Our Lady's dress, the pigment painstakingly washed from lapis lazuli. The fabric dye is less precious but no less special to me, not least because of its name: Alessandrina.

Of course, as the daughter of a cloth merchant I knew more than most about such things, and I had always been curious. There was a story that when I was five or six I had begged my father to take me to the place "where the smells came from." It was summer—that much I remember—close to a great church and piazza near the river. The dyers made up a shantytown all of their own, the streets dark and jammed with slum houses, many of them teetering on the edge of the water. There were children everywhere, half naked, splattered with mud and streaked with color from stirring the vats. The foreman of my father's work looked like the Devil, parts of his face and upper arms wizened from where boiling water had scalded him. Others, I remember, had scratched patterns into their skins, then rubbed different dyes into the wounds so their bodies were marked with bright signs. They were like a tribe from a pagan land. Though their work kept the city alive with color, they were the poorest people I had ever seen. Even the monastery that gave the district its name, Santa Croce, was home to the Franciscans, who chose the most destitute areas in which to build their churches.

What my father felt about them I never knew. Though he might be stern enough with my brothers, he was not a hard man. The ledgers of his company included an account in God's name through which he gave generous alms to charity, and in recent years he had paid for two stained-glass windows in our church of Sant' Ambrogio. Certainly his wages were no worse than any other merchant's. But it was not his job to alleviate poverty. In our great Republic, man made his fortune by the grace of God and his own hard work. If others were less fortunate that was their business, not my father's.

Still, something of their desperation must have infected me during that visit, because while I grew up yearning for the colors of the warehouse, I also remembered the cauldrons, their steamy heat like the pots of hell where they boil sinners. And I did not ask to go again.

My sister, however, had no such pictures to cloud the pleasure of the cloth and was at this moment more interested in how the blue might complement the swell of her breasts. Sometimes I think that when it comes to her wedding night she will enjoy her nightdress more than her husband's body. I wondered how much that would bother Maurizio. I had only met him once. He seemed a sturdy enough fellow, with some laughter and force, but there was not much sign of the thinker in him. That might make it better, of course. What did I know? They seemed satisfied with each other.

"Plautilla. Why don't we leave this for now?" my mother said quietly, pushing back the fabrics and sighing slightly. "The afternoon is particularly warm today, and some sun on your hair might further develop its fairness admirably. Why don't you go out onto the roof with your embroidery?"

My sister was taken aback. While it was well known that fashionable young women regularly addled their brains with sun in a futile attempt to turn dark into light, it was a vanity their mothers were not supposed to know about.

"Oh, don't look so surprised. Since you will do it regardless of what I think, it seems easier to give you my blessing. You will not find much time for such fripperies soon anyway."

My mother had recently gained the habit of saying things like this, as if somehow all natural life for Plautilla would end with her marriage. Plautilla herself seemed to find this prospect rather exciting, though I must say it put the fear of hellfire into me. She gave a small squeak of delight and flapped around the room in search of her sun hat. When she found it, she took an interminable time to fit it, pulling her hair out through the central hole to make sure that while her face was in shade every strand would be exposed to the sun. Then she gathered up her skirts and went swooping out. If you had tried to paint her exit, you would have had to fling swaths of silk or gauze cloth around her body to suggest the wind in her speed, as I had seen some artists do. Either that or give her bird wings.

We watched her go. I got the impression it made my mother rather sad. She sat for a moment before she turned to me, which meant I caught the glint in her eyes too late.

"I think I'll join her." I got up from my chair.

"Don't be ridiculous. You hate the sun, Alessandra, and anyway your hair is black as a crow's. You would do better to dye it if you were so inclined, which I doubt you are."

I saw her eyes slide to my ink-stained fingers and curled them up hastily.

"And when did you last treat your hands?" My appearance was one of many things about me that tested her sorely. "Oh, you are impossible. I will send Erila out this afternoon. Do them before you go to bed, you hear? And stay now. I want to talk to you."

"But Mama—"

"Stay!"

Three

I BRACED MYSELF FOR THE LECTURE. HOW MANY TIMES had we been here before? We would never sort it out, she and I. I had almost died at birth. She had almost died giving birth to me. Eventually, after two days of labor I was hauled out with tongs, both of us screaming all the way. The damage done to her body meant there would be no more children, and long before she began to see something of herself in me there was a powerful bond between us. I asked her once why I hadn't died, as so many others I had heard about. "Because God willed it so. And because He gave you a curiosity and spirit that made you determined to survive, come what may."

"Alessandra, you should know your father has started talking to prospective husbands," she said now.

I felt my stomach curdle at the words. "But how ... I am not even bleeding yet!"

She frowned. "You are sure of that?"

"How could you not know? Maria checks my laundry. It's hardly a fact I could keep secret."

"Unlike other things." Her voice was quiet. I looked up. But there was no sign that she would go any further. "You know I have shielded you for a long time. I cannot go on doing so forever."

Such was the seriousness of her voice that it made me almost frightened. I looked at her for guidance as to how we should continue this conversation, but she gave me none. "Well," I said moodily, "it seems to me that if you did not want me this way, you should not have allowed it."

"And what would we have done otherwise?" she said gently. "Kept you from books, taken away your pens? Chastised it out of you? You were too loved too early, child. You would have taken such treatment badly. Anyway, you were always so stubborn. In the end it seemed easier to keep you occupied by sending you to your brothers' tutors." She sighed. By this time she must have realized that the solution had proved as troublesome as the problem. "You were so eager in their place."

"I doubt they would thank you for it."

"That's because you have yet to learn the power of humility," she said, more sharply this time. "As we have discussed before, such a lack sits loudly in a young woman. Perhaps if you spent as much time in prayer as you do in study."

"Is that how you did it, Mama?"

She gave a short laugh. "No, Alessandra. In my case my family put a stop to any temptations of vanity."

She seldom referred to her childhood but we all knew the stories: how the children, male and female, had been educated together at the order of a scholastic father committed to the new learning. How her eldest brother had grown up to become a great scholar himself, favored by the Medici and living off their patronage, which allowed the sisters to be married well to merchants who accepted their unusual education when sweetened by generous dowries. "When I was your age it was even less acceptable for a young woman to have such learning. If my brother's star hadn't risen so far, I might well have had trouble finding a husband."

"But if my birth was God's will, then you must always have been meant to marry Papa."

"Oh, Alessandra. Why is it you always do this?"

"Do what?"

"Push your thoughts further than they need or ought to go."

"But it is logic."

"No, child. That is the point. It is *not* logic. What you do is more irreverent: questioning things so deep and coherent in God's nature that human logic is imperfect to understand them anyway."

I said nothing. The storm, which was not unfamiliar to me, would pass quicker if I demurred.

"I do not think you have learned that from your tutors." She sighed, and I could feel her exasperation with me was acute, though I still did not quite know why. "You should know that Maria has found drawings in a case under your bed."

Ah, so that was it. No doubt she had come across them while searching for hidden blood-soiled rags. I skimmed the case in my mind, trying to predict where her wrath was going to fall.

"She is convinced that you have been wandering the city without a chaperone."

"Oh, but that is impossible! How could I? She barely lets me out of her sight."

"She says there are sketches of buildings that she has never seen and images of lions devouring a boy in the Piazza della Signoria."

"So? She and I went together for the feast day. You know that. We all saw the lions. Before they killed the calf they had a tamer who stood in the cage with them, and the lions never touched him. Then someone told us—maybe it was Erila—how a little boy had got in the cage the year before, after everyone had gone home, and been mauled to death. Maria must surely remember that. She swooned at the news."

"That is as may be. But the fact is she knows you could not have drawn all of that then and there."

"Of course I didn't. I made some sketches later. But they were awful. In the end I had to copy the lions from an image in the *Book of Hours*. Though I am sure their limbs are not right."

"What was the lesson?"

"What?"

"The lesson. In the *Book of Hours*...around which the lions were woven?"

"Er...Daniel?" I said lamely.

"You remember the image but not the lesson. Oh, Alessandra." She shook her head. "What about the buildings?"

"They are from my own head. When would I get the time to draw them?" I said quietly. "I just bring bits that I have remembered together."

She stared at me for a moment, and I'm not sure that either of us knew what she was feeling. She had been the first to recognize my facility with the pen, when I was so young I barely understood it myself. I had taught myself to draw by copying all the votive paintings in the house, and for years my passion was a secret between the two of us, until I was old enough to appreciate the nature of discretion. While it was one thing for my father to indulge a precocious child in an occasional sketch of the Virgin, it was quite another to have a grown daughter so possessed that she raided the kitchen for capon bones to grind for boxwood dust or goose feathers for a dozen new quills. Art might be a way to God, but it was also the mark of a tradesman and no pastime for a young woman of good family. Recently Erila had become my accomplice in deceit. What my mother thought, I no longer had any idea. Two years before, when I was floundering in the skill of silverpoint—the stylus so fine and hard that it leaves no room for mistakes of the eye or the hand—she had asked to see my attempts. She had studied them for a while, then handed them back without saying a word. A week later I found a copy of Cennino Cennini's *Treatise on Technique* in the chest under my bed. My hand has grown much steadier since then, though neither of us ever referred to the gift again.

She sighed. "Very well. We shall talk no more about it." She paused. "I have something else to discuss. The painter has asked to sketch you."

I felt a small explosion of fire somewhere inside me.

"As I said, he has been visiting churches. And as a result of what he has seen he is ready to continue. He has done your father's likeness already. I am too busy with Plautilla's marriage to waste time with him now, so he must move on to the children. He has asked for you first. You have, I presume, no idea why?"

I looked directly at her and shook my head. It may sound strange but it made a significant difference to me then, not using words to lie to her.

"He has set up a temporary studio in the chapel. He says he must see you in the late afternoon when the light is right. He is most insistent about this. And you will take Ludovica and Maria with you."

"But—"

"There is no argument, Alessandra. You will take them both. You are not there to distract him, or to debate the finer points of Platonic philosophy. In which subject I think anyway there might be some difference of language."

And though her words were strict the tone was gentler, which made me feel comfortable with her again. Which of course meant that I misjudged the risk. But who else could I talk to about it now, when the matter was becoming so imminent?

"You know, Mama, I have this dream sometimes. I must have had it maybe five or six times now."

"I hope it is a godly affair."

"Oh, yes, indeed it is. I dream . . . well, I dream that, strange though it may sound, I don't get married after all. That instead you and Papa decide that I should go into this convent—"

"Oh, Alessandra, don't be a dolt. You don't have the capacity for a convent. Its rules would shrivel you in a moment. Surely you must know that."

"No . . . yes, but—but you see in my dream *this* convent is different. In this convent the nuns can celebrate God in different ways, by doing—"

"No. Alessandra Cecchi, I am not listening to this. If you think your bad behavior will force us into any change of mind about a husband, you are gravely mistaken."

Here it came, the beginning of her anger, like the jet of a hot spring erupting from the earth.

"You are a willful and sometimes deeply disobedient child, and despite what I said, I wish I had broken it out of you earlier because it will do none of us any good now." She sighed. "Nevertheless, we will find a way. I will use the word we have spoken about often: duty. Your duty to your family. Your father is a rich man now, with a record of public service to the state. He has money for a dowry that will bring our name much honor and prestige. When he finds the right man, you will marry him. Is that clear? It is the greatest thing a woman can do, marry and have children. You will learn that soon enough."

She stood up. "Come, child. We will have no more of this. I have much to do. Your father will speak to you when we have made a choice. Then for a while after that nothing will happen. For a while," she repeated softly. "But you should know that I cannot keep him talking forever."

I grabbed the olive branch greedily. "In which case make him choose one that will at least understand," I said, and I looked directly into her eyes.

"Oh, Alessandra." She shook her head. "I am not sure that will be possible."

Four

I POUTED MY WAY THROUGH SUPPER, PUNISHING MARIA with my silences, and went early to my room, where I pulled a chair fast against the door and dug into my wardrobe chest. It was important to keep one's treasures scattered. That way if a single haul is discovered another still remains. Rolled away under my shifts at the bottom was a full-scale pen-and-ink drawing on tinted paper.

For this, my first sustained work, I had chosen the opening moment of the Annunciation. Our Lady is taken unawares by the Angel, and her awe and distress show in the way her hands flutter around her body and her torso twists half in flight, as if both she and Gabriel are being pulled by invisible threads toward and away from each other. It is a popular subject, not least because the strength of their movement offers such a challenge to the pen, but I identify with it most because of Our Lady's palpable disquiet—though the later stages of submission and grace are the ones my tutors always press upon me for spiritual study.

For the setting I had used our own grand receiving room, the window frame behind to emphasize the perspective. It was, I thought, a good choice. The way the sun refracts through the glass at a certain time of day is so beautiful that one might indeed believe that God is carried in its shafts. I had once sat there for hours waiting for the Holy Spirit to reveal Itself to me: eyes closed, my soul warm in the light, the sun like a beam of holiness piercing through my eyelids. But instead of divine revelation all I got was the thud of my own heartbeat and the incessant itch of an old mosquito bite. I remained stubbornly—and now I look back on it almost excitedly—unblessed.

But my Madonna is more worthy. She is rising from her seat, her hands flying up like nervous birds to defend herself against the rushing wind of God's arrival, the perfect young virgin disturbed at prayer. I have taken the greatest care with both of their garments. (While much of the world was closed to me, the fabrics and fashions at least I could study at will.) Gabriel is dressed in a long chemise made from my father's most expensive lawn, its soft cream falling in a thousand tiny pleats from the shoulders and gathered loosely at the waist, the material light enough to follow the speed of his limbs. Our Lady I have made quietly fashionable, her sleeves split open at the elbow to show her chemise poking through from underneath, her waistline high and belted, and her silk skirt falling in a waterfall of pleats around her legs and across the floor. When the outline drawing is complete, I will begin work on the shading and the highlights, using various degrees of ink solutions and a wash of white lead paint applied by brush.

Mistakes at this stage are not easily corrected, and my hand was already unsteady with nerves. I was becoming decidedly more sympathetic to the plight of the apprentices in Bartolommeo's workshops. To gain myself a little time I was filling in the receding floor tiles to practice my skill at perspective when the door handle moved and the wood rattled against the chair.

"Not yet!" I grabbed a sheet from the bed and threw it across the drawing. "I am...undressing."

Once, a few months before, Tomaso found me here and "accidentally" knocked the bottle of linseed oil, which I use for making tracing paper, into a pestle of white lead powder that Erila had managed to find for me in the apothecary's shop. His silence had been bought at the cost of my translations of the Ovid poems he was struggling with. But it wouldn't be Tomaso now. Why waste his evening tormenting me when he could be prettifying himself for the fallen women of the streets with their regulation bells and high-heeled shoes calling young men to attention? I could hear him upstairs, the boards creaking under his footsteps as he no doubt procrastinated over which color hose would go best with the new tunic the tailor had just delivered to him.

I unhooked the chair top and Erila swept in, a bowl in one hand and a pile of almond cakes in the other. Ignoring the drawing—though she is my accomplice, it is better for her to pretend she is not—she settled herself on the bed, divided the cakes, and pulled my hands toward her, stirring up the paste of lemon and sugar and applying it thickly to my skin. "So. What happened, did Maria snitch on you?"

"Lied, more like. Aah. Careful . . . I've got a cut there."

"Too bad. Your mother says if they're not white by Sunday she'll make you wear chamois gloves for a week."

I let her work for a while. I love the feel of her fingers pushing their way deep into my palms, and even more I love the fabulous contrast of her jet-black skin against mine, though it always taxed my charcoal supply when it came to sketching her.

She says she remembers nothing of her homeland in North Africa except for the fact that the sun was bigger there and the oranges tasted sweeter. Her history might be the stuff of a modern Homer. She was brought to Venice with her mother when she was, she thought, five or six years old, and sold at the slave market there to a Florentine merchant whose business later collapsed when he lost three ships from the Indies. My father took her in lieu of a debt. I was still a baby when she came, and she was given charge of Plautilla and me at times, which was easier than the manual work that otherwise would have crushed her. She has a keen intelligence mixed with common sense and from my earliest years could both rule and amuse me. I think my mother saw in her an answer to her prayers when it came to the molding of her singular daughter, so from early on she had become mine. But no one could really own Erila. Though in law she was my father's property to do with as he wished, she has always had the independence and stealth of a cat, wandering the city and bringing back gossip like fresh fruit and making money on its resale. She has been my best friend in the house for as long as I can remember, my eyes and ears for all the places I cannot go.

"So. Did you get it?"

"Maybe I did, maybe I didn't."

"Oh, Erila!" But I knew better than to rush her.

She grinned. "Now here's a good one. Today they hanged a man at Porta di Giustizia. A murderer. Chopped his wife's lover into bits. After he'd swung for half an hour, they cut him down and put him on the death cart, whereupon he sat right back up again, complaining of a great ache in his throat and demanding a drink of water."

"He did not! What did they do?"

"Took him to hospital, where they're feeding him bread soaked in milk till he can swallow and they can hang him again."

"No! And what did the crowd do?"

She shrugged. "Oh, they yelled and cheered him on. But then this fat Dominican with a face like a pumice stone barged in with a sermon about how Florence was a cesspit so overflowing with evil that the wicked flourished while the good suffered."

"But what if it wasn't evil? I mean, what if it was an example of God's boundless mercy, even for the grossest sinners? Oh, I wish I had been there to see it! What do you think?"

"Me?" She laughed. "I think the hangman got the knot wrong. There, you're done." She held my hands, surveying her handiwork. They were clean for the first time in days, the nails shining and pink, but how much whiter my skin was was hard to tell.

"Here." From her pocket she fished out a small bottle of ink (what my brothers use on their studies in a month went on my drawings in a week) and a thin brush of miniver tails, delicate enough to add the highlights to Our Lady's face and costume. I flung my arms around her neck.

"Hmm. You're lucky. I got them cheap. But don't use the ink till after Sunday, or I'll be the one in trouble."

AFTER SHE HAD GONE I LAY THINKING OF THE MAN AND THE NOOSE and how one could tell the Lord's mercy from a mistake in knotting, or if perhaps they might be the same thing. I asked God forgiveness, in case such thoughts are impure, and then appealed to the Virgin to intercede on my behalf to make my hand steadier as I capture her goodness for the page. I was still awake when Plautilla opened the canopy and crawled in, reeking of hair oil, liberally applied to counteract the drying power of the sun. She said her prayers under her breath, a rapid litany that seemed more about words than feelings but perfect nevertheless, and settled down, pushing me to the side so she could get the larger share of the bed. I waited until her breathing was even before pushing her back again.

After a while I heard the massing of mosquitoes. The smell of her oil was everywhere, like honey to the bee. The burning herb pomade hanging from the ceiling would be overwhelmed by it. I reached for the vial of citronella I kept under my pillow and smeared it over my hands and face.

Zzan...zzan...zap! A mosquito landed on my sister's plump white wrist. I watched it making itself comfortable before pricking her skin. I imagined it drawing up her blood like a long draft of water, then unsucking itself from her body, zooming out of the window, and flying across town to Maurizio's house, where it would enter his bedchamber, find an exposed limb, and pierce deep into his skin, whereupon the blood of the two lovers would instantly be mingled. The power of the idea was almost unbearable, even if it was only the lumpen likes of Plautilla and Maurizio. But then if such a thing were possible—and having made a study of mosquitoes, it seemed to me it must be: I mean, what could that be but our blood? When you killed them at the begin-

ning of the night their bodies were just black smears, yet later
they splatted the reddest of red juice—if such a thing were possible then surely it might also be capriciously done. There were
a thousand windows in the city. How many ill-suited gouty old
men had already mingled their blood with mine? I wondered. It
made me think again that if I were going to have to have a husband, I would want one that would come to me, not with a fine
leg and pearls on his brocade but in the shape of a swan, wild
wings beating like a storm cloud, as in Zeus and Leda. And that if
he did that I might indeed love him forever. Though only if he
would let me draw him afterward.

As so often happened on such nights, the activity of my
thoughts drove me further awake until eventually I slid out from
under the sheets and made my way out of the bedroom.

I love our house in the dark. There is so much blackness and
its internal geography is so complex that I have learned to measure it out in my mind, knowing where to find the doors and
which angles of turn are necessary to avoid intrusive bits of furniture or unexpected stairs. Sometimes as I glide from room to
room, I imagine I am out in the city itself, its alleyways and corners unfolding like an elegant mathematical solution in my mind.
Despite my mother's suspicions, I have never walked the city
alone. Of course there have been moments when I have escaped
the clutches of a chaperone to move down a side street or loiter
at a market stall, but never for long and always in daylight. Our
few evening excursions for festivals or late mass showed a place
still wide awake. How its atmosphere might change when the
torches went out I had no idea. Erila was a slave, and yet she knew
more of my city than I ever will. I had as much chance to travel
the Orient as I did streets alone at night. But I could dream.

Below me the main courtyard was a well of darkness. I made
my way down the stairs. One of the house dogs raised a sleepy
eye as I passed him, but he was long used to my nocturnal wanderings. My mother's peacocks in the garden were more to be

feared. Not only had they sharper hearing but their shrieks were like a chorus of souls in hell. Wake them and you woke everyone.

I pushed open the door into the winter receiving room. The tiles were polished and smooth under my feet. The new tapestry hung like a heavy shadow and the great oak table, my mother's pride and joy, was laid for ghosts. I curled myself onto the stone windowsill and slipped the catch carefully. From here the house looked out over the street and I could sit and watch the nightlife. The torches in their great iron baskets on the wall illuminated the front of the house. It was a sign of the new wealth of the neighborhood that there were households rich enough to light latecomers home. I had heard stories of how on moonless nights in the poorer parts of town people died from falling down pits in the cobbles, or drowned in overflowing gutters. Though their blindness was probably made worse by the wine.

No doubt my brothers' sight would be similarly impaired by now. What they lacked in vision they make up for in noise, their drunken laughter hitting the cobbles and bouncing in exaggerated echo up to the windows above. Sometimes the racket woke my father. But there was no such excitement tonight and my eyelids were beginning to droop when I noticed something down below.

From the side of our house a figure emerged into the main street, his body briefly illuminated in the glow of the torches. He was long and lanky, with a cloak pulled tight around him, but his head was bare and I caught that certain flash of whiteness in his skin. So. Our painter was going out into the night. He would see little enough art at this hour. What was it my mother had said? That he was finding the city raucous after the stillness of the abbey. Maybe this was his way of sucking in silence, though there was something in the manner in which he walked, head down, eager to lose himself in the dark, that spoke more of purpose than of atmosphere.

I was torn between curiosity and envy. Was it that simple? You wrapped yourself in a cloak, found the right door, and just stepped out into the night. If he moved fast he could be at the Cathedral of Santa Maria del Fiore in ten minutes. Then cross by the Baptistery and head west toward Santa Maria Novella or south to the river, from where you might be able to hear the chatter of the women's little bells. Another world. But I did not like to think of that, remembering his Virgin, so filled with grace and light she could barely keep her feet upon the ground.

I set myself to keep watch until he returned, but after an hour or so I grew sleepy and, not wanting to risk being found there in the morning, I went back upstairs to my room. I slid under the sheet, noticing with uncharitable satisfaction how the bite on Plautilla's wrist was starting to swell. I curled myself round her warm body. She gave a whinnying little snort, like a horse, and slept on.

Five

IN ITS RAW STATE THE ROOM HAS LITTLE OF GOD ABOUT it. He has cordoned off a small part of the nave where the sunlight comes through the side window, falling directly in a broad band of gold. He himself sits in the shade, by a small table on which is paper, pen and ink, and some newly sharpened stalks of black chalk.

I come in slowly, with old Ludovica behind me. Maria, alas, has been struck by an acute attack of indigestion. You must believe me when I say that though I wished her ill enough that day I had nothing to do with the amount of food she consumed or the sickness it left her with. Looking back, it has made me wonder at the strange ways in which God works. Unless you believe that this, like the hangman's noose, was not an example of His handiwork.

He stands up as we come in, his eyes on the ground. Ludovica's gouty age makes our progress slow, and I have already asked for a comfortable chair to be placed for her nearby. At this time of day it will only be a matter of time before she falls asleep and then no doubt forgets that she has done so. She is of invaluable assistance to me during such moments.

If he remembers our last meeting he does nothing to show it. He gestures me to a small dais in the light, with a high-backed wooden chair placed at an angle so that our eye lines will not cross. I take a step up, already self-conscious about my height. I think we are as nervous as each other.

"Shall I sit?"

"As you wish," he mumbles, still not looking at me directly. I arrange myself in a pose I have seen from the women in the chapel portraits, back straight, head high, my hands folded across my lap. I am not sure what to do with my eyes. For a while I look straight ahead, but the view is dull and I drop my gaze to the left, from where I can see the lower half of his body. The leather at the bottom of his hose, I notice, is badly worn, but the shape of his leg is good, if a little long. Like my own. As I sit there I become aware of the odor of him, much stronger this time: an earth smell, mixed with sourness, almost a kind of rotting about it. It makes me wonder what he has been doing the night before to have such a stench upon him. Clearly he does not wash enough—it is something I had heard my father remark about foreigners—but to draw attention to it now would stop any chance we might have of conversation. I resolve to leave it to Plautilla. The stink will almost certainly drive her mad.

Time passes. It is warm there, under the sun. I glance up at Ludovica. She has brought some embroidery, and it is sitting on her lap. She puts her needle down and watches us for a while, but she has never shown much interest in art even when her eyes were good enough to see it. I count slowly to fifty, and by thirty-nine I hear her breathing start to rumble in her chest. In the silence of the chapel she sounds like a great cat purring. I turn to look at her, then glance across at him.

In today's light I can study him better. For a man who has spent the night wandering the city he looks well enough. His hair is brushed, and if its style is too long for current Florentine fashion, it is still thick and healthy, his complexion even paler against its richness. He is long and thin, like me, but it is less a fault in a man.

He has broad fine cheekbones, and his eyes are almond shaped and have almost a marble effect, gray-green flecked with black, so that I am reminded of the stare of a cat. He is not like any man I have seen before. I do not even know if he is good-looking, though that may be more to do with the way he keeps himself hidden inside. Apart from my brothers and my tutors he is the first man I have ever been in such close proximity to, and I can feel my heart thudding inside my chest. At least sitting I am less like a giraffe. Though I am not sure he notices. While he is looking at me, he doesn't seem aware of me at all. The light shifts around the dais to the intermittent scratching of the chalk on the page, each line careful, considered, the result of a singular communion between the eye and the hand. It is a vibrant kind of silence that I am familiar with. I think of all the hours I have spent in similar pinpoint concentration, my fingers bent around a sharpened pebble of black chalk, trying to capture the head of a sleeping dog on the stairs or the strange ugliness of my own naked foot, and it makes me more patient than I might otherwise have been.

"My mother says you have had the fever?" I say at last, as if we were relatives who had been talking for an hour and just fallen silent that very second. When it is clear he is not going to answer I think about bringing up his nocturnal wanderings, but I can't decide what to say. The sound of his chalk continues. I move my eyes back to focus on the chapel wall. The quiet is now so profound that I begin to think we will be here forever. Though eventually Ludovica will wake and then it will be too late....

"You know, if you are to succeed here, painter, you may have to speak a little. Even with women."

His eyes flick to one side so that I know he takes the words in, but even as I say them they seem too crude and I feel embarrassed for myself. After a while I stir in my seat, shifting my pose. He stops, waiting for me to be still again. I make a little noise. The more I try for stillness the more uncomfortable I feel. I stretch myself farther. He waits again. Only now I am alert to the possibilities of mischief. If he will not talk, I will not sit properly. As I settle I bring my left hand up in front of my face, deliberately obscuring his view. Hands. They are always difficult. So bony and yet fleshy at the same time. Even the greatest of our painters have trouble with them. Yet immediately he is drawing again, this time such insistent scratching that the noise makes me hungry for paper.

After a while I get bored with my failure and put my hand back into my lap, flexing the fingers upward till they stand up like monstrous spider legs upon my skirts. I watch the knuckles go white and see a single vein throb up against the skin. How strange the body is, so full of itself. When I was younger we had a Tartar slave girl, a fierce character who suffered from fits; when they came upon her she would fall rigid on the ground in spasm, her head flung so far back that her neck strained and stretched till it looked like that of a horse and her fingers clawed at the floor. Once she made foam come out of her mouth and we had to put something between her teeth so she did not swallow her own tongue. Luca, who I now think was always more interested in the Devil than God, believed she had been entered by a demon, but my mother said she was ill and should be left to recover. My father sold her later, though I am not sure he was entirely honest about her health. Even if it was illness it could have easily passed for possession. If one had to paint Christ casting out devils, she would have made a perfect model.

Ludovica is snoring loudly. It will take a thunderbolt to rouse her. It is now or never. I stand up. "May I see what you have made of me?"

I feel his body go rigid. I can see he wants to hide the paper, but he also knows it would not be proper. What can he do? Pick up his equipment and run out? Attack me again? He would be on a mule back to the northern wastes if he did that. And underneath all the silence I do not think he is stupid.

My courage deserts me at the table edge. He is so close I can see the dark stubble on his face, and the sweet rank smell of him is acute now. It makes me think of decay and death, and I remember his violence from the time before. I glance nervously at the door. What would happen if someone came in? Maybe he is thinking the same thing. In one awkward move he pushes the board across the table, face up, so that I can see it without moving any farther toward him.

The page is filled with sketches: a study of my full head, then parts of my face, my eyes, the lids half lowered, in a manner caught between shy and sly. He has not flattered me, as I do sometimes with Plautilla as a way of buying her silence when she sits for me, but instead I am myself, alive with both mischief and nerves, as if I cannot speak but cannot stay silent. Already he knows more of me than I do of him.

And then there are the sketches of my hand held up to my face, palm and back, my fingers rounded little columns of living flesh. From nature to the page. His skill makes me giddy.

"Ah," I say, and there is pain as well as wonder in my voice. "Who taught you this?"

I look at my fingers again, real and drawn. And I want more than anything to see how he does it, to watch the way each mark goes onto the page. For that alone I would risk being closer. I look at his face. If it is not arrogance, it has to be shyness that keeps him so silent. What must it be like to be so shy that you find it hard to speak?

"It must be difficult for you here," I say quietly. "I think if I were you I might be homesick."

And because I do not expect him to reply it registers like a small thrill inside me to hear his voice, which is softer than I remember.

"It's the color. Where I come from everything is gray. Sometimes you can't tell where the sky ends and the sea begins. The color makes everything different."

"Oh, but surely Florence is as it must have been then. I mean in the Holy Land, where Our Lord lived. All that sunlight. That's what the Crusaders tell us. Their colors must have been as bright as ours. You should visit my father's warehouse sometime. When the bolts of cloth are finished and stacked together it is like walking through a rainbow."

It strikes me that this is probably the longest speech that he has ever heard from a woman. I feel the panic rising in him again and remember his earlier wildness, the way his whole body had shaken in front of me. "You mustn't worry about me," I blurt out. "I know I talk a lot but I am only fourteen, which makes me a child rather than a woman, so I cannot possibly harm you. And besides, I love art as much as you do."

I put out both my hands and lay them gently on the table between us, spreading my fingers loosely on the wood so there is both tension and relaxation to the pose. "Since you are studying hands, perhaps you would like to have a record of them resting? They are easier to see than in my lap." And I think my mother would have approved of the humility in my voice.

I stand very still, eyes lowered, waiting. I see the board slide off the table and a crayon move from nearby. When I hear its sounds on the page I risk looking up. I can only see the paper at a slant but it is enough to watch it take shape: dozens of tiny fluid strokes raining down onto the page, no time for thought or consideration, no breath between the seeing and the doing. It is as if he is reading my hands from under the skin, building the image from the inside out.

I let him work for a few moments. The silence between us seems a little easier now. "Mother says you have been visiting our churches." He gives the slightest of nods. "Which frescoes did you like most?"

The hand stops. I watch his face. "Santa Maria Novella. *The Life of John the Baptist*," he says firmly.

"Ghirlandaio. Yes, his Capella Maggiore is one of the wonders of the city."

He pauses. "And . . . another chapel across the river."

"Santo Spírito? Santa Maria del Carmine?"

He nods at the second name. Of course. The Brancacci

Chapel in the convent of the Carmine. My mother has directed him well, no doubt using her connections and his status as a lay monk to gain him access to usually forbidden areas. "The frescoes of the life of Saint Peter. They are also highly thought of here. Masaccio died before he could complete them you know. He was twenty-seven years old." I can see this fact impresses him. "I was taken there once as a child, but I barely remember it. Which did you like best?"

He frowns as if the question is too hard. "There are two scenes from the Garden of Eden. In the second, when they are expelled, Adam and Eve are both crying—no, more...howling—as they are banished. I have never seen such sorrow at the loss of God's grace."

"What about before the Fall? Are they as joyful as they are later sad?"

He shakes his head. "The joy is not as strong. It comes from a different painter's hand. And the serpent hanging from the tree has a woman's face on it."

"Oh, yes, yes." I nod, our eyes meeting, and for the moment he is too interested to look away. "My mother has told me of this. Though you know there is no scriptural evidence for such a rendering."

But the mention of the Devil in woman has pulled him back into himself again, and he falls silent. The scratching starts again. I glance down at the board. Where did such talent come from? Is it really God-given?

"Did you always have such skill, painter?" I ask softly.

"I don't remember." His voice is a murmur. "The father who taught me told me I was born with God in my hands to make up for my lack of parents."

"Oh, and I am sure he was right. You know in Florence we believe that great art is the study of God in nature. That is the view of Alberti, one of our foremost scholars. Also Cennini, the artist. Their treatises on painting are very widely read here. I have copies in Latin if you would like...." And while I know such knowledge is a way of showing off, I still cannot resist it. "Alberti tells how the beauty of the human form reflects the beauty of God. Though of course he owes such insight partly to Plato. But then you may not have read Plato either. If you are to be noticed here in Florence you cannot ignore him. Though he never knew Christ, he has much to say about the human soul. The understanding of God in the Ancients has been one of our great Florentine discoveries."

My mother, had she been here, would by now have had her head in her hands at my lack of modesty, both for myself and my city, but I know he is listening. I can tell from the way his hand has stopped on the page. I think he might have spoken more had not Ludovica given a sudden loud snort, which went some way toward waking her up. We both freeze.

"Well," I say quickly, stepping back, "perhaps we should stop now. But I can come again and you can practice on my hands if you like."

But as he puts down the board and I look at the drawing, I realize he has already taken everything he needs.

Six

I TOOK THE COPIES OF ALBERTI AND CENNINI OUT OF MY chest and placed them on the bed. I could not part with Cennini. I depended on it for everything from the fall of drapery to the colors I would never get to mix. But Alberti he could have.

I made Erila my messenger, with the offer of a red silk scarf.

"No."

"How can you say no? You love this color. And it loves you."

"No."

"But why? It is simple. You just go down and give it to him. You know the room as well as I."

"And if your mother finds out?"

"She won't."

"But if she does. She will know it is from you and she will know it is by me. And she will have my skin for a pouch."

"That is not true." I search for the words. "She...she will understand that we are both about the business of art. That our acquaintance has only God's purpose about it."

"Ho! That's not how old Ludovica tells it."

"What do you mean? She was asleep. She couldn't see any-thing." She is silent now, but I have jumped too quickly and she begins to smile. "Oh, you cheat, Erila. She didn't tell you any-thing."

"No. But you just did."

"We talked of art, Erila. I mean it. Of the chapels and the churches and the colors in the sunshine. I tell you he has God in his fingers." I paused. "Though his manners are impossible."

"That's what worries me. You've too much in common, you two."

But she took the book anyway.

THE FOLLOWING DAYS WERE FRANTIC ONES. WHILE MY MOTHER AND the maids prepared Plautilla's wardrobe, Plautilla spent endless hours on the preparation of herself, lightening her hair and bleaching her skin until she began to look more like a ghost than a bride. The next night when I got to the window it was late; I remember because Plautilla was in such a state of agitation that it took her hours to fall asleep and I heard the bells of Sant' Ambrogio strike the hour. The painter appeared almost immedi-ately, dressed in the same enveloping cloak, sliding into the gloom with the same determined stride. But this time I was equally determined to wait up for him. It was a clear spring night, the sky a full map of stars, so when the thunder arrived later it seemed to come out of nowhere, the lightning that followed it scorching a gigantic cross-stitch in the sky.

"Whoa!"

"Yeah!"

I saw them as they rounded the corner, my brothers and their entourage, like a gang of pirates unsteady on dry land, slapping and hugging one another as they tottered down the street. I slid back from the window, but Tomaso has eyes like a falcon and I heard his insolent whistle, the one he uses to summon the dogs.

"Hey, little sister?" His voice boomed off the cobbles. "Little sister!"

I shoved my head out and hissed at him to be quiet. But he was too drunk to register. "Whoa . . . Look at her, boys. A brain as big as the inside of Santa Maria del Fiore, and a face like a dog's arse."

Around him his friends yelped their approval of his wit. "Keep your voice down or Father will hear you," I spit back, covering my injury with anger.

"If he does, you'll be the one in trouble, not me."

"Where have you been?"

"Why don't you ask Luca?" But Luca was having trouble standing unaided. "We found him with his hands on Santa Caterina's stone tits, spewing his stomach out over her feet. He'd probably have been arrested for blasphemy if we hadn't got to him first."

The next flash of lightning lit up the sky like daylight. The thunder that followed was close, not one but two cracks, the second truly deafening, as if the very ground itself had split beneath it. Of course we all knew of such things: the way that sometimes the earth can slice open and the Devil grab a few lost souls through the gashes in between. I got to my feet in sudden terror, but it was already over.

Down below they were similarly startled, though they covered it with whoops and fake horror. "Yeah! Earth shake," yelled Luca.

"No. Cannon fire." Tomaso was laughing. "It's the French army come over the Alps on their way to conquer Naples. What a glorious prospect. Think of that, Sister, rape and pillage. I hear the uncouth French are hot to pluck young virgins from the new Athens."

From the garden at the back of the house the peacocks started up, a screeching fit to wake the dead. Along the street I saw windows opening, and in the direction of the cathedral a glow of light appeared. The painter would have to wait. I was back across the floor and up the stairs within seconds. As I slid into my bed I heard my father's voice rise up in anger from below.

Next morning the house was alive with the news. How in the deepest night a shaft of lightning had struck the lantern of the great dome of Santa Maria del Fiore, cracking open a block of marble and hurtling it to earth with such force that half of it crashed through the roof, the other half crushing a nearby house though miraculously leaving the family untouched.

But worse was to come. For that same night, Lorenzo the Magnificent, scholar, diplomat, politician, and Florence's most noble citizen and benefactor, was lying in his villa in Careggi, crippled by gout and stomach pain. When he heard what had happened in the city, he sent to find out which way the stone had fallen, and when they told him he closed his eyes and said, "It was coming this way. I shall die tonight."

And so he did.

THE NEWS HIT THE CITY HARDER THAN ANY THUNDERBOLT. THE morning after, my brothers and I sat in an airless study as our Greek teacher stumbled over the words of Pericles' funeral oration, his tears watermarking the pages of the specially copied manuscript, and though we later made fun of his lugubrious tone, I know at the time even Luca was moved. My father closed his business for the day, and from the servants' quarters I heard Maria and Ludovica wailing. Lorenzo de' Medici had been the city's foremost citizen since before I was born, and his death blew a cold wind through all of our lives.

His body was brought down to the monastery of San Marco for the night, where the nobler of the citizenry were allowed to view it. Our family was one of those who made the pilgrimage. Inside the chapel the casket was so high up I could barely see into it. The corpse was dressed modestly, as befits a family which, though it ruled Florence in private, had always sought to appear otherwise in public, and his countenance was peaceful, with no sign of the stomach agonies he was said to have suffered at the end (for which Tomaso gossiped that his doctor had prescribed pulverized pearls and diamonds; later, those who disliked him would say he died swallowing what remained of his private wealth so the city could not get its hands on it). But my central memory was how ugly he was. Though I must have seen his profile on a dozen medallions, it was much more arresting in the flesh: the way his flattened nose reached down almost to his lower lip and his chin jutted up like the headland on a rocky coast.

As I stood gawping, Tomaso whispered in my ear that his hideousness was its own aphrodisiac, driving women wild with desire, while his love poetry ignited fire in the coldest of female hearts. The sight of him made me think again of that day in Santa Maria Novella when my mother had drawn attention to the making of history with Ghirlandaio's great chapel. And because this was clearly such a moment, I turned to find her in the throng and so caught her unawares, her tears shining like crystal drops in the candlelight. I had never seen her cry before, and the sight of it disturbed me more than the corpse.

San Marco's monastery where the body lay had been Lorenzo's grandfather's favorite retreat, and the family had spent a fortune endowing it. But its new prior had marked himself out as an independent thinker, railing against the Medici for promoting the works of pagan scholars over the word of God. Some said he had even refused to give Lorenzo absolution on his deathbed, but I think that was scurrilous rumor, the kind that spreads like fire through a crowd on a hot afternoon. Certainly that day Prior Girolamo Savonarola confined himself only to the most respectful of words, preaching a passionate sermon on the transience of life compared to the eternity of God's grace and exhorting us to live each day wearing the eyeglasses of death so we would not be tempted by earthly pleasures and thus be ever ready for our Savior. To which there was much nodding and agreement in the pews, though I suspect those who could afford it still went back to the smells of rich food and good living. I know we did.

Because both our own and Plautilla's future family were well-known Medici supporters, the wedding was postponed. My sister, never one to be willingly upstaged, and whose nervous system was already teetering on the edge of collapse, now wandered round the house with a face as bleached as a bedsheet and a temper as black as the Baptistery Devil.

But that wasn't the worst of it. Lorenzo's death put the city out of sorts in many ways. In the coming weeks Erila brought back all manner of cruel stories: how two of the lions, the very symbol of our greatness, had fought and killed each other in their cages behind the Piazza della Signoria the day before his death, and how the next day a woman had gone crazy during mass in Santa Maria Novella, running down the aisles screaming that a wild bull was charging toward her with its horns on fire and threatening that it would bring the building down on top of them all. Long after they took her away, people said they could hear her screams echoing around the nave.

But worst of all was the body of the young girl that the night watches of Santa Croce found in the marshland between the church and the river a week later. Erila wove it in all its gory detail for Plautilla and me as we sat over our embroidery in the garden under the shade of the pergola, the yellow spring broom all around us and the smells of lilac and lavender making the stench of the story somehow even worse.

"The corpse was so rotten that the flesh was falling off the bones. The watchmen had to hold camphored cloths to their noses just to search it out. They say she'd been dead since the night of the thunderbolt. Whoever did it hadn't even buried her properly. She was rank in a pool of her own blood and the rats and dogs had got to her. Half her stomach was eaten away and there were bite marks everywhere."

The proclamation they read out later in the market square said she had been grossly assaulted, and it called upon the perpetrator to come forward for the sake of his own soul and the good reputation of the Republic. That young girls were violated and sometimes even died of it was a sad but acknowledged truth of the city. The Devil found his way into many men's hearts through their loins, and such outrages only proved the efficacy of the traditions that kept respectable men and women so strictly separated until married. But this crime was different. According to Erila, the damage done had been so dreadful, her sexual organs so cut and torn about, that no one could be quite sure if it was man or beast that had been responsible.

GIVEN THE HORROR OF IT, IT DIDN'T REALLY SURPRISE ANYONE when, months later, the notices fell from the boards, streaked with rain and trampled underfoot by pigs and goats, and no one had come forward to confess to the outrage that left such a stain upon the city's soul.

Seven

PLAUTILLA'S WEDDING, WHEN IT FINALLY TOOK PLACE, was a testament to my father's cloth and our family fortune. When I think of her it is always on this day. She is seated in the receiving room, dressed for the ceremony. It is early, the light tender and sweet, and the painter has been called in for a last sitting to capture her for the future decoration of our walls. She ought to be tired (she has been awake most of the night, despite the sleeping draft my mother gave her), but she looks as if she has just risen from the Elysian fields. Her face is full and soft, her skin fabulously pale, though with the rouge of excitement lighting up the cheeks. Her eyes are clear, their inner edges shining and red like a pomegranate seed against the white, her eyelashes neither too thick nor too dark—no box hedges here—and her brows full in the middle, then tapered like a painter's line toward the nose and the ears. Her mouth is small and pouty like a Cupid's bow, and her hair—what can be seen of it under the flowers and the jewels—reflects her admirable commitment to indolence and a host of afternoons spent staked out in the sun.

Her dress is in the latest fashion: the neckline scalloped, show-

THE BIRTH OF VENUS 55

ing off her plump flesh and my father's cunning Flemish lawn, already madly in demand; her underskirts soft and full as angels' wings so that when she glides past you can hear the material sighing across the floor. But it is the overdress that makes you want to weep for its beauty. It is made of the finest yellow silk, the shade of the brightest crocuses grown especially for their dye in the fields around San Gimignano, and its skirt is embroidered, not grossly like some of the dresses you see in church, which try to compete with the altar cloth, but subtly so that the flowers and the birds seem to entwine through the stitching.

In such a garment my sister is so lovely that, if Plato is to be believed, one would expect her to be shining with goodness, and certainly she is nicer than usual this morning, almost floaty with excitement. But while she wants her likeness recorded, she is far too impatient to be sitting for long. With everyone else in the house occupied I am brought in as companion and chaperone to amuse her, while on the other side of the room our painter's hands move steadily on the page.

Of course, I am as much interested in him as in her. Everyone in the house has been given new robes in celebration of the day, and he looks handsome though not particularly comfortable in his. It is weeks since I sent him the Alberti, but I have heard nothing from him. He is fatter (our kitchen is renowned) and is it my imagination or does he hold his head a little higher? Our eyes meet as I come in and I think there might even be a smile there, but on this of all days he must also practice humility. The only thing that has not changed is his hand, as concentrated as ever, each line bringing her more alive, then marking the fabrics with numbers so he can tell which colors to add later.

What he does on his nights away I still have no idea. Even my queen of gossip has nothing to tell me. In the house he is still a loner, shunning the company of others, only now they see him as snobbish rather than sick, placing himself above them, which given his status as the family artist is of course fitting. It is only much later I realize it is less snobbery that stops him from talking than the fact that he does not know what to say. Children brought up in a monastery, in the company of adults, learn better than most the power of solitude and the pure but harsh discipline of speaking only to Our Lord.

I catch his eye and realize that his hand has moved on to me. But my likeness is not within his instructions and his attention makes me blush. As the younger sister, it is important I do not outshine the bride, though there is little enough chance of that. Despite all my mother's ointments, my skin is as dark as my sister's is fair, and recently my giraffe body has begun to sprout in ways that all of Erila's skills with lacing and the thick box pleats of the tailor's design cannot hide. He has no time to finish me. The room is suddenly awash with people, and we are being bustled out. In the courtyard below, the main gates are open and Erila and I watch as Plautilla is hoisted onto the white horse, her dress arranged so it flows like a golden lake around her, and the wedding chest is lifted to the shoulders of the grooms (Erila says it takes as many men to carry as Lorenzo's coffin), and so the procession to the house of her in-laws begins.

As we parade through the streets a crowd gathers, which gives my father particular pleasure, but then he knows that our fortune grows from spinning women's desire into fabric and that waiting to greet us at Maurizio's house are dozens of Florence's more affluent families, each with an appetite for fine cloth.

The façade of their palazzo is hung with ornate tapestries especially hired for the occasion. Inside, the wedding banquet is laid out on long trestle tables in the courtyard. If my father is the master of the cloth, his in-laws rival him with the food. There is not an animal within hunting distance of Florence that hasn't lost at least one member of its family to the oven that day. The greatest delicacy is the roasted peacocks' tongues, though given the screeching of their cousins at our house I can't bring myself to pity them too much. I feel more sorry for the turtledove and the chamois deer, both of which are much less glorious dead than alive, though the smell of their spiced flesh is enough to make the old men dribble over their velvet jerkins. Along with the game there is poultry—boiled capon and chicken—followed by veal, a whole roasted kid, and a great fish pie flavored with oranges, nutmegs, saffron, and dates. There are so many courses that after a while you can smell the belches as much as the food. Of course, such culinary excess is officially frowned upon. Florence, like all good Christian cities, has laws to limit luxury. But just as everyone knows that a woman's marriage chest is a way to hide her excess jewels and rich fabrics from the authorities, so the feast that follows the ceremony is a private affair. Indeed, it's not unknown to see the very people whose job it is to police the law stuffing their faces with the rest of the gluttons, though what the pious new prior of San Marco would make of such hypocrisy and decadence doesn't bear thinking about.

After the food comes the dancing. Plautilla is the true bride at this moment, turning a sweep of her hand into an invitation of such subtle coquetry that it makes me despair anew at my own clumsiness. When she and Maurizio lead the "Bassa Danza Lauro," Lorenzo's own composition (and its own statement of allegiance danced so soon after his death), it is impossible to take one's eyes off her.

I, in contrast, am all left feet. On one of the more complex turning moves I lose my place completely and am only saved when my partner of the moment whispers the next steps in my ear as we pass. As I recover, my rescuer, a man of older years, holds my eye firmly during the next move, steering me through, and as we interlace for the last time—with a certain elegance, I am proud to say—he bows his head toward me again and says quietly, "So tell me—is it better to excel at Greek or at dancing?" before turning on his heel in time to pay court to the girl standing next to me.

Since it is only my family who are so intimately acquainted with my failings, and my brothers in particular who would be spiteful enough to use them as gossip, I feel myself flush with sudden shame. My mother, of course, has been following the whole encounter like a hawk. I anticipate a rebuke in her eyes, but she simply looks at me for a moment, then glances away.

The festivities last far into the night. People eat until they can hardly walk, and the wine flows like the Arno in flood so that many of the men become quite rude on it. But what they say to each other I cannot tell you, because by now I am banished to one of the upper rooms with two fat chaperones and a dozen girls of my own age for company. The segregation of unmarried young women at these moments is accepted custom (flowers still in bud must be protected from any forced advent of summer), but recently the gap between the other girls and me feels wider than our age, and as I looked down on the party that night, I vowed that this would be the last time I would be an observer rather than a participant.

And I was right, though I was yet to understand the cost.

TO MY SURPRISE I MISSED PLAUTILLA. AT FIRST THE EXPANSE OF white linen and my undisputed sovereignty over what had been our room gave me pleasure. But after a while the bed began to feel too big without her. I would no longer hear her snoring or grow tired of her chatter. Her babble of words, however trivial or annoying, had been a backdrop to my life for so long that I could not imagine what the silence would be like. The house began to echo around me. My father went abroad again, and with his absence my brothers took more often to the streets. Even the painter was gone, to a workshop near Santa Croce where he could practice the art of fresco, which he would need for the altar. With the right teacher and with my father's purse behind him, he would buy himself entrance into the Doctors and Apothecaries Guild, without which no painter could work offi- cially in the city. Just the thought of such elevation made me ache with longing.

When it came to my own future, my mother proved as good as her word and there was no immediate talk of marriage negotia- tions. My father's mind when he returned was on other things.

Even I could see that in the wake of Lorenzo's death the geometry of influence in the city had begun to shift. Florence was noisy with speculation as to how far Piero de' Medici could fill his father's shoes and, if not, whether the family's enemies would, after so many years of suppression, gain enough support to tip the balance. While I knew little of politics at that time, it was impossible to miss the venom now spurting forth from the pulpit of Santa Maria del Fiore. Prior Savonarola had recently outgrown his church at San Marco and now delivered his weekly sermons to an increasingly packed cathedral. The holy friar, it seemed, was in direct contact with God, and when they looked down together on Florence they saw a city corrupted by privilege and intellectual vanity. After so many years spent daydreaming my way through sermons full of scriptures but no fire, I found his lava flow of words spellbinding. When he railed against Aristotle or Plato as pagans whose works undermined the true church while their souls rotted in eternal fire, there were arguments I could find to defend them, but only afterward, when his voice was no longer ringing in my ears. He had a passion that felt like possession, and he painted pictures of hell that curdled one's insides with the smell of sulfur.

What all this meant for my future marriage plans was hard to tell, though married I must clearly be. In Savonarola's vision of this bleak, stained city, virgins were more at risk than ever before—just think of that poor girl whose body had been destroyed by lust and left for the dogs to ravage on the banks of the Arno. My brothers, who would remain single till their thirties, at which point they would be deemed sober enough to become husbands, having ruined God knows how many virgin servants on the way, made it their business to taunt me about the whole marriage business.

I REMEMBER ONE ENCOUNTER IN PARTICULAR THAT TOOK PLACE IN the summer of 1494. The house was full again, my father busy with the affairs of another journey and the painter, recently arrived home from his apprenticeship, barricaded in his room

intent on completing the designs for the chapel. I was sitting in
my room, a book open on my lap, my mind filled with schemes as
to how I might visit him, when Tomaso and Luca swaggered past
me on their way out. They were dressed for pleasure, though the
new cut of the tunic high up the thigh did more for Tomaso's leg
than for Luca, who wore my father's cloth with all the elegance of
a bullock cart. Tomaso, in contrast, had a fast eye for fashion and
from an early age had walked as if the world were watching him
and approving what it saw. His vanity was so naked it made me
want to laugh, but I knew better than to make fun of him. He had
bloodied me too many times in the past.

"Alessandra, dearest," he said, sweeping me a mocking wide
bow. "Look, Luca, our sister is reading another book! How
charming. And such a modest pose. You had better be careful,
though. While husbands like meek wives who keep their heads
down, you will have to lift your eyes up to them sometimes."

"I'm sorry? What was that you said?"

"I said you're going to be next. Isn't she, Luca?"

"Next for what?"

"Shall I tell her or will you?"

Luca shrugged. "Rolling and plucking," he said, making it
sound like something the cook does in the kitchen. While they
might be slow at Greek grammar, my brothers had a talent for the
most recent street slang, which they used whenever my mother
was out of earshot.

"Rolling and plucking? And what is that, pray, Luca?"

"It's what Plautilla's been doing." He grinned, referring to the
fact that our sister had recently set the household alight with the
announcement of her pregnancy and the promise of a male heir.

"Poor little sister." Tomaso's sympathy is worse than his spite.
"Didn't *she* tell you what it is like? Well, let's see. I can only speak
for the man. With a ripe one, it would be—like the first suck of a
juicy watermelon."

"And what do you do with the skin?"

He laughed. "Depends how long you want it to last. Though maybe you should ask your precious painter the same question."

"What's he got to do with it?"

"You don't know? Oh, dear Alessandra, I thought you knew everything. That's what the tutors always tell us."

"They only mean it in comparison to you," I retorted, before I could stop myself. "What are you saying about the painter?"

But I am too eager, which gives him an advantage.

He makes me wait. "What I'm saying is that our apparently devout little artist has been spending his nights poking around the Florentine slums. And he's not there to paint pictures. Isn't that right, Luca?"

My elder brother nods, his face fat with a silly grin.

"How do you know?"

"Because we met him, that's why."

"When?"

"Last night, sneaking back over the old bridge."

"Did you speak to him?"

"I asked him where he'd been, yes."

"And?"

"And he looked guilty as sin and said he was 'taking the night air.' "

"Maybe he was."

"Oh, little sister. You have no idea. The man was a mess. Face like a ghost, stains all over him. He was positively reeking of it— the stink of cheap cunt." Though I had not heard the word before, I knew from the way he said it something of what it must mean, and while I chose not to show it, he shocked me by the contempt in his voice. "So. You had better be careful. If he paints you again, keep your cloak wrapped tight around you. He might take more than your likeness."

"Have you told anyone else about this?"

He smiles. "You mean have I snitched on him? Why should I? I think he probably paints better on the juice of a good whore than he would on a diet of the Gospels. Who was that artist you so love? The one who plucked the nun for his Madonna."

"Fra Filippo," I say. "She was very beautiful. And he offered to marry her afterward."

"Only because the Medici made him. I bet old Cosimo took a bit off the price of the altarpiece though."

It is clear that Tomaso has inherited something of my father's business acumen.

"So what bargain did you strike with the painter in return for your silence, Tomaso?"

He laughs. "What do you think? I made him promise to give Luca and me a good leg and a wide brow. Our beauty for posterity. And to give you a harelip—and a shortened leg, to explain your dancing."

Though I am expecting it, of course, his cruelty still takes me aback. It always comes to this moment in our arguments: his need to punish me for the humiliations of the study room; my refusal to be crushed. I sometimes think the trajectory of my whole life was played out in my battles with Tomaso. That each time I won I also somehow lost.

"Oh, don't tell me I've hurt your feelings! If you only knew... We're doing you a favor, aren't we, Luca? It's not easy finding a husband for a girl who quotes Plato but falls over her own feet. Everybody knows you're going to need all the help you can get."

"You better be careful, both of you," I say darkly, thickening my voice to cover my hurt. "You think you can do what you like. That Father's money and our coat of arms give you license. But if you opened your eyes you'd see things are changing. The sword of God's wrath is rising above the city. He stalks the streets at night in your footsteps and sees what evil you commit."

"Whoa, you sound just like Savonarola." Luca laughs nervously. I am good at voices when I put my mind to it.

"You laugh now"—I turn on him, drilling his eye as I have seen the prior do from the pulpit—"but you'll be crying soon enough. The Lord will send plague, flood, war, and famine to

punish the ungodly. Those who clothe themselves in righteousness will be saved; the rest will choke on the fumes of the sulfur."

For a moment I swear even my lumpen brother can feel the
heat of hell.

"Don't listen to her, Luca." Tomaso is harder to scare. "He's a
madman. Everyone knows that."

"Not everyone, Tomaso. He knows how to preach and he
quotes the scriptures well. You should listen to him sometime."

"Ah ... I do start listening, but then my eyelids grow heavy."

"That's because you've been out too late the night before.
Look behind you and see the effect he has on those who have
slept in their own beds. They have eyes as big as hosts. And they
believe him." I can see Luca is listening hard now.

"War? Famine? Flood? We see the Arno in the streets every
other year, and if the crops fail people will be hungry again. It
doesn't have to be God's will."

"Yes, but if Savonarola predicts it and then it happens, people
will connect the two. Think about the pope."

"What? He tells us that a sick old man is going to die, and then
when he does everyone calls him a prophet. I would have thought
it would take more than that to impress you. Anyway, you should
be more worried than most. If he's suspicious of learning in men,
he believes the Devil resides in women. He doesn't even think
women should speak. Because, if you remember, dear Sis, it was
Eve who used her words to beguile Adam and—"

"Why is it when there are voices raised in this house it is always
you two?" My mother sweeps into the room dressed for traveling,
Maria and another servant trotting behind carrying a set of
leather bags. "You brawl like street fighters. It is an offense to hear
you. You, sir, should not taunt your sister, and you, Alessandra, are
a disgrace to your sex."

We all bow to her. Halfway down I catch Tomaso's eye, and he
gives my unspoken request for a truce some thought. There are
still some moments when our need to help each other is greater
than our differences.

"Dear Mama, forgive us, we were simply discussing religion," he says, with a charm that might undress certain women but was lost on my mother. "How far we should pay heed to the good friar's recent sermons."

"Oh!" She let out an angry breath. "I would hope my children would follow God's will without Savonarola's words to sting them into action."

"But surely you don't agree with him, Mama?" I said urgently. "He believes the study of the ancients is a betrayal of Christ's truth."

She stops and stares at me, her mind still half on other things. "Alessandra, each day I pray that you will find a way to contentment by questioning less and accepting more. As to Girolamo Savonarola—well, he is a holy man who believes in the kingdom of heaven." She frowned. "Still, I do wonder that Florence should have had to find a friar from Ferrara to hold a mirror up to her soul. If one has to listen to bad news, it is better to come from one's own family. Like now." She sighed. "I have to go to Plautilla."

"To Plautilla? Why?"

"There is some problem with the baby. She has asked for me. I will almost certainly stay the night and send word back with Angelica. Alessandra, you will stop brawling and get ready for your dancing teacher, who apparently still believes that miracles are possible. Luca, you will go to your studies, and Tomaso, you will stay and speak to your father when he gets in. He is at a meeting of the Security Council in the Signoria, and it is likely that he will be late."

"But Mother—"

"Whatever it is that you have planned to do this evening, Tomaso, it will wait until your father returns. Is that clear?"

And my pretty brother, who always has an answer to everything, remained silent.

Eight

I STAYED UP LATE, EATING MILK PUDDINGS FILCHED FROM the pantry—our cook adored me for my appetite, and such theft was viewed only as the sincerest form of flattery—and playing chess with Erila for gossip. It was the only game where I could ever beat her. At dice and cards she was a master gambler, though I suspect it was as much her skill in cheating as in playing. On the streets she could probably have made a fortune, though gambling was one of the sins that Savonarola was now breathing fire on from the pulpit.

When we had tired of playing, I made her help me mix up my ink washes and then pose for me in my Madonna's silk Annunciation dress. I set the lamp to the left of her, so the shadows created came nearest to the effect of daylight. Everything I knew of such techniques came from Cennini. Though he was long dead, he was the nearest I would come to a teacher and I studied him with the devotion of a novitiate to the scriptures. Following his lore on drapery, I used the richest ink wash to create the darkest part of the shadow, then graduated the ink lighter until it reached the tops of the folds, where I added a streak of watered white lead so the ridge of cloth seemed to capture the shine of the light. But while it gave Our Lady's costume a certain depth, even I could see it was crude, more a trickery of the brush than an expression of truth. My limitations made me despair. As long as I was both my own master and apprentice I would be forever caught in the web of inexperience.

"Oh, keep still. I can't capture the fold if you move."

"You should try standing here like a piece of stone. My arms are falling off, they ache so."

"That's from the speed with which you move your chess pieces. If you were sitting for a real painter you would have to be statue-still for hours."

"If I were sitting for a real painter my purse'd be heavy with florins."

I grinned. "I'm surprised they haven't plucked you off the streets. Your skin shines so when the sun is on you."

"Ha! And what story would they put my color in?"

Looking back on it now, I wish I had had the courage to make her my Madonna, just to capture that coal-black sheen. There were those in the city who still found her skin strange; they would turn and gawp at her as we walked together back from church, half fascinated, half repulsed. But she would have none of it, holding their stare until they broke first. For me her color had always been glorious. There had been times when I could barely stop my brush from tracing a line of white lead along her forearm just to marvel at the contrast between the light and the black.

"What about our painter? Mother says the chapel frescoes will be the life of Santa Caterina of Alexandria. There would be room enough for you there. Has he never asked you?"

"My likeness done by Skinnyboy?" She looked at me intently. "What do you think?"

"I . . . I don't know. I think he has a great eye for beauty."

"A young monk's fear of it, too. For him I'm just another shade he wants to capture."

"So you think he is impervious to women?"

She snorted. "If he is, he'll be the first one I've ever met. He's just rigid with purity."

"In which case I wonder why you go to such lengths to keep me out of his company!"

She stared at me for a moment. "Because in the right hands innocence can spring more traps than knowledge."

"Well, that shows how much you know," I said, triumphant that for once my gossip was fresher than hers. "From what I hear he spends his nights with women whose souls are blacker than your skin."

"Who told you that?"

"My brothers."

"Pah! They don't know their arse from their elbows. Tomaso loves himself too much, and when it comes to a woman's body Luca couldn't find a crow in a bowl of milk."

"You say that, but I remember a time when he looked on you eagerly enough."

"Luca!" She laughed. "He's only got the stomach for sin when he's halfway down an ale cask. When he's sober I'm the Devil's creation."

"And so you are. Oh—Stop moving! How can I get the shadow right if you shift so?"

Later, when she was gone, I developed a throbbing in my belly that came and went in uneven rhythm, though how much that was a surfeit of milk pudding was hard to tell. The summer heat was upon us now, and it could curdle the brain. I wondered about Plautilla. Could it be her pain I was feeling? She would be at most only four to five months gone with child. What did that mean? Between Erila's gossip and my brothers' crudeness I probably knew more about the act of sex than most closeted girls of my age, but for every fact there was a small ocean of ignorance, and the growth of a baby was one of them. Still, I could read my mother's anxiety enough to know when it was serious. The ache came back like a fist squeezing my bowels. I got up and started to walk around to try and ease it.

I could not get the painter out of my mind. I thought about his talent, the way he had captured my hands at rest, how peaceful he had made them seem, how full of soul. Then I saw him stumbling across the Ponte Vecchio with my brother's gang splayed out in front of him, and try as I might I could not equate the two images. Yet whatever Erila's doubts, the fact that he had been there at all was deeply incriminating. The old bridge had a fearful reputation: the butchers' and candlemakers' shops with their womblike interiors and thick smells of rotting meat and boiling wax drifting out onto the street. Even by day there were dogs and beggars everywhere, sniffing around for scraps or offal, while at night on either side of the bridge the city splintered into a maze of alleyways where darkness hid all manner of sins.

The prostitutes themselves were careful enough. There were rules as to how they should conduct themselves. The bells they carried and the gloves they wore were the law as well as props of enticement. But again, it was a law gently implemented. As with the Sumptuary Police, there was an accepted difference between the spirit and the letter. Erila was forever coming home with stories about how women accosted by officials for wearing fur or silver buttons argued their way out of a fine by a cunning use of semantics: "Oh no, sir, this is not fur, it is a new material which is only *like* fur. And these? These are not buttons. There are no buttonholes, see? They are, rather, clips. Clips? Yes, you must have heard of them. Surely Florence is the wonder of the world, to have such new things in it." But from what one heard, such wit was now lost on certain of the new officers. Purity was coming back into fashion, and the blind eye of authority was getting back its vision.

I had only seen a courtesan once. The Ponte alle Grazie had been closed with flood damage and we had had to cross at the Ponte Vecchio. It was dusk. Ludovica walked in front of Plautilla and me, with Maria herding in the rear. We passed by an open shop door, a candlemaker's, I remember, gloomy inside but with a window at the back looking out over the river, the sunset behind it. A woman was sitting in silhouette, her breasts bare, and at her feet a man kneeling with his head between her skirts, as if in worship. She was lovely, her body lit up by the setting sun, and at that moment she turned her head to look out toward the street and I am sure she saw me staring. She smiled and seemed so... well, sure of herself. I know that I felt both excited and disturbed and had to look away.

I wondered later about her palpable beauty. If Plato was right, how could it be possible for a woman of no virtue to have such looks? Filippo Lippi's mistress had at least been a nun serving God when the call came to be his Madonna. And in a way she still served God afterward, her image calling others to prayer. Oh, she was beautiful! Her face lit up dozens of his paintings: clear-eyed, calm, shouldering her burden with gratitude and grace. I liked her more than Botticelli's Madonna. Though Fra Filippo had been his teacher he had taken a different model, a woman everyone knew to have been Giuliano de' Medici's mistress. Once you knew her face you began to see it everywhere: in his nymphs, his angels, his classical heroines, even his saints. Botticelli's Madonna, you felt, might belong to anyone who looked at her. Fra Filippo's belonged only to God and herself.

My stomach stabbed at me again. My mother kept a bottle of digestive *liquore* in the medicine chest in her dressing room. If I took some now it might ease the pain. I left my room and moved silently down one flight of stairs, but as I turned toward my mother's quarters I was drawn to something else, a flickering line of light coming from under the door of the chapel room to my left. The chapel was out of bounds to servants, and with my mother and father gone there was only one person it could be. I can no longer remember if that thought halted or spurred me on.

INSIDE, A FLICKERING WAVE OF CANDLELIGHT ILLUMINATES THE apse, but immediately the light contracts, then eclipses altogether as the last candle is capped. I wait, then close the door behind me, deliberately letting its hinges moan, before letting it slam noisily shut. Whoever I am, as far as he is concerned I have left again.

For the longest time we stand in the dark, the silence so raw that when I swallow I can hear the sound of my saliva inside my ears. Finally, a pinprick of light appears where the candles had been. I watch as the concealed taper fires one wick, then another and another, until the apse is awash with tongues of orange and he comes into focus, his tall lanky body revealed inside the semi-circle of light.

I take the first steps toward him. My feet are bare and I am practiced at night walking. But so, it seems, is he. His head lifts sharply, like an animal reading a night scent. "Who's there?" And his voice is harsh enough to do damage to my heartbeat, though I know it comes from fear rather than anger.

I walk to the edge of the light. The glow of the candles throws shadows onto his face and his eyes glint, a true cat in the dark. We are neither of us dressed for company. He has no tunic on and his undershirt is open so I can see the ridge of his collarbone and the smooth bare flesh beneath, pearl-shiny in the candlelight. I am a frozen gawky figure in a crumpled chemise, my hair unbraided down my back. That same yeasty smell about him that I remember from our portrait sitting is heavy in the air around us. Except now I know where it comes from. What did my brother call it, the stink of cheap cunt? But if Erila is right, how could a man so frightened of women be so drawn? What if he is come here to confess?

"I saw the candlelight from the corridor. What are you doing?"

"I am working," he says gruffly.

Now, behind him, I can see the *cartone* stuck to the east wall of the apse, a full-sized drawing of the fresco with the outline pricked out so it can be transferred to the wall in charcoal. The art of fresco: what I know so much about in theory he is now familiar with in fact. His new knowledge makes me want to cry. I know I should not be here. Whether he is profligate or not, if we were to be found together now both our lives would be torn apart. But my hunger and my curiosity override my fear, and I move past him to read the drawing better.

I can still see it now: the glory of Florence conjured up in a hundred deft pen strokes. In the foreground, two groups of people are gathered on each side, staring down at a stretcher on the floor on which a girl's body is laid. They are marvelous, these spectators: flesh-and-blood men and women of the city, their characters captured in their faces—age, kindness, serenity, or stubbornness in turn. His ethereal pen has come down to earth. But his journey is most noticeable in the girl. She draws your eye in immediately, not just because she is the focal point in the composition but because of her intense fragility. With Tomaso's obscenities buzzing in my head, I cannot help but wonder where he has found the model. Perhaps he only seeks them out to paint them. Were there really prostitutes so young? That she is a girl rather than a woman is obvious; under her night shift you can feel her breasts budding and there is a clumsy angularity about her frame, as if womanhood is coming too soon. But the singular most arresting thing about her body is its complete lifelessness.

"Oh!" I am speaking before I have given myself permission. "You have learned a lot in our city. How do you do that? How is it I know she is dead? When I look at her it seems so clear. But which are the lines that tell me that? Show me. Whenever I draw bodies, I can't distinguish sleep from death. Many times they just look awake with their eyes closed."

So there. It is out at last. I wait for him to laugh in my face or show his contempt in a million other ways. The silence grows and I am as scared as when we were both in the dark.

"I should tell you that this is not a confession in the face of God, sir, since He already knows," I say quietly. "But it is a confession in front of you. So perhaps you might say something?"

I look past him into the gloom of the chapel. It is as good a place as any. Its walls will surely hear worse in years to come.

"You draw?" he says softly.

"Yes. Yes! But I want to do more. I want to paint. As you do."

Suddenly it seems as if it is the most important thing in the world to tell him. "Is that so terrible? If I were a boy and had talent, I would already be apprenticed to a master—just as you have been. Then I too would know how to light up these walls with paint. But instead I am stuck in this house while my parents look for a husband for me. Eventually they will buy one with a good name and I will go to his house, run his household, have his children, and disappear into the fabric of his life like a pale thread of color in a tapestry. Meanwhile the city will be full of artists constructing glories to God, and I shall never know if I could have done the same. Even though I don't have your talent, painter, I have your desire. You have to help me. Please."

And I know he has understood. He does not laugh or dismiss me. But what can he say? What could anyone say to me? I am so arrogant, even in my despair.

"If you need help, you must ask God for it. It is a matter between you and Him."

"Oh, but I *have* asked. And He has sent me you." His face shifts in the candlelight so I can no longer see his expression. But I am too young and too eager to bear his silence for long. "Don't you understand? We are allies, you and I. If I had wanted to harm you, I could have told my parents how you attacked me that first afternoon."

"Except I think you sinned as much against propriety as I did that day," he says quietly. "As we do now, being here together." And he starts to gather up his stuff in preparation for blowing out the candles and I watch it all slipping away from me.

"Why do you dismiss me so? Is it because I am a woman?" I take a breath. "Because it seems to me you have learned enough from them in other ways." He stops, though he does not turn or in any other way acknowledge my words. "I mean . . . I mean your girl on the stretcher. I wonder how much you paid for her to lie down for you."

Now he turns and looks at me, and his face is bloodless in the candlelight. But there is no going back.

"I know what it is you do at night, sir. I have watched you leaving the house. I have spoken to my brother Tomaso. I think my father would be most unhappy to discover that his chapel painter spends his nights whoring in the slums of the city."

At that moment I think it possible that he might cry. For all that God might be in his fingertips, he is sorely inadequate when it comes to dealing with the cunning of our city. How disillusioning it must have been for him, arriving in the new Athens only to find it so noisy with compromise and temptation. Maybe Savonarola is right, after all. Maybe we have indeed become too worldly for our own good.

"You don't understand anything," he says, and his voice is dark with pain.

"All I am asking is that you look at my work. Tell me what you think, without lying. If you do this simple thing I will not breathe a word. More—I will protect you against my brother. He can be much more vicious than I, and—"

We both hear it: the crash of the central door opening below us in the house. The same lightning rod of horror runs through us together and without thinking we start to extinguish the candles around us. If someone were to come in now... What did I think I had been doing, taking such a risk?

"My father," I whisper, as the darkness engulfs us. "He was at a meeting of the Signoria late."

On cue I hear his voice, calling up into the stairwell; then, from nearer, another door opening. Tomaso must have fallen asleep waiting for him. Their voices mingle and another door closes. It is quiet.

Close by in the darkness the red speck of his taper light glows like a firefly. We are so close to each other that his breath grazes my cheek. His smell is all around me, hot and sour, and I feel a sudden sickness in the pit of my stomach. If I put out my hand now I could touch the skin on his chest. I step back as if he has scalded me and send a candle spinning over the flagstone floor. The noise is awful. A moment earlier, and...

"I'll go first," I say, when I have regained my balance, and my voice sounds dry with fear. "Stay until you hear the door close."

He grunts assent. A flicker of candlelight appears next to the taper glow, with his face illuminated above it. He lifts it and hands it to me. Our eyes meet in the glow. Do we have an agreement? I have no idea. I retrace my footsteps hurriedly to the main door. When I reach it I look back to see his figure in enlarged silhouette against the wall as he pulls the paper down from the apse wall, his arms outstretched like a man crucified.

Nine

B ACK IN MY ROOM, THE SOUND OF MY FATHER'S AND brother's voices echoed up the stone staircase from his study below. The pain in my stomach corkscrewed again so that I could barely stay upright. I gave the argument time to end, then made my way out again, determined now to reach my mother's medicine chest.

But I was not the only one up who shouldn't be. Tomaso was coming down the stairs with about as much finesse as a wounded bull. But at least he was trying to be quiet. He was so intent on stepping on air that he walked straight into me, then looked guilty as sin as he straightened up—all of which meant I had something to barter.

"Alessandra! God's teeth, you gave me a fright," he said, in a cracked whisper. "What are doing here?"

"I heard you and Father arguing," I lied smoothly. "It woke me up. Where are you going? It's nearly morning."

"I—have to see someone."

"What did Father say?"

"Nothing."

"Did he have news about Plautilla?"

"No, no. There's no news from her."

"So what did you talk about?" His lips closed a little tighter. "Tomaso?" I said, with soft threat. "What did you and Father talk about?"

He gave me a cool stare, as if to show that while he understood the bargain, this particular surrender would not cause him much grief. "There's trouble in the city."

"What kind of trouble?"

He paused. "Bad. The night watchmen of Santo Spírito have found two bodies."

"Bodies?"

"A man and a woman. Murdered."

"Where?"

He took a breath. "In the church."

"The church! What happened?"

"No one knows. They found them this morning. They were laid out beneath the pews. Their throats had been slit."

"Oh!"

But there was more. I could see it in his eyes. God help me, though I didn't mean to, my thoughts strayed to the body of that young woman with dog bites all over her. "What else?"

"They were both naked. And she had something stuffed in her mouth," he said grimly, then stopped, as if he might have said enough.

I frowned to show I didn't understand.

"It was his cock." He watched my confusion, then gave a grim little smile and put his hand down to grab hold of his own crotch. "Understand now? Whoever killed them cut off his cock and stuck it in her mouth."

"Oh!" I know I must have sounded like a child, because at that moment I felt like one again. "Oh, who would do such a thing? And in Santo Spírito!"

But we both knew the answer. The same madman who had cut the marsh girl's body to pieces just by Santa Croce church.

"That's what Father's meeting was about. The Signoria and the Security Council have decided to move the bodies."

"Move them? You mean—"

"So they'll be found outside the city."

"That's what Father told you tonight?"

He nodded.

But why would he have done that? If you were going to keep such a horror secret, you didn't do so by telling people. Especially not young men like Tomaso, who spent half their lives out on the streets. Young men who might therefore find themselves at risk if they didn't change their behavior. Of course. My stomach pain must have addled my brain.

"But—why should they move them? I mean, if that's where they were found, shouldn't—"

"What happens, Alessandra, do you get stupid at night?" He sighed. "Think about it. The desecration would cause a riot."

He was right. It would. Only a few weeks before, a young man had been found chipping bits off the statues in the niches outside the old church of Orsanmichele and had barely escaped with his life after the mob had got hold of him. Erila said he had been touched by madness, but Savonarola had made the city nervous about such blasphemy and, after a summary trial, the hangman had dispatched him three days later with less violence and equally little ceremony. A sacrilege such as this one now would offer fine ammunition to the friar. What were his words about Florence? *When the Devil rules a city, his uncrowned consort is lust, and thus does evil proliferate until there is only filth and despair.*

I felt so sick and so frightened that I had to pretend not to be. "You know, Tomaso," I said with a small laugh, "there are some brothers who would protect their younger sisters against such stories."

"And there are some sisters who spend their days worshipping their brothers."

"But what fun would you get from them, pray?" I said softly. "They would surely bore you."

For the first time as we looked at each other I wondered how our lives might have been if we had not been cast as enemies. He shrugged slightly and started to move past me.

"You can't go out now, not knowing that. It could be dangerous." He said nothing.

"That's what you and Father were rowing about, right? He forbade you to go?"

He shook his head. "I have an appointment, Alessandra. I *have* to go."

I took a breath. "Whoever she is, you can wait."

He looked at me in the gloom for a moment and then smiled. "You don't understand, little sister. Even if I could, *she* can't. So. Good night." He said it quietly and made to leave.

I put a hand on his arm. "Be careful."

He let it rest there for a while before he lifted it off carefully. Was he on the verge of saying something more, or did I only imagine it? He took a sudden step back from me. "God, Alessandra, what's happened? You're hurt!"

"What?"

"Look at you, you're bleeding."

I looked down. Sure enough, on the front of my shift there was a fresh dark stain.

And suddenly it all made sense. It wasn't Plautilla's pain I was feeling but my own. It had come. The moment I most dreaded in my life. I felt a great flush of shame rise up like fever. My face grew hot with it and I clutched my hands over my night shift, scrunching it up between my fingers until the stain disappeared. And as I did so I felt a trickle of hot liquid run down the inside of my thigh.

Tomaso, of course, read it all. I felt even sicker with terror at the prospect of his revenge. But instead he did something I have never forgotten. He leaned toward me and touched my cheek. "So," he said, almost gently, "it seems we both have secrets now. Good night, little sister." He moved past me down the stairs, and I heard a door below him close quietly.

I went to bed and felt my blood flow.

Ten

MY MOTHER ARRIVED HOME BEFORE ANY OF US HAD RISEN. She and my father ate behind closed doors. At ten o'clock Erila woke me to say I had been summoned to his study. When she saw the blood she gave me a sly smile, changed my sheets, and brought me cloth to bind into my undergarments.

"Not a word," I said. "Do you understand? Not a word to anyone until I say so."

"Then you'd better say so fast. Maria will sniff you out in no time."

Erila dressed me quickly and I presented myself. At the dining table I met Luca, bleary-eyed, stuffing himself with bread and pork jelly. I felt too sick to eat. He scowled at me. I scowled back. My mother and father were waiting. Tomaso arrived a few minutes later. Despite a change of clothes, he had the look of someone who had not been to bed.

My father's study was situated at the back of his showroom at the side of the palazzo, where the ladies of the town would bring their tailors to pick the latest fabrics. The place reeked of camphor and other salts suspended in pomades from the ceiling to keep away the moths, and the smell permeated his room. These areas were usually out of bounds for us children, particularly for Plautilla and me, and for that reason of course I loved them even more. From his small parchment-lined office my father ran a small empire of trade throughout Europe and parts of the East. As well as wool and cotton from England, Spain, and Africa, he imported many of the rainbow dyes: vermilion and realgar from the Red Sea, cochineal and *oricello* from the Mediterranean, gall nuts from the Balkans, and, from the Black Sea, the rock alum with which to fix them. Once the cloth was finished, the bolts that did not go into Florentine fashion went back onto the ships to feed the luxury markets in the countries they came from. When I look back on it now, I think my father lived with the weight of the world on his shoulders, because while we prospered I know there were times when the news was bad—when the loss of a ship to storms or piracy had him in his room through the night and my mother kept us on tiptoe next day lest we should wake him. Certainly in my memory he was forever at his ledgers or his letters, tallying the columns of profit and loss and sending dispatches to merchants, agents, and cloth manufacturers who lived in cities with names I could barely pronounce, sometimes in places where they didn't believe that Jesus Christ was the son of God, though their heathen fingers understood beauty and truth enough within a bale of cloth. Such letters flew daily out of our house like carrier pigeons, signed, sealed, and wrapped in waterproof cloths against the elements, painstakingly copied and filed in case of mishap or loss on the road.

With such business upon him, it was no wonder that my father had so little time for matters of the home. But that morning he looked particularly weary, his face more jowly and lined than I remembered it. He was seventeen years older than my mother and would have been in his fifties at this time. He was rich and well thought of and had twice been chosen for minor offices of state, the most recent his place on the Security Council. Had he been more strategic with his influence he might have promoted himself quicker, but while he was shrewd at business he was also a simple man, more suited to the transport of cloth than politics. I believe he loved us children and he was good enough at lecturing Tomaso and Luca when their behavior demanded it, but in some ways he was more at ease in his factories than his home. His education had only been sufficient unto the fact of his trade—his father had done it before him—and he had none of my mother's knowledge or her golden tongue. But he could tell if the color in a bolt of cloth was uneven from a single glance, and he always knew which shade of red would please the ladies most when the sun shone.

So the speech he gave that morning was, for him, long and one to which he, and I suspect my mother, had given much thought.

"First I have good news to give you. Plautilla is well. Your mother stayed the night with her, and she is recovered."

My mother sat back straight, hands folded in her lap. She had long since perfected the art of female quiescence. If you had not known, you would think she was feeling nothing.

"But there is other news, which, since you will hear it soon enough from gossip, we have decided that you should learn first at home."

I shot a glance at Tomaso. Was he really going to talk of naked women with cocks in their mouths? Not my father, surely.

"The Signoria have been meeting through the night because there are events abroad that affect our security. The king of France is arrived in the north at the head of an army to pursue his claim on the Duchy of Naples. He has destroyed the Neapolitan fleet at Genoa and signed treaties with Milan and Venice. But to go farther south he must come through Tuscany, and he has sent envoys asking for our support of his claim and safe passage for his army."

I could see from Tomaso's smirk at me that he had known more than he'd told me all along. But then of course women are not fit for politics.

"So will there be fighting?" Luca's eyes shone like gold medallions. "I hear the French are fierce warriors."

"No, Luca. There will not be fighting. There is more glory in peace than in war," said my father sternly, no doubt aware of how the demand for fine cloth diminishes during conflict. "The Signoria, with the advice of Piero de' Medici, will offer neutrality but no support for his claim. In that way we shall show strength mixed with prudence."

Had Piero's name been spoken even six months before it would probably have soothed us all, but even I knew that his reputation had crumbled since his father's death. Rumor was that he had trouble pulling on his own boots without whining or losing his temper. How was he possibly going to have the charm or the cunning to negotiate with a king who didn't need to flatter our city-state when he could just walk in and trample all over it? Though such thoughts were not for me to voice.

"If we pin our hopes on Piero, we might as well open the gates today and welcome them in."

My father sighed. "And which gossipmonger tells you that?" Tomaso shrugged. "I am telling you the Signoria has faith in the Medici name. There is no one else who commands such a level of respect with a foreign king."

"Well, I don't think we should let them just walk through. I think we should fight them," said Luca, as usual having listened but not heard a thing.

"No, we will not fight them. We will talk to them and make terms with them, Luca. Their battle is not with us. It will be an agreement among equals. They might even give us something in return."

"What? You think Charles will fight our disputes for us and deliver Pisa into our hands?" I had never heard Tomaso so outrightly quarrelsome in front of my father before. My mother was looking at him sternly, but he did not or would not notice. "He will simply do what he pleases. He knows he only has to threaten and our great Republic will cave in like a house of cards."

"And you are a boy trying to speak like a man and making a risible job of it," said my father. "Until you have the years to take on such matters, you would do better to keep such treacherous opinions to yourself. I will not hear them in this house."

There was a shimmering little silence where I kept my eyes away from both of them. Then Tomaso said sullenly, "Very well, sir."

"And if they do come?" said Luca, still oblivious. "Will they come inside the city? Would we let them go that far?"

"This is something to be decided when we know more."

"What about Alessandra?" my mother asked quietly.

"My dear, if the French come upon us, Alessandra will be sent to a convent with all the other young girls of the city. Plans have already been discussed—"

"No," I blurted out.

"Alessandra—"

"No. I don't want to be sent away. If—"

"You will do as I see fit," said my father, his tone very angry now. He was not used to this level of rebellion in the family. But then he had forgotten how we had all grown older.

My mother, more pragmatic and wiser, simply looked down at her folded hands again and said softly, "I think before we say any more you should know that your father has other news to deliver."

They glanced at each other and she smiled slightly. He took her guidance gratefully.

"I...it is possible that within the foreseeable future I will be called to the honor of the office of Priore."

One of the Council of Eight. Honor indeed, even though his early knowledge of such elevation was proof that the selection process was corrupt. Looking back now I can still feel the pride in his voice as he said it. So much so that it would have been churlish even to think that at a time of such crisis our city might have been better served by wiser, more experienced men, because to acknowledge that would have meant also acknowledging that something was seriously wrong within the state, and I don't think any of us at that moment, even Tomaso, wanted to go that far.

"Father," I said, when it was clear that neither of my brothers was going to, "you do our family great honor by this news." And I came and knelt before him and kissed his hand, a dutiful daughter again.

My mother glanced approvingly in my direction as I rose.

"Why, thank you, Alessandra," he said. "I will remember that, if and when I take my place in the government."

But as we smiled at each other I couldn't help thinking of those butchered bodies and all the blood they would have left under the pews of Santo Spírito, and how Savonarola could use them powerfully against a city where the threat of a foreign invasion now made him an even greater prophet in the people's eyes.

MY MOTHER IS SITTING BY THE WINDOW IN HER ROOM. FOR A moment I think she might be praying. For as long as I can remember, she has had a way of being alone with her stillness that makes her seem almost absent. But whether it is thought or prayer I cannot always tell, and I do not have the courage to ask. Watching her from the door I see how beautiful she still is, though she is well past her youth and her beauty is more fragile in the harsh morning light. How does it feel when your family is slipping away from you and your first daughter is to become a mother? Is there triumph that you have navigated her through the waters of Scylla and Charybdis, or do you wonder what you will do with yourself now she has gone? Lucky for her that she still had me to worry about.

I waited till she noticed me, which she did without turning.

"I am very tired, Alessandra," she said quietly. "If this is not important I would prefer if it could wait till later."

I took a deep breath. "I want you to know that I won't go into a convent."

She frowned. "That decision is still some way off. Though if it comes to it, you will do as you are told."

"But you said yourself—"

"No! I am not talking about this now. You heard what your

father said: *If* the French come—and as yet that is by no means certain—the city will not be safe for young women."

"But he said they wouldn't come as enemies. If we make a truce—"

"Look," she said firmly, turning to me at last. "It is not women's business to know about the affairs of state. And you in particular will only add to your burdens by showing that you do. But it does not mean you should stay stupid in private. No army occupies a city without having some rights over it. And when soldiers are at war, they are not citizens, only mercenaries, and young virgins are most at risk. You *will* go to a convent."

I took a breath. "What if I was married? No longer a virgin, and with the protection of a husband? I would be safe then."

She stared at me. "But you don't want to be married."

"I don't want to be sent away."

She sighed. "You are still young."

"Only in years," I said. Why, I thought, must there always be two conversations, one that women have when there are men present and one we have when we are alone? "In other ways I am older than all of them. If I have to get married in order to stay, that is what I will do."

"Oh, Alessandra. That is not a good enough reason."

"Mama," I said, "it's all changed anyway. Plautilla is gone, I am at war with Tomaso, and Luca lives in his own thick fog. I can't study forever. Maybe that means I'm ready." And for that second I think I really believed it.

"But you know you are *not* ready."

"I am now," I said bluntly. "I started to bleed last night."

"Oh." Her hands went up and then down to her lap, in the way they always did when she sought to steady herself. "Oh!" And then she laughed and stood up, and I could see that she was also crying. "Oh, my dear child," she said, as she took me into her arms. "My dear, dear child."

Eleven

WITH CHARLES AND HIS ARMY ON THE TUSCAN BORDER AND panic sniffing around the city gates, Florence took herself to church. There were so many people in Santa Maria del Fiore that Sunday that the crowd spewed out onto the steps below. My mother said it was the greatest gathering she had ever seen for a service, but it felt to me as if we were waiting for Judgment Day. Gazing up into the dome, I felt—as I always did—a sudden vertigo, as if its very scale unbalanced one's mind.

My father says Brunelleschi's wonder is still the talk of Europe—how such a great structure could have risen without the traditional help of supporting beams. Even now when I imagine the final coming I think of Santa Maria del Fiore filled with the mass of the godly risen from the grave, the dome alive with the beating of angel wings.

Still, I would hope Judgment Day might smell better, since the stink of so many bodies hung in the air like a fog of foul incense that day. Already a number of the poorer women had fainted, but then the more devout had apparently begun fasting, on Savonarola's orders, to bring the city back to God. It would take longer for the rich to swoon, though I noticed they had been careful to dress down; this was not the time to risk being found guilty of vanity.

By the time Savonarola climbed into the pulpit the place was humming with godliness, but it fell deathly silent upon his arrival. It was the supreme irony of the age that Florence's ugliest man was also her most godly. Yet it was a testimony to his eloquence that when he preached you forgot his dwarf body, his drilling little eyes, and the nose hooked like an eagle's beak. Together he and his archenemy Lorenzo would have been the stuff of gargoyles. One could almost imagine the diptych in which their profiles confronted each other, their noses as powerful as their personalities, the city of Florence—their battle-field—in the background. But who would risk such a painting now? Who would dare to commission it?

His enemies said he was so small that to raise himself up he stood on books, translations of Aristotle and the classics that his monks procured for him so his feet could despoil them. Others claimed he used the stool from his cell, one of the few pieces of furniture that he allowed himself in a life of extreme asceticism. It was said that his was the only cell in San Marco without a devotional painting, so much suspicion did he have about the power of art to undermine the purity of faith, and that he stilled any cravings of the flesh by whipping himself daily. While there had always been those in the church with an appetite for flagellation, it was a delicacy of suffering that did not appeal to everyone. Looking back on it now, I think we Florentines were always a people more interested in pleasure than pain, though at times of crisis fear bred its own desire for self-punishment.

He stood for a moment in silence, his hands clutching the edge of the stone, his eyes raking the great crowd around him. "It is written that the shepherd should welcome his flock. But today I do not welcome you." The voice that came out began as a hiss, growing louder with each succeeding word until it filled the cathedral and rose up unto the heaven of the dome. "For today you crowd into God's house only because fear and despair lick at your feet like the flames of hell and because you long for redemption.

"So you come to me, to a man whose own unworthiness is matched only by the Lord's generosity in making him His mouthpiece. Yes, the Lord shows Himself to me. He blesses me with His vision and unveils the future. The army that waits on our border was foretold. It is the sword I saw hanging above the city. There is no fury like the fury of God. *'They shall cast their silver in the streets and their gold shall be removed: all their silver and gold shall not be able to deliver them in the day of the wrath of the Lord.'* And Florence lies like a carcass swarming with flies in the burning path of His vengeance."

Even for those who knew their scriptures well it was hard to see the seams. He was working up a sweat now, his hood thrown back, the nose moving to and fro like a great beak pecking at sparrows. At first, when he began preaching, it was said that his voice was thin and wheezy and that, in response to his sermons, old women would fall asleep and dogs would howl at the church door. He had found his voice now, and it rolled out like thunder. The Greeks might call it demagoguery, but there was more to it than that. He spoke to everyone; in his godliness, sin was the great leveler, undermining power and wealth. He knew how to mix his message with the yeast of politics, which is why the privileged feared him so much. But these thoughts came later. At the time you just listened.

From out of his robes he pulled a small mirror. He held it up toward the crowd. At a certain angle it caught a blaze of candlelight and sent it spinning around the church. "See this, Florence? I hold up a mirror to your soul and what does it show? Decay and rot. This, which was once a godly city, now pours more filth down its streets than the Arno on a flooding tide. *'Enter not the path of the wicked and go not in the way of evil men.'* But Florence has blocked her ears to the words of the Lord. When the night comes down, the beast starts to walk and the battle for her soul begins."

Next to me I felt Luca shift in his seat. In the study room the only texts he ever showed any interest in were the ones that had war and bloodshed in them. If there was fighting to be done, whoever the enemy, he would want to be there.

"In each dark alley where the light of God has been blown out there is sin and violation. Remember the broken body of that pure young woman. There is outrage and sodomy. *'Burn out their foulness, Lord, and let their bodies renounce sin in torment and everlasting fires.'* There is lust, there is fornication. *'The lips of strange women drop as honeycomb, but her end is bitter as wormwood, sharp as a two-edged sword. Her feet go down into death and her steps take hold on hell.'*"

Even Tomaso was paying attention now, spoiled, pampered Tomaso, whose looks drew women like moths to the candle flame. When had he last thought about hell? Well, he was thinking about it now. You could see it in his eyes. For all of his usual insouciance, the thought of those mutilated bodies and the threat of a French army at the gates were inside him now. I stared at his face, intrigued by this new anxiety. He felt my gaze and, scowling at me, dropped his head.

As he did so, another face from across the rows of pews came into focus above his: a man staring directly at me with a clear shine in his eyes. He was immediately familiar, but it took me a moment to place him. Of course: Plautilla's wedding. The man who had talked of Greek and then helped me through the steps. As the look between us connected he nodded slightly, and I thought I saw a slight smile move across his face. His blatant attention confused me and I turned back to the pulpit.

"Ask yourself, men and women of Florence. Why does God march the French army toward us now? It is to show us that our city has forgotten Christ's message. A city that has become dazzled by false gold, that has put learning above piety, the so-called wisdom of pagans over the word of God."

As the river of wrath poured over us again, from the body of the church there came a low moaning of voices, a kind of chorus of despair. " *'Behold, because you have set at nought all my counsel I will laugh at your calamity,'* saith the Lord. *'I will mock when your fear cometh as desolation and when destruction arrives as a whirlwind; when distress and anguish cometh upon you I will not answer.'* O Florence. When will you open your eyes and return to the ways of God?"

The moaning got louder. I could even hear the rattle starting in Luca's throat. I glanced back up toward the man. He was not listening to Savonarola. He was still looking at me.

Twelve

FOUR DAYS LATER, THE MUTILATED BODIES OF THE MAN and the woman were found outside the city walls, in an olive grove off the road between Florence and the village of Impruneta.

The weather had been hot for so long that there were fears of drought and the harvest being ruined, and the church had organized a procession to bring the miraculous statue of Our Lady of Impruneta down into the city for prayers and a mass. If God was angry with Florence, He might still listen to the intercession of Our Lady. But as the procession gathered bigger and bigger crowds on its way to the city gates, stragglers fanned out from the path and into the fields—and so it was that a boy found himself wandering on the edge of a vineyard and he spotted bloody flesh under the vines. If I had been my father on the Security Council, I might have asked what fool had allowed the transportation of the bodies to a place so obvious, but of course no one said a thing.

Because the crime had taken place outside the city walls, it was not strictly a Florentine affair so there were no damning proclamations in the City Square. Still, the news of the murders traveled like the plague. The woman was a prostitute and the man her client and their corpses were stinking, the wounds alive with maggots. Ours was not a queasy city. If the woman had been prosecuted for licentiousness, a healthy crowd would have gathered to watch her nose cut off. Those same people had probably seen entrails split in the name of justice before now, but the blasphemous punishment in this violence burned its way into people's minds and brought the friar's dark prophesies echoing back. What man could possibly have done such a thing? It was an act of such depravity that it was easier to read it as retribution: the Devil pulling himself up from hell and stalking the streets to claim his own early.

At home my father brought us together again to report how the French envoys had come and gone, laden with gifts and honeyed promises of neutrality, but no safe conduct. Would it be enough, or would Charles have the nerve to invade Tuscany? All we could do was wait. And still the heat continued. Our Lady's intercession, it seemed, was not enough.

I sat in my room. My Annunciation was finished, but I was already dissatisfied with it. Our Lady's discomfort was captured well enough and the Angel had a certain verve to his movements, but their world was monochrome and my fingers were itching for color. In the past I had done my best with household alchemy. I had used egg yolks filched from the kitchen (my love of meringues was legendary with the cook), which, mixed into white lead, could produce a shade close to that of skin. I had made my own black out of the grounds of burned almond shells and soot gathered from the linseed-oil lamp, and once I had even forged a passable shade of verdigris by pouring strong vinegar into copper bowls. But there had been uproar in the kitchen when the stained bowls had been discovered, and the quality of the paint produced was feeble. Anyway, what stories could you illustrate using black, white, and green?

It was almost a week since the painter and I had parted company in the chapel. The workmen had begun erecting the scaffolding for him to begin. I could not wait any longer. I called for Erila.

Since the news of my bleeding she had become excited on my behalf. Once a husband was selected for me, she would find herself in a house in which her mistress would be *the* mistress and her new influence would know no limits. She had much more of an appetite for life than many slaves. But then it had not been as cruel to her as to others. There were some houses where as she got older she would have been taken advantage of—the city was littered with big-bellied slaves who served their masters in the bedroom as well as the dining room—but my father was not like that, and though Luca had tried his luck she had sent him away with a flea in his ear. Tomaso, as far as I knew, had never bothered. He had too much respect for his own vanity to put himself through anything that didn't lead to certain victory.

"And when I find the painter, what do I say to him?"

"Ask him when I can deliver them. He'll know what that means."

"And do you?" she said sharply.

"Erila, please. Just do this one thing for me. There's not a lot of time left."

And though she looked at me sternly enough she went anyway, and when she arrived back later and told me he would be in the garden early tomorrow morning I thanked her and told her I would go myself.

I rose at dawn. The smell of fresh baking hung in the air and turned my stomach with hunger. The garden in the back courtyard was my mother's greatest joy. It was young still, the growth of barely half a dozen summers, but my father had stocked it with plants brought from his villa so there was an air of maturity to it even then. There was a sprouting fig, a pomegranate and a walnut tree, a run of box hedge shot through with aromatic myrtle, an herb garden rich enough to service the kitchens with quantities of sage, mint, rosemary, stonewort, and basil, and a colorful show of flowers that changed with the seasons. My mother, with an ear for Platonic sweetness, thought gardens were close to God, and she was always extolling the virtues of contemplation for the growing mind. I used it mostly for copying shrubs and flowers, of which there were enough varieties to supply a dozen separate Annunciation and Nativity scenes.

There was, however, one drawback. To the plants my mother had added wildlife: doves with clipped wings and her beloved peacocks, two cocks and three hens. For her alone they reserved their respect, even affection. They could tell her footfall, and as she arrived, usually with a bag of seed, the cocks would rush to her. After they had eaten they would strut away, spreading their fans for her. I hated them, both their vanity and their viciousness. Once, when I was younger and entranced by their colors, I had tried to pet one and it had bitten me, and since then their beaks had been the stuff of my nightmares. When I thought of the corpses in the field or the young girl covered in animal bites, I couldn't help but imagine what the peacocks' beaks might have made of their eyes.

But that morning they found other prey. The painter was seated on the stone bench, a set of brushes and a dozen tiny pots of mixed paint by his side. In front of him the two cocks stood pecking at tossed seed, both tails stubbornly closed and drooping behind them, and he was watching them intently. But when they saw me one of them let out an irritable shriek, and its plumage exploded up in a dance of threat as it turned on me.

"Ah...don't move," he said, grabbing the brushes, his hands flying over the pots, mixing the colors in his mind before they reached his fingers.

But my paralysis was real enough. "Please!" I said. Now it was his turn to see me in distress. He stared at me for a moment, caught between his brush and my panic, then took some seed from a pouch and held it out, making a strange chucking noise at the back of his throat. The bird jerked its head as if in recognition and strutted toward the outstretched palm.

"You have no need to be scared of them. They are harmless."

"That's what you think. I still have the scars to prove different." I stood watching him. It took a certain spirit to have such birds eating out of one's hand. My mother and he were the only ones I had ever seen manage it. "How do you do that? It's so unfair that God has given you the fingers of Fra Angelico *and* the touch of Saint Francis."

He kept his eyes on the cock. "In the monastery it was my job to feed the animals."

"Not this kind," I muttered.

"No," he said, his eyes fixed on their outrageous plumage, "I've never seen these creatures before. Though I've heard stories."

"Why do you need to paint them? I didn't think Santa Caterina communed with animals."

"Angel wings," he said, as its cruel little beak darted to and from his hand, "for the Resurrection on the ceiling of the chapel. I am in need of feathers."

"In which case you had better be careful your angels don't outshine God." And as I said it I thought how much easier it was for us today, speaking to each other in this way, as if the discord of the chapel darkness had been burned off by the morning sun. "What did you use in the North?"

"Doves . . . geese, and swans."

"Of course. Your white Gabriel." And I saw again the billowing wings of the crude fresco in his room. But he was learning fluency in color now. I could see it on his hands. What would I not give to have my nails caked with the dried blood of so many shades? The cock, having pecked its fill, sauntered away, paying me the final insult of ignoring me. The bright morning air was still between us, my yearning as fresh as the dew on the leaves. He picked up his brush again. I moved closer. "Who mixes your colors, painter?"

"I do."

"It is hard?"

He shook his head, his fingers moving fast. "At first maybe. Not now."

I could feel my fingers itching with the need to touch the colors, so much so that I had to clench my fist by my side. "I can name every shade on every wall in Florence, and I know the recipes for a dozen of them. But even if I could get the ingredients I have no workshop to mix them and no time that is my own without supervision." I stopped. "I am so tired of pen and ink. It gives shade without life, and everything I capture with it looks somehow melancholy."

This time he looked up at me and our eyes met. And as in the chapel I swear that he understood. The roll of drawings was burning the palm of my hand. Inside was my Annunciation and a dozen others picked as much for their ambition as their precision. It was now or never. I could feel fear like sudden sweat on my palms, and it made me harsher toward him than I intended. I held them out to him now. "I do not want diplomacy, do you understand? I want the truth."

He didn't move, and in the silence after my words I knew that I had damaged something that had been growing between us, but I was too nervous to know how else to behave.

"I'm sorry. I cannot judge them for you," he said quietly. "All I can do is my own work."

Though he did not say it unkindly, his words were like the peck of the peacock's beak into my soul. "Then my father was mistaken in your talent. And you will always be an apprentice and never a master." My hand was still outstretched. I let the papers fall onto the bench by his side. "Your opinion or your reputation. You leave me no choice, painter."

"And what choice does that leave me?" This time he didn't look away. The gaze lasted a long time, well beyond politeness, until in the end it was I who dropped my eyes.

At the end of the garden Erila appeared. For the sake of appearances I whirled upon her, though I knew she had been keeping watch over us. "What are you doing?" I switched to Italian. "Spying on me—"

"Oh, madam, please don't stamp your foot at me," she said

meekly, her humility blatantly fake. "Your mother is looking for you."

"My mother! At this time? What did you tell her?"

"That you were in the garden drawing leaves."

"Oh!" I turned on him. "Oh, you must go." I said in Latin. "Quickly. She mustn't find you here with me."

"What about your leaves?"

His Italian was getting better. He took up a piece of charcoal. My mother's orange bush grew underneath his fingers, the fruit so heavy you could feel it ready to drop. As he handed me the paper I didn't know whether to laugh or cry. He gathered his paints and put them in a bag by his side. Then he took the sheaf of drawings and slipped them in too.

"I don't care what you say," I called after him. "Just don't lie to me."

THE COOK'S FRESH BREAD WENT WELL WITH SLICES OF QUINCE preserve. I ate too much while my mother, unnaturally fluttery with nerves, drank only watered wine. The letter had come by an early messenger, though she must surely have known about it in advance; my sister Plautilla had invited family and friends to a small gathering. The baby was due within a few months and now was the time to show off all the fine linen and clothes bought in preparation for the event. I didn't give it a second thought. My mother, on the other hand, seemed to do nothing but think about it. She ordered Erila to do my hair and lay out a selection of my wardrobe in advance.

"If you don't approve of him, you'd better find some good reason fast," Erila said with a mouthful of pins, as she scraped my hair back under the heavy pearl combs.

"What do you mean?"

"I mean when did you last get trussed up like a banquet chicken to visit your sister?"

She teased the second ringlet out of the hot tongs and we watched in the glass as it curled down the side of my face. For a second the two sat in perfect symmetry; then the left slipped resolutely lower than its partner.

When my mother saw me, she didn't even try to hide her anxiety. "Oh, dear. Your hair is very dark, isn't it? Perhaps we should have used dye after all. Still, I am sure we can do better with your dress. Let's see. The gold shot is still in fashion, but I think your father would approve more of one of your brighter silks. The Brazil red from the Western Indies goes well with your complexion."

My father, though he believed in the efficacy of wearing the business, had never knowingly made a remark on my wardrobe that I could remember.

"You don't think it is a little grand?" I said. "We would not want to provoke the wrath of the godly on the streets."

"The preacher does not rule the city yet," my mother retorted, and I think it was the first time I had heard a note of disdain toward him. "We may still dress as we please where the family is concerned. The shade suits you. And put some effort into your face. Maybe just a touch of white powder to lighten your complexion. Erila can do it for you if she doesn't waste too much time gossiping."

"Mama," I said, "if by any chance this is about a man, it would be easier to pick one who was blind. That way he couldn't see my defects."

"Oh, my dear, but you're wrong. You are lovely. Lovely. There is great bloom and shine to your spirit."

"I am clever," I said sourly. "It is not the same thing, as I have been told many times."

"And who has told you that? Not Plautilla. She is not so cruel."

I hesitated. "No, not Plautilla."

"Tomaso."

I shrugged.

She thought about it. "Your brother has an acid tongue. It would perhaps have been better not to have made an enemy of him."

"It was none of my doing," I said sullenly. "He finds it easy to take offense."

"Well, no matter. When it comes to important things, blood is thicker than water," she said firmly. "So let us think about the shoes."

Thirteen

PLAUTILLA WAS LIKE A SHIP IN FULL SAIL. EVEN HER FACE was plump. It was almost as if she were disappearing inside her own flesh. Her hair had lost its fairish tint. No time for dyeing now. With that bulk she probably couldn't make it as far as the roof anymore. She didn't seem to mind. She was thick and placid, like an animal slumped at the water hole, too big to move. But then it was very hot.

We were the first to arrive. My mother brought sweetmeats and sugared almonds, and Plautilla showed us round the newly decorated bedroom. There were new tapestries on the walls and on the bed a set of hand-embroidered sheets, monogrammed with the family crest and a border pattern all around. The baby's crib was to the side, filled with a white damask coverlet fringed with gold and silver. The wedding chest sat in a place of honor, the dancing Sabines looking too energetic now for the stifling heat. Does men's lust grow sluggish at such times? Certainly a child conceived in high summer was considered suspect; something to do with the double heat of the air and the lust, but then

I was not old enough to have been taught the inner rubric of such things. No doubt it was an education to come.

I had heard from Tomaso that Maurizio had wagered 30 florins against 400 that the baby would be a girl. That way his disappointment might be compensated by his winnings, though I doubt it would have covered what he had paid out for all the accessories. Everything was according to the fashion: fragrant white wines for the mother-to-be and a brace of young pigeons for after the birth, because their flesh was easy to digest. You could hear the birds cooing, oblivious of their fate, in the courtyard below. The midwife was retained, the search was on for a suitable wet nurse, and the room was furnished with objects of taste: small devotional paintings and statues so that during her labor Plautilla might look on only beautiful things and so increase the beauty and character of the child. I was impressed. Maurizio, it must be said, had done everything his chubby pigeon of a wife could wish for.

"Mama tells me the painter has done the birthing tray," she added breathlessly, as we reached the end of her inventory. "She says it is wonderful. I asked for the Garden of Love on one side and the grid of a chessboard on the other. Maurizio does like to play," she said, then giggled girlishly at her own words.

Would I too be saying things like this when I was married? I stared at my fleshy, happy sister in a kind of horror. She knew so much more than I did. How could I ever get around to asking her?

"Don't worry," she said, poking my arm conspiratorially. "Now you are bleeding you will understand it all soon enough." She made a face. "Though I must tell you it is not like reading books at all."

So what is it like? I wanted to say. Tell me. Tell me everything. "Does it hurt?" I said, almost as if I hadn't intended to.

She pursed her lips and looked at me, savoring the moment of power. "Of course," she said simply. "That is how they know you are pure. But it passes. And then it is not so bad. Really." And I thought looking at her that she meant it, and for the first time I realized that my vain, silly sister might have actually found something she could do well in life. It made me glad for her and even more terrified for myself.

Our conversation broke up as new guests arrived, friends of the family, all bringing their small offerings. Plautilla moved around them, laughing and smiling. Then the gentleman joined us.

He was wearing a wine-colored velvet cloak, finer than the one in church, the like of which my father would definitely have approved. He looked older than the other times I had seen him, but daylight is crueler than candles and oil. He noticed me as soon as he came in, but paid his first compliments to my mother. I saw her fold her hands over each other and give him her full attention. It was presumably not the first time they had met. Was I surprised? You know, I am still not sure. Someone told me much later that you always know the people who are going to make a difference in your life, from the very first time you set eyes on them, even if you do not like them at all. And I had noticed him, as he had me. God help us.

I caught Plautilla in one of her billowing sidles across the room and pinned her to the nearest wall, or as near as her belly would permit.

"Who is he?"

"Who?"

"Plautilla, I cannot pinch you as I used to. You might go into labor and I could not bear your screams. But once your baby is born I can pinch *it* with impunity, since it will be years until it can blame me."

"Alessandra!"

"So. Who is he?"

She sighed. "His name is Cristoforo Langella. He comes from a noble family."

"I'm sure," I said. "So why would he be interested in me?"

But there was no time for further gossip. He had already left my mother's side and was heading our way. Plautilla broke away from me and sallied across the room, smiling. I stood rigid and studied my feet, my posture defying all rules of charm and femininity.

"Madam," he said, bowing slightly in front of me, "we have not, I think, been formally introduced."

"No," I muttered, darting him a glance. There were heavy crow's-feet around his eyes. At least he knows to laugh, I thought. But can he do it with me? I looked at the floor again.

"So, how are your feet today?" he said in Greek.

"Maybe you should ask them yourself?" I answered, in a voice that reminded me of my childhood tantrums. I could feel my mother watching me, willing me to behave. While she couldn't hear what was going on, she would know my facial gestures well enough to mark sarcasm from acquiescence.

He bowed again, much lower this time and addressed the hem of my gown. "How are you, feet? You must be relieved there is no music." He stopped, then looked up and smiled. "We saw each other in church. What did you think of the sermon?"

"I think if I were a sinner he would have me smelling the boiling oil."

"Then you are lucky that you are not. Do you think there are many who hear him and don't smell it?"

"Not many. But I think if I were poor I would hear the screams coming from my betters first."

"Hmm. You think he preaches rebellion?"

I thought about it. "No. But I think he preaches threat."

"True. Yet I have heard him vent his spleen on everyone, not just the rich and the frightened. He can be very critical of the Church."

"Perhaps the Church deserves it."

"Indeed. You know that our present pope has a picture of the Madonna painted above the entrance to his bedroom? Only she has the face of his mistress."

"Really?" I said, momentarily seduced by such superior gossip.

"Oh, yes. It is said his table groans under the weight of so many roasted songbirds that the woods around Rome are silent now, and his children are welcomed into the house as if sin were no sin at all. But then, to err is human, wouldn't you say?"

"I don't know. I suppose that is what the confessional is for."

He laughed. "Do you know of the frescoes of Andrea Orcagna in the refectory of Santa Croce?"

I shook my head.

"He paints the Last Judgment with nuns' heads between the Devil's teeth. And Satan looks as if he is suffering indigestion from the number of cardinal's hats he has swallowed."

Despite myself, I started to giggle.

"So tell me, Alessandra Cecchi. Do you like the art of our fair city?"

"Oh, I adore it," I said. "And you?"

"The very same. That is why Savonarola's words don't freeze my soul."

"You are not a sinner?" I said.

"On the contrary. I sin often. But I believe in the power of love and beauty as an alternative route to God and redemption."

"You follow the ancients?"

"Yes," he said, in a theatrical whisper. "But tell no one, because the definition of heresy is getting wider every minute."

And naïve though I know it was, I found his conspiratorial manner rather thrilling. "Your secret is safe with me," I said.

"I knew it would be. So tell me, what defense should one proffer when our mad monk lectures us on how illiterate old women know more of faith than all the Greek and Roman thinkers put together?"

"One should give him a copy of Boccaccio's *Defense of Poetry*. His translations of the tales of the classical gods find only the most Christian of virtues and moral truths."

He stood back and looked at me, and I swear I did not misread the admiration in his eyes. "I had heard that you were your mother's daughter."

"I shouldn't take much comfort in that, sir. My brother is fond of telling everyone that while she was carrying me she saw violence in the streets and it curdled me in her womb."

"Then your brother is cruel."

"Yes. But he may still be honest."

"Still, in this case he has made a mistake. You enjoy your studies. There is nothing wrong in that. Is it just the classics, or do you favor our own writers too?"

"I think Dante Alighieri is the greatest poet Florence has ever produced."

"Or ever will. We would have no argument there. Can you recite *The Divine Comedy?*"

"Not all of it!" I said. "I am barely sixteen."

"Just as well. If you could recite it all, we would still be here at the Second Coming." He looked at me for a moment. "I hear that you draw?"

"I . . . who told you that?"

"You must not be so nervous with me. I have already entrusted my secret to you, remember? I only bring it up because I am impressed. It is unusual."

"It wasn't always. In ancient times—"

"I know. In ancient times, Varro's daughter Maria was celebrated for her art." He smiled. "You are not the only one to be familiar with Alberti. Though he couldn't know then that Florence's own Paolo Uccello had a daughter who worked in her father's workshop. The littlest sparrow, they called her." He paused. "Perhaps you might let me see your work sometime. I would like that."

A servant appeared at his elbow offering sweetmeats and spiced wine. He took a glass and handed it to me. But the spell had been broken. We stood silent for a while, both of us looking somewhere else. The silence grew, if not uncomfortable, then rich. Then he said, in the quiet voice he had used in the dance, "You know, Alessandra, why we are meeting here today?"

I felt sick to my stomach. Of course I should say no, as my

mother might have taught me. But the fact was I did know. How could I not?

"Yes," I said. "I think so."

"Would that be acceptable to you?"

I looked up at him. "I was not aware that my feelings would be taken into consideration."

"Well, they are. That is why I am asking you now."

"You are kind, sir." And I know I blushed.

"No. Not really. But I would like to think myself fair. We are both strange fishes in this sea. The time for fighting alone is drawing to a close. Talk to your mother. No doubt we will see each other again."

He moved away from me and soon after took his leave.

Fourteen

T HERE IS MUCH TO RECOMMEND HIM, ALESSANDRA. HIS father and mother are both dead, so you will be mistress of your own house. He is well educated. He writes poetry and is a connoisseur and patron of art."

My mother was too agitated to keep her hands in her lap. I had had a night and a day in which to become more anxious. "He sounds like the city's most desired suitor. Why is he not already married?"

"I believe he was writing something and put all his energies into that. Then recently two of his brothers died, both without heirs. The name is important and he needs to preserve it."

"He needs a son."

"Yes."

"Which is why he needs a wife."

"Yes. But I think he may also want one."

"He hasn't wanted one before."

"People change, Alessandra."

"He is old."

"Older, yes. But it is not always a fault. I would have thought you of all people would understand that."

I sat looking at the wooden carvings on the settle. It was midafternoon and the rest of the house was asleep. The summer loggia at the top of the house was open to what little breeze the weather could offer, and its walls were painted the coolest of green to remind one of nature. But even here it was too hot to think. By this time of year we would usually be in the country, at my father's farm. Our continued presence in the city was the sternest sign yet of his civic anxiety.

"What do you think of him, Mama?"

"Alessandra, I don't know a great deal. The family is good; in that respect it would be a most honorable match. For the rest, all I can say is that he saw you at Plautilla's wedding and a few weeks ago he made an approach to your father. He is not part of our circle. I hear that while he espouses learning he does not involve himself in politics. But he is cultured and serious, and given the tensions of the moment that may be more sensible. Other than that he is almost as much a stranger to me as he is to you."

"So what is the *gossip* about him? What does Tomaso say?"

"Your brother speaks ill of everyone. Though interestingly, now I think about it, he has spoken no ill of him. I am not sure he knows him. But, Alessandra, the man is forty-eight years old. He will have lived his life up until now, of that there is no doubt."

"Men live, women wait."

"Oh, Alessandra. You are too young to sound so old," she said, in the same voice with which she had calmed a thousand of my tiny storms. "It is not such a tragedy. You will see how to make it work for yourself. He may well enjoy his own company as much as you enjoy yours."

"So it will be a marriage based on absence?"

"And none the less satisfying for that. You know there are things you do not understand yet, though you may find that hard to believe."

We smiled at each other. This pact of ours had been forged early. The virtues that I didn't have—how long was the list? silence, obedience, modesty, timidity—she would overlook in private as long as I did not humiliate her in public. She had taught me as well as she could. And I had tried. Really.

I wondered if this was the conversation that daughter and mother were meant to have before marriage and, if so, when we would come to the wedding night. I tried to jump the great chasm in my mind. I saw myself waking up in a strange bed, next to a strange man, opening my arms to greet another day....

"I want Erila as part of my dowry," I said.

"You shall have her. He will have his own slaves, but I am sure he will look favorably on ways to make you feel at home. When your father talked to him he was quite solicitous about that."

There was a long pause. It was so hot. My hair was damp with sweat and my skin felt as if someone had sprayed it with warm water. In the streets there was already talk that this too was God's punishment: He had stopped the seasons to show us the extent of His displeasure. I wanted nothing more than to bathe, then lie on my bed and sketch the cat as it lay sprawled across the coverlet, too indolent to move. Of my own volition, my life was about to be blown apart and I was almost too tired to care.

"So are you saying we are decided, Alessandra?" asked my mother gently.

"I don't know. It feels so fast."

"It was your decision. Your father says if the French come they will be here within the month. There will be little time for ceremony then."

"Yet I thought the point of marriage was that it allowed us to prove our status to the rest of Florence. There won't be much time for that now."

"That's true. Though in the present climate your father thinks that may be no bad thing. I find it hard to believe: Do you actually *want* to parade through the streets with everyone looking at you, having been scrubbed and groomed for weeks before?" And I thought for a second how frightening it would be to live without the one person who knew me almost as well as I knew myself, even if she could not always admit it.

"Oh, Mama. If it was up to me I would prefer to stay here, read my books, paint my paintings, and die a maid. But," I said firmly, "I know I cannot do that, and therefore since I have to take someone, it might as well be him. I think he will be"—I roamed a little for the word—"I think he will be kind. If I turn out to be wrong, then he's old and maybe he'll die soon and I'll be free."

"Oh, don't even wish that in jest." Her voice was fierce. "He is not that old, and you should know there is no freedom in widowhood. You would do better to get used to the convent now."

I stared at her. Had it ever been an option for her? "You know I still have that dream." I sighed. "About the place where I would be allowed to do what I want. While honoring God for the privilege."

"If there were such a convent, Alessandra, half the women in the city might wish to be in it," she said, with quiet tartness. "So. It is decided? Good. I shall tell your father. I believe your husband-to-be would be equally ready for an early ceremony. There will not be time for us to commission a *cassone*, which means we must get a secondhand chest or use one that passed down through the family. If he asks, do you have any preferences for what the paintings might be?"

I thought about it. "I don't mind which story, as long as it's not that sad girl in the Nastagio story, chased by dogs and disemboweled. Let there be a lot in the art to look at." I was back in a strange bedroom in a stranger's house, and suddenly all my courage seemed to trickle away. "When I am married and gone from here, who will I talk to then?" I said, and I heard my voice split along the seam.

She looked taken aback, and I knew it had cut her too. "Oh, my dear Alessandra, you will talk to God. As you surely must. It will come easier there because you will be alone. And He will listen. As He does. As He did to me. He will help you to talk to your husband. In that way you will become a good wife and a good mother. And it will not all be pain, I promise you." She paused. "I would not let that happen to you." And I think as far as she could, she really believed that.

So it was that she spoke to my father that night, and the contract of consent between our families was drawn up that week, with the stipulation that the dowry requirements would be met within the month and the marriage celebrated and consummated on the same day.

WHICH WAS JUST AS WELL, BECAUSE FIVE DAYS AFTER OUR CONVERSA-tion Charles VIII gave Florence his answer to her offer of neutrality. Having crossed the Tuscan border, he marched on the fortress of Fivizzano, sacked the town, and massacred the entire garrison.

In the cathedral the congregation moaned under Savonarola's tongue: "For behold, Florence, the scourge has fallen; the prophecies are being fulfilled. It is not I but God who foretold it, God who is leading the armies. The Sword has descended.... Now it is coming. Now."

Fifteen

I DID NOT SEE MY FUTURE HUSBAND AGAIN UNTIL THE morning of our wedding. These were awful days. The government was on the verge of daily collapse and fatalism hung like a heavy-bellied storm cloud over the city. Piero de' Medici was agitating for Florence to defend herself, but even his closest followers were deserting him now and openly talking about negotiating with the enemy. My father was distraught, but still the call to government did not come. The Medici influence was waning so fast that it would soon be its own ruin to be associated with them.

Finally, at the end of October, Piero left the city with his personal entourage and headed for the French camp.

In the study room our tutor made us pray for his safe return. From the pulpit Savonarola openly preached welcome to Charles, hailing him as God's instrument for saving Florence's soul and denouncing Piero as a Medici coward whose family had destroyed our godly Republic. The waiting city vibrated with anxiety. Three days before, my father had come home with news of a proclamation from the Signoria that if the French army entered the city certain households would be billeted upon. Officials came round and chalked so many doors with white crosses that it looked like the plague had hit again. As with the pestilence, wealth and influence proved no protection. Both my old and my new home were chosen. If the French did come, their arrival would mark my first role as hostess in my married house.

Each day there was a story of another family dispatching their daughters—indeed, sometimes even their wives—to the safety of cloisters, though as I heard my mother mutter one day when the panic was running high, "When did any invading foreign army respect the sanctity of convent walls?"

And the date of my wedding, 26 November, was less than two weeks away.

The heat had finally broken the day before and the rain had come. I sat at my window, my possessions around me, watching the dirt flow down the gullies, wondering if this too was God's plan to wash the city clean. Erila helped me pack my chest.

"All this is happening very fast."

"Yes," I said, meeting her gaze. "Does that worry you?"

She shrugged slightly. "Maybe you didn't need to take the first one they offered."

"Oh, really. Did I miss the queue outside the house? Or would you have preferred to see me fingering my rosary beads in some damp cell in the wilds of the country? I could have asked to take you with me there too."

She said nothing.

"Erila?" I waited. "He will be your master as well. If you know anything I don't, it would be better to tell me now."

She shook her head. "We are both sold already. We shall just have to make the best of it."

It felt as if my life were running out like the sands in an hourglass and there would soon be no time unaccounted for. I had heard nothing from the painter. His silence was like an ache that I tried to ignore, yet sometimes in bed when the heat had been at its worst I found myself succumbing to it, and then I would be back in the cool of the chapel, his skin pearly in the candlelight, or in the freshness of the dawn garden, watching his fingers flying over the page, entranced by the way angels' wings grew under his touch. On those nights I slept badly and woke in a sweat that was cold as well as hot.

I decided that honesty was the best method of deceit and asked my mother's permission to visit the chapel, seeing as I would be leaving soon. She was too busy to join me, and of course there was less need for chaperones now. Erila would do.

The chapel was transformed. The apse was halfway between a building site and a sorcerer's cave: there were scaffolding and beams lashed into place to create a series of walkways and platforms at every height, reaching high up the walls, while in the middle a small fire clogged the air with fumes. Above it, strung across the roof, was a grid of what looked like thick black wire, the shadow of which was thrown up by the light of the flames onto the vaulted roof above. The painter was hoisted high into the space on a harness. He was suspended close to the surface of the roof and was intent on drawing the shadow grid lines onto the ceiling itself. When he completed one, he called down for the men to slacken or tighten the rope to move him from one side to another, in and out of the heat.

Erila and I stood and watched transfixed. He was so concentrated and deft, like a gangling spider spinning a crude but geometrically perfect web. He moved fast, doing the best he could to avoid the heat of the flames. Already one wall showed figures in outline painted in earthy red sinopia in readiness for the plastering to take place. On the ground a boy, probably no older than myself, was working at a table with pestle and mortar, grinding the outline paint. When the fresco work began in earnest there would be more than one, but for now he would suffice. From above the painter called to him. The boy looked in our direction and left what he was doing to join us.

He bowed low. "The master says he cannot stop now. The fire will scorch the ceiling if it burns too long, so he must finish the grid this afternoon."

"What is he doing?" Erila muttered, clearly horrified by the spectacle.

"Oh, he is gridding the roof so he has the reference points for the fresco," said the boy eagerly. I stared at him. His face was grimy but his eyes shone. At what age had he first felt the itch in his fingers?

Erila shrugged, as confused as before.

"The curve of the roof is deceptive when you are painting it," I explained. "It is impossible to gauge the perspective correctly. The grid lines will help him keep to his original drawing. His sketch will have the lines superimposed, like a map, so that he can then transfer the whole picture accurately from one to the other."

The boy shot me a look. I shot it straight back. Don't argue with me, it said. I have read and know more than you will ever know about this, even if it is you and not me who will finally cover our ceilings with visions of heaven.

"Then tell your master that we will watch and wait for him," I said evenly. "Perhaps you might bring us some chairs."

He looked a little scared but said nothing, scuttling back to the apse and hunting around for suitable chairs. As he pulled two across the floor the painter yelled for him and he was caught for a moment between orders. I was pleased to see the painter won and he left them in the middle of the floor to get back to his work. Erila retrieved them.

It was the best part of an hour before he came down. The fuel was straw, cheap and capricious, so that it would flare up within seconds. He cried out once or twice as the flames flew too high and the workmen damped them down, which only caused the smoke to make him cough. I had heard of awful injuries at this stage, so the skill of the hoisters needed to be as great as the skill of the painter. Eventually he gave a signal for them to winch him down. The rope twirled and spun as it descended to the floor. He almost fell out of the harness and flung himself flat onto the ground coughing uncontrollably and retching up phlegm, which he spit out in great gobbets as he struggled to get his breath back.

How would it ever be possible for women to do such things? Uccello's daughter might have painted squares of drapery in *The House of Mary Magdalene*, but she would not have found herself hoisted up into the vaulted skies. Men perform, women applaud. I was beginning to lose faith. From the pulpit, Savonarola was agitating to sending us back to our houses. There were rumors that he would only preach to men soon, and if the French came the women not barricaded in convents would be hidden behind locked doors. God help us then.

He sat up with his head in his hands, then looked across the chapel and saw us still there waiting. He got up, smoothing down his clothes as best he could, and walked over. He seemed somehow different, as if his body had grown stronger with his spider walking, his former shyness absorbed into the work. Erila stood up to meet him, making an instant barrier between him and me. His face was blacker than hers and his smell was all sweat and burn, as if there were almost something of the Devil's confidence about him.

"I cannot stop now." His voice was cracked with the fumes. "I need the daylight as well as the fire."

"You are mad," I said. "You will injure yourself."

"Not if I work fast enough."

"My father has some mirrors that he uses to make the candle-light brighter when he works at night. I will ask him to send you one."

He bowed his head. "Thank you."

From the apse the workmen called out a question, and he answered in clear dialect.

"You speak Tuscan now."

"Fire makes a fast learner." Amid the grime of his face there was the ghost of smile.

The silence grew. "Erila," I said, "would you leave us for a moment."

She glanced fiercely at me.

"Please." Because I did not know what else to say.

She glared at him, then dropped her eyes and moved away

toward the apse, her hips swaying carelessly, as she sometimes did when she wanted men to look at her. The boy could not take his eyes off her, but the painter did not notice.

"You have looked at them?"

He nodded slightly, but I could read nothing in his eyes; they were too bloodshot with smoke. He glanced back hurriedly to the fire.

"So if not now, then when? I leave within a few days."

"Leave? For where?"

It was clear he had not heard. "I am about to be married. You did not know?"

"No." He paused. "No, I did not know."

His isolation was so profound that it screened him even from servants' gossip. "Well, then, perhaps you have also not heard that our city is threatened with invaders. And that the Devil is on the streets, murdering and mutilating."

"I...I have heard stories, yes," he mumbled, and his confidence seemed to desert him for a moment.

"You go to church, right? So you have heard him preach."

This time as he nodded he wouldn't meet my eyes.

"You should be careful. The monk would put a prayer book where your paintbrush should be. I—"

But Erila was back at my side now, her tongue clicking in irritation. Her job was to see me delivered pure to my husband's marriage bed, and she had not come this far to be foiled by my intrigues with an artisan.

I took a breath. "So when, painter? This evening?"

"No." His voice was harsh. "No, I cannot this evening."

"You have another appointment perhaps?" I let the question hang in the air. "Tomorrow, then?"

He hesitated. "The day after. The grid will be finished and the fire cleared by then."

From the apse one of the men called out. He bowed, then turned and walked back. From where we were standing we could still feel the warmth of the flames.

Sixteen

O F COURSE I WAITED FOR HIM. HE WAS LATE, LEAVING
after the torches had gone out, and if I hadn't had the
window open I might not have heard the side door
groan or had a glimpse of him as he scuttled into the
black. How many times had I followed him in my
imagination? It was easy enough. I knew every step
and uneven cobblestone as far as the cathedral, and unlike most
girls my age I was not afraid of the dark. What harm could possibly befall someone with cat's eyes such as mine?

All that evening I had tormented myself with pictures of my
own bravery. I had deliberately stayed dressed to push myself
nearer to the edge. Within days I would be locked in someone
else's life, in a house for which I had no internal map, and so my
beloved nocturnal freedom would be over. On the window seat
next to me was one of Tomaso's hats I had filched from his dressing room. I had spent hours trying it on, so I knew just how to
place it in a way that made it impossible to see my face. Of course
there were still my skirts, but I could hide them in one of my
father's longer cloaks, and walking fast in the darkness I would
only be spotted if I met with...with what? A light? A figure? A

gang of men? I stopped the thoughts. Mine was an elaborate game, a pact I had made with myself. If I were to be married and buried alive, I would not die without seeing even a little of my Orient. I owed myself that much. And if the Devil was out there, surely he would have worse sinners to punish than a girl who disobeyed her parents to breathe in the night air for a memory of freedom.

I went down the stairs and crossed into the back courtyard from where the servants' door let out onto the side street. It would usually be bolted from the inside at this time of night and he took a risk, leaving it unfastened when he went out. If someone were to wake and find it now...? I could, I realized, scupper his life simply by pushing the bolt back across. Instead, I followed him out.

I took a step outside. The door was still ajar behind me. I pulled it shut, then tried it to make sure it opened.

I stood for a while waiting for my heartbeat to quieten.

When I felt calmer I moved a half-dozen steps into the darkness. The door dissolved into black behind me. But at the same time my eyes started to work better. There was a thin moon, enough to make out the cobbles directly in front of my feet. I made myself walk farther: fifteen, twenty steps now, then thirty. To the end of one street and the beginning of another. The silence was deeper than the dark. I had almost reached the next corner when I heard a scuffle and something ran over the hem of my dress. I gasped involuntarily, though I knew it must be a rat. What was it the friar said? How the cloak of night brings out the vermin of the city. How it pours lust, like poison, into men's veins. But why? Though men's foulness might be hidden from each other, God's eye would presumably see it just as clearly in the dark. Could it come upon anybody? Were prostitutes ordinary women who stayed out too long in the night? A ridiculous idea. Still, I felt a shiver of fear like frost around my heart.

I took a few deep breaths. The smell of freedom was mixed with the sour tang of urine and rotting food. The Florentines left their mark on the streets like spraying cats. Savonarola might strive for purity of thought, yet decay and dirt were all around us. Still, I would not be frightened into stopping. My brothers, who were rude and stupid by degree, danced their way through the city darkness every night without mishap. I would simply ape their confidence, walk the streets to the Duomo, and from there to the river. Then I would come back. Not so far as to be lost, but far enough so that when my own daughters came to me with fantasies of freedom I could tell them that there was both nothing to fear and nothing to miss. It was simply the same city without light.

The street was broader now. I walked faster, my shoes tapping over the uneven cobbles, my father's cloak sweeping the ground around me. Where, I wondered, would the painter be by now? I had waited awhile before following him. He would surely have crossed the bridge long ago. How long would it take him, there and back? That depended on what he was doing in between. But I would not think of that now.

As I turned the corner, the great mass of the cathedral revealed itself at the end of the street ahead of me, the curve of the great dome blacker than the night reaching high up into the sky. The closer I got the more improbable its size became, as if the whole of the city lay crouched under its shadow. I could almost imagine it lifting off from the ground in front of my eyes, rising slowly like a vast black bird above the houses, out of the valley, up toward the heavens: an ascension of brick and stone marking the final miracle of its construction.

I kept my fancies at bay as I crossed the square quickly, head down. Past the Baptistery I took the street south, passing the church of Orsanmichele, its saints staring down at me stone-eyed from their niches. During the day the market here was filled with cloth dealers and the green baize tables of bankers and money-lenders, their raised voices mingling with the snap of the abacus. When my father's business was still young he had had a stall here and I had come once with my mother to visit, marveling in the hustle and the noise. He had been so pleased to see me. I remember that I had buried my face in the mounds of velvets, the daughter of an aspiring merchant, proud and spoiled by turns. But now the place was echoingly deserted, with pockets of blackest shadow under the arches.

"You're out very late, little master. Do your parents know where you are?"

I froze to the spot. The voice, thick like molasses, came from somewhere deep inside the dark. If I turned back I could be in the Baptistery square within a few moments. But to run away would show my fear.

I saw the figure of a monk emerge from the night, a big man in dark Dominican robes, his head covered by his cowl. I quickened my pace. "There's nowhere you can hide where God cannot see you, sir. Take off your hat and show me your face." His voice was harsh now, but I was almost to the corner and his words chased after me as I plunged into the darkness. "That's it. Run home, boy. And be sure to say your prayers and beg forgiveness, lest you die in the night and the devil take your soul."

It took a lot of swallowing to get the saliva back in my throat. I distracted myself by concentrating on the map in my head. I took a turn to the left and then another. The alley was high and narrow. I must have been nearly to the cathedral again when I heard the laughter and made out the shadow of two men coming out of the darkness ahead of me. My blood went icy. They were walking arm in arm, so engrossed in each other that for a while they did not pick up my presence. Going back would lead to the friar and there were no further side streets between them and me. The quicker I walked the quicker it would be over.

One spotted me before the other. He removed his arm from his companion's waist and took a step away in my direction. Within seconds the other followed, until they were both deliberately walking toward me in a scissors movement, with a gap of only a few feet between them. I put my head down until Tomaso's hat entirely covered my face and pulled my cloak fast about me. I heard rather than saw them grow closer. I was having trouble breathing and the blood was roaring in my ears. They were upon me before I had time to think, one to either side of me. I wanted to run but was scared it might provoke them. I hunched my shoulders down and counted the steps in my head.

As they reached me I heard their voices whispering like animal sounds moving around me, all sibilance and threat—*Tschuck, shuck, hsss, tschuck, schuck, tschuck, schuck, hsss*—followed by a set of almost girlish giggles. It was all I could do not to scream. As they passed I felt their bodies brushing mine.

Then, just as suddenly, they were gone. I heard their laughter rise up, raucous and confident, mischief in the sound, and as I glanced behind I saw the two of them come together again like flowing water, linking arms, the game forgotten, already intent on their own business.

I was safe, but my remaining courage had disintegrated under the strain. I waited till they were out of sight, then turned and ran for home. Less sure of my steps, in my haste I tripped over the stones and almost went sprawling. Eventually the rusticated façade of our palazzo appeared ahead of me with its corner shrine of the Virgin welcoming weary travelers, and I ran the last bit to the entrance. As the door closed behind me I felt my legs give way. Stupid, stupid girl. I had walked a dozen streets and come running home, scared off by the first signs of life. I had no courage, no spirit. I deserved to be locked up. The Devil may take the reckless, but the good will surely die of boredom. Boredom and frustration.

I could feel the tears coming, nerves and fury mixed together. I started to pull myself up from the ground and was halfway across the yard when I caught the sound of the door opening again.

I sank back into the shadows. It had to be him. The door closed again, quietly this time, and I heard the sound of the inside bolt being drawn across. For a second there was silence, then padded footsteps crossed the courtyard. I waited till he was almost directly in front of me. He was breathing heavily. Maybe he had been running too. If I stayed still he would have just moved past me and away. Why did I do it? Because I had been such a coward? To prove to myself that I was not all talk? Or maybe it was more unkind than that: the need to see someone as frightened as I had been.

"Did you have a good time?"

I stepped into his path at the same time as I spoke. He lifted off the ground with the shock and I heard something fall, a dull slam like a hard object hitting the ground. He seemed more agitated by the loss of it than by my presence as he flung himself down onto the ground, feeling desperately around him. But I had got there first. My fingers closed over the rough cover of a book. Our hands met. He withdrew his instantly as if the touch had scalded him. I pushed the book back toward him and he grabbed it.

"What are you doing here?" he hissed.

"Watching you."

"Why?"

"I told you. I want your help."

"I can't help you. Don't you understand?" And I heard the fear in his voice.

"Why? What is out there? What have you seen?"

"Nothing. Nothing. Get away from me."

He pushed me to one side as he got up and stumbled out of the way. But we had made too much noise, and a voice came rolling out of the darkness somewhere off the courtyard nearby, freezing us both to the spot. "Shut up, whoever you are. Go screw somewhere else."

I stayed crouched in the darkness. The voice died away and after a few seconds I heard the painter stumble off. I waited till everything was quiet, then used my hands to push myself up. As I did so I found something on the ground nearby, a paper that must have slid out of the book. I grasped it tightly in my hand and made my way silently back across the courtyard, up the servants' staircase to the main body of the house.

Once in the safety of my room I fumbled to light the oil lamp. It took awhile for its glow to grow vivid enough for me to see.

I unfolded the paper and smoothed it out on the bed.

It had been torn in half, so the image was cut through the middle, but there was enough to read it. It was part of the body of a man, naked legs and most of the torso, the paper ripped below where the neck would have been. The chalk strokes were rough and crude, as if there had been barely enough time to capture it, but what it showed was unforgettable. From the collarbone to the groin, his body was split open by a single deep knife wound, the flesh peeled backward like an animal carcass on a butcher's stall and the innards pulled out and exposed.

My hands came up to my mouth to stifle the quick moan, and as they did so I registered the smell on my fingers: that same sweet stench of decay that had come off his body the day of the portrait session in the chapel, a session which I now remembered had taken place after another of his night journeys into town. And so I learned that what our devout artist did with his nights had more to do with death than sex.

Seventeen

I T MUST HAVE BEEN ONLY A FEW HOURS LATER WHEN the shouting in the streets woke me. I had fallen asleep fully dressed on my bed, the paper in my hand. The oil lamp was still burning and the sky was streaked with swaths of pink. Someone was banging on the main door of the palazzo. I pulled on a gown over my clothes and met my father halfway down the stairs.

"Go back to bed," he said tersely.

"What is happening?"

But he ignored me. Below us in the courtyard a servant had already saddled his horse. I saw my mother on the landing still in her dressing robe.

"Mother?"

"Your father is called for. Piero de' Medici is arrived back at the Signoria."

Of course there was no sleep to be had after that. Since there was nowhere else, I put the paper for safekeeping with my own drawings, already packed in my marriage chest. I would think about what I should do with it later. For now there were more pressing matters. Downstairs, Tomaso and Luca were about to leave. I met my mother and followed her into her bedroom to plead with her, though I knew it would be to no avail.

"You told me once that history must be noted. We stood together in Ghirlandaio's chapel and you said those words to me. Now something even more momentous is happening in our city. Are we not allowed to be witnesses?"

"It is out of the question. Your father says Piero has come into the city with a sword in his hand and men at his heels. There will be bloodshed and violence. It is not for women to witness such things."

"So what do we do, sit and embroider our shrouds?"

"Don't be melodramatic, Alessandra, it doesn't suit you. Yes, you can sew if you like. Though it might do you better to pray. For yourself as well as the city."

What could one say? I did not know any more what was right. Everything that had once seemed safe and certain was unraveling before my eyes. The Medici had ruled our city for fifty years, but they had never in all that time raised arms against the state. At best Piero was a bad politician, at worst he was a traitor. Tomaso was right. The Republic was falling like a house of cards. Where had it gone? All that glory and wealth and learning? Could it be that Savonarola was right? All the art in the world could not keep out an invading army. Was it our sins and our pride that had brought us to this?

My mother busied herself about the house.

Halfway down the stairs I met Erila slipping out.

"There is talk of bloodshed on the streets," I said. "You should be careful. Mother says it is no place for women out there now."

"I'll remember that," she said, grinning as she pulled her cloak around her head.

"Oh, take me with you," I whispered as she moved away. "Please." And I know that she heard me, because I saw her hesitate before she went, moving swiftly toward the door.

. . .

I KEPT VIGIL ON MY WINDOW SEAT IN THE RECEIVING ROOM. Just after midday the great bell of the Signoria started to toll. I had never heard it before yet I knew immediately what it was. What had my tutors called it? La Vacca, the cow, because its tone was so mournful and low. But while its name was comical, its sound marked the end of the world, for it was rung only at moments of deepest crisis: a call for the citizenry of Florence to gather in the Piazza della Signoria because the government was under threat.

My mother came rushing in and joined me at the window. Already there were people pouring out onto the street. Now she was as agitated as I. I thought for a moment she was ill, she looked so faint.

"What is it?"

She said nothing.

"What is it?" I insisted.

"I haven't heard it for so long," she said dimly. She shook her head as if clearing her thoughts. "They rang it the day of the assassination of Giuliano and the attack on Lorenzo in the cathedral. The city was in uproar, people screaming and shouting everywhere." She stopped and I could feel her struggling to continue. It made me think of her sudden tears at Lorenzo's body. Who was she then? "I . . . I was carrying you near to term, and the moment the bells started I felt you move violently. I think you probably wanted to be watching then too." She smiled weakly.

"What did you do?" I said, remembering the below-stairs tales of her transgression.

She closed her eyes. "I went to the window, just like you."

"And?"

"And I watched as the mob dragged one of the assassins, the priest De Bagnone, through the streets to the gallows. He was bleeding from where they had castrated him."

"Oh." So it was true. I had been turned in the womb by fear

and horror. I moved away from the window almost without thinking. "And so I grew monstrous from the shock."

"No. You are not monstrous, Alessandra, only curious. And young. Like I was." She paused. "If it makes you feel better, I was not so much shocked or frightened as consumed by sadness for him. That anyone should be in so much pain and terror... I know what is said by others about such things, but I have thought about it much since that day, and I think that if I gave you anything in the womb it would have been compassion for the suffering of man."

I came and sat down next to her, and she put her arm around me. "What will happen to us, Mama?" I said, after a while.

She sighed. "I don't know. I fear Piero has neither the wit nor the power to save the government, though he may yet save his own life."

"And the French?"

"Your father says they are on their way. Piero has made humiliating concessions. He has given them the freedom of the city, the fortress of Pisa, and a great loan to Charles's war chest."

"So much! How could he do that? When will they get here?"

"It's only a matter of days." And she looked at me, almost as if she were seeing me for the first time. "I think we should accept that your wedding may come sooner than we think, Alessandra."

As always, it was Erila who brought the news. It was so late by then I think even my mother was worried, and for once she didn't have the heart to banish me to my room.

"Piero's gone, madam. Taken his men and fled the city. When the Signoria heard the terms he'd made they threw him out. But he refused to leave the square and his men had their swords out. That's when they rang the bell. You should have seen the crowds. Half of Florence was there within minutes. They took a vote to form a new government then and there. The first thing it did was to exile him and put a price of two thousand florins on his head. I came back through Via Tornabuoni. The Medici Palace is already under siege. It's like a war out there."

So Savonarola had been proved right. The sword was upon us.

. . .

I ROSE AT 6 A.M. I REFUSED MARIA, AND ON THIS OF ALL DAYS I WAS given my way. Erila dressed me and decorated my hair. We were both exhausted. For me it marked the second night of sleeplessness. In the courtyard the grooms were harnessing the horses, and a group of men my father employed as guards were being fed in the kitchens. Half the city was still on the streets and there was talk of looting at the Medici Palace. It was nobody's idea of a wedding day.

I considered myself in the mirror glass. There had been no time for my husband to supply my new wardrobe, as was the custom, so I had had to make do with my own. In recent months I had grown large for my best crimson brocade, but I was stuffed into it nevertheless and could barely move my arms, the sleeves were so tight. No sign of my sister's sighing silk skirts and pale skin now. I had neither beauty nor grace. But then this was not the time for proud family portraits anyway. It was just as well. How could I sit calmly in front of a man whose chalk captured sliced flesh and the contours of disemboweled innards?

I felt sick even at the thought.

"*Tss...* Hold still, Alessandra. I can't weave the flowers in place if you jiggle so."

It was not my twisting but their wilted condition that was the fault. Yesterday's flowers for today's bride. I caught her eye in the glass. She did not smile, and I know she was frightened too.

"Erila—?"

"Shhh... There's no time for this now. We'll be fine. It's a marriage, not a coffin. Remember, it was you who chose this over the nunnery."

But I think she was only sharp to keep her own spirits up, and when she saw my tears she held me, and when my hair was finished she offered to slip out to fetch me some soft-roasted chestnuts and wine. Only as she was leaving did I remember the painter and our appointment for later that day.

"Tell him—" But what was there to tell? That I was gone from my father's house while he spent his nights amid the stink of death and bloody evisceration? "Tell him it is too late now." And so it was.

The door opened soon after she left and Tomaso stood in the entrance, as if afraid to come any closer. He was still in last night's clothes.

"How is it out there, brother?" I said evenly, into the mirror.

"As if the invasion is come already. They are ripping down the Medici crests from all the buildings and painting up the sign of the Republic in their place."

"Will we be safe?"

"I don't know."

He took off his cloak and wiped his face with it. "I trust you are not dressed for my wedding," I said, almost glad for a reason to spat with him. "You won't make any conquests with that much dirt upon you. Though I think the guest list will be somewhat reduced by circumstances."

He gave a little shrug. "Your wedding," he repeated softly. "I seem to be the only one who has not congratulated you." He paused, and we looked at each other in the mirror glass. "You look... handsome."

And it was so incongruous to hear even such a simple compliment from his lips that I couldn't help laughing. "Good enough to roll and pluck, you mean?"

He frowned, as if my crudeness upset him. He moved farther in so he could see me directly, out of the reflection of the mirror this time. "I still don't know why you did it."

"Did what?"

"Agreed to marry him."

"To get away from you, of course," I said lightly, but again he did not react. I shrugged. "Because I would die a slow death in a convent, and I have no life here. Maybe with him I will get one."

He made a small noise in his throat, as if the answer had not helped him. "I hope you will be happy."

"Do you?"

He hesitated. "He is a cultured man."

"So I hear."

"I think ... I think he will give you the freedom you desire."

I frowned. It was similar to something my mother had said. "And what makes you think that?"

He shrugged.

"You know him, yes?"

"A little."

I shook my head. "No. More than a little, I think." Of course. There had been so much going on, I had not been thinking straight. How else had he known about my studies and my painting? Who else would have given him such ammunition? "It was you who told him about me, right?" I said. "About my Greek. And my drawing. And my dancing."

"Your dancing tells itself, and your knowledge, sister—well, your knowledge is legendary." And there was a flash of the old Tomaso back again, the knife dipped in sarcasm.

"Tell me something, Tomaso. Why is it we always fight?"

"Because..." He stopped. "Because ... I cannot remember anymore."

I sighed. "You are older than I, you have more freedom, more influence, you dance better"—I paused—"and you are a good deal prettier." He did not say anything. "Or you certainly look in the mirror more often," I added, with a laugh.

He could have laughed back. There was an opportunity for that. But instead he said nothing.

"Well," I said softly, "maybe we would do well not to make peace now. I think it would shock us too much, and the world is already full of such shocking things."

There was nothing left to be said, but still he stayed, loitering. "I meant it, Alessandra. You do look handsome."

"I look ready," I corrected. "Though I am not sure that I am. Anyway... The next time we meet after today, I will be a wife and Florence will be an occupied city. You could do better than to brawl in the streets for a while. You might find yourself at the end of a French sword."

"I shall come and visit you instead."

"You will always be welcome in my home," I said formally. I wondered how long it would be before the word stopped sounding strange in my mouth.

"In which case I shall come often." He paused. "Give my regards to your husband."

"I will."

I know now, of course, that the conversation meant more to him than it did to me.

YOU COULD HARDLY CALL IT A MARRIAGE PROCESSION. I RODE A horse, but you could barely see me for the surrounding guards, and no one on the streets stopped to admire my costume. The city was jumpy. There were knots of men huddled together on street corners, and when we got to the cathedral we were stopped and ordered to take another route because the square in front of the church was cordoned off.

But the cordon was not complete, and through the gap I had a clear view.

There was a figure lying on the steps of the Baptistery, his body slouched against Ghiberti's shining sculptured doors. A cloak covered his head, but from the length of his leg and the colors of his cloth he was clearly a young man. He might almost have been asleep after a night's drinking, had it not been for the pool of black blood that was seeping like floodwater from underneath his body.

The groom pulled my horse onward, but the smell of blood must have got into its nostrils because it refused suddenly, snorting, its feet chopping on the cobbles. I held on to the saddle, staring at the corpse. And as I did the cloak slipped down and I saw a mangled bloody face, the head half severed from the torso and a gaping hole where the nose had been. Above him the doors told the story of the Angel of God staying Abraham's hand in the Sacrifice of Isaac, but there was no such mercy here. Another mutilated corpse by another church. Savonarola was right: Florence was at war with herself, and the Devil was running the city during the hours of darkness.

The groom pulled the horse's head to, and we continued on our way.

Eighteen

M Y HUSBAND'S PALAZZO WAS OLD AND DRAFTY, A SMELL OF damp about the very stones. My instinct about the guest list proved correct. It was not simply timing that had thinned the ranks, but a nervousness about past allegiances. With the government changing hands, it would not do to be seen at a wedding of the old guard, and my father, though he might not have been as prominent as he would have liked, was most certainly aligned. I can't say it worried me. What need did we have of spectators? The ceremony was simple and brief. The notary was more agitated than we were, looking over his shoulder every time there was a shout or a noise from the street. But he did the job, supervising the signing of the contracts and the exchange of rings between the two of us. In the rush there had been no time for my husband to have brought the counter dowry, but he had done what he could and I think my mother was touched by the small amber brooch he gave her, an heirloom from his mother. For Luca there was a drinking flask and for Tomaso a silver belt, rather handsome, I thought, with promises of more things to follow.

While the city shook with crisis, the inside of Cristoforo's old house was quiet and refined. He had a calm way with him and throughout the ceremony treated me with polite attention, more like an acquaintance than a wife, but then of course so I was. I found it rather reassuring, proof of his honesty as well as his goodwill. We stood side by side, and he was tall enough that I did not have to hunch my shoulders to complement him as I would with many other men. He looked good: better than I, it must be said. When he was younger I daresay he would have been a spectacularly attractive man, and amid the lines and slightly florid complexion there was still enough haggard beauty in place to catch the eye.

After the ceremony there was a simple meal of cold meats, pork jelly, and fresh roasted pike stuffed with raisins. Not much of a wedding feast, though I could tell from my father's face that the wines, from the cellar, were superior. After we ate there was dancing and music in the winter receiving room. Plautilla puffed and sweated her way through a few rounds, but her gazelle grace was gone in the swell of her belly. After a while she sat on the side and watched as others played. When my new husband led me into the "Balli Rostiboli," I didn't fall over or miss the steps of any of the dances. My mother watched quietly. My father, beside her, feigned a certain interest, but his mind was on other things. I tried to imagine the world through his eyes. He had built his entire life on the advancement of his family and the glory of the state. Now his daughters were dispersed, his sons wild on the streets, the Republic in crisis, and the French army a day's march away. While here we were, intent on dancing as if there were nothing better to do.

The festivities broke up early in accordance with the curfew. My family took their leave, embracing first me and then my new husband. My mother kissed me solemnly on the forehead and, I think, would have spoken to me further but I would not look her in the eye. I was nervous now and willing to blame everybody but myself for my predicament. "You must be brave," she had told me hurriedly that morning as she checked my dress, no time for the full briefing. "He will know you are young and he will take care. The marriage night might hurt a little, but it will be over soon. This is a great adventure, Alessandra. It will change your life and I believe, if you can embrace it, it will give you a stillness and a satisfaction that the future might otherwise deny you."

I'm not sure she believed it either. As for myself, I was so distracted by then that I was not even listening properly.

"SO, ALESSANDRA LANGELLA, WHAT SHALL WE DO NOW, YOU AND I?" He stood surveying the quiet debris. The silence after the music was alarming.

"I don't know."

I knew he must be feeling my nerves. He poured himself another drink. Oh, please don't get drunk, I thought. Ignorant as I was, even I knew that while a husband should not come to his bride in uncontrolled lust (and there had been no sign of anything like that; indeed, the only time he had touched me since the ceremony had been during the dancing), neither should he come to her in drink. As to the other forbiddens—well, I would no doubt learn them as we went along.

"Perhaps we should explore some mutual interest for a while. Would you like to look at some art?"

"Oh, yes!" I said, and I think my face must have lit up because he laughed at my gaucheness as one might laugh at the over-eagerness of a child. I remember thinking as he did so that he seemed like a good man and that, once we had become man and wife, we could go back to talking as we had done at Plautilla's house and spend our spare time sitting next to each other reading and studying affairs of the mind, like the brothers I had never really had. And in that way, though the state might crumble around us, we would keep something of the old Florence within ourselves, and so out of all of this horror would come something good.

As we climbed the stairs I noticed it got colder.

His sculpture collection was on the second floor. He had given over an entire room to it. There were five statues: two satyrs, a Hercules with muscles like knotted rope under marble skin, and a memorable Bacchus whose body, though stone, looked fleshier than my own. But the most beautiful was the young athlete: a naked youth, his weight taken on the back foot, his torso twisted in readiness for the thrust of the discus he held cupped in his right hand. Everything in his body spoke of fluidity and grace, as if Medusa had caught him at the very second before thought and action connected. Surely even Savonarola would have been moved by him. Sculpted long before Christ, there was palpable divinity in his perfection.

"You like him?"

"Oh, yes," I breathed. "I like him very much. How old is he?"

"He is modern."

"No. He is—"

"—classical? I know, it's an easy mistake. He is evidence of my philistinism."

"What do you mean?"

"I bought him in Rome from a man who swore he had been unearthed on the island of Crete two years before. The torso still bore the marks of earth and fungus. See the chipped fingers on the left hand? I paid a fortune for him. Then, when I got him back to Florence, a friend with connections to the Medici sculpture garden told me he was the work of a young artist. A copy from a piece that Cosimo had owned. Apparently it was not the first time that such a deceit had taken place."

I stared up at the young man. One could almost imagine him turning his head toward us, smiling at the discovery of his own fraud. It would be a charming smile, though.

"What did you do?"

"I congratulated the artist and kept the statue. I think he is worth whatever money I paid for him. Come. I have things that I think will interest you even more."

He took me into a smaller room. From a locked cupboard he took out a rich malachite cup and two agate vases, reset by Florentine goldsmiths in special gilded stands with his name engraved on the bottom. Then he pulled out small inlaid wooden drawers, revealing a set of Roman coins and jewelry. But his real prize he kept till last: a large portfolio that he placed carefully on a table in front of me. "They are illustrations of a text waiting to be bound into a book. Can you imagine what glory they will bring when it is finished?"

I slid them out, one by one, until maybe a dozen of them lay in sequence across the table. The parchment was thin enough for me to see the writing on the back, but I didn't need to read the words to know what book it was. The ink sketches showed glimpses of heaven: a sublimely delicate Beatrice holding Dante by the hand and guiding him up through a swarm of tiny spirits toward the Godhead above.

"*Paradiso.*"

"Indeed."

"And is there also *Purgatorio* and the *Inferno*?"

"Of course."

I went farther back, canto by canto. As the drawings descended toward hell they became more complex and wild, some of them teeming with naked figures tormented by demons, others capturing men frozen into tree structures or violated by snakes. Though I knew Dante, my imagination could never have dreamed such a rolling river of images to go with the words.

"Oh! Who did these?"

"You don't recognize his style?"

"I have not seen as much art as you," I said quietly.

"Try this." He flicked through the pile and pulled out a particular canto from *Paradiso* in which the tendrils of Beatrice's hair waved around her face with the same exuberance as the folds of her gown swept over her body. In her face, half coy, half serene, I thought I saw the hint of a more calculated mistress, one who pulled all manner of men's desires away from their wives.

"Alessandro Botticelli?"

"Very good. She is indeed his Beatrice, don't you think?"

"But...but when did he draw these? I didn't know that he had illustrated *The Divine Comedy.*"

"Oh, our Sandro has almost as great a love for Dante as he does for God. Though I hear that is changing under the lash of Savonarola's words. These were done some years ago, after he came back from Rome. At the start they were a labor of love rather than a commission, though he always has a patron. They took him a long time. And as you see, they remain unfinished."

"How did they come to you?"

"Ah, sadly I am only their guardian. I hold them for a friend who has been busy with politics and fears his collection might become vulnerable to the violence abroad."

Of course I was curious as to who this friend might be, but he said nothing more. I thought of my mother and father. While she was cleverer than he was in so many ways, there were all manner of things he didn't share with her and about which she did not ask. No doubt I would learn soon enough where the frontiers lay.

I went back to the sketches. The journey through *Paradiso* was graceful, even profound, but my attention was continually drawn back to the *Inferno.* These pages crawled with suffering and sorrow: bodies drowning in rivers of blood, armies of lost souls rushing through eternity pursued by winds of fire, while Dante and Virgil, in some of the illustrations clothed in fiercely bright colors, walked along a precipice of cool stone licked by flames.

"So tell me, Alessandra," my husband said, looking over my shoulder, "why is it, do you think, that hell always holds more fascination than heaven?"

I thought back to all the other paintings and frescoes I had seen, didactic in their horror: squatting imps with bat wings and claws, gouging flesh and crunching bone. Or the Devil himself, his great animal body thick with hair, stuffing screaming sinners into his mouth as if they were carrots. Compared with that, what images did I remember of heaven? Hosts of beatified saints and angels in serried ranks, united in wordless serenity.

"Maybe it is because we have all felt pain," I said. "Whereas it is harder for us to understand the sublime."

"Ah? You would see sublime as the opposite of pain? What about pleasure?"

"I think ... I think pleasure is too weak a word for union with God. Surely pleasure is an earthly concept: it is what comes from giving in to temptation."

"Precisely." He laughed. "So the pain of hell reminds us of earthly pleasure. A potent connection, wouldn't you say? Because it reminds us of life."

"Though it should also remind us of sin," I said sternly.

"Alas, yes." He sighed. "Sin." Though he did not sound too saddened by the thought. "The two do grow together like ivy round the bark."

"So which place will you go to, sir?" I asked, but the sternness had gone and I wondered how it would feel if next time I used the word *husband*.

"Me? Oh, I shall go where I can find the best company."

"And will you be looking for gossip or philosophy?"

He smiled. "For philosophy, of course. Give me classical scholars for eternity."

"Ah, then you are disqualified already. For those great minds remain in limbo, since they were born before the birth of the true Savior. And while they feel no pain, they suffer the despair that comes from having no hope of transcendence. Even purgatory is denied them."

He laughed. "Well done. Though I must tell you I smelled your trap. It was my compliment to spring it for you." And of course as he said it I found myself wondering at the very pleasure of our conversation and how, if he was right, that in itself made it a candidate for sin. "Though I would add," he continued, "that if Dante is to be our Virgil through the afterlife, I am sure we could both agree that there are places in hell where one might find good debating companions. In between torments, his sinners manage some penetrating discourse."

He and I were standing closer now, a hundred naked bodies at our fingertips. Dante's hell had an elegant metaphysical symmetry about it: for each sin, the apposite torture. So gluttons suffered eternal hunger, thieves who could not tell their property from another's found their bodies metamorphosing into snakes and serpents, and sinners consumed by the heat of lust were blown in endless flight by flaming winds, no satisfaction from the burning itch however much they scratched.

Yet here we were studying them: husband and wife, our desire sanctified by the act of marriage. If there was to be bodily contact between us it could, rather than sin, be a stepping-stone to divinity. We had both read our Marsilio Ficino. *Vinculum Mundi:* love binding all of God's creation together, Plato and Christianity in joyous union. So the physical act of love of man and woman was the first rung on a ladder that might lead to a final ecstatic union with the Godhead. I, who had so often dreamed of transcendence, now felt a slip-sliding sensation in my womb, a mixture in itself of pain and pleasure.

Perhaps God had had a hand in this after all. If my husband up till now had chosen lust over love, then surely my purity might bring us both to salvation. Through our minds we might find our bodies, and through our bodies we would aspire to God.

"Where did you meet my brother?" I said, because if ours was to be a meeting of souls I would need to know.

He paused. "I think you know where."

"In a tavern?"

"How much does it shock you?"

"Not much," I said. "You forget I have lived with him a long time. I know he spends much of his life in such places."

"He is young, though." He paused. "I have no such excuse."

"It is not my business what you did before me," I said, and I was pleased by my own meekness.

"How sweetly you put it." And he smiled.

Yes, I thought. Women would find him attractive. Though he has presence, he does not pursue. Given the incessant way lust drives some men, I could see how this would be its own subtle seduction.

We fell silent. I think we both knew the time had come. Despite his courtliness I wished he would touch me. Some simple contact: a brush of clothes or hands meeting across the parchment. Though I might want him purer, I had need of his knowledge now. I yawned.

"You are tired?" he said immediately.

"A little. It has been a long day."

"Then we shall retire. I shall call for your slave. What is her name?"

"Erila."

"Erila. She can help you get ready."

I nodded, finding it hard to speak now, such was the pressure in my windpipe. I moved to the side, concentrating on the paintings, while he rang the bell. Hell's bodies were all around me, writhing and rolling in savage memories of pleasure. This was a man at home with naked flesh. As his wife, I would have the advantage of his years of experience. Yes. I could have done worse.

FIRST SHE TOOK OFF MY SHOES, EXTRACTING FROM INSIDE THE sole the gold florin my mother had placed there to bring my union wealth and fertility. As I held it in my palm I feared for a moment it might make me cry, so much was it the symbol of my lost home. Then she undid my laces and I stepped out of my dress and my chemise until I stood in front of her naked. My wedding night shift was ready on the bed. The room was cold, and as I shivered the surface of my skin rose up like the corpse of a plucked chicken. She stood with the gown in her hands, studying me. She had dressed me since I was a child and had watched the changes in me year by year. Now we both wondered where the thickened hips and the sprouting thatch of pubic hair had come from.

"Oh, my lady," she said, trying to be light and using the term in jest. "Look at you—such a ripe peach."

Despite myself I laughed. "I think fat, more like. I am puffed up like a diseased bladder."

"It's flesh that comes and goes with the moon. But it suits you. You are ready."

"Oh, not you too, Erila. I have had enough of it from Tomaso. The only thing that has changed in me is that I bleed like a stuck pig now. Otherwise I am the same as before."

She smiled. "Not quite the same. Mark my words."

I wished again that she had been my mother. Then I could have asked her all the things I didn't know and that might save my life or at least my dignity over the next few hours. But it was already too late. I grabbed the gown and pulled it over my head. The sheet of silk fell to the floor, my father's profits caressing my naked hips and legs. Inside it I looked almost graceful.

I sat while she took down my hair. It was so thick and unruly that when the last few pins came it fell heavily down my back.

"It is like a river of black lava," she said, as she began brushing and tugging its tangles free.

"A field of squabbling crows, more like."

She shrugged. "Where I come from the color is beautiful."

"Oh! Then can I go and live in that country too? Or I have an even better idea." I caught her eye in the mirror. "Why don't you go to him tonight in my place? Really. It is perfect. It will be dark so he'll never know the difference. We've barely exchanged twenty words together. No, stop laughing, I mean it. You are nearly as plump as I am. As long as he doesn't talk Greek to you it'll be simple."

Her laughter has always been a benign contagion, and for a while now we were both unable to stop. If he heard us, what would he think? I took a deep breath, held it in, and closed my eyes. When I opened them again she was smiling at me.

"Do you think I am too young for this, Erila?" I said anxiously.

"You are old enough."

"When did it happen to you?"

She pursed her lips. "I can't remember."

"Really?"

"No." She paused. "I can remember."

I sighed. "At least give me some tips. Please. Tell me what to do."

"Don't do anything. If you do he'll think you've done it before and ask for the contract back."

And we both laughed again.

She went about her business, tidying the room, picking up my wedding gown, and holding it to her in front of the mirror with a secret smile and a flounce. It would look better on her than it had on me. When she gets her freedom or a husband, whichever comes first, I will give her such a dowry, something majestic to go with that velvety skin and mane of crinkled hair. God help the man.

"What did you tell me once? Before Plautilla's wedding... That it was not as bad as having a tooth pulled but that it could be as sweet—"

"—as the top string vibrating on a lute."

I laughed. "And which poet said that?"

"This one," she said, and pointed between her legs.

"So how about... like the first suck of a juicy watermelon."

"What?"

"That's what my brother Tomaso said."

She shrugged. "Your brother knows nothing about it," she said more sternly.

"Well, he makes a good pretense at it."

But she had stopped playing now. "Come. Enough of this," she said, smoothing down my dress and finishing my hair. "Your husband'll be waiting."

"And where will you be?" I said, a little frantic.

"Downstairs with the other slaves. Where, I have to tell you, it is dank and colder than your father's house. You're not the only one who will need ways to warm herself in our new home." But she still took pity on me. "You'll be all right," she said, and she grabbed my cheek. "It won't kill you. Stop thinking about it. Clever women don't die of it. Remember that."

Nineteen

I SLID INSIDE THE CRISP EMBROIDERED SHEETS, CAREFUL to keep my gown from ruffling up around me. Of my husband there was no sign. I waited. Yesterday I had not even known what the inside of this house looked like. In an hour's time I would know everything about what I did not know now. Was an hour enough? Truly, despite all the gossip, I did not know anything.

The door opened. He was still dressed. It looked as if he were going out rather than coming to bed. He went to the table, where a flagon of wine had been left, and poured two glasses. For a moment I wasn't sure he had even seen me. He came over to the bed and sat down.

"Hello," he said. I could smell the wine on his breath. "How do you feel?"

"Well. Perhaps a little weary."

"As you say. It has been a long day." He took a sip of the wine and handed me the other glass. I shook my head. "You should drink it," he said. "It will relax you." I thought at that moment that I was relaxed. Or as relaxed as I was going to get. But I did as I was told. The taste was different, stronger than the wine I was used to. I had eaten little at supper and that was now some hours ago. The liquid burned its way down my throat. I felt slightly woozy. I shot a glance at him over the top of the glass. He was looking at the floor, as if his mind was on something else entirely. He put down the glass. Certainly he seemed a little unsure. If I was not his first virgin, then certainly I would be his first virgin wife.

"You are ready?" he said.

"Sir?"

"You know what happens now, yes?"

"Yes." I said, dropping my eyes and blushing, despite myself.

"Good."

He moved closer and lifted the sheet away from me, folding it neatly to the bottom of the bed. I sat in my silk finery with my toes peeping out from the bottom of the hem. For some reason they made me think of Beatrice, her naked little feet flying God-ward under the joyful strokes of Botticelli's pen. But Dante had loved her too much to have carnal knowledge of her. Of course, there was also the fact that she was someone else's wife. What had Erila said? Stop thinking ... clever women don't die of it.

He laid a hand on my lower leg, connecting with my skin through the silk, and his touch felt clammy. He left it there for a while. Then, using both hands now, he lifted up the material of my nightgown and carefully folded it upward until my legs were revealed almost to my sex. Now when his hand went to my calf it met my bare flesh. I swallowed, watching his fingers rather than his face, trying to stop my body from going rigid. He traced a line up over my knee and my thigh to the edge of the ruffled gown, then pushed it farther, until my bush started to show, the hair as dark if not darker than that on my head. Had Plautilla dyed there too? Too late now, I thought frantically. My instinct was to cover myself again. I had been taught modesty for too long to discard it so suddenly. He took his hand away and sat for a moment study-ing me. It felt like something was wrong. As if something had dis-pleased him. But whether it was me or him I couldn't tell. I thought of his statues: the smooth marble flesh so perfect, so young. Maybe he was embarrassed by the imperfections of my gawkiness and his age.

"Will you not get undressed?" I asked. To my distress, my voice sounded like a child's.

"That won't be necessary," he said, almost stiffly.

I had a sudden image of the courtesan and the man with his head buried in her lap, and I felt sick. I wondered if he would kiss me now. Surely this would be the moment. But he did not.

Instead he shifted himself farther to the edge of the bed and with one hand started to unbutton his doublet. When the clothing was freed he dipped his hand inside and pulled out his penis, letting it sit limply in his palm. I sat, frozen with panic, not knowing whether to watch or look away. Of course I had seen penises on statues before and, like all young girls, had been both amazed at their scrawny ugliness and confused as to how something so sluglike and shriveled could grow into a weapon hard enough to pierce inside a woman's hole. Now, though I couldn't look, I also couldn't keep my eyes away. Why did he not come to bed? Erila had said there were many ways that a man and woman could do this, but this was not one that I recognized. He clasped his fist around himself and started pulling and stroking, running his hand up and down the stem with a regular almost rhythmic movement. His other hand lay inert on my leg.

I watched transfixed. He seemed to go into a trance. He was no longer looking at me. Instead he seemed to be watching himself, his eyes half closed and his mouth half open, and there were small half-grunting noises coming out of him. After a while he took his other hand off me and applied it to the task too. He glanced back at me once but his eyes were glazed, and though I think he was smiling it left his teeth slightly bared, more like a grimace. I tried to smile too, but there was such a rising panic in me now that I am sure he could see it. I felt my legs glued together.

He was working harder now, and under his fingers his penis

began to swell. "Ha, ha…" He took a half-laughing series of breaths and looked down. "That's better," he muttered, taking air in bigger gulps now.

He maneuvered himself farther up the bed toward me, all the time working his member to keep it stiff. He freed one hand to pull something out from the cabinet nearby. It was a blue glass jar. He fumbled with its lid, then plunged his fingers in, drawing up some clear substance. He rubbed it over himself, then dipped his hand in again and moved toward me. I recoiled involuntarily.

"Don't move," he said sharply. I froze. His fingers reached inside my thatch, fumbling for the opening. The ointment was greasy and icy, so icy that it made me cry out.

"It can't hurt," he said, between breaths. "I haven't done anything yet."

I shook my head, trembling. "It's cold," I said. "It's cold." And I was trying not to cry.

He laughed out loud. I laughed too from sheer terror.

"Oh, God, don't laugh now, we'll lose all my good work," he said hurriedly, and started pummeling himself again. The laughter stuck in my throat.

"You are a virgin, right?"

"Yes."

"So, I am going to break the hymen. It will make it easier when I push myself inside. Do you understand?"

I nodded. What was the teaching they gave to young women? *Virtue is a more valuable dowry than money.* But there was no comfort in such advice now. Nothing to make sense of the awful confusion unfolding before me.

He started to slide two fingers inside me. And just before he did so I saw a shiver pass over his face. This time he could not hide his distaste. Then he pushed in. I cried out. It hurt: a scalding tearing pain, like the cutting of a layer of flesh. I thought of teeth pulling, but could feel no sign of the lute.

"Good girl," he muttered thickly. "Good girl. That's it." He pushed again and once more I yelped, though quieter this time, because this time there was less pain. "Good girl," he said again. It felt like he was talking to an animal, a dog or a cat in labor. He withdrew his hand from me, and I noticed a filmy layer of blood on his fingers. I also noticed that his penis had started to droop. "Damn it," he said, and now he used both his hands to pull at it. "Damn it." And he seemed almost angry now.

When he had coaxed it back into life he climbed on top of me, maneuvering himself into a position where his cock was above my sex, and fiddled and started to push to fit it in. It began to soften as soon as it touched me, but he stiffened it with his fingers and finally managed to push them and it in together. But though my virgin skin was broken I was neither big nor slippery enough to handle the size of him. My mother's transgression had deformed me after all and I cried out again, only this time I could not stop crying. He pushed farther. I closed my eyes tight shut, like a child waiting for the danger to pass, and felt a flush of shame run through me, dark and giddy. But he was too busy to take note of me now.

He was hard at work, grunting and thrusting and swearing slightly under his breath. "God damn it, God damn it. . . ." And even in my pain I felt him swell inside me. He removed his finger and thrust some more, his breath coming now in large pants, like a horse snorting his way uphill with a full load. I opened my eyes to see his face above me, eyes screwed up, a grimace like a death's-head upon him, every muscle strained and pushing as if it would snap. Then suddenly there came a great grabbed snort and yell, and I felt him go limp both inside and out, and a hot stream of liquid came spurting half down my legs as he slid out of me and rolled heavily onto the other side of the bed, gasping for air, like a man rescued from the edge of drowning.

He lay getting his breath back, half laughing, half gasping.

It was over. I was plucked. Erila was right. I had not died of it. But of *Vinculum Mundi* there was no sign at all.

After a while he pulled himself up off the bed and walked across the room. I thought for a moment he was going to leave. Instead, he went over to the table where there was a jug of water and cloth. He stood at a half angle to me, wiping himself off and then sliding his penis back into his clothing. He seemed to have forgotten me already. He gave a heavy sigh, as if to put the memory of it all behind him, and when he turned his face was calm again and I swear he looked almost pleased with himself.

The sight of me must have alarmed him though. I know I was still crying. It hurt too much inside for me to close my legs, so I pushed my gown down over myself and leaned over for the sheet, wincing as I moved and noting the pinkish stain spreading like my shame across the white sheet underneath me.

He studied me for a moment and then filled another two glasses and took a long swig. He came to the bed and held out the second one to me.

I shook my head. I could not look at him.

"Drink it," he said. "It'll help. Drink." His voice, though no longer unkind, was firm and brooked no disagreement.

I took it and gulped. But the liquid got caught up with my tears and I coughed violently. He waited for it to subside.

"Again."

I did as I was told. My hand was shaking so violently that I spilled some of it on the sheet. More red blood everywhere. But this time the liquor connected, sending a river of warmth into my throat and stomach. He stood watching me carefully. After a while he said, "That's enough," and took it from me, putting it on the side table. I lay back against the pillows. He looked down at me for a while, then sat down on the bed. I think I must have recoiled.

"Are you all right?" he said, after a while.

I nodded.

"Good. Then maybe you could stop crying. I didn't hurt you that much, did I?"

I shook my head. I held in the sob that was coming and swallowed it back down. When I was certain I had it under control, I said, "Will I . . . will I have a baby now?"

"God. Let's hope so." He laughed. "Because I can't imagine either of us would want to go through that again." And I think he must have seen the blood drain from my skin because the laughter froze in his throat and he looked at me closely.

"Alessandra?"

But I still couldn't meet his eyes.

"Alessandra," he said, quieter this time. And I think it was then that I realized something was wrong. Even more wrong than what had already happened between us. "I . . . are you telling me you didn't know?"

"Know what?" I said, and to my horror the sobbing started again. "I don't know what you're talking about."

"I'm talking about *me*. I'm asking you if you knew about *me*?"

"Knew what about you?"

"Oh, God's blood." And now he buried his head deep in his hands, so that I could barely make out the next words. "I thought you knew. I thought you knew everything." He looked up. "He didn't tell you?"

"Who didn't tell me? I don't know what you're talking about," I said again helplessly.

"Ah." And now he was angry, a quick violent anger that made me frightened.

"Did I not please you?" I said, and I was surprised by how small my voice sounded.

"Oh, Alessandra." He groaned. He leaned over and made a move to take my hand, but I was shaking now and pulled it back. He didn't try again.

We sat for a moment, united in confusion and despair. Then he said, more quietly but firmly, "Listen to me. You must hear this. Are you listening?"

And everything suddenly seemed so important. I nodded, the trembling notwithstanding.

"You are a splendid young woman. You have a mind like a new-minted florin and a soft young body. And if soft young women's bodies were what I desired, I would no doubt desire you." He paused. "But I don't."

He sighed. "The fourteenth canto. *'The wasteland was a dry expanse of thick burning sand.... Many herds of naked souls I saw all weeping desperately, each group assigned a different penalty.... Some stretched out flat upon their backs, while others—the greater number— wandered, never stopping, round and round.*

'And over all that sand land a fall of slowly burning broad flakes of fire showered steadily...and without a moment's rest the dance of wretched hands went on, this side, that side, brushing away the freshly fallen flames.'"

As he spoke I could see the illustration, the tortured male bodies pitted and scarred from the endless burning of the flesh.

"I prefer Dante to Savonarola," he said. "But our monk is perhaps the clearer of the two. 'And so the sodomites shall rot in hell, which is too good for them, for their perfidy does destroy nature itself.'" He paused. "Do you understand now?"

I swallowed and nodded. Once it was said, what was there not to understand? Of course, I had heard stories. Who hadn't? Crude stories and cruel jokes. But even more than usual fornication, this had been kept locked away from children as the grossest of man's sins: unspeakable to the purity of family and the honor of a godly state. So my husband was a sodomite. A man who spurned women in favor of the Devil in other men's flesh.

But if that were the truth, then more than ever it did not make sense. Why should he want to do what we had just done? Why should he want to put himself through the gross distaste I had seen so clearly on his face?

"I don't understand," I said. "If that is how you are, then why—"

"Why did I marry you?"

"Yes."

"Oh, Alessandra. Use that sharp young brain of yours. Times

are changing. You have heard the poison that leaks from his pulpit. I am surprised you have not noticed the denunciation boxes in the churches. There was a time when you might find only a few names in there, most of them already familiar to the Night Police, and even then as long as enough money changed hands all would be forgiven and forgotten. In its own way we were the city's savior. A state filled with young men waiting for wives develops a certain tolerance for lust that doesn't flood the foundling hospitals with unwanted babies. Anyway, isn't Florence the new Athens of the West?

"But not anymore. Now it won't be long before sodomites shall burn on earth before they burn in hell. Young men had better keep their caps on and elder ones will be first to be named and shamed, whatever their status or their wealth. Savonarola has learned his trade from San Bernardino: '*When you see a grown man in good health who is not married, take it as an evil sign.*'"

"And so you needed a wife to detract attention," I said quietly.

"As you needed a husband to find freedom. It seemed like a fair exchange. He told me—"

"He?" My heart felt sick with the word.

He stared at me. "Yes. He. You're telling me you still don't know?"

But of course I did.

It was, as was true of so much in our fair city, a family affair.

Tomaso. My pretty, stupid brother. Except now I was the stupid one. Tomaso, who so liked to swagger the night streets in fine clothes, who so often came back heavy with sex and the pleasure of conquest. There had been times when if I had thought about it I might have read into his coquetry more desired than desiring. How blind could I have been? A man who talked of plucking and taverns but held women in such contempt that he could barely bring himself to spit out the word *cunt,* it caught so in his throat.

Tomaso, my pretty, fawning brother, who never lacked for rich new garments or even for special silver belts at his sister's marriage. And I saw him staring at me in the mirror that morning—was it really still the same day?—uncomfortable for once with whatever it was he couldn't quite bring himself to say.

"No," I said. "He didn't tell me."

"But he—"

"I think perhaps you might have underestimated how much my brother dislikes me."

He sighed, rubbing his face with his hands. "I do not think it is so much dislike as a certain fear. I think he might be scared of your intelligence."

"Poor thing," I said. And for that second even I could make out the Devil in my voice.

Of course. The longer I knew, the more it all fell into place: the stranger who, when he danced with me, had inside information about both my clumsiness and my Greek. Tomaso's glee the night he spotted the blood on my robe and saw a way to save his lover and pay his sister back at the same time. The morning in church when he had bent his head under Savonarola's accusations and I had encountered Cristoforo's eyes looking straight into mine. Except of course I had not been the one he was gazing at. No. That shining little smile of worship had been reserved for my brother. My stupid, pretty, fawning, vain, vulgar, vicious brother.

I started to cry again.

He had enough compassion not to try and stop me. He sat watching over me; then after a while he put out his hand, and this time I let it cover mine. "I am so sorry. It was not meant to be like this."

"You should never have trusted him to tell me," I said, when I could find the breath. "What lies did he spin you about me?"

"Only that it would be doing both of us a favor. That you wanted freedom and independence more than a husband. That you would do anything that was necessary to get it."

"He was right," I said softly. "Though not anything."

We sat again for a while. Outside in the night we caught the sound of shouting, men running through the streets, then a sudden sharp cry of pain, and it brought back the gruesome sight of the young man adrift in his own blood by the Baptistery doors. Florence was turned against herself now, and safety was gone forever.

"Despite my sins, you should know that I am not a bad man, Alessandra," he said, after a while.

"What about in the eyes of God? You don't fear the burning sands and storms of fire?"

"As we said, at least in hell there will be a memory of pleasure." He paused. "You'd be surprised how many of us there are. The greatest civilizations of antiquity have found transcendence in the arsehole of a man."

I winced.

"Forgive my crudity, Alessandra. But it is better that you know me now. For we are going to have to spend time together."

He got up to fill his glass again. I watched him walk across the room. Now his haggard beauty and studied elegance seemed almost teasing. Why had I not noticed it before? Was I so locked in my own mind that I could not read the signs around me?

"As for Judgment Day," he continued, "well, I will take my chances. In those same burning sands are blasphemers and usurers, and worse torments are reserved for them. I think even if I had never yearned for the taste of young boys, heaven would still have not been mine. At least I will have the comfort of sharing the flames with fellow sinners. And I will be in religious company. Believe me, if that army of sodomites had not been so constantly in flight, I wager you would have seen a host of tonsured heads among their numbers."

"No!"

He smiled. "For a sophisticate, Alessandra, you are charmingly naïve."

Though not for much longer, I thought. I looked at him. Now he was without distaste, his humor and goodwill were back, and I couldn't help but like him a little again.

"At least you will not be able to claim your wife's reluctance drove you to it," I said quietly. He looked bemused. "The sodomite that Dante talks to in the sixteenth canto. Doesn't he say something like that? I cannot remember his name."

"Of course. Jacopo Rusticucci. A man of no public merit whatsoever. Rumor has it he was a merchant rather than a scholar." He smiled. "Tomaso told me he would find me a wife who knew her *Divine Comedy* as well as I." I dropped my eyes. "I am sorry. His name brings you pain."

"I'll live," I said quietly. But I could feel hot tears pricking at the back of my eyes.

"I hope so. I would hate to be the cause of death to such a sweet intellect."

"Not to mention such a perfect smoke screen."

He laughed. "Welcome back. I like your wit more than your self-pity. You are a remarkable young woman, you know."

I looked at my husband and wondered what it might have been like if his compliments had warmed my body as much as my mind.

"So—perhaps we should talk of the future. As I told you, this house is yours now. Its library, its art. With the exception of my study, you may treat it as you please. That was part of the bargain."

"What about you?"

"I shall not bother you often. In public we might be seen at a few state events, if indeed there is still a state with enough independence to command them. Other than that I will be out much of the time. That is all you need know."

"Will he come here?" I said.

He looked at me steadily. "He is your brother. As family it would be only natural." He smiled a little at the last word. "The fact is, the city is no longer as safe as it was." He paused. "Let us say there may be times when he comes here. But not for a while."

"You are diplomatic," I said.

He shrugged. *"Man must rule his slaves like a tyrant, his children like a king, and—"*

"—his wife like a politician." I closed the sentence for him. "I am not sure this is what Aristotle had in mind."

He laughed. "Indeed. As for the rest, well, it is up to you. Your choice. Don't let this destroy your life, Alessandra. You'd be surprised what goes on in the bedrooms of our godly city. Such marriages have worked before. You wouldn't want to be like the others anyway. If my attentions burdened you with a dozen children, you would sink beneath the waves. Only give me a single heir and I will leave you alone forever." He paused. "As to your own pleasure—well, that too is your affair. All I ask is that you be discreet."

I stared down at my hands. My insides hurt less than they did, though a deeper burning sensation remained. How did one know when there was a baby in one's womb? My own pleasure? What did I want most in life?

"You will let me paint."

He shrugged. "I have said. You can do as you want."

I nodded. "And I want to see the French," I said firmly. "I mean really see them. When Charles's army marches in, I want to be there on the street, witnessing it as history is made."

He made a small gesture. "Very well. That is what you shall do. It will no doubt be a triumphal entrance."

"You will come with me?"

"I hardly think it would be safe without."

The silence sat between us, yet his name was everywhere. "And what of Tomaso?"

"You and I are man and wife. It will be only proper for us to be seen together." He hesitated. "I will talk to Tomaso. He will understand."

I dropped my eyes so he could not see the spark of pleasure that ignited there.

"So? Do you have any more requests, wife?"

"No"—I paused—"husband."

"Good." He got up from the bed. "Shall I send your slave to you now?"

I shook my head. He leaned over, and for a second I wondered if he might kiss me on the forehead, but instead he brushed his fingers lightly across my cheek. "Good night, Alessandra."

"Good night."

So he left me, and a few moments later I heard the main doors of the house open and close behind him.

AFTER A WHILE THE BURNING SENSATION BETWEEN MY LEGS COOLED and I got up to clean myself. It hurt a little to walk and my skin was crusty where his spouting liquid had dried on my thigh, but his fastidiousness had saved my gown from staining and it fell softly about me as I walked.

I washed carefully, too scared to examine myself. But after I let the gown fall again I moved my hands over my body, just to feel the silk against my skin. And from my breast and hips my fingers strayed downward toward my cleft. What if he had indeed torn me there and there was now a wound that would not heal? Both my mother and her sister had been ripped apart by big children. Could that have happened to me already?

I hesitated, then moved my hand a little farther, separating my fingers to discover that my middle one slipped most easily inside toward my sex. And as it did so my fingertip encountered what felt like a small mound of exposed flesh, which as I touched it sent a raw shiver through me. I felt my breath sharpen and I moved my finger carefully back and across it again. I could hardly tell if the sensation was pleasure or pain, but it made me catch my breath and left me trembling. Was this the way his penis had damaged me, uncovering some nerve end in the very mouth of my sex?

Who could I ask? Who could I possibly tell what had taken place between us? I withdrew my hand quickly, my face flushed with remembered shame. But my curiosity was greater than my pain, and this time I lifted the material of my gown before my fingers roamed back to find the place again. Across my inner thigh a streak of watery blood, pink as the dawn sky, sat like ink wash against my skin. I traced its line back toward my thatch of hair, and the tenderness of my own caress brought tears back to my eyes. I hooked my finger inside me and now when I came upon it, the flesh seemed almost raw. I honed down the point of sensation, then gently applied more pressure, bracing myself for more pain. It seemed to swell under my touch and there came instead a rush of such intense sweetness that it made me gasp out loud and I doubled over slightly on myself. Again I pushed my fingertip. Again it came, and again, like a series of fast ripples on the surface of water, till all I could do was hold on to the table nearby for fear that I might lose my balance as I let the gasps come, so lost was I in the pleasure of my pain.

When it was over my legs were so weak I had to sit down on the bed. There was a strange sense of loss that the feeling was no more, and to my surprise I found myself crying again, though I do not quite know why, because I do not think that what I felt was sadness anymore.

It wasn't long before the anxiety flowed in. What on God's earth would become of me now? I had left my home, my city was in turmoil, and I was newly married to a man who could not bear the sight of my body but who swooned at the thought of my brother. If it had been written as a moral tale, I would probably be sacrificed now, dying of shame and sorrow so that my husband could be brought to penitence and God.

I went over to my marriage chest, a monster of a thing that had once belonged to my husband's mother. It had been carried from his house to mine and then finally back again that afternoon (and to my father's satisfaction it had been as heavy as my sister's, though its riches were weighed in books rather than silks and velvets). From its depths I now brought out my mother's prayer book, over which she and I had first deciphered letters when I was barely able to talk. What was it she had said to me that day the government fell? That when I was alone in my husband's house I would find it easier to talk to God. And that these conversations would make me a good wife and a good mother.

I knelt by the bed and opened the book. But I, to whom words came so easily, could not think of which ones to use now. What could God and I possibly have to say to each other? My husband was a sodomite. If it was not my own arrogance that had brought me to this, it was my duty to bring him to justice for the sake of his own soul as well as my own. Yet if I exposed him I would bring the whole house of lust down with him, and while I might hate my brother how could I possibly destroy my own family in the process? The shame would surely kill my father.

No. The truth was I had brought this upon myself, and while their punishment would be that there would be no salvation, mine would be to have to live with it. I put the prayer book back in the chest. God and I were beyond words.

I cried a little more, but the night had used up all my tears and after a while I took refuge in surer comfort, digging deeper under the cloths and the books to where I had hidden my drawings and my pens and ink.

SO I PASSED THE REST OF MY WEDDING NIGHT IN THE PURSUIT OF art. And this time my pen strokes fell, if not like rain then with ease and fluidity, and gave me quiet pleasure. Although if you had seen the image that grew under my quill, you might have thought that it itself was a sign of my estrangement from God.

On the paper in front of me, a young woman clothed in fine silk lay quietly in her marriage bed, watching as the man at her side sat with his doublet undone and his naked cock held in his hands. On his face there was a look between pain and ecstasy, as if at that moment the divine had entered into him, bringing him to the very edge of transcendence.

It was, even if I say so myself, the truest drawing I had done for some time.

· · ·

CHARLES VIII AND HIS ARMY MARCHED INTO FLORENCE ON 17 November 1494. While history would remember it as a day of shame for the Republic, on the streets it was more like a pageant than a humiliation.

The route from Porta San Frediano over the river past the Cathedral of Santa Maria del Fiore with its great dome to the Medici Palace was choked with people. And among those who found themselves spectators of this grave moment was the newly wedded Langella couple: Cristoforo, scholar and gentleman, and his tender bride, Alessandra, younger daughter of the Cecchi family, who, flush from her nuptials, went on her husband's arm through the swelling crowd, her eyes shining like cut glass as she took in the pulsating color of the streets around her, until they reached the square of the cathedral, where he had to hold her tight as he propelled her through the mass of people toward a set of wooden tiers hastily constructed against a far wall.

There he palmed two florins to a man below (an outrageous price, but Florence was a city of commerce even at times of crisis), and husband and wife climbed to the top and settled themselves, so their view took in not just the façade of the cathedral but the road down which, within barely an hour, Florence would bear witness to the arrival of her first, and surely her only, army of conquest.

And thus did my husband prove as good as his word.

PART II

Twenty

H E HAD ARRIVED HOME THAT MORNING WHILE ERILA AND
I were unpacking my chest, with occasional breaks to
peer from the window at the tide of people flowing
toward the square, and while he did not come to me
immediately, he sent word via his servant that I should
not worry: I was missing nothing, as he had it on good
authority that the king and his army were great but so weary that
they came sluggishly toward the city and would not arrive till
near sunset.

His news was so fresh even Erila was impressed. Which was
good because she and I were a little lost in our new roles as mistress and servant in this drafty gray house.

Our communication since the wedding night had been muted.
I had sketched till dawn and slept long into the day, and not surprisingly she had mistaken my late rising for a sign of connubial
energy. When she inquired as to my health I said I was well and
dropped my eyes, making it clear that I did not wish to say more.
Oh, I would have given anything in the world to tell her. I was
desperately in need of a confidante and till then I think I had told

her everything that had happened to me. But such secrets as I had had were small rebellious ones, harmful to no one but myself. While she and I were close, she was also a slave, and even I could see that, given such temptation, the forces of gossip might prove stronger than her loyalty. Or anyway, that was the excuse I had given myself when I woke that afternoon in my wedding bed, my sketches scattered around me. Perhaps the greater truth was that I could barely bring myself to remember what had happened, let alone share it with anybody else.

So when Cristoforo had come upon us sitting at the window arranging linen and watching the crowds, she already had reason to be suspicious and had got up and taken her leave of us without even looking at him. He had waited till the door was closed behind her before he spoke. "She is close to you, your slave?"

I nodded.

"I am glad. She will be company for you. But I would think that you do not tell her everything?"

While it was a question it was also a statement.

"No," I said. "I do not."

In the silence that followed I busied myself with the folding of cloth, my eyes meek to the floor. He smiled as if indeed I were his beloved new wife and held out his arm to me, and so we walked together down the stairs and out into the throng.

IF I HAD BEEN THE KING OF FRANCE I WOULD HAVE BEEN WELL pleased by the impact my entrance made upon my new vassal state. Though I might have chastised my generals for not starting our triumphal march earlier, since by the time Charles arrived at the square the sun was almost set, which meant there was less light to shine off his gilt armor or illuminate the great gold canopy held above him by his knights and bodyguard. The fading sun also meant that when he descended to climb the steps to the cathedral he could barely be seen by the mass of people, though I suspect that was also because for a king he was unexpectedly short of stature, especially after he had dismounted from his great black horse, chosen no doubt because it made him look taller than he was.

Certainly that was the only moment when the fickle Florentines wavered in their groveling enthusiasm for their sovereign invader. Not least because as this little king began to walk up the entrance of our great cathedral, he limped like a man deformed, which in a way he was, his feet being of noticeably larger proportion than the rest of his body. So it wasn't long before all of Florence knew that the conqueror sent to absolve us of our sins was in fact a dwarf with six toes on each foot. I am pleased to say that I was one of the crowd who spread the rumor around the square that day. And thus did I learn something of how history is written: that while it is not always accurate, one can still be part of the making of it.

Despite the gossip, it was impossible not to be in awe of the spectacle. Hours after the king had left the square to cries of *Viva Francia!* rising up like choral evensong behind him and was safely ensconced in the Medici Palace, Florence was still bursting with the arrival of the infantry and the cavalry. There were so many horses that the air was high with their dung, ground into the cobbles by the artillery guns they pulled behind them. But the most impressive of all were the archers and crossbow men: thousands upon thousands of armed peasants, such numbers that I worried that France might be a country now guarded only by its women until my husband told me that most of the army was not French at all but mercenaries hired for the campaign, expensively in the case of the Swiss Guard, much cheaper for the warriors from Scotland. And I was glad that these were not the men who would be billeted upon us, because I had never seen anything like them: giants from the North with great manes of straw hair and beards as red as my father's dyes, so matted and filthy that one could only wonder that their bows did not get caught in them as they fired.

THE INVASION LASTED ELEVEN DAYS. THE TROOPS BILLETED UPON US were well enough behaved: two knights from the city of

Toulouse with their servants and entourage. We dined with them the night after their arrival, laying out my husband's best plate and cutlery—though they had no idea how to use the forks they were presented with—and they treated me with due deference, kissing my hand and commenting on my beauty, by which I knew they were either blind or liars, and since they could see their way to the wine flagon well enough I concluded the latter. I heard later from Erila that their servants had the similar table manners of pigs but that in other ways they kept their hands to themselves, instructions that must have been issued to the army as a whole, because nine months later there was no obvious epidemic of foundling French babies turned on the wheel at the Ospedale degli Innocenti, though we were later to discover another gift from their occasional courtship that was to cause us more grief than a few extra souls on earth.

Over dinner they spoke with passion about their great king and the glory of his campaign, but when they were better lubricated they confessed to a certain longing for home and weariness about how far their warmongering would take them. The final destination was the Holy Land, but you could see they had their eyes set more on the comforts of Naples, where they had heard the women were fair in their darkness and the riches theirs for the taking. As for the greatness of Florence—well, they were men of battle rather than art and while my husband's statue gallery impressed them, they were more interested in where they could buy new cloth. (I learned later that there were those Florentines who made small fortunes from the invasion by swallowing their patriotism in favor of their pockets.) To be fair, one of the knights spoke with enthusiasm about the marvel of the cathedral and seemed interested when I told him he could find a gilt statue of Saint Louis, the patron saint of his home city, by our great Donatello above the door of the façade of Santa Croce. But whether he sought it out or not, I do not know. What I do know is that they ate and drank a great deal during those eleven days, because the cook kept records of the amounts consumed, since it had been agreed by the truce that the army would pay its own maintenance.

AT FIRST THE CITY PUT ON HER BEST FACE TO IMPRESS HER conquerors. A special performance of the Annunciation was staged at San Felice and my husband managed to get us places, a considerable feat, seeing as I could find no other Medici supporters in the congregation. I had been taken as a child to such an event once at the Carmine monastery, where I had a memory of gossamer clouds strung across the nave of the church and how, at a certain moment, a chorus of little boys had been revealed suspended among them, dressed as angels, one of them so patently terrified that when everyone else began to sing he howled so loudly that he had to be lowered down.

There were boy angels in San Felice this day too, but none of them cried. The church was transformed. A cupola like a second roof had been built and hung from the beams above the central nave, its interior painted the deepest blue with a hundred tiny lamps suspended inside so that you seemed to look up into the night sky with stars in the firmament. Around its base in the heavens stood twelve shining child angels on little plinths. But that was the least of it. For when the moment came for the Annunciation, a rotating second sphere was lowered carrying eight angels, older boys now, and then, from inside that, a further sphere encasing a final, older Angel Gabriel. As he descended he moved his wings to and fro, causing a myriad of lights to flicker around him, as if he brought the very stars of heaven down with him.

While I sat, more astonished even than Mary, my husband made me look up again and note how each sphere of angels could be read as an accentuated lesson in perspective: the biggest at the bottom moving to the smallest at the top. So in this way we could appreciate not only the glory of God but the perfection of the laws of nature and our artist's mastery over them. He told me that this elaborate stage device had been the invention of none other than the renowned Brunelleschi, its secret handed down through the years since his death.

While there is no record of what the king of France thought of it all, I know we Florentines were mightily proud and impressed. Yet when I look back on it now I find it hard to distinguish between my joy at the spectacle and the quieter pleasure that came from my husband's erudition and the way he taught me to look deeper into things I might otherwise have missed. When we headed back that night through the crowded streets, he guided me by the elbow so we moved like two sleek fishes through a tumbling sea. After we reached our house, we sat talking for a while of all we had witnessed and he accompanied me to my room, where he kissed me on the cheek and thanked me for my company before retiring to his study. As I lay in bed thinking back on all that I had seen, I could almost believe that my freedom had been worth whatever sacrifice I had made to get it. And that Cristoforo, whatever he might do in the future, had made an honest start to our bargain.

In the days that followed, the government was kept busy swapping compliments with the king and ratifying a treaty that made his occupation look like an invitation and gave him a great loan for his war chest, presumably in thanks for not sacking the city. While the officials were polite enough to one another, on the streets the atmosphere soured faster and a few would-be young warriors started to pitch stones at the invaders, who in turn gave sword blows back, and in this way a dozen or so Florentines were killed. Not exactly a massacre, or even glorious resistance, but a reminder at least of the spirit we had lost. Aware that his welcome was growing thin and advised by Savonarola that God would go with him if he went fast, Charles mobilized his army and they marched out at the end of November, with a good deal less ceremony and crowd to cheer them on their way—which could have had something to do with the fact that they left without paying their bills—our own good Toulouse noblemen included—liars to the end.

Two days later, my husband, who had slept in the house for the whole time, a gentleman, for his wife's safety, left also.

Without him and our invaders, the palazzo suddenly felt cold and stern. The rooms were dark, the wood paneling stained with age, the tapestries moth-eaten, and the windows too small to let in much light. And because I was scared that my solitude might tumble me into a pit of self-pity, the next morning I woke Erila at dawn and together we set out to test the new freedom of my married life on the streets.

Twenty-one

THE BODY ON SANTA TRINITÀ BRIDGE SPOKE AS MUCH OF madness as blood lust. It was hanging from a post next to the small chapel, and by the time the monks discovered it the dogs were already halfway through their meal. Erila said the only mercy was that he would have been dead by the time his body was disemboweled, though it was hard to know that for sure, since even if he had screamed as his intestines unraveled, the gag in his mouth would have muted the worst of it. The scavengers must have arrived soon after the murderer left, because by the time we got there—the news reached the market soon after first light; all we had to do was follow the flow—what remained of his insides was already on the cobbles. The watchmen had beaten the dogs away by then, though the wildest of them were still loitering, heads down, bellies crouched to the ground, feigning disinterest, their paws twitching with energy. At one point as the crowd gathered, one of them streaked in from the side, snatching a piece of offal between his snapping jaws before a kick landed him, yowling but still attached to his prize, halfway across the bridge.

The watchmen were almost as rough with the crowd, but it

was impossible to keep people away. Erila held us well to the back, her arm linked tightly with mine. While she found my curiosity alarming, that was more to do with the trouble it might get her into than any faintheartedness on her part; had she been there alone she would already have wormed her way to the front. As for me: well, of course the sight of that ravaged body turned my stomach—I had been so sheltered at my parents' home I had never even seen a public execution—but I made myself get over it. I had not come this far in the pursuit of freedom to be sent whimpering home at the first sign of blood or violence. Anyway, despite the sweetness of my sex, I was indeed curious, if curious is the right word....

"Don't you see, Erila," I said to her urgently, "this is now the fifth."

"The fifth what?"

"The fifth body since the death of Lorenzo."

"What d'you mean?" she said, clicking her tongue at me. "People die on the streets every day. You just have your head sunk too far into books to notice."

"Not like this. Think about it: the girl in Santa Croce, the couple in Santo Spírito whose bodies were moved to Impruneta, and then the boy by the Baptistery three weeks ago. Each killed in or near a church and each mutilated in some awful way. There has to be a connection."

She laughed. "How about sin? Two tarts, one client, a sodomite, and a pimp. Maybe they were all on their way to confession. At least whoever did this one saved the priests an earful."

"What do you mean? Do you know him?"

"Everybody knows him. Why d'you think there's such a crowd here? Marsilio Trancolo. Anything you want, Trancolo can get it for you. Or he could. Wine, dice, women, men, young boys—he had a stock of all of them ready, at the right price. Florence's most prominent procurer. From what I heard he's been working overtime for the last two weeks keeping the foreigners supplied. Well, he'll be in good company in hell now, that's for sure. Hey!"

she yelled, taking a swipe at a man who had careered into us in his eagerness to get closer to the front. "Watch where you put your hands, scum."

"Then move your black snatch out of the way," he shouted, shoving her back. "Slut. We don't need women of the Devil's color on our streets. Watch your step or you'll be next for his knife."

"Not before your balls are hanging alongside the Medici crest," she muttered, as she started to push me out through the back of the crowd.

"But Erila—"

"But nothing. I told you, this is no place for a lady." She was angry now, so it was hard to tell her concern from fear. "If your mother found out she'd have me strung up on the post next to him."

She maneuvered us off the bridge. The crowd thinned out along the river, then grew again as we crossed down into the Piazza della Signoria. In the days after the French left, the square had been heaving with citizens eager to vote in the new government, with Savonarola its ruler in all but name. Now his supporters were sitting grandly inside the Town Hall, formulating new laws by which they hoped to turn a godless city into a godly one. From the council chambers they would have a bird's-eye view of Santa Trinità bridge. To have a lesson on the Devil's punishment so close at hand would concentrate their minds wonderfully on the task before them.

OVER THE ENSUING DAYS, ERILA GREW IMPATIENT WITH MY HUNGER for the streets. "I can't be out with you every minute of the day. I've work to do in the house. And so have you if you are to become its mistress." Of course, she was still angry with me for keeping my own counsel about my wedding night and was taking it out on me in small but powerful ways. She was not the only one. The servants watched me strangely now. In the opening days of my marriage I had playacted the role of the wife, inquiring about the accounts and ordering around anyone who would listen. But my lack of confidence betrayed me, and a household that had run for years without a wife did not take kindly to my childish interventions. There were times when I could almost hear them laughing at me behind my back, as if they knew about the tawdry game being played out for the benefit of my husband's reputation.

To keep despair at bay I retreated to the library. Tucked under the loggia on the top floor, away from damp and flooding, it was the only room in the house that offered any real comfort. There must have been close to a hundred volumes here, dating back in some cases to the beginning of the century. The most extraordinary was a copy of the first translations of Plato by Ficino commissioned by Lorenzo de' Medici himself, not least because inside I found a notation in an exquisite hand.

To Cristoforo,
whose love of learning is almost as great
as his love of beauty.

The date was 1477, the year before my birth. As the signature was a work of art in itself, who else could it have been but Lorenzo himself? I sat staring at the ink. Had Lorenzo lived, he would have been almost the same age as my husband. My husband's knowledge of his court was greater than I had realized. If he ever came home, what conversations we might have about it!

I read a few chapters of the text, entranced by its provenance, but I am ashamed to say that while even a few months before its wisdom would have dazzled me, now such volumes of philosophy had the air of old men about them: venerable but having lost the energy to influence a world that had moved on from them.

From books I turned to art. Surely Botticelli's evocation of Dante would still inspire. But the great cabinet in which my husband kept the portfolio was locked and when I called his servant for the key he denied all knowledge of it. Was it my imagination, or did he smirk at me as he said it?

He brought me richer news an hour later.

"You have a visitor, madam."

"Who is it?"

He shrugged. "A gentleman. He didn't give a name. He is waiting downstairs."

My father? My brother? The painter? The painter... I felt a flush rise in me and got up quickly. "Show him into the receiving room."

He was standing by the window, staring across the narrow street to the tower opposite. We had not seen each other since the night before my wedding, and if thoughts of him had ever strayed into my mind since then I had snuffed them out as firmly as altar candles capped at the end of mass. But now, in his presence again, I felt myself almost trembling as he turned to me. He did not look well. He was grown thin again. His complexion, always pale, was like goat's cheese, and there were heavy circles under his eyes. His hands were stained dark with paint and I saw he was holding a roll of drawings wrapped in muslin. My drawings. I found it hard to breathe.

"Welcome," I said, arranging myself carefully on one of my husband's hard wooden chairs. "Won't you sit down?"

He made a small noise, which I took to be a refusal since he stayed standing. What was it that kept us so nervous in each other's company, the one as gauche as the other? What had Erila said to me once about the dangers of innocence over knowledge? Surely I was innocent no longer. And when I thought of the innards of the eviscerated man in his nighttime sketches, I knew that in some way or another neither was he.

"You are married," he said at last, his almost sulky shyness back as his shield.

"Yes, I am."

"In which case I hope I do not disturb you."

I shrugged. "What is there to disturb? My days are my own now." But I could not keep my eyes off the roll in his hand. "How is the chapel? You have started?"

He nodded.

"And? It goes well?"

He mumbled something I did not hear properly, then: "I . . . I brought you these," he said, and thrust out the drawings awkwardly in front of him. As I put out my hand to take them I could feel it shaking slightly.

"You have looked at them?"

He nodded.

"And?"

"You understand I am no judge . . . but I think . . . I think that both your eye and your pen have truth about them."

I felt a wild jump in my stomach, and though I know it is blasphemous to even think it, I felt for that moment as if I were Our Blessed Lady in the Annunciation, hearing news of such magnitude that it conjured up as much terror as joy. "Oh . . . you think so! . . . So you'll help me?"

"I—"

"Oh, but don't you see? I am married now. And my husband, who is solicitous for my well-being, would, I know, give permission for you to instruct me, show me techniques. Perhaps I might even assist you in the chapel. I—"

"No, no!" His alarm was as fierce as my excitement. "It's not possible!"

"Why not? There are so many things you know, you—"

"No. You don't understand!" His vehemence stopped me. "I cannot teach you anything." And such was his horror that one might think I had propositioned him with some act of gross indecency.

"Is that cannot? Or will not?" I said coldly, looking directly at him.

"Cannot," he muttered, then repeated it louder, each word broken, as if he were telling himself as well as me. "I cannot help you."

I was finding it hard to breathe. To have had so much offered and then taken away. "I see. Well"—I rose to my feet, too proud to let him see the depth of my distress—"no doubt you have business to attend to."

He loitered for a moment as if there was more to say, then turned and moved toward the door. But there he stopped. "I... there is something else."

I waited.

"The other night... the night before your wedding, when we... when you were in the courtyard..."

But though I knew what he was going to say, I was too angry to help him now. "What of it?"

"I dropped something... a piece of paper. A sketch. I would be grateful to have it back."

"A sketch?" I could hear my voice grow distant. Just as he had dashed my hopes, so I would do the same to him. "I'm afraid I don't remember. Perhaps if you reminded me what it was of?"

"It was... nothing. I mean, nothing important."

"Important enough to get it back, though?"

"Only because... it was done by a friend. And I... must give it back to him."

It was such an obvious lie—the first and maybe the only one I ever heard him tell—that he didn't dare look at me as he said it. The torn piece of paper rose up in front of me: the man's body ripped open from neck to groin, his innards exposed as on a butcher's hook. Only now of course it had a companion in my mind: the city's most notorious pimp hanging from the chapel post, the dogs snapping at his entrails. While the drawing pre-dated the body by weeks, the evisceration was almost identical. My brother's words echoed in my mind. "Your precious painter was a mess, face like a ghost and stains all over him." A gaunt face and bloodshot eyes could be the signs not just of a man who walked the streets at night but someone who even when he rested could not sleep.

"I'm sorry," I said, my words in cold homage to his own. "I cannot help you."

For a moment he remained frozen; then he turned, and I heard the sound of the door closing behind him. I sat with the roll of drawings in my lap. After a while I picked them up and threw them across the room.

Twenty-two

I HAD PRECIOUS LITTLE TIME TO THINK ABOUT IT. MY husband returned a few days later, his timing coolly precise. Savonarola's Christmas sermons were due to begin the next morning, and the godly should be seen to go to church from the beds of their wives and not their lovers.

He even made it his business to take me with him out walking that same evening, so we could be noted together in public. It had so long been my dream: to wander the streets in that magic hour between dusk and dark, the life of the city lit by the setting sun. But though the light was beautiful, the streets were somehow lackluster. There were fewer people than I imagined, and almost every woman I saw was veiled and—to an eye fed by my father's bright fabrics—drearily dressed, while the few who were unaccompanied had their heads down, intent on reaching their homes. At one point, under the loggia in the Piazza Santa Maria Novella, we passed a young cockerel of a man in a fashionable cloak and feathered hat who, I thought, tried hard to catch my husband's attention, but Cristoforo dropped his gaze immediately and maneuvered me away and we soon left him behind. By the time we reached home in the dark, the city was almost empty. The curfew of the mind was making as much impact as any new law. It was the greatest irony that I had negotiated my freedom just when there was no Florence left to explore it in.

That night, we sat together in the drafty receiving room, warmed by a myrtle-wood fire, discussing affairs of state. While there was a wounded part of me that wanted to punish him for his absence, my curiosity was too acute and his company too interesting for me to resist him for long. I believe the pleasure was mutual.

"We should be there early to secure a good place. I would lay you a wager, Alessandra—except of course a wager itself would be illegal now—that the cathedral will be overflowing tomorrow."

"Do we go to see or be seen?"

"Like many, I suspect, a mixture of the two. It's a wonder how suddenly the Florentines have become such godly people."

"Even sodomites?" I said, proud of my own courage with the word.

He smiled. "I do believe you get a rebellious pleasure from saying that word out loud. Though I would suggest you expunge it from your vocabulary. Walls have ears."

"What? You think servants will betray their own masters now?"

"I think when slaves are offered their freedom in return for informing on their masters, Florence has become a city of the Inquisition, yes."

"Is that what the new laws say?"

"Among other things. The punishments for fornication are made severe, for sodomy even more so. For the younger ones, flogging, fining, and mutilation. For older and more practiced sinners—the stake."

"The stake! Dear God. Why such a difference?"

"Because, wife, young men are held to be less responsible for their actions than older ones. Just as deflowered virgins are considered less guilty than their seducers."

So Tomaso's inviting swagger would be classed as less damning than my husband's quiet hunger for him. Though he was my flesh and blood, the cruel truth was I cared less for his welfare than for the man who lusted after him.

"You must be careful," I said.

"I intend to be. Your brother asks after your welfare," he added, as if reading my thoughts.

"What do you tell him?"

"That he would do better to ask you himself. But I think he fears to see you."

Good, I thought. I hope he lies quaking in your arms. I found myself shocked by the image, which I had not let myself conjure up before: Tomaso in my husband's arms. So my brother was the wife now. And I . . . well, what was I?

"It has been quiet with the house so empty," I said at last.

He paused. We both knew what was to come. Savonarola might police the night, but in the end all he would do was drive the sins farther into the dark.

"If you prefer, you need not see him," he said quietly.

"He is my brother. If he comes to our house it would be strange if I did not."

"That is true." He was staring into the fire, his legs pushed out in front of him. He was an educated, cultured man who had more brains in his little finger than my brother did in the whole of his soft coquettish body. What was this lust made of, that it made him risk everything for its consummation? "I don't suppose you have any news for me?" he said, after a while.

Oh, but I did. That very afternoon I had felt shooting pains in my womb, but rather than an early baby I had given birth to streaming ribbons of blood. But I didn't know how to say that, so I simply shook my head. "No. No news."

I closed my eyes and saw again my drawing of our nuptial night. When I opened them again he was looking at me intently, and I swear the pity had something of affection in it. "I hear you have been using the library in my absence. It pleased you, I hope."

"Yes," I said, relieved to be back on the dry land of learning. "I found a volume there of Plato by Ficino with an inscription to you inside it."

"Ah, yes. Praising my love of beauty and learning." He laughed. "It is hard now to imagine there was a time when our rulers believed such things."

"So it *was* Lorenzo the Magnificent! You actually knew him?"

"A little. As the inscription suggests, he liked his courtiers to be men of taste."

"Did he . . . did he know about you?"

"What—my sodomy, as you so enjoy calling it? There was not much that Lorenzo did not know about those around him. He was a student of men's souls as much as of their intellects. You would have been enthralled by his mind. I am surprised your mother has not told you of him."

"My mother?"

"Yes. When her brother was at court she came sometimes to visit."

"She did? Did you know her then?"

"No, I was—er, busy with other things. But I saw her a few times. She was very beautiful. And she had something of her brother's wit and erudition when it was called upon. She was much appreciated, I remember. She has not told you anything of this?"

I shook my head. In all my life she had never said a word. To have such secrets from your own daughter! It made me think again about her story of watching the Medici assassins pulled through the streets, drowning in the blood of their own castration. No wonder the horror had turned me in her womb.

"Then I hope I haven't spoken out of turn. I hear you also asked about the keys to the cabinet. I'm sorry to disappoint you, but I think the manuscript will be gone soon."

"Gone? Where?"

"Back to its owner."

"Who is he?" And, when my husband said nothing, "If you

believe I cannot keep your secrets, sir, you have made a bad choice of a wife."

He smiled at the logic. "His name is Piero Francesco de' Medici, Botticelli's sometime patron."

Of course. Lorenzo the Magnificent's cousin and one of the first to flee to the French camp. "I count him as a traitor," I said firmly.

"Then you are more foolish than I thought." His voice was sharp. "You should be more circumspect with your words, even here. Mark me, it will not be long before those who support the Medici will go in fear of their lives. Besides, you know only half the story. There is reason enough for his disloyalty. When his father was assassinated, Piero Francesco's estates were left in the care of Lorenzo, who leeched money from them when the fortunes of the Medici bank fell. His resentment is hardly surprising, but he is not a bad man. Indeed, as a patron of art, history may put him alongside Lorenzo himself."

"I have seen nothing he has given to the city."

"That is because as yet he keeps it for himself. But his villa at Cafaggiolo has paintings by Botticelli that the artist himself might live to regret. There is a panel in which Mars lies conquered by Venus, prostrate with such languor that it's hard to tell whether it is his soul or his body she has just vanquished. And then there is Venus herself, rising naked in a shell from the waves. You've heard of her?"

"No." My mother had told us once about a set of screen paintings of the Nastagio legend that Botticelli had done for a wedding, and how all who saw them marveled at their detail and life. But, like my sister, I was resistant to tales of woman's flesh torn apart, however fine the artist. "What is she like, his Venus?"

"Well, I am no connoisseur of women, but I suspect you would find in her the chasm between the Platonic and the Savonarolan vision of art."

"Is she beautiful?"

"Beautiful, yes. But she is more than that. She is a joining of the classical and the Christian. Her nakedness is modest, yet her gravity is playful. She both invites and resists at the same time. Even her knowledge of love seems innocent. Though I imagine most men who look on her think more of taking her to bed than to church."

"Oh! I would give anything to see her."

"You should hope that no one sees her for a while. If news of her were common, our pious friar would almost certainly want to destroy her along with his sinners. Let's hope Botticelli himself does not feel bound to give her up to the enemy. From what I hear he is leaning heavily toward Savonarola already."

"No!"

"Oh, yes. I think you would be surprised by how many of our great figures will follow. And not just the artists."

"But why? I don't understand. We were building a new Athens here. How can they bear to see it pulled down?"

He stared into the fire, as if the answer might be found there. "Because," he said at last, "in its place, this mad and clever monk will offer them a vision of something else. Something that talks directly to all men, not just the rich and the clever."

"And what will that be?"

"The building of the New Jerusalem."

My husband, who seemed to have always known that he was bound for hell, looked for that moment almost sad. And I knew he was right.

Twenty-three

S O MANY OF THE SERVANTS ASKED TO ATTEND THE sermon next morning that there was almost no one left to guard the house. It was a story repeated through the city. A smart thief could have made away with cart-loads of wealth that Sunday, though he would have to have had a strong stomach for hell to sin at such a moment—like using the darkness after Christ's crucifixion to pick the pockets of the crowd.

While the poor put on their best clothes, it was the rich who dressed for the occasion, turning their fur collars inward and making sure their jewels were well hidden, in keeping with the new Sumptuary Laws. Before we left, Erila and I inspected each other for anything dubious or frivolous that might be revealed under our cloaks. Our modesty proved not to be enough. As we crossed the square toward the cathedral it was clear something was wrong. The place was awash with people and there were angry voices, punctuated by the sound of women crying. We had barely got to the steps when our way was blocked by a heavyset man in rough clothing.

"She can't come in," he said rudely to my husband. "Women are barred."

And there was such aggression in his voice that for a moment I wondered if he knew something more about us and it made my blood run cold.

"Why is that?" my husband said coolly.

"The friar preaches on the building of the godly state. Such matters are not for their ears."

"But if the state is godly, what could he possibly say that could offend us?" I said loudly.

"Women are barred," he repeated, ignoring me and addressing my husband. "The business of government is for men. Women are weak and irrational and should be kept in obedience, chastity, and silence."

"Well, sir," I said, "if women are indeed—"

"My wife is a vessel of exemplary virtue." Cristoforo's fingers pinched a line of flesh under my sleeve. "There is nothing even our most diligent Prior Savonarola could instruct her on that she does not practice naturally."

"Then she would better go home to tend the house and let the men be about their business," he said. "And that veil of hers should have no edging and cover her face properly. This is a state of plain virtue now, not messed with rich man's fancies."

Six months before he would have found himself whipped home for such disrespect, but now his insolence was so confident that there was nothing to reply. As I turned I saw the same scene being played out at a dozen points on the steps around us: prominent citizens being humiliated by this new coarse piety. It was easy to see how it worked: As the rich dressed down, so the poor had less reason to look up to them. And it struck me, not for the last time, that if this was indeed the beginning of the New Jerusalem, it had a smell of more than spiritual revolution about it.

My husband, however, who would have seen it as clearly as I, wisely chose not to take offense. Instead he turned and smiled at me. "My dear wife," he said, with studied sweetness and silly language, "go you now home with God and pray for us. I will join you later and relate what, if anything, is said that does affect you."

So we bowed and parted like players in a bad rendition of Boccaccio's tales, and he disappeared into the cavernous interior.

AT THE FOOT OF THE STEPS, ERILA AND I FOUND OURSELVES IN A sea of women torn between piety and indignation at their exclusion. I recognized a few whom my mother might have counted as equals, women of grace and means. After a while a group of boys, their hair cut short, and dressed more like penitents than youths, came up and started herding us away to the edge of the square. It seemed to me they used the excuse of their holiness to prod and demean us as they would never have been allowed to do before.

"This way." Erila grabbed me and pulled me to one side. "If we stay here we'll never get in."

"But how can we? There are guards everywhere."

"Yes, but not every door is for the rich. With luck they'll have picked lesser thugs for lesser people."

I followed her out of the crowd and around the side of the cathedral until we found a door where the river of people was less grand but moving with such force that it was impossible for the vergers at the entrance to police everyone surging inside. As we pushed ourselves forward we could hear a rising tide of sound from within. It seemed that Savonarola had appeared at the altar, and suddenly the crush was heavier and the momentum faster as the great cathedral doors began to close.

Inside, Erila pulled me quickly backward, so that we pressed ourselves into the space between the second screen door and the church wall. Any earlier and someone would have spotted us. Any later and we would not have got in. I sneaked a glance out over the mass of bodies and saw we weren't the only women to defy the ban, because a few moments into the mass there was a great commotion to the left and an elderly woman was rough-handled out the doors, the men hissing at her as she went. We kept our heads down, folding ourselves into the gloom of the interior.

When the service reached the sermon, the whole cathedral fell silent as the little monk made his way to the pulpit. This would be the first time he had preached publicly since the new government had been formed. While it might not have added to his stature (though to be fair from where I stood I couldn't see him anyway), it had clearly blown a greater force into him. Or maybe it was indeed God. He spoke with such an easy familiarity about Him.

"Welcome, men of Florence! Today we meet to do great business. As the Virgin made her way to Bethlehem in preparation for the coming of our Savior, so our city takes the first steps along the road that will lead it to redemption. Rejoice, citizens of Florence, for the light is at hand."

An opening ripple of approval ran through the crowd.

"The voyage is begun. The ship of salvation is launched. I have been with the Lord these days, seeking His advice, begging His indulgence. He has not left my side, day or night, as I have prostrated myself before Him awaiting His orders. 'O God,' I have cried, 'give this great duty to another. Let Florence guide herself through this stormy sea and let me go back to my solitary haven.' 'It is impossible,' the Lord replies. 'You are the navigator and the wind is in the sails. There can be no turning back now.' "

Another roar rose up around him, louder this time, further urging him on, so that I could not help but think of Julius Caesar, who each time he spurned the crown incited the mob to offer it him again with even more fervor.

" 'Lord, Lord,' I say to Him, 'I will preach if I must. But why need I meddle with the government of Florence? I am but a simple monk.' Then the Lord says in a terrible voice. 'Take heed, Girolamo. If you would make Florence a holy city, its godliness must be built on deep foundations. A government of true virtue.

This is your task. And though you may fear it, I am with you. As you speak, so my words flow over your tongue. And thus the darkness will be penetrated, until there is no place for the sinners to hide.

" 'But never mistake the severity of the journey. The very fabric is rotten, eaten away with the wormwood of lust and greed. Even those who think themselves godly must be brought to justice; those men and women of the church who drink my blood from gold and silver chalices and care more for the cups than for me, they must be taught again the meaning of humility. Those who worship false gods through pagan tongues must have their mouths sealed. Those who stoke the fires of the flesh must have the lust burned out of them.... And those who look at their faces before my own must have their mirrors smashed and their eyes turned inward to see the stain on their souls....

" 'And in this great work men will lead the way. For as the corruption of man began with the corruption of woman, so their vanity and frailty must be guided by stronger hands. A truly godly state is one where the women stay behind closed doors and their salvation rests in obedience and silence.

" 'As the pride of Christendom goes to war to win back my Holy Land, so the glorious youth of Florence will take to the streets to wage battle on sin. They will be an army of the godly. The very ground will sing with their footsteps. And the weak, the gamblers, the fornicators, and the sodomites, all those who flout my laws shall feel my wrath.' Thus saith the Lord to me. And thus I obey. Praise be His name, in heaven and on earth. Praise be to this our great work in building the New Jerusalem."

And I swear, if it were not God then I do not know who was inside him, because he did indeed seem like a man possessed. I felt a shudder go through me, and for that moment it made me want to tear up my drawings and ask for forgiveness and God's light, though the yearning came more from fear than any joy of salvation. Yet even as I felt it and the congregation rose up with one voice to praise him, I could not help but also be reminded of the sound that rose from Piazza Santa Croce on the day the city held her annual football contest, and the way the men in the crowd roared out their approval at every instance of sudden skill or aggression.

I turned to Erila to see how she was affected, and as I did I lifted my head a fraction, just as the man in front of me chose that moment to shift his weight to get a better view. And so his sideways glance caught mine and I knew instantly we were discovered. A whisper went up toward us, and Erila, more attuned than I to the speed of male violence, grabbed and pulled me through the crowd until we reached the crack in the door and spit ourselves out, safe but shaking, into the cool sunshine of a bright December morning in the New Jerusalem.

Twenty-four

WHILE SAVONAROLA PREACHED HIS GODLY CITY FROM THE pulpit, Erila and I took to the streets. The idea of living behind closed doors with only seclusion and piety for company made me cold with fear. Even without the stain of my husband's sins I would fail every test that Savonarola's God would set me, and I had risked too much to go meekly into that darkness now.

Most days we went to the market. Though women may be temptation on the streets, the business of shopping and cooking must still be done, and if the veil was thick enough it was sometimes hard to tell the curious from the obedient. I do not know what Florence's Mercato Vecchio is like now, but then it was a wonder: a circus of sensation. Like everything else in our city it was stained with the mess of living, but that also gave it its vibrancy and style. Inside the square were elegant airy loggias, each constructed by and decorated for the trades they housed. So under the medallion portraits of animals were the butchers and under the fish the fishmongers, vying for the attention of your nostrils with bakers, tanners, fruit sellers, and a hundred steaming food stalls, where you could buy anything from stewed eel or roasted pike fresh from the river to chunks of pork stuffed with rosemary and sliced off the carcass as it dropped its juices off the spit. It was as if all the smells of life—the yeast, the cooking, the death, and the decay—had been thrown together in a great stew-pot. I have found nothing to compare to it, and during those first dark winter days of God's kingdom in Florence it felt like all that I had craved and was most afraid to lose.

Everyone had something to sell, and those who had nothing sold their nothingness. There was no loggia for the beggars, but they had their pitch nevertheless—on the steps of the four churches that stood like sentinels around the square. Erila said there were already more beggars since Savonarola had taken control. But whether that was because there was more hardship or more piety—and therefore greater expectations of charity— it was hard to know. The one who really captivated me was the wrestler. He was standing on a plinth near the western entrance to the square and a crowd had already gathered around him. Erila said she knew him of old. Before he was a mountebank he had been a professional fighter who took on all comers in the mud reaches by the river. In those days he had had a manager who took bets for him, and there was always a crowd to be found shouting on the contestants, as they stumbled and groaned in the black quicksand until both parties emerged looking like devils. She told me later that she had once seen him bury another man's head so deep in the mud that he could only signal his surrender by the waving of his arms.

But such spectacles had been built on gambling, and in the wake of the new laws he had no option but to find another use for his magnificent body. He was naked to the waist, the cold sending his breath out as smoke. His upper torso was more like an ani-mal's than a man's, his muscles so prominent and thick that his neck reminded me directly of a bull. He made me think of the Minotaur and its howling attack on great Theseus in the center of the labyrinth. But his was a different aberration of nature.

His skin had been oiled until it shone, and along his arms and across and around his chest was a painting (though what paint could adhere to such oily human skin?) of a great serpent. And as he flexed his muscles, making his skin ripple, so its thick green and black curves gleamed and slithered along his upper arms and across his torso. It was a most monstrous and magical sight. I was entranced, so much so that I pushed my way rudely to the front till I was standing right below him.

The richness of my cloth drew attention to my purse and he leaned over toward me. "Watch carefully, little mistress," he said, "though you may have to lift your veil to see the wonder properly." I moved aside my muslin and he grinned at me, a gap as wide as the Arno between his front teeth, then lifted out his arms toward me so this time, when the snake crawled, it was so close I could almost touch it. "The Devil is a serpent. Beware of the hidden sins in the pleasure of a man's arms."

By now Erila was tugging at my sleeve, but I threw her off. "How did you do that to your body?" I said eagerly. "What paints did you use?"

"Put some silver in the box and I'll tell you." The snake leaped upward onto his other shoulder.

I dug into my purse and threw half a florin in the box. It sat glimmering there amid the dull copper. Erila gave a theatrical sigh at my gullibility and grabbed my purse out of my hand, stuffing it inside her own bodice for safekeeping.

"So tell me!" I said. "It cannot be paint. In which case it must be dye?"

"Dye and blood," he said darkly, squatting down now so he was indeed close enough to touch, close enough to see the film of sweat and oil on his skin and smell the sourness of his body. "First you cut into the skin, little cuts, snip snip snip, then one by one you prick in the colors."

"Oh. Does it hurt?"

"Hah. I screamed like a baby," he said. "But once it was started I wouldn't let them stop. And so every day my snake grows prettier and more lithe. The Devil serpent has a woman's face, you know. To tempt men. Next time I go under the knife I'll ask them to give it your features."

"Ach!" Erila's voice, sniping with contempt. "Listen to this flattery. He just wants another coin."

But I shooed her away. "I know who did this," I said quickly. "It was the dyers of Santa Croce. You're one of them, yes?"

"I was," he said, and he stared at me more closely. "How did you know that?"

"I have seen their skin patterns. I went there once, as a child."

"With your father, the cloth merchant," he said.

"Yes! Yes!"

"I remember you. You were small and bossy and had your nose into everything."

I laughed out loud. "Really! You really remember me!"

Erila tutted loudly. "I've got her purse already, bonehead. There's no more silver to be had."

"I don't need your money, mistress," he growled. "I make more waving my arms than you do on the streets after dark when they can't tell your color from the black of the night." And he turned his attention back to me. "Yes, I remember you. You had fine clothes and this ugly scrunched-up face. Still, you weren't afraid of anything."

I registered his words like a small knife jab. I might have taken a step back but his face came closer. "But I tell you something. I didn't think you were ugly. Not at all. I thought you were luscious." And as he said the word he sent the snake rippling languidly across his body toward me, at the same time flicking his tongue around his lips till the tip came out and waggled at me. It was a gesture of such naked lust that I felt my stomach turn with queasy excitement. I moved away quickly and pushed toward Erila, who was already free from the crowd, and as I went I heard his crude laughter ringing out over my head.

She was so angry at my disobedience that for a few moments she wouldn't talk to me. But as the crowd thinned, she stopped and turned to me. "You all right?"

"Yes," I said, though I suspect it was clear I wasn't. "Yes."

"So now maybe you see why ladies on the streets take chaperones. Don't worry about him. His days are numbered. Once the new army finds him they'll have him strung up so fast that both of his precious snakes will go limp with terror."

But I could not shrug off either the beauty of his body or the truth of his observations about my own.

"Erila?" I stopped her again.

"What is it?"

"Am I really so ugly that he would recognize me after all these years?"

She snorted and grabbed me to her in a fast hug. "Aah, it wasn't your ugliness he remembered, it was your courage. God help us, it'll get you into more mischief than your looks ever will."

So she pulled me down the narrow streets toward home.

BUT THAT NIGHT I COULD NOT GET HIS SKIN OUT OF MY MIND. I slept badly, the muscles of the snake squeezing my dreams into nightmares until I woke in a sweat, fighting its coils off my body. My gown was soaked cold on my skin. I peeled it off and stumbled to my wardrobe chest to find another. In the dim light from the outside torches, I caught the reflection of my upper torso in the small burnished mirror on the paneled wall. The sight of my nakedness held me there for a moment. My face was full of heavy shadow and my curves trapped darkness under my breasts. I thought of my sister on her wedding day, shining with the confidence of her beauty, and suddenly I could not bear the contrast. The mountebank was right. There was nothing in me to delight the eye. I was so ugly that men remembered me only for my hideousness. I was so ugly even my husband found me distasteful. I remembered the painter's description of Eve as she fled Paradise, howling into the darkness, newly ashamed of her own nakedness. She had been wooed by a serpent also, its forked tongue piercing her innocence as its coils squeezed life from its prey. I climbed back into my bed and curled in on myself. After a while my finger strayed toward my cleft, seeking a comfort from my body that no one else would ever give. But the night was full of sin now and my fingers were afraid of the sweetness they might find, and instead I cried myself to sleep with my loneliness for company.

Twenty-five

OVER THE NEXT FEW WEEKS, GOD AND THE DEVIL FOUGHT it out in the streets of the city. Savonarola preached daily while gangs of young boys appeared as his warriors of the new church, chastising Florentines for their lack of piety and sending women home to keep their own counsel.

My sister Plautilla, on the other hand, who had always had a talent with appearances, chose this moment to surpass herself. Erila woke me at dawn on Christmas morning with the news. "There is a messenger from your mother's house. Your sister gave birth this night to a baby girl. Your mother is with her now and will call on us on her way home."

My mother. I had not seen her since my marriage six weeks before. While there had been times in my life when her love had felt strict and implacable, there was no one else who both understood my perversity and cared for me despite or even because of it. Yet this same woman now had a past that connected her with my husband and a son who had orchestrated his own sister's downfall. By the time she arrived that afternoon, I had become almost frightened to see her. My fragility was not helped by the fact that my husband had left the night before and was not yet returned.

I welcomed her in the receiving room, like a good wife should, though the room felt cold and loveless compared with the one she had furnished with such grace. I stood up as she came in and we embraced. After we were seated she studied me with her usual eagle eye.

"Your sister sends her love. She is proud as a peacock and in excellent spirits. The baby is in good voice too."

"Praise be to God," I said.

"Indeed. And you, Alessandra? You look well."

"I am."

"And your husband?"

"He is well too."

"I am sorry to miss him."

"Yes... I am sure he will be back soon."

She paused. "So. Things between you are..."

"—magnificent," I said firmly.

I watched her register the rebuff and try again. "The house is very quiet. How do you spend your time?"

"I pray," I said. "Just as you suggested. And to answer your next question, I am not pregnant yet."

She smiled at my naïveté. "Well, I would not worry. Your sister was faster than many in that regard."

"Did the baby come easily?"

"Easier than you," she said gently, and the reference to my birth was, I know, an attempt to make me softer toward her. But I was having none of it.

"Maurizio will be a rich man today."

"Indeed. Though no doubt he would have preferred a boy."

"Still, he wagered four hundred florins on a girl. No heir, but a good start for a dowry. I must talk to Cristoforo about doing the same thing. When my time comes."

I was pleased with myself for this sentence, for it sounded very like the way I thought a wife should talk.

My mother stared at me. "Alessandra?"

"Yes?" I said brightly.

"Is everything all right, my child?"

"Of course. You have no need to worry about me anymore. I am married, remember."

She paused. She wanted to say more, but I could see that she was disconcerted by this brittle, self-possessed young woman who now sat in front of her. I let the silence grow.

"How long were you at court, Mother?"

"What?"

"My husband has been sharing his memories of the days of Lorenzo the Magnificent. He tells of how the whole court sang the praises of your beauty and your wit."

I think if I had physically attacked her she would not have been more taken aback. I had certainly never seen her struggle so for words before. "I didn't...I was never at court. I simply visited...a few times...when I was young. My brother took me. But—"

"So you did know my husband?"

"No. No...I mean, if he had been there I might have seen him, but I didn't know him. I...it was all a long time ago."

"Still, I am surprised you never speak of it. You who are so keen for us to acknowledge history. Didn't you think we would be interested?"

"It was a long time ago," she repeated. "I was very young...not much older than you are now."

Except right at that moment I felt very old indeed. "Was my father at court too? Is that how you met?" Because it seemed clear to me that if my father had rubbed shoulders with such greatness, we, his children, would never have heard the end of it.

"No," she said, and with the word I could feel the change in her voice as she regained her composure. "Our marriage came later. You know, Alessandra, while your passion for the past is admirable, I think we would do better to talk of the present." She stopped. "You should know that your father is not well."

"Not well? How?"

"He is...he is under some strain. The invasion and the changes in Florence's fortunes have gone hard with him."

"I would have thought he would have made good business out of it. From what I heard, the only thing the French were willing to pay for was our cloth."

"Yes. Only your father would not sell it to them." And when I heard that, I loved him all the more for it. "I fear his refusal will have marked him out as a man of the opposition. I trust it will not cause us grief in the future."

"Still, he must have known he could no longer expect to be called to the Signoria. Our great hall of government will be filled with Snivelers from now on," I said, using the slang word for Savonarola's followers. She looked alarmed. "Don't worry. I don't use such words in public. My husband keeps me well abreast of the changes in the city. Like you I have heard of the new laws—against gambling and fornication." I paused. "Against sodomy."

Once again my words stopped her breath. I could feel it. The air between us grew very still. Surely it was not possible. That my own mother would have let such a thing happen.

"Sodomy," I repeated. "Such a grave sin that I have only recently understood its meaning. Though I feel my education in such matters was rather lacking."

"Well, it is not something that a good family need take notice of," she said, and now she was every bit as brittle as I. In those words, the enormity of her betrayal was made clear to me and, while I could hardly believe it, I also felt such fury that it was difficult to be in the same room with her. I stood up, making some excuse that I had work to do. But she did not move.

"Alessandra," she said.

I stared at her evenly.

"My dear child, if you are unhappy—"

"Unhappy? Why? What could there possibly be in my marriage that makes me unhappy?" And I continued to stare at her.

She rose up, defeated by my aggression. "You know your

father would like it if you came to visit. He is much weighed
down by the matters of business these days. Ours is not the only
state to be in turmoil, and too much politics is bad for trade. I
think it would distract him a little to be visited by his favorite
daughter," she said gently. "As it would myself."

"Really. I would have thought the house would be full of my
brothers, now we are becoming tougher on young men's follies."

"Well, it is true that Luca has changed his ways," she said.
"Indeed, I fear Savonarola has made a new conquest in your
brother. You should be aware of that in your dealings with him.
And Tomaso—" She broke off and I saw again the tremor in her.
"Well, we do not see a great deal of Tomaso these days. I think
that is another thing that worries your father." And she dropped
her eyes.

She had got as far as the door and still I had said nothing, when
she turned. "Oh, but I have forgotten. I have brought you something. From the painter."

"The painter?" I felt the familiar sweet pain rise and curl in my
stomach, though such had been the drama of our lives that I had
not thought of him for some time.

"Yes." She pulled out something from her bag, a parcel
wrapped in white muslin. "He gave it to me this morning. It is his
wedding gift. I think he may have been put out that we did not
use him for a marriage chest, though your father did explain to
him there had been no time."

"How is he?"

She gave a shrug. "He has begun the frescoes. But we are not
to see them till they are finished. He works by day with his
helpers, then on his own at night. He leaves the house only to
attend service. He is a strange young man. I have said no more
than fifty words to him in all the time he has been with us. I think
he was probably better suited to his monastery than our worldly
city. But your father still believes in him. We must hope his frescoes are as rich as his faith."

She stopped. Maybe she was hoping she might have softened

my silence with the promise of further gossip. But still I would do nothing to help her, so she embraced me quickly and went.

The room grew cold around my new aloneness. I would not let myself think about what I had learned, because if I did I would surely fall into a chasm of pain from which I would never emerge. Instead, I turned my attention to the painter's present.

I unwrapped the muslin carefully. Underneath, painted in tempera on a panel of wood about the size of a large church Bible, was a portrait of Our Lady. The scene was vibrant with the color palette of the Florentine sun, and the background detail showed off elements of the city: the great dome, the complex perspectives of its loggias and piazzas, and a wealth of churches. At the center sat the Virgin, her hands (such beautifully painted hands) folded gently in her lap and her gold-leaf halo shining out to the world, defining her as the Mother of God.

That much was certain. What was less certain was the moment of her life in which he had chosen to capture her. Her youth was paramount, and from the way she was staring boldly out past the viewer's gaze it was clear that she was looking at someone. Yet there was no sign of any eager angel bringing her glad tidings and no dancing or sleeping baby to bring her joy. Her face was long and full, too full to be beautiful, and her skin nowhere near pale enough to be fashionable, but despite her looks there was something about her: a gravity, an intensity almost, that made you look twice.

That second look revealed something else. Mary was less of a supplicant than an inquirer; there was a questioning in her eyes, as if she were yet to satisfactorily understand or accept everything that was being asked of her—and that, without understanding, it was possible she might choose not to obey.

In short, there was a kind of rebellion to her, the like of which I had never seen in a Madonna before. Yet despite her transgression I knew her well enough. Because her face was my own.

Twenty-six

I STAYED UP INTO THE NIGHT, MY MIND CAREERING between the guilt of my mother and the transgression of the painter. How could she have been capable of such betrayal? What was he thinking to create such a work? I sat at my bedroom window looking out onto a city that was more forbidden to me now than when I had been a virgin in my father's house, and I wondered about the journey of my life, which had taken me from such hope to such despair. As I sat there I caught the first flakes of snow rushing up out of the darkness past the window. And because snow was something that happened rarely in the city, I was, despite myself, entranced and stayed up to watch. So it was that I witnessed the arrival of the great blizzard.

It raged for two nights and two days, the snow so thick and wind-driven that in daylight it was hard to see even to the other side of the street. When it finally blew itself out, the city was transformed: the streets more like the contours of the country-side, with dips and dunes that buried many houses up to the second floor, while so much rain had turned to ice from the over-hangs of the roofs that Florence looked as if it had been hung with curtains of cascading crystals. It was so beautiful it could almost have been the work of God, a vision to celebrate our new purity. Though others said it was a sign that Our Lord had joined with Savonarola and, having failed to burn our sin away with the heat, now sought to freeze it out of us with the cold.

The weather became our lives for a while. The river froze deep enough for children to build bonfires on its surface, and the boatmen were the first to starve as Florentines learned to walk on water. Years before, when I was a child and there had been a snowstorm strong enough to cover the city, people had taken to the streets to build snow sculptures, and one of the apprentices at Lorenzo's sculpture school had constructed a lion as a symbol of Florence in the garden of the Medici Palace. It was so lifelike that Lorenzo had opened the gates to let the citizenry see it. But there were no such fripperies now. Each evening as darkness fell the city grew so silent that you would think the people had been frozen into the landscape. My husband's house was drafty enough that we might as well have been on the street, and indeed, some people did die in their homes. We at least had fires, which burned the front of our legs while leaving our backs freezing.

By the second week the snow turned to black ice and became so perilous that no one went out unless they had to. The winter darkness began to seep into our souls. It seemed to last forever. The days had scarcely any daylight to them yet they were achingly long, and my husband's growing impatience with his separation from my brother was so overt that after a while his longing began to overrule his politeness and he started to withdraw from me, keeping himself to his study long into the night. His absence upset me more than I could bear to admit. Then, one morning, the weather notwithstanding, he left the house and did not return with the dark.

But if he could go, then so could I. Next day, leaving a note for Erila, I headed out alone to visit my sister.

On the streets, the air was so cold you could only take small breaths, it so cauterized your nostrils. People walked slowly, their

whole attention focused on where they put their feet. Some carried bags of dirt—earth and grit—that they scattered like seed
corn in front of them. Salt would have done better, but it was far
too valued a commodity to waste on one's footsteps. I had neither,
and as a result my way was treacherous and, while the distance
between our two houses was not far, my skirts were torn and
crusted black before I had traveled a hundred yards.

Plautilla welcomed me with astonished but open arms, setting
me down by the fire and clucking over the daring and stupidity of
her precipitate younger sister. Her house felt so different from
mine. It was less grand and more recently built so there were fewer
cracks to let the cold in. There were also more fires, and it had that
relentless busyness of family that I remembered so fondly from my
childhood. In contrast to my raw nose and pinched face she looked
comfortable and warm, though it has to be said she was almost as
fat without the baby as she had been with.

Despite the wonder of its timing, my sister's nativity had
clearly been a good deal less humble than Our Lady's. In her
defense one could argue that since her confinement had coin-
cided with the invasion, Plautilla had not been out in public for a
while and no one had broken the news to her about how much
things had changed. Nevertheless, if the Sumptuary Police had
chosen to pay a visit to the nursery they would have had the baby
out of most of her clothes and much of the furniture on the
street. Fortunately, we had not come to that. Yet.

She let me hold my bawling, scrunched-up little niece, who
dutifully screamed in my arms until the wet nurse took her and
fixed her onto the breast, where she gorged herself like a young
lamb, so that you could hear the greedy suck and gulp of her
jaws, while Plautilla sat in plump serene silence, replete with her
triumph and soft nipples.

"I understand now that this is what women were made for."
She sighed. "Though I wish Eve had saved us some of the agony
of birthing. You would not believe the pain. I think it must be

worse than the strappado. God showed Our Lady great mercy in relieving her of that particular burden." She popped another sweet into her mouth. "But look at her, will you? Doesn't Papa's cream cloth make the most beautiful swaddling? See what you have to look forward to. She is a much greater creation than all your scribbling, don't you think?"

I agreed that she was, though—since Plautilla only held her three or four times during my visit and spent the rest of the days sorting out baggage that would accompany the baby and the wet nurse to the country within the week—I couldn't quite see how significant a difference she was going to make to her life. As for Maurizio, from the brief few moments I saw him he seemed rather bored by the whole affair, but then the men of the state were about bigger business than babies. And she was only a girl.

"Mother says you are well but grown humble. I must say you look a little plain."

"Very plain," I said. "But then the world is grown plain. I am surprised they have not told you."

"Oh, why should I leave the house? I have everything I need here."

"And after the baby goes? What will you do then?"

"I will tidy up, and when I'm rested we will set about making another," she said, with a coy smile. "Maurizio will not rest until we have a fleet of boys to lead the new Republic."

"Good for him," I said. "If you get them out quickly they could become the new warriors for God."

"Yes. Talking of warriors, have you seen Luca recently?"

I shook my head.

"Well, let me tell you he is changed. He came to see Illuminata just two days ago. Don't you love that name? Like a new light in the sky. He said it was a fitting name for our time and that blessed was the fruit of my womb." She laughed. "Imagine our Luca using such language. Mind you, he looked awful. His nose was blue from the cold of the street patrol. He had all his hair cut off, like a monk. Though I've heard there are younger ones who really do look like angels."

Though I bet they poke like devils, I thought, remembering the group in the square. I cast a glance at the wet nurse, who had her eyes fixed on Illuminata, who in turn was staring unblinking back up at her. Was she too a follower of the new state? It was hard to know what one could say in front of whom these days.

"Don't worry," Plautilla whispered, catching my look. "She's from outside Florence. She barely understands us."

But I saw a small flash in the hooded eyes that made me think otherwise.

"Guess what Luca bought me as her birthing present? A book of Savonarola's sermons. Fancy that! Straight from the printing press. Imagine, they are printing them now. Three new printer's shops opened in the Via dei Librai in the last few months, he said, all to deal with the new words. Do you remember when Mother used to say it was vulgar to buy books that came from mechanical means? That the beauty of the words was—" She stumbled.

"—half in the strokes of the pens that copied them," I said. "Because the copyists added their love and devotion to the original text."

"Ooh. You do remember everything. Well, no more. Even gentlemen buy printed books now. I hear it is all the rage. Just think. No sooner does he say things than they are in our hands. So those who cannot read can have them read aloud. No wonder he has such a devout following."

Though she could be easily distracted by flurries of fashion, she was not stupid, my sister, and I believe that had she been in church listening to the passion of his words during this time, she too might have felt a certain fear as well as wonder. But the pleasures of marriage and motherhood were softening her brain. "You are right," I said quietly. "Still, I would give it some time before you read them to Illuminata."

I saw the wet nurse shift her gaze slightly, pulling the baby off the breast for a moment so that its indignant screams momentarily disrupted the conversation. For the rest of my stay I did not bring the subject up again.

WHEN I ARRIVED HOME SOME DAYS LATER, THE ICE WAS MELTING.

On the corner of our street the thaw had revealed a half-frozen body of a dog, its insides slit open and its black entrails coming to life as the first maggots began to survive the cold. I could not tell if the stink was of life or of death. My house also smelled different, as if some foreign animal had entered it. Or it could have been that I spotted Tomaso's horse tethered next to Cristoforo's in the courtyard. They were both glistening with sweat, standing companionably close, waiting for the groom to finish brushing them. The boy broke off from his task to greet me with a quick nod. I nodded back. Why did I feel so sure that he had ministered to both animals like this many times before?

Erila met me before I could get as far as my room. I expected her to berate me for my absence, but instead there was almost an exaggerated jollity to her.

"How was your sister?"

"Plump," I said. "In many ways."

"And the baby?"

"Hard to tell. It was covered in milk vomit. But it has a voice on it. I think it'll survive."

"Your brother is here. Tomaso." Was it my imagination or was she looking at me rather keenly?

"Really," I said casually. "When did he arrive?"

"The day after you left," she said, and her studied casualness felt about as real as my own. So did she know too? Had she always known? Had everyone known but me?

"Where are they now?"

"They just got in from riding. I...I think they are in the receiving room."

"Perhaps you would tell them I am home. No. No, on second thought I will go to them myself."

I sidestepped her and climbed the stairs quickly before I lost

my courage, feeling her eyes on my back as I went. The day after
I had left. My husband's naked desire made me ashamed for him.
And for myself.

I pushed open the door quietly. They had made themselves at
home. The table was still laid from supper with a good wine
opened, and the air was heavy with the smell of spices. It would
seem the kitchen had done them proud. They were standing at
the open grate, close to the fire and closer still to each other,
though not touching. To the unobservant eye they might have
been two friends sharing the warmth, but all I could feel was the
charge between them, leaping like the crack of energy between
two burning logs of wood.

Tomaso was less ostentatiously dressed now, clearly mindful
of the new codes, though it seemed to me that his good-looking
face was going a little to fat. He would be twenty next birthday.
Not exactly manhood, but old enough to warrant heavier punishments. Was it yesterday Plautilla had been recounting stories
of how in Venice younger men convicted of sodomy regularly
had their noses cut off, a prostitute's punishment, befitting their
emasculated status and designed to ruin their vanity? It had
made me understand the meaning of that mutilation of the boy
on the steps of the Baptistery the day of my marriage. In all my
years of conflict with Tomaso I had never harbored such cruel
thoughts toward him, and it scared me that I should do so now.

He was the first to see me, catching my eye over my husband's
shoulder. We had spent our lives as each other's tormentors: he
the mule with the thick kick, me the mosquito, scoring half a
dozen red blisters to his one occasional thump.

"Hello, sister," he said, and I swear his triumph was tinged with
fear.

"Hello, Tomaso." I knew my voice must be strange because I
could barely find enough breath to get his name out properly.

My husband turned immediately, moving away from his lover
and toward me in the same sleek move. "My dear. Welcome
home. How was your sister?"

"Plump. In many ways." Thank God for the power of memory.

There followed a confused few steps of dance as we arranged ourselves in the room, Cristoforo in one chair, me in another, and Tomaso on a small settee nearby: husband, wife, and brother-in-law, a charming family group of Florence's more cultured elite.

"And what of the baby?"

"Fine." There was a pause. What was Savonarola's great wisdom when it came to women? After obedience, a wife's greatest virtue is silence. But then to be a real wife you have to have a real husband.

"Plautilla has missed you," I said to Tomaso. "She says you are the only one not to visit."

He dropped his eyes. "I know. I have been busy."

Snipping the frills off your garments, no doubt, I thought, though as I did so I noticed he was wearing the silver wedding belt. The fact of it registered like a punch in my stomach. "I am surprised you have been out so much. I would have thought the city less inviting for you these days."

"Well"—he shot the fastest look at Cristoforo—"I don't really..." He trailed off with a slight shrug, obeying the instruction he had clearly been given to humor me.

The silence returned. I looked at my husband. He looked at me. I smiled, but he did not quite return it.

"Tomaso reports that they are clearing the convents," he said mildly, "removing any art that doesn't conform to the monk's vision of decency and any ornaments or vestments that are too rich."

"What will he do with all the confiscated wealth?" I asked.

"No one knows. But I wouldn't be surprised if we don't start smelling woodsmoke before too long."

"He wouldn't dare, surely?"

"I think it is not a question of dare. He can do as he pleases, as long as he takes the people with him."

"What of the remainder of the Medici collection?" I said. "He wouldn't destroy that?"

"No. More likely he will suggest that they auction it off."

"Then keep an inventory of everybody who buys it," I said tartly. "You will have to temper your urge for acquiring more beauty, Cristoforo, or we shall find ourselves marked out for other reasons."

He nodded slightly, acknowledging the wisdom of my logic. I shot a glance at Tomaso. "And what is your opinion of our friar's attitude to the Rinascimento?" I said, eager to show up his shallowness. "I am sure it must occupy your mind continually."

He gave a slight scowl. Don't thumb your nose at me, I thought. You have done far more hurting in your life than you have ever been hurt.

"So," I continued, after it was clear that he would not. "I hear that Luca has gone for God's warrior. Let us hope you haven't made an enemy there."

"Luca? No. He just likes armies. You never saw him on the streets in the old days. He likes brawling. If it isn't fighting the French, it's fighting sinners. It's where he gets his pleasure."

"Well, we all get it in different places." I paused. "Mother says you are never home." I paused again. Longer this time. "She knows about you, yes?"

And he looked up alarmed. "No. What makes you say that?"

"Because that's the impression she gives. Maybe Luca has felt the need to confess on your behalf."

"I told you. He wouldn't betray me," he said moodily. "Anyway, he doesn't know enough."

Whereas I do, I thought. The temperature between us was rising. I could feel it coming up like vomit in my throat. And I could feel my husband, *our* husband, tensing up on the other side of the room. Tomaso sent him another look, a more obvious one this time, one that had laziness to it and spoke of conspiracy, sweat, and desire. While I had been cooing over babies and swaddling clothes, they had been rolling each other in the glorious security of my absence. This might be my home now, but at this moment I was the interloper. It made me mad with pain.

"Still, you must admit it has a certain symmetry: one son goes to God while the other goes to the Devil. Lucky for our parents, both daughters are married. How delighted they must have been when you suggested my suitor, Tomaso," I said quietly, but not the less viciously for that.

"Oh, and you of course were so blameless," he said, fast as a magnet snapping onto metal. "Maybe if I'd had a sweeter little sister, things might have been different."

"Ah." I turned my body away so I couldn't read the warning signs I would be getting from my husband. "So that was how it happened. You were born a pure soul ready to fly to God, and then this vile young girl arrived and so humiliated you—because you could not be bothered to learn anything—that you turned against all women, and so she set you on the path to sodomy."

"Alessandra." Cristoforo's voice behind me was quiet. I might almost not have heard it.

"I told you, there was no point," Tomaso said bitterly. "She doesn't forgive."

I shook my head. "Oh, I think you are more guilty of that sin than I, sir," I said icily, and I could feel the control slipping away. "You know we talk of you, Cristoforo and I? Does he not tell you that? Quite often, actually. About how pretty you are. And how stupid."

I felt my husband rise from his chair. "Alessandra," he said, more severely this time.

But I could not stop now. It was as if a dam had burst inside me. I turned to him too. "Of course, we do not use those actual words, do we, Cristoforo? But each time that I make you think or laugh with some piece of learning or an observation of art, rather than some simpering gesture or fluttering of eyelashes... each time I see your eyes light up with the pleasure of our conversation, and your mind is distracted for a moment from his body... then I think I have scored a small victory. If not for God, then at least for humanity."

Oh, but I did not want it to be like this. I had imagined it all so different: how I would be courteous and witty, would smile and reassure and so, little by little, lure them both into a conversation where I could quietly, subtly, expose my brother's shallow vanity for what it was, while I watched my husband's eyes shine with involuntary pride at my intelligence and humor.

But I couldn't do it. Because of course hate, or maybe it was love, isn't like that.

I watched them staring at me, a mixture of pity and disdain in their eyes, and suddenly it all slid away: my recklessness, my courage, my monstrous, monstrous confidence leaking out from the wound that, I realized now, I had inflicted on myself. What should have been their shame had become my own. I think at that moment I would have even joined the Snivelers if someone could have taken away the pain.

I got up from my seat and could feel that I was shaking. My husband's eyes were cold. It struck me that he looked older suddenly, or maybe it was simply the contrast with Tomaso's overripeness.

"I am sorry, husband," I said, looking directly at him. "I seem to have forgotten my side of our bargain. Forgive me. I shall go to my room. Welcome, brother. I do hope you enjoy your stay."

I turned and walked to the door. Cristoforo watched me go. He did not follow me. He could have said something, but he did not. As I closed the door I imagined them coming together like a long sweet sigh, entwining and fusing into each other like Dante's thieves and serpents, so that I could no longer tell my brother from my husband. And I did myself further damage by the tenderness and violence of the image.

Twenty-seven

S HE OPENED THE DOOR AND STOOD AT THE END OF THE room, and even in my hysteria I could see she was frightened to come in. Which scared me even more, because she had never been frightened of me, even when as a child I had been at my meanest to her.

"Go away, Erila!" I shouted, burying my head in the covers, but that only decided her. She crossed the room and climbed onto the bed and put her arms around me. I pushed her off. "Go away."

Still she stayed.

"You knew. Everybody knew, yet you didn't tell me."

"No!" And this time she held on to me till I had to look at her. "No. If I had known would I have let you marry him? Would I? Of course not. I knew he was profligate. That he plucked where he could. That much I knew. But men stick it in all manner of holes when nothing else is available. It's common knowledge, and your mother and I did you wrong if we protected you so much you didn't know that. But those same men usually turn from one to the other without blinking. So, yes, they will fuck a man if a woman is not available. That is how it is. It may not be how your God would have it, but it is how it is." There was something in the very violence of her language that made me feel better. Or at least made me listen. "But for the most part, all that ends when they get married. The boys dry up and the women stay wet for them. Or at least for the children. So I thought—maybe because I wanted to think—that that was how it would be with him. In which case, why tell you? It would only have made that first night worse."

That first night. Clever women do not die of it. But we would not go into that now. "And Tomaso?" I said, gulping back my sobs. "Did you know about him?"

She sighed. "There were rumors. But he is a tease, your brother. It could all just have been part of his games. Maybe I should have listened more. But not the two of them. I knew nothing about that. If it had been gossip I would certainly have heard it and I didn't."

"What about my mother?"

"Oh, God forgive us, your mother didn't know."

"Oh, but she did! She knew Cristoforo at court when she was younger. He said he saw her there."

"And what of it? She was a young girl. She would have known even less of such things than you. How could you even think such a thing about her? It would break her heart."

Instead, though, it had broken mine. "Well, if she didn't know, she does now. At least about Tomaso. I saw it in her face."

Erila shook her head. "Many secrets are no longer secrets now. It seems the Snivelers make good whisperers too. From the stuff I'm hearing, even the confessional box has no back to it anymore. Most likely Luca, the new angel of God, said something."

So much for Tomaso as a judge of character. "But... if no one knew... I mean, how did you find out?"

"I live here, remember?" and she gestured to the walls.

"Do they all know?"

"Of course. Believe me, if he didn't pay them so well they would probably not be the only ones by now. They like him. Even for his sins." She paused. "And so do you. That's the worst of it."

· · ·

SHE STAYED WITH ME TILL I SLEPT, BUT THE PAIN HAD SEEPED into my dreams and that night the snake coils came in to torment me again. The mountebank's leer was the Devil's mouth; the serpent rose up from it, full of color and hissing lascivious rage, crushing and cursing me until I woke up screaming, though I think my voice was only in my sleep because the house was deathly calm around me.

Erila's pallet by the door was empty. The darkness howled in my ears and I swear I could hear the rustle of the snake inside it. My skin was wet with the sweat of fear. I was abandoned in a house of sin, and the Devil was come to get me. I forced myself to get up and light the lamp. The shadows retreated to the corners of the room, lapping there like a rising tide. I dug desperately into my chest, pulling out my drawings, chalks, and pens from the bottom. Prayer comes in many forms. If sleeping brought the Devil and my husband's sins took away my words, then I would stay awake and try to pray to God through my pen, conjuring up an image of Our Lady to intercede for me.

My hands were shaking as I took out the lump of black chalk. It had been weeks since I had used it and its edges were blunt. I found my blade, wrapped in a piece of my father's cloth, and started to sharpen the end, the sound of the scraping gently familiar. But the semidarkness and the moisture of my fingers made me clumsy and the blade slipped suddenly, slicing a fast long furrow across my hand and down my inner arm.

The blood welled up instantly, bright against my sallow skin, a vibrancy of color that no dye could capture. I stared in fascination as the line grew thicker, spreading out across my arm till it started to drip onto the floor. What story had Tomaso told me once? About a madman in prison who had opened his own veins to write the testimony of his innocence on the walls, and how, once started, he could not stop and they had found him next morning, bloodless, shriveled in the corner, the walls covered with crusted black words. What stories might I tell now if I could find the right color for them? The thought made me shiver. The blood was flowing quicker now. I should stanch it as Erila had taught me. But not yet. I grabbed the small ceramic dish used to hold herbs from the summer pomade and held it under the wound. The drops flowed into each other on my skin, then splashed fat and hard into the dish. It was not long before they formed a shallow pool. The liquid of life (God's ink). Too precious for paper. The pain would come soon. I would need cloth to bind the skin tight. But the fabric from the blade was too small and my other garments too precious. I slipped my gown over my head. I would use that. Soon... First I must choose my brush, the one made from the fattest miniver tails, its end thick as a sunbeam. My body faced me in the burnished glass. I saw again the serpent dancing its way across the mountebank's oiled arms, the sun playing off its coils. In the lamplight I was pearly with sweat. My husband and my brother were even now entwined together, greedy with lust. I would never feel what they were feeling. My body would remain a foreign land to me, uncharted and untouched. No one to caress my skin or marvel at its beauty. I dipped the tails into the blood and with a flourishing stroke traced a cool wet line from my left shoulder down over my breasts. The color was like a scarlet banner across my skin.

"In God's name!"

She had hold of me immediately. The dish went cracking to the floor, the blood splattering.

"Leave me be!"

She snapped the brush out of my hand, seizing my arm above the elbow and holding it up high, her fingers like a vice gripping my flesh, applying pressure to stem the flow.

"Leave me be, Erila," I yelled again, my voice high and angry.

"I will not. You are in the grip of the dream still. It had you so thrashing and moaning I went to fetch you a draft." And she snatched the gown with her other hand and started to wrap it tight around the wound.

"Ah! You hurt me. Let me alone, I tell you; I am fine."

"Oh, yes, as fine as a madwoman."

And I did not sound so fine either, because we could both hear my laughter now even though there was little enough to laugh at. I saw her eyes wide with shock as she pulled me to her, holding me so tight that I could barely breathe.

"I am fine, I am fine," I said, over and over again, as the laughter turned to tears and the pain of the cut came in like a branding iron, offering me something more powerful than self-pity to fight against.

Twenty-eight

AFTER THAT NIGHT I WAS ILL FOR A WHILE. ERILA WAS SO worried that she took away my blades and brushes until my wildness left me. I slept a lot and lost my appetite for food as well as life. The wound swelled and pussed and brought a fever in its wake. Erila nursed me with herbs and poultices until the skin joined back together and the healing started, though it left a scar which journeyed from angry red to the white raised line that I still have today. And all the time she watched over me with the ferocity of a hellhound at the gate, so that when my husband came to inquire after my health later that first day, I heard their raised voices outside the door but there was never any question as to which one of them would win.

Later, when my calmness had earned her trust again and my sense of humor was restored enough to hear her quips, I asked her what had passed between them and she had acted out the scene for my amusement: he the hangdog, posturing, then harassing and threatening; she the half-witch black slave, spinning tales of heartbreak and sudden bloody miscarriage.

It was such a shocking lie that I found it almost pleasing.

"You didn't say that!"

"Why not? He wants a child. It's about time he realized he's not going to get one from poking your brother."

"But—"

"No buts. From what you say he made a deal with you. You make him stick to it. If he likes the smell of arse that's his affair. Tomaso is just his whore on the side. You are the mistress of the house, and he had better treat you as such."

"What did he say?"

"Oh . . . that he had no idea, that he was sorry, and . . . blah blah. They never know what to say about women's stuff. The first mention of that kind of blood and even the ones who like cunt go queasy."

"Erila!" I had laughed. "Your language is worse than Tomaso's."

She shrugged. "At least my behavior is better. You 'ladies' don't know the half of it. You should hear the things they say about you. Either you're standing under your halos, eyes up to heaven, or you're munching apples in their faces and flashing your bush. I'm not even sure *they* know which they prefer. The best you can do is choose when you change your costume." She had grinned at me. "My mother used to say that in our land there were enough gods for women to have at least one on their side, while your religion has three in one and they are all men. Even the bird."

It was such a shocking way to describe the Holy Spirit that I found myself wanting to giggle. "I hope she did not spout such blasphemy in public."

She shrugged. "If she did, who would care? You forget the laws of slavery mean she had no soul to save."

"So what? She died a heathen?"

"She died in bondage. That was all that mattered to her."

"But you go to church, Erila," I said. "You know your prayers as well as I. Are you telling me that all this time you don't believe?"

She looked down. "I grew up in another language, under another sun," she said. "I believe what I need to believe to get by."

"And when you are free. Will that change things?"

"Let's talk about that when it happens."

Though we both knew that siding with me against him was not the way to see freedom come any faster.

"Well," I said, "I think whatever secrets are in your heart, God will see them and He will know that you are a good person and look kindly on you."

She stared at me. "And which God is that, yours or the monk's?"

She was right. When I was a child it had all seemed so simple. There had been one God, who, though He had a voice like thunder when angry, also had enough love to keep me warm at night when I spoke to Him directly. Or so it seemed to me. And the more I learned and the more complex and extraordinary the world became, the deeper His capacity to accept my knowledge and rejoice with me. Because whatever man's achievement, it came first and foremost from Him. But this no longer seemed true. Now man's greatest achievements seemed to be in direct opposition to God, or *this* God, the one who was now ruling Florence. This God was so obsessed with the Devil that He seemed to have no time for beauty or wonder, and all of our knowledge and art was condemned as just another place for evil to hide. So now I no longer knew which God was the true one, only which was louder.

"All I know is that I don't want to live with a God who would send you or even my husband to hell without hearing their story first," I said quietly.

She looked at me fondly. "You were always soft, even as a child when you tried to be hard. Why should you care for him?"

"Because . . . because in some way I don't think he can help it. And because . . ." I paused. Did I really believe what I was about to say? "Because in some way I think *he* cares for *me*."

She shook her head as if we were indeed a foreign race that made no sense to her. "For what it's worth, you may be right.

Though he's not to be forgiven for that reason." She paused, then got up and offered me her hand.

"What is it?"

"There's something you should see. I have been waiting for the right moment."

And she walked me out of my dark cavernous bedroom across the stone landing to a smaller room, which in another household would have been waiting as a nursery.

She slipped a key from her pocket into the heavy lock, and the door fell open.

In front of me was a newly fashioned workshop: a desk and a stone sink with a few buckets to the side and on the table near the window a row of bottles, boxes, and small soft parcels all labeled, next to sets of different-sized brushes. Close by was a porphyry slab for grinding, and two generous panels of wood ready for sizing and priming and the first strokes of the paint.

"He had it brought here while you were ill. And I fetched that from your chest." She pointed to my dog-eared manuscript of Cennini's handbook, over whose pages I had shed such bitter tears because it offered me knowledge without the wherewithal to turn it into paint. "It's the right one, yes?"

I nodded dumbly and moved toward the table, slipping open the catches on a few of the boxes, sliding my fingers into the powders: the thick black, the fierce yellow of the Tuscan crocus, and the deep giallolino with the promised shades of a hundred trees and plants within a solid lump of rock. The shock of so much color was like the first sunlight on the frozen city after the snow. I could feel myself smiling, but there may also have been tears.

So. If we could not have love, my husband and I, then at least I could have alchemy.

OUTSIDE, THE ICE MELTED AND TURNED TO SPRING AS I COOKED UP a feast of colors, my fingers growing calloused with grinding and dark with paint stains. There was so much to learn. Erila helped me, measuring and mixing the powders and preparing the surface of the wood. Nobody bothered us. Around us the house ran itself, and if there was gossip it was surely no more damning than for the sins already at large. It took me the best part of five weeks to transfer my Annunciation onto the wood panel. My life became absorbed in the swirling folds of Our Lady's skirts (no lapis still, but a fine-enough shade of blue mixed from indigo and white lead), the deep ocher of the floor tiles, and a gold-leaf halo for my Gabriel, in luminous contrast to the dark surround of the window frame beyond. At first my hand was much less steady with the brushes than with the pen, and my clumsiness made me despair at times, but little by little my confidence grew, enough so that by the time it was finished I wanted immediately to start again. And in this way I forgot the pain and madness of my brother and my husband and healed myself.

Eventually my curiosity returned and I began to chaff against my self-imposed exile. Erila played her part well, bringing me nutritious bits of gossip, like a mother bird regurgitating food to her young until it is strong enough to go catch its own prey.

Still, our first outing together shocked me. It was late spring now, yet the city was dreary with its own piety. The tap of prostitutes' heels had been replaced by the click of rosary beads, and the only boys on the streets were there to save souls, by whatever means they chose. We passed a gang of them in the square practicing their marching: children as young as eight or nine in God's militia, encouraged by parents who, Erila said, were buying up bales of white cloth to make their angelic robes. Even the rich had muted their dress so the very color palette of the city had become bleached and monochromatic. Foreigners who came in and out of the city for trade and business were amazed by the changes, though they couldn't decide if they were indeed witnessing God's kingdom on earth or something more sinister.

The pope, it seemed, had no such doubts. While Florence championed purity, Erila brought gossip that the Borgia pope had installed his mistress in the Vatican Palace and was handing out cardinal's hats like candied fruit to his children. When he stopped making love he started making war. The French king and his army, gorged on Naples and too weary for the Holy Land, were returning north. But Alexander VI was not a pope to suffer the humiliation of a second occupation, however temporary, and had raised an army from a league of city-states to chase them home with their tails between their legs.

With one exception. From his pulpit in the cathedral, Savonarola declared Florence exempt from such duty. What was the Vatican after all but a richer, more corrupt version of the convents and monasteries he had pledged himself to purge?

DURING THOSE LONG EVENINGS WHEN THE CITY HAD BEEN FROZEN and before Cristoforo's lust had taken him away from me, he and I had talked much about this conflict. How Savonarola's aggressive piety not only threatened the pope's lifestyle but the very fabric of the Church. The glory of God was not just in the number of souls saved but in the influence wielded, the power of the buildings, and the art, the way foreign dignitaries stared in awe at the paintings crawling up the walls of the Sistine Chapel. But such wonder needed income to sustain it, and no hunched-up hawk-nosed prior with an urge for self-flagellation was going to get in the way of that.

It was the only challenge that might stop him. In recent months, opposition within Florence itself had collapsed like mud houses when the floods come in. I could barely believe how easily an old order could be swept aside. Cristoforo had said something else wise then: that just as there were those who feared and hated Savonarola now but would do nothing to try and stop him because his power was so great, so equally there had been people who had felt the same way about the Medici, men who had truly believed that that benign dictatorship—despite or even because of its glories—had been sapping Florence of her republican strengths and purity. But that when a state is so confident it takes wild or stupid men to stand up directly against it. Dissent, he argued, was an art best conducted in the shadows.

Yet even the shadows had gone silent now. The Platonic Academy, once the pride and joy of the new learning, had crumbled. One of its greatest exponents, Pico della Mirandola, was an open follower of Savonarola, waiting to take his Dominican vows, and Erila said there was even talk that men from families as loyal as the Rucellai were leaning toward the cells in San Marco.

Such gossip made me think again of my own family.

This new fad for whiteness would give little work to the dyeing vats of Santa Croce. I remembered the children down by the river with their stick legs and patterned skins. Take the color from the cloth and you took the food from the workers. For all that Savonarola might preach equality, he had little understanding of the ways in which the poor get richer without charity. This too was my husband's observation. I must say there were times during our conversations when I wondered what good he might have done for the state if he had been more interested in politics than the contours of boys' buttocks. See—in my bitterness I was even learning my brother's language.

But in the end what hurt the dyers also hurt my father, for while he might have more fat to live off than his workers, not even his profits could last forever.

"Your father would like it if you came to visit. He is much weighed down by the matters of business these days.... I think it would distract him a little to be visited by his favorite daughter," my mother had said.

Even if she had offended me, I could not forget my father. And as soon as I began to think of them, of course I also thought about the painter and how much more we would have to share now I too had begun to wield a brush.

Twenty-nine

T HE OLD SERVANTS WELCOMED US AS IF I WERE THE prodigal daughter returned. Even Maria with her beady eyes and mean little mind seemed pleased to see me. No doubt the house had got quieter since my leaving. I may have been trouble, but I was also life. I must have looked different in some way, too. Everyone who saw me told me the same. I think my face might have changed with my illness, its shape starting to show more through the pillows of my cheeks. I wondered what my father would say—his younger daughter with the face of a woman rather than a girl.

Well, I would have to wait to find out. Both he and my mother were at the hot springs taking the waters and unlikely to be back for some weeks. I should have sent ahead to tell them I was coming.

The house felt strange to me, like somewhere I had visited only in a dream. Maria told me Luca was home eating lunch and would I like to join him? I got as far as the entrance to the dining room. He was hunched over a plate, stuffing his face. For an Angel he looked terrible. Plautilla was right; the haircut was a disaster. It made his face look huge, like a lump of porous rock, his pockmarks speckled like tiny water holes over the surface. He was chewing with his mouth open, and I could hear the sound of the food squelching.

I crossed to the table and sat down beside him. Sometimes it is worth knowing your enemy. "Hello, brother," I said, smiling. "You have changed your clothes. I am not sure that gray suits you as a color."

He frowned. "I am in uniform, Alessandra. You should know I am in God's army now."

"Oh, and a great thing it is. Though I think you should probably still wash occasionally. When white gets too dirty it can tend toward black."

He sat with the words for a moment, separating out the wit from the meaning. If I had a florin for the time wasted in lessons waiting for Luca to arrive at a place I had already left, we would be a richer family than we were today. "You know what, Alessandra? You talk too much. It will be your damnation. Our life is but a short walk to death, and those who listen to the sound of their own voices rather than the word of the True Christ will rot in hell. Is your husband with you?"

I shook my head.

"Then you should not be here. You know the new rules of our godly state as well as I. Wives without their husbands are vessels of temptation and must stay behind closed doors."

"Oh, Luca," I said. "If only you had always had such facility for remembering things that matter."

"You would do well to watch your tongue, sister. The Devil is in your false learning, and it will bring you to the flames faster than a poor woman who knows nothing but the Gospels. Your precious ancients are an outlawed caste now."

I had never heard my brother so fluent. Still, he was itching to make words into deeds. I could see his fist clenching on the table. His cruelty to me as a child had always been more physical than Tomaso's. My mother hardly ever caught him red-handed and the bruises only came up later. Tomaso was right. He had always been a thug. The only difference now was that he was less beholden to his elder brother. Though what problems his changed loyalties might cause us all had yet to be tested.

I got up from the table, my eyes to the floor. "I know," I said sweetly. "I am sorry, brother. I will go to confession when I get home and ask the Lord's forgiveness."

He stared at me, wrong-footed by my sudden meekness. "Hmm. Very well. If you do so humbly enough, He will give it."

Before I got to the door he had his face back in the plate again.

WHEN I ASKED ABOUT THE PAINTER, MARIA GOT FLUSTERED. "WE don't see him anymore. He lives in the chapel."

"What do you mean, he lives in the chapel?"

She gave a little shrug. "I . . . I mean he lives there now. All the time. He never goes out."

"What of the frescoes? Are they finished?"

"No one knows. He sent the apprentices away last month." She paused. "They seemed eager to leave."

"But . . . I thought he went to church. That he had become a follower. That's what Mother told me."

"I . . . I don't know about that. He used to go, I think. But not now. He hasn't been out of the chapel since the thaw."

"Since the thaw? But that's weeks ago! Why hasn't my father done something?"

"Your father . . ." She paused. "Your father has not been quite himself."

"How do you mean?"

She glanced at Erila. "I . . . I can't really say any more."

"And my mother?"

"Er . . . she is looking after him. And then there's Tomaso and Luca. She has no time to be dealing with tradesmen." Maria, like Ludovica, had never been one to champion the elevation of art. Too much fuss over a few colored scribbles. Better to say your prayers with your eyes closed and not let your imagination get in the way.

"I wonder that she didn't ask for my help," I said quietly, but I already knew the answer. She had, but I had been so angry I had shunned her.

Maria was looking at me, waiting to know what I would do. Everybody had seen me as the baby of the family, precocious, maybe, but barely able to look after myself, let alone anyone else. What could have happened to make me change? I am not sure even I knew.

"I will see the painter," I said. "Where are the keys?"

"They don't work. He bolts the door from inside."

"How about the other entrance, from the sacristy?"

"The same."

"What about food?"

"We leave a plate outside once a day."

"The main door or the sacristy?"

"The sacristy."

"How does he know it's there?"

"We knock."

"And he comes out?"

"Not while anyone's there. The cook waited once, but he never came. No one bothers now. We've got better things to do."

"So no one has seen him?"

"No. Though at night sometimes he makes a noise."

"What do you mean?"

"Well, I don't know, but Ludovica—she doesn't sleep so well—said she's heard him crying."

"Crying?"

She shrugged, as if it was not her place to say any more.

"And the boys? Have they tried?"

"Master Tomaso is hardly ever here. And Master Luca... well, I suppose he thinks he's in church."

Which I suppose in a way he was.

In the upstairs kitchen the cook was phlegmatic about the whole business. If the man didn't want to eat, he didn't want to eat. The last four days of food had been left untouched. Maybe

God was feeding him. John the Baptist had lived on locusts and honey for months, after all.

"I bet it wasn't as good as your pigeon pie, though," I said.

"You always ate well, Miss Alessandra." He grinned. "It's quiet around here without you."

I sat for a while, watching his fingers dice a dozen fat cloves of garlic faster than a moneylender divvies up his coins. My childhood was all here in the smells and tastes of this kitchen: black and red pepper, ginger, cloves, saffron, cardamom, and the pungent sweetness of our own crushed basil. An empire of trade on the chopping block. "Prepare him a plate of something special," I said. "Something whose smells will make his juices flow. Maybe he'll be hungry today."

"Maybe he'll be dead."

He didn't say it cruelly, more as a matter of fact. I thought back to my father's careful chivalry toward the painter when he first arrived on that cold winter night years ago. I remembered the excitement we had all felt: a real live artist living under our own roof, capturing our family for posterity. Everyone had seen it as a mark of the family's prestige, a statement of our status, our future. Now it just seemed to be about the past.

I left Erila and the other servants in the kitchen gossiping with the cook and made my way down the stairs and out across the back courtyard to the painter's quarters. I had no idea what I was looking for. The journey was filled with my younger self skipping out in front of me, sneaking her way down from the main house during the heat of the siesta to confront the new arrival in his den with her boundless enthusiasm and curiosity. If I met her now what advice would I give her? I could no longer work out at what point it had all gone wrong.

The door to his room was closed but not locked. Inside, the atmosphere was musty, a whiff of neglect in the air. The exuberant figures of the Angel and Mary on the wall of the outer chamber had peeled off the unprepared plaster like a relic from an earlier age. The table on which he had kept his sketches was empty and the crucifix gone from the wall. Inside the inner room, the bed was a wad of tossed straw with a grimy cloth thrown across it. Whatever few possessions he owned had gone with him to the chapel.

I'm not sure I would have even bothered with the bucket if it hadn't been for the smoke stains above it. It was sitting in the corner as I turned to leave, and at first I thought the marks might be a rough painting of sorts: a mass of dark curling shadows crawling up the wall and onto the ceiling. But when I got closer and put my hand out to them my palm came back covered in soot, so I turned my attention to the bucket positioned underneath.

The fire had not been successful with the crucifix. Though it was smashed in two, the wood was barely burned at all and it was hard to tell whether he had broken it first and then tried to incinerate it or, irritated with the failure of the flames, had taken it out and smashed it against the wall. The cross was fractured and Christ's legs had broken off, the nails still attached to the feet. His upper torso hung painfully from the T of the cross. I held him carefully in my hands. Even in its damaged state, the sculpture carried passion.

Part of the reason it hadn't burned was that the fire in the bottom of the bucket hadn't been strong enough. He had fed it with paper but carelessly, the leaves too packed together to allow enough air in. There was a feeling of haste to the whole affair, as if something or someone had been nipping at his heels. I scooped my hands in and pulled out the charred remains. The pages at the bottom fell apart in my fingers, bits of feathery ash breaking loose and floating through the air like gray snow, their content lost forever. But the pages nearer to the top were only partly damaged or, in some cases, simply charred around the edges. I carried them into the outer chamber where there was more light and laid them gently down upon the desk.

They divided into two kinds: the drawings of me and the drawings of the bodies.

The ones of me were everywhere, practice sketches for the Madonna, my face repeated one, two dozen times, variations of the same grave, quizzical look that I didn't quite recognize as my own, partly I suppose because I was never that still or silent to myself. He had been searching for the right angle for my head, the right focal point of interest outside the frame, and in passing he had drawn one with me staring straight out at the watcher. It was only a matter of a few degrees in the shift of the eyes, but the effect was enormous. This young woman seemed so—I don't know—so aggressive, almost as if she were challenging the viewer. I think if the face had not been my own, her look would have been almost improper.

Then came the bodies. First the man with no stomach who I had already seen, half a dozen further sketches with his innards more exposed. Next came another torso: this one had been strangled, the body laid out flat on the ground, as if it had just been cut down, the ligature still buried in his neck and the face bloated and bruised, with a trail of what might have been shit dripping across his legs.

After that there were the women. One was old, again naked, her stomach muscles slack and sagging, lying sideways with one arm curled over her head as if she was trying to protect herself from death. There were wounds all around her body and the other arm lay at a strange angle, the elbow pointing the wrong way, like a broken doll. But it was the younger one who scared me most.

She was stretched out on her back, naked, and she too I had seen before. Her body was that of the young girl laid out in the fresco design for the chapel, lying on her stretcher. But in these sketches, not only was she dead, she was also mutilated. Her face was caught in a rictus of agony and terror, and the whole bottom half of her stomach was ripped open and exposed. Among the mess of gobbets and blood was the small but unmistakable form of an early fetus.

. . .

"COOK SAYS THE MEAL IS READY, MISS ALESSANDRA."

Maria's voice sent my heart colliding into my rib cage. "I...I'll be there in a moment," I said, folding the sheets of paper hurriedly into my skirts.

Outside in the sunlight Maria and Erila stood waiting. Erila gave me a look of blunt suspicion. I refused to meet her eyes.

"So what was it you found in there?" she asked, as we climbed the narrow staircase leading to the sacristy door, she going first, holding the tray in front of her.

"Er...a few sketches, that's all."

"I hope you know what you're doing," she said gracelessly. "Half the servants think he's twisted round his own charcoal. They say he spent most of the winter drawing animal carcasses they had thrown out. In the kitchen they think he's got devil eyes."

"That's as may be," I said. "But we still can't let him starve to death."

"Well, as long as you know you're not going in there alone."

"It's all right. He won't hurt me."

"And what if you're wrong?" she said firmly, turning to me as we reached the top. "What if something's gone wrong in his head? You've seen them on the streets. Too much God brings on brain fever. Just because he's seduced you with his paintbrush doesn't mean he isn't dangerous. You know what I think? I think this is not your business. You have a home of your own now and enough trouble there to occupy an army. Leave this to someone else. He's just a painter."

She was frightened for me, of course, remembering that night of my own madness when for a moment my blood had become my paint. And because she is not stupid, my Erila, I did consider what she said. Of course the pain and terror of that young woman's face had clawed its way off the page into my brain. That she and the others were drawn from life there was no doubt. Or rather, drawn from death. But where he had been when the one state turned into the other was the real question. I thought again about his mix of panic and sweetness. I remembered my taunts to him that first day and his clumsy fury back. I remembered also his slow, shy unfolding when I had sat for him, and the way he talked of God crawling into his hands as a child. Somehow I knew that—however lost and crazy he might be—he wouldn't hurt me.

As for my own home? Well, there was no warmth to be had there anymore. I was an outsider. It would be better for me to hunt down like-minded companions in pain to ease my loneliness.

"I know what I am doing, Erila," I said, with quiet force. "I'll call if I need you. I promise."

She gave that little click of her tongue, which I love because it speaks so much while saying so little, and I knew she would let me go.

She set the tray near the entrance so the smell of the newly cooked flesh would creep under the wood. It brought back the echo of a thousand mornings as a child when I had fasted through mass, guilty because the prospect of God's body on my tongue was less arousing than the aroma of roasting meats coming from the kitchen when I arrived home. What it must be like to smell it after days without food I could not imagine.

I stood back and signaled to her. She knocked loudly.

"Your food is here," she said in a booming voice. "The cook says if you don't eat this, he'll stop sending it. It's roast pigeon, spiced vegetables, and a flagon of wine." She knocked again. "Last chance, painter."

Then I signaled again and she stomped off down the stairs, her footsteps heavy on the stones. At the bottom she stopped and looked up at me.

I waited. For a while nothing happened. Then finally I heard a scraping noise from somewhere behind the door. The locks clicked and the door opened a fraction. A shambling figure came out and bent down to pick up the tray.

I stepped out of the shadows, just as I had that night in the house when I had sent his drawings scattering to the ground. He had been scared by me then, and so he was again. He backed into the room and tried to close the door behind him, but he was holding the tray at a strange angle and his coordination seemed to have gone. I rammed my foot in the gap and started to push myself through. He pushed back, but though I had been ill, he had been fasting and the door gave with my weight. As he staggered back, the tray and its contents went flying, an arch of red wine spraying the walls. The door slammed behind me.

We were both inside.

Thirty

H E LEFT THE TRAY WHERE IT HAD FALLEN IN THE DARK-
ness and scrabbled away like a cockroach, through the
sacristy and into the body of the chapel. I picked up
the wooden platter and saved what I could of the food.
The wine was lost as wall paint.

Then I followed him.

The smell inside the room was vile, excrement and urine.
Even when you don't eat you carry on pissing and shitting, for a
while at least. Fearful of where I might put my feet, I hesitated
until my eyes became accustomed to the gloom. The apse was
cordoned off, the scaffolding still in place but tarpaulins and
sheets up all around. The tables were laid out in working order:
paint powder, pestles and mortars, and brushes, all prepared.
Next to them sat a large concave mirror similar to one my father
kept in his study, the better to reflect what remained of the daylight when his eyes grew dim. In a farther corner there was
another bucket with a makeshift wooden lid on it. I assumed the
smell was coming from there.

It was cooler than the rest of the house. And damp, the kind of
damp that seems to ooze out of the stone when there are no

human bodies to heat it. He had been brought up amid stone and cold light. What had my father said about him? That he had painted every space around him till there were no more walls to fill. But not now. Not here. Here, apart from the closed-off apse, there was nothing. I wondered again what was behind the tarpaulins.

Now I saw him. He was sitting in the corner, hunched over himself. He wasn't looking at me. He didn't seem to be looking at anything. He was like an animal cornered by the hunt. I approached him gently. Despite my brave words I was scared. Erila was right. With so much religion abroad, holy madness was on the increase: people who lived so much with God that they didn't know any longer how to be with humans. You came across them in the streets sometimes, chattering to themselves, laughing, crying, their vulnerability vibrating like a halo around them. For the most part they were benign souls, more like lost hermits. But not all. When God was fermenting inside them they could be very frightening.

I stopped a few yards in front of him. The Madonna with my face and the bodies with their bowels unraveled between us. As I opened my mouth I still didn't know what words would come out.

"You know what they call you in the kitchen?" I heard myself say. "Uccellino. Little bird. After the painter, in reverence to your talent, but also because they are scared of you. They think you wait till nightfall and then fly out the window. The cook is convinced you won't eat his food because you have found better somewhere else. He is offended, as all good cooks are."

He gave no indication that he heard me. He was rocking slightly, his arms crossed around him, his hands curled and cradled under his armpits, his eyes closed. I moved closer to him. It didn't seem right, being so tall above him. I sat down on the ground, feeling the cold stone through the folds of my gown. He looked so alone and lonely, I wanted to warm him with the company of words. "When I was growing up and all the talk was of the beauty of our city, there used to be a story about an artist who worked for Cosimo de' Medici. Fra Filippo was his name." I made my voice gentle and even, as I remembered Erila's when she used to talk me into sleep as a child. "You have seen his work. He paints his Madonna with such serenity that you would think his very brush was dipped in the Holy Spirit. He was a monk, after all. But no. Our good brother was so full of carnal thoughts that he would break off from his painting to range around the city at night, accosting any woman who would have him. The great Cosimo de' Medici got so frustrated with him—as much because the paintings stayed unfinished as because of his sins, I think— that he locked him into his studio at night. But when he came in the second morning he found the window open, the bedsheets tied together, and Filippo gone. After that he gave him the key back. Whatever Filippo needed to do for his art he accepted, even if he didn't understand or approve."

I paused. Though nothing obvious about him had changed, I knew now he was listening. I could feel it in his body.

"To have such a fire inside oneself must be very hard some-times. I think it must make you behave in ways that you only barely understand. When I have been at my worst I wonder later why I did the things I did. Except that they seemed necessary at the time. And I have no talent at all. Not compared with yours."

I could see that his whole body was shaking. There had been times—like that first afternoon in his room—when the very physicality of him had made me shake, but not as he did now. This was a different kind of fear.

I put the remains of the supper between us and slid the plate toward him. "Why don't you eat something?" I said. "It's good."

He shook his head, but his eyes flicked open. Not ready yet. I caught a quick glimpse of his face. His skin was the same color as the white on a Della Robbia ceramic. I remembered him crawl-ing around the ceiling, flush with the heat of the flames as he sketched the grid that would become heaven. He had enough energy and vision then. Whatever happened to heaven?

"I have probably talked to you more than anyone in this house has," I said. "Yet I don't even know your name. You have been 'the painter' for so long that that is how I think of you. I know nothing about you, except that you have divinity in your fingers. More than I will ever have. I have felt such envy of you that I think I might have missed your pain. In which case I am sorry."

I waited. Still nothing.

"Are you ill? Is that it? Has the fever come back?"

"No." It was so quiet I could barely hear him. "I am not hot. I am cold. So cold."

I reached out to touch him, but he jerked backward. As he did so, I saw a flash of pain shoot across his face.

"I don't understand what's happened to you," I said gently. "But whatever it is, I can help."

"No. You cannot help me. No one can help me." Then another silence, and this time a whisper. "I am abandoned."

"Abandoned? By whom?"

"By Him. By God."

"What do you mean?"

But he only shook his head violently and clasped his arms more tightly around him. Then, to my horror, he started to weep, sitting there frozen with a slow flow of tears running down his face, like those miraculous statues of the Virgin that cry blood as a way to bring the doubting back to faith.

"Oh, I am so sorry."

And now for the first time he looked directly at me, and as I stared into his eyes it seemed as if he, the painter, that shy young man from the North, was no longer there, and in his place was just a great pit of sadness and terror.

"Tell me," I said. "Please. There is nothing so terrible it can't be told."

Behind me the door opened and I heard soft footfalls. It would be Erila. I had been in here too long and she would be beside herself with worry.

"Not now," I muttered, without moving.

"But—"

"Not now."

"Your parents are expected soon."

It was a good lie, as much to warn him as to help me. I tilted my head toward her and the look she gave me contained a lecture within it. I nodded slightly in recognition of its advice. "Then come back for me. Please."

I turned away. Her footsteps retreated and the door closed.

He still hadn't moved. I took a risk. I pulled out the sketches from inside my gown and laid a few of them on the ground near to the plate, so the man's innards sat next to the remains of the roasted meat. "I have known for a long time," I said softly. "I have been to your room. I've seen them all. Is this what you can't tell?"

A shudder passed through him. "It's not what you think," and his voice was a sudden growl. "I didn't hurt them. I didn't hurt anybody—" He broke off.

This time I went toward him, and if it was the wrong thing to do then I was not the one to judge. I was living in a world where a husband pokes his wife as if she were a cow and men embrace and penetrate each other with a passion and devotion that would make the saints blush. There was no such thing as correct behavior anymore. I put my arms gently around his body. He let out a sharp moan, though whether it was from pain or despair I could not tell. His flesh was cold and stiff like a corpse, and he was so thin I could feel every bone through his skin.

"Tell me, painter. Tell me...."

His voice when it came was low and halting, the penitent searching for the right words. "He said that the human body was God's greatest creation and that to understand it you had to go under the skin. Only that way could we learn how to bring it to life. I wasn't the only one. There were six or seven of us. We met at night in a room in Santo Spírito hospital, by the church. The corpses belonged to the city, he said, people who had no family to claim them or criminals from the gallows. He said God would understand. Because His glory would live on in our art."

"He? Who is this 'he'?"

"I didn't know his name. He was young, but there was nothing he couldn't draw. Once they brought in a boy—fifteen, sixteen. He had died from something in the brain but his body was perfect. He said he was too young to have been corrupted. He said he would be our Jesus. I was going to put him in the fresco. But before I could paint him he came back with his Crucifixion. It was sculpted in white cedar. The body was so perfect, so alive, you could feel every muscle and sinew. I was sure it was Christ. I couldn't—"

He broke off again. I released him and sat back so I could look at him, assess the damage that his words had caused him. "And the more God flowed through him, the more He drained out of you," I said quietly. "Is that what happened?"

He shook his head. "You don't understand.... You don't understand. I should never have been there. It was all a lie. It wasn't God in that room but something else. The power of temptation. After the army came, *he* went away. Disappeared. The corpses stopped coming. The room closed. There was talk of bodies being found in the city. A girl with her womb cut out, the couple, the man disemboweled. Our bodies...we didn't know...I mean...I didn't know...." He shook his head. "It wasn't God in that room." He said again, angrily this time, "It was the Devil. Don't you see? The friar says the more we paint man rather than God, the more we take away His divinity. The body is His mystery. His creation. It is not for us to understand it, only to worship. I gave in to the temptation to know. I disobeyed, and now He has abandoned me."

"Oh, no, no! This is Savonarola's voice speaking, not you," I said. "He wants people to be scared, to think that God will leave them. That way he keeps them in his grip. This painter, whoever he was, was right. How can it be evil to understand God's wonder?"

But he didn't reply.

"And even if it were, He would not abandon you for such a

thing," I prodded, terrified that I might lose him again. "Your talent is too precious to Him."

"You don't understand," he said again, and he had his eyes screwed tight shut. "It's gone, gone.... I stared into the sun and my eyes are burned out. I can't paint anymore."

"That's not true," I said softly, putting out my hands toward him. "I have seen those drawings. They have too much truth about them to be godless. You are lonely and lost and you have frightened yourself into despair. All you need is to believe that you can see again and you will. Your hands will do the rest. Give them to me, painter. Give me your hands."

He stayed rocking and sniveling for a moment, then slowly uncurled them from around his body and extended them toward me, palms down. I took hold of them, and as I did so he let out a sharp yelp of pain as if my touch had burned him. I shifted my grip to the ends of his fingers, cold as ice, and gently turned them over.

Oh! But all my gentleness could never be enough. In the middle of his palms were two great wounds, dark holes of caked blood, the flesh swollen around the edges where infection was setting in. The holes where the nails would have gone in. I thought of Saint Francis waking up in his stone cell filled with the ecstasy of God. And of my own intoxication that night, when the pain of my body had seemed like almost a relief to the pain of my mind. But mine had been an accidental self-mutilation, neither as deep nor as lost as this.

"Oh, dear God," I breathed. "Oh, dear God. What violence have you done to yourself?"

As I said it I felt despair like a poisoned fog seep over him again, filling his mouth and his ears and his eyes, choking his spirit with its fumes. And now I felt really scared, because I could no longer be sure it wouldn't leak into me too.

Of course I had heard stories of melancholy. How even pious men sometimes got lost on their journey to God and gave in to self-destruction to ease the pain. One of my early tutors had fallen into such a pit, wasted away with lack of hope and meaning, until even my kindly mother had dismissed him, fearful of the impact of his sorrow upon our young minds. When I had asked her about him she had told me that some believed such sorrow to be the work of the Devil, but that she thought it was a disease of the mind and the humors, and that while it did not usually kill, it could debilitate a soul for the longest time, and there was no easy remedy.

"You are right," I said quietly, pulling myself away from him, working more on instinct now than reason. "You have sinned. But not in the way you think. This is not truth, it is despair, and despair is a sin. You cannot see because you have put out the light inside you. You cannot paint because you have been lured into self-destruction."

I stood up.

"When did you do this to yourself? How far had you got with the frescoes?" I said, and my voice was fierce.

He sat for a moment, staring at the ground.

"If you don't tell me I shall look for myself."

I pulled him up. Roughly. I know I hurt him.

"You are too selfish, painter. When you had talent, you wouldn't share it. Now you are without it you are almost proud of that too. You have not just embraced despair, you have sinned against hope. The Devil deserves you."

I walked him up through the chapel to the left-hand wall of the apse. He came without resistance, as if his body were more under my control than his own, though it was my own heart that I felt thudding in my chest.

The tarpaulins covering the walls and ceiling were connected separately by double ropes running to a pole at the floor. "Come. Show me these God-forsaken works," I said. "I want to see."

He looked directly at me for a moment. And in that instant I saw something underneath the despair, a kind of recognition of me, an understanding that if there was no one else I would have to do. Then he turned to the ropes and, unknotting them, let the first tarpaulin slip.

There was not a great deal of light that day, so it is hard for me to explain adequately why the impact was quite so great. Of course I was expecting something different, something lost or bad or defiled, and had tensed myself for shock. But instead I was undermined by beauty.

The newly painted frescoes glowed off the wall: the life of Santa Caterina, divided into eight parts, her serene willowy figure moving in vibrant color through her early years. Like his Virgin on the wall, she seemed to contain not just the peace of God but an exuberant human sweetness all her own.

I stared at him, but he would not meet my gaze. The brief moment of connection had slid away and he was in the grip of his own demons again. I went myself to the next panel and unleashed the ropes, letting the tarpaulin slide slowly to the ground. The second wall took her from her triumphs to her death. It was here that the heresy started to seep in.

Like every good Florentine I knew the stories of a thousand saints, had read the parables of their temptations and their bravery and final martyrdoms. Some went more or less willingly; not all had beatific smiles at the moment when the fire caught or the knives were sharpened, but somewhere, in some shape or form, as death came they radiated a certainty of heaven in their pain. But this Santa Caterina did not seem certain of anything. In her cell awaiting execution, in place of serenity there was only agitation, and in the final scene where, having destroyed the wheel, she is dragged toward the executioner's sword, the face that stared accusingly out at the spectator was lit with palpable fear, reminding me of the agony to come in the young girl of the drawing.

The final tarpaulin covered both the back wall and the vaulted roof above. As I walked toward the winch that held it in place I felt sweat at the base of my neck.

As it fell I strained my head upward. The back wall offered a host of angels, their wings splayed out in a feathery glory plucked from doves and peacocks and a thousand imaginary birds of paradise, their eyes looking up to Our Father who art in heaven.

Sure enough, there he was in the middle of the ceiling, on the golden throne, shining and glorified, surrounded by saints filled with their own sublime lightness—the Devil, his black hairy body splayed out over the seat, his three heads exploding out of his neck, each with its own halo of bat wings, and in his claws the figures of Christ and Mary, stuffed halfway into his mouth between his doglike teeth.

Thirty-one

W E TOOK HIM IN MY FATHER'S CART. HE DIDN'T MAKE a
fuss. Whatever fight might have been in him was gone
by then, and he seemed grateful for any show of kindness. By the time Maria realized what we were doing
I think she wanted to stop me, but she had already
ceded her authority by then and could only stand by
and fret. When she asked me, as she did repeatedly, what was
happening, I told her the same thing that I told my mother in the
letter I left for her: that I had found the painter ill in the chapel
and was taking him to my house to tend to him.

It was the truth anyway. That he had some kind of malady was
obvious to everyone who saw him as we helped him out from the
chapel down into the courtyard. He seemed to crumble as the
sun hit him, a fearful shaking coming upon his body and his teeth
chattering till you thought it would rattle the bones in his skull.
Halfway down he collapsed altogether and had to be carried the
last flight of stairs.

We wrapped him in blankets and put him gently in the back of
the cart. Before we had removed him from the chapel, Erila and I
had winched the tarpaulins back into place and locked both

doors and pocketed both sets of keys. If she thought anything about what she had seen on the walls and ceiling, she said nothing of it to me.

By the time we rode out of the gates it was almost dark. I sat in the back of the cart; Erila was driving. She was nervous. I think it was the first time I had ever seen her so. It was, she said, a bad moment to be out on the streets. Dusk was when Savonarola's young warriors came out to impose their curfew, shooing men and women twice their age across the city into their homes away from the temptations of the streets. And since they also took it upon themselves to divide up the stalwart from the tempted, and help the latter by making their journey home swifter and often more painful, it was necessary to have a good story ready, just in case.

They came upon us as we turned the corner by the mighty flanks of the Palazzo Strozzi, a building that would have been the greatest palazzo in the city had it not been left unfinished since the death of Filippo Strozzi. It was a death Savonarola had used frequently as preaching material to illustrate the absurdity of prizing wealth over the promise of everlasting life. Meanwhile, the city had grown so used to the palazzo's half-finished façade that I could no longer begin to imagine what it would look like if it were ever completed.

They had used the great cornerstone as their temporary border post. There were about two dozen of them fanning across the street, their tunics grubby and their resemblance to angels distinctly far-fetched. The eldest one—would this have been Luca's role?—stepped out from the rest and put his hands up in front of us. Erila pulled the cart to a halt, so close that the horses' breath was steamy in his face.

"Good evening, godly Florentine women. What brings you out on the streets after dark?"

Erila bowed her head low as she did when she was playing the slave. "Good evening, sir. My mistress's brother is ill, and we are taking him home for treatment."

"So late and without a chaperone."

"My master's driver is at fasting prayer across the city. We started in the light but the cart wheel caught a rut and we had to wait to be pulled out. We are almost home now."

"Where is your invalid?"

She gestured to the back of the cart.

The leader signaled to a couple of the gang and they came over to where I was sitting with the painter half concealed under the blanket asleep in my lap. One of them pulled back the covers from his body, and the other poked him with a rod he was carrying.

He came to with a start, yanking himself out of my arms and frantically scrabbling away from them to the back of the cart. "Don't come near, don't come near me. I have the Devil in me. He has Christ between his teeth and he will swallow you too."

"What's that he says?" The boy, who had a nose as sharp as his rod, was poised for another poke.

"Can't you understand the language of the saints when you hear it?" I said rudely. "He speaks in Latin of Christ's mercy and the love of our Savior."

"But what did he say of the Devil?"

Of course: thanks to Savonarola his name was more famous than God's these days. "He says Christ's mercy and love will drive the Devil out of Florence with the help of the godly. But we can waste no time. My brother follows the friar. He is destined to take his robes at San Marco. The investiture is planned for next week. Which is why we must get him home and healed before the ceremony."

The boy wavered. He took a step closer and the point of his nose registered the painter's self-neglect. "Phew! Well, he don't look much like a friar to me. Look at him—he's lousy with filth."

"He's not ill, he's drunk," said the other one, and I saw the leader start toward us.

"Keep him still there, mistress," Erila's voice sang out, edgy and loud from the front of the cart. "If he moves the boils may burst. And the contagion is great within the pus."

"Boils? He's got the boils?" The boy with the rod took a hasty step back.

"Why didn't you say so to begin with?" The leader spoke now, taking charge, as all good leaders should. "Keep away from him, all of you. And you, woman, get him out of here. And make sure he doesn't go near any monastery till he is healed."

Erila snapped the reins hard and the cart lurched forward, the barricade melting away before the threat of contagion. The painter curled himself back under the blankets, moaning at our clumsy speed. I waited till they were out of sight before climbing my way up to the pillion.

"Whoa, watch your skin," she said, as I slipped down by her side. "I don't want any of that pus over me."

"Boils!" I laughed. "Since when is our godly army afraid of a few boils?"

"Since the infection came." She grinned. "Your trouble is you still don't get out enough. Mind you, those who do are beginning to regret it. No one knows where it came from. Rumor is the French left it in the holes where they put their juices. It started with the prostitutes but it's begun to spread. When it was only the women who got it, it was known as the Devil's disease, but now that the faithful are starting to blister and bubble, the talk is of God testing their patience like . . . who was that Bible man he sent the plagues to?"

"Job," I said.

"Job. That's the one. Though I bet Job never had anything like French boils: great balls of heat and pus, which hurt like hell and leave fat scars. Still, from what I hear, it's keeping its sufferers out of the sack with more success than the friar's teaching ever did."

"Oh, Erila!" I laughed. "Your gossip is gold-plated. I swear you should have let me teach you your letters better. You could do a history of Florence that would rival Herodotus' tales of Greece."

She shrugged. "If we live long enough to grow old together, I'll talk and you can write. I just hope we get that far. Which depends on you knowing what you're doing now," she said, gesturing to the back of the cart and cracking the reins above the horses' heads so they picked up speed as the dark settled in over the city.

Cristoforo and Tomaso's horses were not in the courtyard and there was no lamp on in his room. I ordered the grooms to carry the painter to the workplace next to my bedroom, where we made up a pallet for him, explaining that he was a holy man of our family taken ill while my parents were away. I caught Erila's sharp look but ignored it. The alternative was to quarter him with the servants and, while his Latin ramblings might have been safe enough there, if he started screaming about the power of the Devil in Tuscan it would be wiser to have him out of earshot of believers.

Once he was settled we called for the groom's elder brother, Filippo, to tend to him. He was a sturdy young man, born with ruptured eardrums, which made him appear slower and more stupid than he actually was. But it also gave his dumb strength a kind of gentleness, and as such he was the only one of my husband's servants that Erila had had any time for. In the months since we arrived she had taught herself enough signing to make him her willing slave (though how she paid him for his services I did not ask). Now she gave him instructions to start preparing a bath for the painter before stripping him out of his clothes. From her room she brought her medicine pouch, passed on from her mother, which even as a child I remember had the smell of the exotic about it. Had her mother had the wisdom to cure stigmata of the mind as well as the hands?

"Tell him we're going to wash and bandage his hands," Erila said quickly. "Make sure he understands."

He was sitting in the chair where they had left him, his body slumped forward, his eyes staring at the floor. I went up to him and crouched by his side. "You are safe now," I said. "We will look after you. Tend your hands and make you feel better. Nothing bad will happen to you here. Do you understand?"

He did not respond. I looked up at her. She gestured me to the door.

"What if—"

"—he makes a fuss? Then we'll crack his skull for him. But one way or another he'll be washed and fed before you come near him again. You can use the time to think up some fancy story for your husband. Because I don't see how the holy relative crap is going to work for him."

And with that she pushed me from the room.

THE FIRST FEW DAYS WERE THE WORST. WHILE THE HOUSEHOLD tiptoed around us, the gossip was noisier than any of their footsteps. For his part the painter lay in a kind of stupor, mute yet in his own way rebellious. While he had allowed Erila and Filippo to bandage his hands and bathe him, he still refused food. Her diagnosis was blunt and to the point.

"He can move his fingers, which means he may paint again, though no one'll ever read his life in his palms. As to the other: there's no plant or ointment I know to cure him. If he carries on not eating, that'll kill him quicker than any loss of God."

All that evening I lay awake listening for him. At the darkest point of the night he suffered a kind of howling fit, a sound of such deep despair, as if all the pain in the world was leaking out of him. Erila and I met at his door, but his wailing had woken others and she would not let me go in.

"But he is in such pain. I think I can help him."

"You'd do better to help yourself," she spit at me. "It is one thing for a husband to break the rules of propriety, another thing entirely for the wife. They are his servants. They've had neither the time nor the wish to grow to love you for your willfulness. They'll betray you, and the scandal will run like a line of fire through both your lives. Go back to bed. I'll see to him, not you."

And because her words scared me, I did.

The next night the crying, when it came, was much softer. I had been awake reading so I heard it immediately but, mindful of her words, waited for Erila to respond. Either she was too tired or sleeping too deeply. Fearful that he might rouse the house again, I slipped out to check.

The landing was empty, Filippo lay fast asleep again outside his door, oblivious to the noise. I moved over him carefully and went in. If it was a foolish thing to do, then all I can say is I am still not sorry I did it.

Thirty-two

THE ROOM WAS LIT BY A SMALL OIL LAMP, ITS GLOW tender like the candlelight in the chapel that night, the smell of paint and the paraphernalia of my work all around. He was lying on the bed, staring straight up into space, sorrow and emptiness like a lake around him.

I walked over and smiled down at him. His cheeks were wet but the crying had stopped. "How are you, painter?" I said gently.

His eyes saw me but made no connection.

I sat myself on the edge of the bed. In the past he would have flinched away from my closeness, but now he didn't react. I could not tell whether his apathy was weakness or the paralysis of despair. I thought of myself on my wedding night, and how my whole world had lain in shattered fragments around me, and how, when my mind could no longer work, my fingers had taken over. But he had deliberately mutilated his one means of salvation. His hands lay awkwardly on the cover, the bandages neat and unstained. But whether or not they would allow him to hold a pen I didn't know.

When there are no pictures, all that is left are words.

"I have brought you something," I said. "If you are to be swallowed up by the Devil, you might as well hear from others who have fought the same battle."

I picked up the volume I had been reading when his cries aroused me. While it did not have Botticelli's illustrations to light it up, the very act of inscribing so many words onto paper was in itself the labor of deepest love. To which I now added my own, speaking slowly as I translated the haunting vernacular Italian into Latin, straining to find the right words with which to speak to him.

> *Midway along the journey of our life,*
> *I woke to find myself in a dark wood,*
> *For I had wandered off from the straight path.*
> *How hard it is to tell what it was like,*
> *This wood of wilderness, savage and stubborn.*
> *Even the thought of it brings back all my old fears.*
> *A bitter place, death could scarce be bitterer....*

I read on through the first canto of the *Inferno*, with its forests of despair and wild animals of fear, but always leading to that first glimpse of the sunlit hill above and a vestige of hope.

> *The hour was early in the morning then,*
> *The sun was climbing up with those same stars*
> *That had accompanied it on the world's first day,*
> *The day Divine Love set their beauty turning:*
> *So the hour and sweet season of creation*
> *Encouraged me to think I could get past....*

I glanced up as I took a breath and saw that his eyes had closed. I knew he was not asleep. "You are not alone, you know," I said. "I think many people at some point in their life feel darkness around them, as if they have fallen from the hand of God, slipped through His fingers onto the rocks below. I believe Dante felt that too. I think his great talent somehow made it harder for him. As if more was expected of him because so much was given. But if he could find his way back again, so can we all."

In truth I, like my husband, had found hell more familiar to enter than paradise, but there had been some moments where the light had always warmed my soul. I went looking for them now in the hope that they might warm his too.

"When I was young," I said, to cover the silence as I searched, "I used to think that God was light. I mean...people would tell me that He was everywhere, but I could never see Him. Yet those who were filled with Him were always painted with a halo of golden light around them. When Gabriel spoke to Mary, his words came into her breast on a river of sun. I used to sit as a child and watch the sun come through the windows at certain times of the day, studying the way it would splinter through the glass and send light spots over the floor. I would think of it as God dividing Himself into a shower of goodness, that each pinprick of light contained the whole world and God, as well as itself. I remember that it used to make my mind shake, just trying to hold on to the thought of it. Later, when I read Dante, I found some verses in *Paradiso* that seem to say the same thing...."

I was still looking when he started to speak.

"Not light," he said quietly. "For me it wasn't light."

My fingers paused on the page.

"It was cold."

He halted.

"Cold?" I said. "How?"

He took a deep breath, as if it were the first he had taken for a very long time, and then let it out again without speaking. I waited. He tried again, and this time the words came through.

"It was so cold. In the monastery. Sometimes the wind came from the sea with ice in it.... It could freeze the skin off your face. Once the snow was so deep we couldn't get out of the doors to the woodshed. A monk jumped from a window. He sank into a drift and took a long time to get up. That night, they made me sleep next to the stove. I was small, thin, like a piece of birch bark. But then the stove went out.

"Father Bernard took me into his cell.... It was he who first gave me chalk and paper. He was so old his eyes looked as if he was crying. But he was never sad. In winter he had fewer blankets than the others. He said he didn't need them because God warmed him."

I heard him swallow, his throat dry with the talking. Erila had left some sweetened wine on the bedside table. I poured him a small glass and helped him to sip it.

"But even Father Bernard was cold that night. He laid me down on the bed next to him, wrapped me in an animal skin, then in his own arms. He told me stories about Jesus. How His love could wake the dead and how with Him in one's heart one could heat the world.... When I woke it was light. The snow had stopped. I was warm. But he was cold. I gave him the skin but his body was stiff. I didn't know what to do. I got out a piece of paper from his chest under the bed and drew him, lying there. His face had a smile on it. I knew that God had been there when he died. That now He was in me, and because of Father Bernard I would be warm forever."

He swallowed again, and again I lifted the glass to his mouth. He took another sip, then lay back down and closed his eyes. We sat together in the monk's cell for a while, waiting for death to turn into life again. I thought of the chest under Father Bernard's bed, and from my worktable I brought paper and chalk sharpened in readiness for the moment when his fingers might work again.

I placed them on his lap.

"I want to see what he looked like," I said firmly. "Draw him. Draw your monk for me."

He looked down at the paper, then at his own hands. I watched the ends of his fingers curl. He pulled himself up in the bed. He moved his right hand to the fat pebble of chalk and tried to cup his fingers over it. I saw him wince with pain. I used the book as a rest for the paper and put it on his knees.

He looked up at me. The despair moved across his face again.

I hardened my heart to his pain. "He gave you his warmth, painter. It's the least you can do for him before you die."

He started to move his hand across the page. The line began, then slipped. The chalk dropped and fell to the floor. I picked it up and put it back into his grasp. Gently I cupped the back of my hand over his, lacing my fingers through his, careful not to touch the wound, offering my muscles as ballast when he came to push the chalk. He let out another sharp breath. I made the first few strokes with him, letting him guide the line. Slowly, painstakingly, the outline of a face grew underneath our strokes. After a while I felt his fingers strengthen and took mine away. I watched as despite the pain he completed the drawing.

An old man's face appeared on the page, his eyes closed, a half smile on his lips, and while it did not quite glow from the love of God, neither was it frozen in emptiness.

The effort cost him, and when he finished and the chalk fell from his fingers his skin was gray with the pain.

I plucked some bread from the table and soaked it in wine, then put it to his lips.

He took it in and chewed slowly, coughing slightly. I waited till he swallowed, then fed him some more. Little by little, bite by bite, sip by sip.

Eventually he shook his head. Too much and he would be sick with it. "I'm cold," he said at last, his eyes still closed. "I'm cold again."

I climbed onto the bed and lay down by his side. I put my arm underneath his head and he turned away from me, curling in on himself, like a child in my grasp. I wrapped myself around him. We lay there and he grew warm in my arms. After a while I heard his breathing even out and felt his body go slack against me. I felt peaceful and very happy. If I hadn't been scared that I too might fall asleep, I think I might have lain there till early morning and slipped out before the household woke.

I started to move stealthily, pulling my right arm gently from under his head to extricate myself. But the movement disturbed him and he moaned slightly, rolling over in his sleep, pinning me further to the bed with the weight of his shoulder and head and throwing his other arm over my body.

I waited for him to settle before trying again. In the glow of the oil lamp his face was close to mine now. While hunger had sharpened his features, his skin seemed almost translucent, more like a girl's than a boy's. His cheeks were hollow, though strangely his lips remained full. I could chart the rise and fall of his lungs by the heat of his breath on my face. Erila and Filippo had done a good job: his skin smelled of camomile and other herbs and his breath had the tang of the sweet wine to it. I stared at his lips. My husband had once pecked me on the cheek while leaving me at my doorway. That was the only kiss I would ever feel in my life from a man. I would be prodded and poked until I produced an heir, but when it came to tenderness or passion I would remain a virgin. Or, to quote my husband, my pleasure would be my own affair.

I leaned over and moved my face nearer to his. His breath came in warm sweet waves. This time the closeness of him did not make me shake. Instead, it made me bold. His body was so dry I could see cracks in the surface of his skin. I put my fingers into my mouth to moisten them. My saliva was hot and secret, a transgression in itself. I ran the tips of my wet fingers lightly over his lips. The touch of him sent a sharp shock down into the pit of me, but thrilling, like the feeling I had had when I discovered my own injury inside me. I could hear my heart thumping in my ears, as in the afternoon when I had looked for God in the rays of sunlight and not found Him. Not all warmth has revelation built into it. Some you have to find yourself. I moved my fingers from his face down to his chest. The robe they had found for him was too big for his emaciated body and his shoulders were bare. My fingertip was the finest of brushes. I remembered the exhilaration of the bright line of my own blood that night in the darkness and imagined colors flowing out of me onto him, his skin turning to trails of indigo blue or wild saffron under my finger. His flesh was hot. He murmured at my touch, stirring in his sleep. My fingers stopped, hovered, then moved again. The saffron turned to hot ocher, then deep purple. Soon he would be alive with color.

I moved my mouth closer to his. And lest you are in any doubt, I should tell you that I knew absolutely what I was doing. By which I mean that I and the doing of it were one. And I was not afraid. My lips met his, and their fleshiness made me turn over inside. I felt him stir against me and he stifled a dark groan as his mouth opened and I found my tongue moving against his.

His body was so thin it was like holding a child. My flesh flowed over him, and as our torsos met I felt his sex rise up against my thigh. Somewhere in me a spark lit up and started to grow. I tried to swallow but I couldn't find enough saliva. My whole life was present in the breath I now started to take. Once I had the air inside me what would I do with it? Would I kiss him again or use it to pull myself away from him?

I never made the decision. Because now *he* moved, pulling himself onto me and kissing me back, the tongue clumsy and eager, fat with the taste of him. Suddenly we were together, fumbling and rolling breathlessly, my insides on fire, my skin like a raw nerve, and what followed was all so quick, his fingers on my flesh so muddled and so clumsy, that when he found his way to my sex I cannot tell whether it was shock or pleasure that I felt, though I know that it made me cry out so loud that I feared we might be discovered.

What I do know, though, is that as I pulled up my gown and helped him to find his way inside me he opened his eyes for the first time and for that brief instant we looked at each other, no longer able to pretend that what was happening was not happening. And there was in that look such intensity that I thought however wrong it might be it was not evil, and that while man might not be able to forgive us, it was surely possible that God might. And I still believe that, just as I believe that Erila was right that innocence can sometimes be as dangerous as knowledge, though there are many who would say such thoughts simply prove the depth of my damnation.

When it was over and he lay across me, winded by the second chance at life he had been given, I held him and spoke to him like a child, saying anything and everything I could to keep him from reconnecting with his fear. Until I ran out of things to say and found myself reciting what I could remember of those verses from the last canto of Dante, while choosing not to think what heresy my recitation might include:

> *In that abyss I saw how love held bound*
> *Into one volume all the leaves whose flight*
> *Is scattered through the universe around;*
> *How substance, accident, and mode unite,*
> *Fused, so to speak, together, in such wise*
> *That this I tell of: one simple light.*

Thirty-three

IN MY ROOM I WASHED MYSELF. IF I HAD HAD TIME I might have thought a million thoughts.

"Where have you been?"

I spun around. "Oh my God, Erila, you scared me!"

"Good." I had never seen her so angry. "Where were you?"

"I ... er ... The painter woke. I thought you were asleep. So ... I went to see if he was all right."

She looked at me, her contempt writ large. My hair was messed and I knew my face was flushed. I put down the cloth and arranged my gown, keeping my eyes on the floor. "I ... um ... I managed to get him to take a little food and wine. He's sleeping now."

She moved fast, grabbing me by the shoulders and shaking me so hard that I cried out. I had no memory of her ever hurting me before. When the shaking stopped she kept her grip on my arms, her fingers digging deep into my flesh. "Look at me." She shook me again. "Look at me!"

I looked. And she held my eyes, as if she couldn't quite believe what she was seeing.

"Erila," I said. "I—"

"Don't lie to me."

I stopped mid-sentence.

She shook me again, then just as suddenly let me go. "Didn't you hear a word I said to you? What? You think I do all this for my own good?"

She grabbed the flannel from where it had fallen by the basin and dipped it in the water. She pulled up my gown and started to flannel my skin, over my breasts and stomach and down my legs and in between, even into my cleft, rough, hurting me, like a mother with a recalcitrant child. After a while I started to cry, as much from fear as hurt, but it didn't stop her.

When she finally finished she tossed the flannel back into the bowl and threw me a towel. She watched while I sullenly dried myself, whimpering, swallowing down the tears, trying not to feel shame.

"Your husband is back."

"What? Oh, my Lord. When?" And we both heard the panic in my voice.

"An hour or so ago. You didn't hear the horses?"

"No. No."

She gave a loud snort. "Just as well I did then. He's asking for you."

"What did you say?"

"That you were tired and sleeping."

"Did you tell him?"

"Which bit of it? No, I didn't say anything. But I'm sure the servants will, if they haven't already."

"Good," I said, trying to sound reassured. "Well, I . . . I'll talk to him tomorrow."

She stared at me for a moment. Then shook her head in clear exasperation. "You don't understand, do you? Dear God, how's it possible that between your mother and me we didn't teach you. Women can't do the same things as men can. It doesn't work like that. They get destroyed by them."

But I was scared now and it suddenly felt that those who weren't with me were against me. "He told me my life was my own," I said angrily. "It was part of the bargain."

"Oh, Alessandra, how can you be so stupid? You don't have a life. Not like he does. He can fuck what he likes when he likes. No one will ever accuse him. But they will accuse you."

I sat chastened. "I . . . I didn't—"

"No. Not again. Don't lie to me again."

I looked up. "It just happened," I said quietly.

"Just happened? Ho!" She blew out her cheeks, half laughter, half fury. "Yes. Well, it always does."

"I didn't . . . I mean, no one need know. He won't tell. Neither will you."

She sighed angrily, as if she were dealing with a child to whom she had told the same fact six hundred times already. She turned on her heel and paced the room, back and forth, marching out her anxiety. Finally she stopped and turned to me.

"Did he come?"

"What?"

"Did he come?" She shook her head. "If your street sense were as fast as your mind you could rule the city, Alessandra. Did his fluid come inside you?"

"I . . . er . . . I'm not sure. Maybe. I think so."

"When did you last bleed?"

"I don't know. Ten days, maybe two weeks ago."

"When did your husband last poke you?"

I dropped my head.

"Alessandra." She hardly ever called me by name, but now she couldn't stop it. "I need to know."

I looked up at her and started to cry again. "Not since . . . not since the wedding night."

"Oh, sweet Jesus. Well, he had better do it again. Soon. Can you arrange that?"

"I don't know. We haven't talked about it for a while."

"Well, talk about it now. And get it done. From now on you

don't go near the painter without a chaperone in the room. You hear me?"

"But—"

"No! There are no buts. The two of you have been star-crossed ever since you first set eyes on each other, only you were too young to know it. Your mother should never have let him in the house. Well, it's too late now. You'll live. And if he's able to find your hole, I expect he'll crawl his way back into life again. It's the kind of resurrection that often sparks an appetite in men."

"Oh, Erila, you don't understand; it wasn't like that."

"Oh, no? So how was it? Did he ask your permission, or did you offer?"

"I started it," I said firmly. "It was my fault."

"And what, he did nothing?" And I think she might have been relieved to find my spirit back again.

I gave a small shrug. She looked darkly at me one more time, then came over and pulled me roughly into her arms, hugging me tight and clucking over me like a mother hen. And I knew that if she ever left me again then so would my courage.

"Idiot, stupid girl." She murmured sweet insults into my ear, then held me at arm's length and stroked my cheek and swept my tousled hair back from my face to study me better. "So," she said softly. "You did it? At last. How was it? Did you hear the sweetness of the lute string?"

"I...Not really," I whispered, though I knew I had felt something.

"Well, that's because you have to do it more than once. They learn slowly, men. They're all fury and fumble and hot haste. Most of them don't get any better at it. They just move on. But there are occasional ones who have the humility to learn. As long as you don't let them know you're teaching them. But first you have to find your own pleasure. Can you do that?"

I laughed nervously. "I don't know. I...I think so. But...I don't understand, Erila. What are you telling me?"

"I'm telling you that if you're going to break the rules, you have to learn to do it better than anyone—*anyone*—who keeps them. That's the only way you beat them at their game."

"I don't know if I can do that...unless you help me?"

She laughed. "When did I not? Now get into bed and sleep. You're going to need your wits about you tomorrow. As are we all."

Thirty-four

H E WAS SITTING AT THE TABLE, READING AND DRINKING wine. The morning was young but the heat was already strong. We had not seen each other for many weeks. I didn't know how much I might have changed, though that morning when I studied my face in my mirror glass I could not see any obvious difference. He, on the other hand, was altered. The lines around his mouth were more prominent, pulling his face into a permanent scowl, and his skin was more flushed. Keeping up with my brother would put a strain on a young constitution, let alone an older one. I sat opposite him and he greeted me. I had no idea what he was thinking.

"Hello, wife."

"Hello, husband."

"You slept well?"

"Yes, thank you. I am sorry I was not here to meet you."

He made a dismissive wave of the hand. "You are fully recovered now?"

"Yes," I said. Then, after a while, "I have been painting."

He lifted his eyes, and I swear I saw pleasure there. "Good." He looked back down at his papers.

"Is my brother with you?"

He glanced up. "Why?"

"I . . . er, I would like to greet him if he is."

"No, no. He is home. He is not well."

"Nothing serious, I hope."

"I think not. Just a touch of the fever."

I would not get such a good opening again. "Sir, I have something to tell you."

"Yes?"

"We have a visitor in the house."

This time he looked up. "So I've heard."

I told it simply, fashioning it into a story about art and beauty: the wonders the painter could create and the fear that he would not be able to do so anymore. I think I did as good a job as I could, though I know I was more nervous than I might have wished. He never took his eyes off me once, even when the silence grew between us after I had finished.

"Alessandra . . . You remember our first conversation, yes? On our wedding night."

"Yes."

"So you will remember that I asked a number of things from you then, to which I remember you agreed. And one of those things was discretion."

"Yes, but—"

"Do you really think this was a discreet act? To bring a crazed man halfway across town in a cart at night, to the palazzo from where your husband is absent, and house him in a room next to your own?"

"He was ill—" I broke off. I knew there was no point. By Erila's own rendition of the rules I had forfeited any sense of right. "I'm sorry," I said. "I can see that it might compromise you. Even if he isn't—"

"What he is or isn't is not the point, Alessandra. The point is how it is perceived. That, my dear, is what this city is all about now. Not reality but perception. You are clever enough to know that as well as I."

This time he let the silence grow.

"He cannot stay," I said after a while, making it a fact rather than a question.

"No, he cannot."

"I...er...I believe he is a little better anyway." I had already heard from Erila that he had taken some sustenance that morning. "In which case he will be eager to return to my parents' house. He has work to finish. He is a wonderful painter, Cristoforo. When you see his apse finished, you will understand."

"I'm sure I shall." He took a sip of the wine. "We will talk no more about it." He put down the glass carefully and sat for a moment watching me. "Now, I have something to tell you." He paused. "Yesterday two acquaintances of mine were arrested on suspicion of indecent fornication. They had been accused through the denunciation box in Santa Maria Novella. Their names are of no importance, though you will hear them soon enough because they are from good families." He paused. "Though not as good as ours."

"What will happen to them?"

"They will be interrogated and tortured in an attempt to verify the accusations and to gain more names as to their associates. Neither of them have direct reason to implicate me, but—well, once the thread starts to unravel, the garment can come apart very fast."

No wonder my transgression had angered him. On the other hand, if I had been Erila I would surely start looking for potential as well as disaster in such a moment.

"Well, sir, maybe we should find a way to protect you more." I paused. "Would a pregnant wife do anything to revive your reputation?"

He smiled wryly. "It would certainly do it no harm. But you are not pregnant, unless I mistook your slave's words. And she seemed to make herself very clear."

"No," I said, "I am not," remembering Erila's lie. "But if I can conceive once, I can conceive again." I let the silence grow just a little. "It is a good time for me now."

"I see. And you would feel ... content about that?"

I looked at him directly and my gaze did not waver. "Yes," I said. "I would."

And I got up and slowly leaned across the table and kissed him lightly on the forehead before leaving the room and returning to my own.

I SHALL NOT BORE YOU WITH DESCRIPTIONS OF OUR SECOND experience of intercourse. My reticence is not meant to tease or intrigue. If there were more to report than the first time I would gladly disclose it. The older I grow the more sure I become that the silence surrounding such matters breeds only more hesitation and misunderstanding. But there was no misunderstanding between us then. Ours was a business partnership between husband and wife. And there was enough respect and care so at least I felt more of an equal.

Unlike the first time, he did not leave immediately. Instead we sat almost companionably together for a while, taking refreshments and talking of art and life and matters of state. And thus as we relaxed we gained some mutual pleasure from our union again, though it came from the caress of words rather than skin.

"When did you hear this? It isn't common gossip yet."

"No? Well, it will be soon enough. Such things can't be kept secret for long."

"Will Savonarola obey?"

"Put yourself in his place, Alessandra. You are the undisputed leader of the city. Florence hangs on your every word. The pulpit is a better place to govern from than the Signoria. Then your enemy, the pope, forbids you to preach on pain of excommunication. What would you do?"

"I think it would depend on whose judgment I feared more, the pope's or God's."

"You wouldn't think that it was heresy to suggest a difference between the two?"

"Well, *I* might think that, yes. But I am Savonarola for the sake of this argument. And he makes no such distinction. God comes first for him. Though"—I broke in on myself—"he is not a fool when it comes to matters of state. But then, neither is the pope."

"So would it interest you further to know that there is a carrot as well as a stick?"

"Which is?"

"A cardinal's hat if he agrees."

"Oh!" I thought about it. "No. He won't take it. He may be mad for God, but he is not a hypocrite. He despises the corruption of the church. A cardinal's hat would be like taking the thirty pieces of silver to betray the true Christ."

"Well, we shall see."

"Cristoforo, how do you know all this?" I asked admiringly.

He paused. "I do not spend all my free time whoring with your brother."

I was taken aback. "But . . . but I didn't think you were involved in such things," I said, remembering my mother's analysis of him.

"At times like this that is the best way to be involved, wouldn't you say?" He paused. "The safest opposition is one that doesn't exist until the right moment."

"In which case I think you should be careful whom you confide in."

"I am," he said, looking at me keenly. "Do you think I have made a mistake?"

"No." My voice was firm.

"Good."

"Nevertheless, you must be careful. This involvement makes you a political enemy as much as a moral one."

"That is true. Though I suspect when they light the straw under me it will not be my politics they are burning."

"Don't speak like that," I said. "That won't happen. However powerful he is, he can't defy the pope forever. There will be many devout Florentines who would feel uncomfortable listening to the preachings of an excommunicated friar."

"You're right. Though the pope will need to pick his time. Too soon and it will only encourage further rebellion. He must wait till the cracks start to show."

"He had better have a long life then," I said. "I see no cracks."

"In which case you are not looking carefully enough, wife."

"You should have been on the streets when his warriors stopped us with the painter." I saw his face darken. "It's all right. They had no idea who we were. Erila scared the wits out of them by evoking French boils."

"Ah, yes, the boils. So our saviors, the French, are shown to have brought more with them than civic liberty."

"Yes, but that's hardly enough to dent his power."

"Not on its own, no. But what if summer continues as hot as the winter was cold? What if there is no rain and the crops fail? We are too pious to pursue prosperity now and the city doesn't have as much fat to live off as she did. And for all his godly army, there is still a madman running round the place using people's intestines as necklaces."

"There's been another body?"

He shrugged. "It is not common knowledge. The watchmen at Santa Felicita found human remains splattered over the altar yesterday morning."

"Oh..."

"Yet when they came back with help they were gone."

"You think his supporters got rid of the body?"

"What body? Reality and perception, remember? When he was in opposition, such desecration was a gift from heaven. Now it smacks of anarchy. Or worse. Think about it. If Florence is godly but God is cruel to Florence, it will only be a matter of time before the friar's supporters start publicly questioning if his is the right kind of piety."

"You think this or you know it?" I said. Because even an opposition that doesn't exist must be in touch with voices from within as well as without.

He smiled. "We shall see. Tell me, Alessandra, how do you feel?"

How did I feel? I had slept with two men in the last few hours. One had fed my body, the other had fed my mind. If Savonarola was indeed God's envoy on earth, then I should already be feeling the flames licking at my feet. But instead I was surprisingly calm.

"I feel . . . full," I said.

"Well, I have heard that summer is a ripe time for conception, if husband and wife meet in respectful love rather than lust." He paused. "So. Let us pray for the future."

THE PAINTER LEFT EARLY THE NEXT MORNING. ERILA SAW HIM before he went. She told me later that he was calm and civil to her and let her tend his hands. The wounds were starting to heal and, while he was still weak, he had eaten enough to give him a certain alertness, as if some of his spirit were returned to him. The last thing she did was to give him the keys to the chapel. My parents were not due home for some weeks; the latest news was that my father was improving with the waters. Either he would find the will and the strength to rework the frescoes or he would not. I could do nothing more to help him now.

After he was gone, I lay in my room wondering which child I would like more: one who had an aptitude for politics or for painting.

PART III

Thirty-five

M Y HUSBAND WAS PROVED RIGHT ABOUT MANY THINGS IN the months that followed, not least the weather. The summer roared on, steamy and fetid as a horse's breath, and the city grew rank with it. Where two years before we had seen the pews from the church of Santa Croce floating down toward the cathedral as the spring rains came in, now those same streets were producing dust storms as the carts rattled by.

In the country, the burgeoning olives shriveled tight as animal droppings and the ground was so hard it might as well have been frozen. As the heat progressed through August into September the word *drought* began to be replaced by the whisper of famine. With no water to wash their whiteness, Savonarola's Angels began to smell less pure. But then they had less to police. It was too hot to sin. It almost felt too hot to pray.

The pope did exactly as my husband had predicted and ordered Savonarola to stop preaching. The private offer of a cardinal's hat had been dismissed with a public utterance that another scarlet hat would suit him better, "one red with blood." Still, Savonarola understood the politics of the moment enough to retire to his cell to ask for God's guidance. Even my husband applauded his acumen, but whether it was politics or sincerity it was impossible to know. For a holy man he was a complex mix of arrogance and humility.

The weather, the power struggle—my husband had predicted it all. He was also right about early summer. It proved a good time for conception.

I lay in my darkened room, throwing up the contents of my stomach day and night into a bowl beside my bed. I was sicker than I had ever been in my life. It had begun two weeks after I failed to bleed. I woke up one morning and tried to get out of bed and, as my legs gave way from under me, so my stomach arrived in my mouth and then out onto the floor. I couldn't even make it to the door. Erila found me there later, retching up saliva because by that time there was nothing else to retch.

"Congratulations."

"I am dying."

"No, you're not. You're pregnant."

"How can that be? This is not a baby, it is a disease."

She laughed. "You should be glad. This level of sickness means the pregnancy is well founded. Women who feel nothing often bleed it away before the end of the third moon."

"And the lucky ones?" I said, between retches. "How long does it last?"

She shook her head, mopping my head with a wet cloth. "Thank God for your build," she said cheerfully. "It will serve you well."

I became consumed by sickness. There were days when I could barely speak, I was so focused on the rise of the saliva level in my mouth. It had its uses. I did not think of the painter, his fingers on the wall or the feel of his body against mine. I did not wonder about my husband or even resent my brother. And for the first time in my life I did not yearn for my freedom. The house was already too big a world for me.

My illness did wonders for my standing with the servants.

Where before I had been cocky and full of myself, now I could barely walk. They stopped whispering about me behind my back and started providing bowls at strategic places around the house so I could vomit wherever the urge took me. They even came to me with suggestions. I ate garlic, chewed gingerroot, and drank earth tea. Erila combed every apothecary in the city for remedies. She spent so long in the Landucci shop next to Palazzo Strozzi that she struck up a relationship with its owner, a man of loquacious gossip to match her own. He sent back a poultice filled with herbs and dried bits of dead animals to lay across my stomach. It smelled worse than my vomit, though it seemed to soothe me for a few days. But only a few days. My husband, who was busier than ever on matters that weren't supposed to exist, became so worried he brought in a physician. He gave me a potion that made me throw up more.

By the middle of September I had been sick for so long that even Erila stopped being jaunty with me. I think she feared I might die. I was so sick there were times I would almost have welcomed it. I became morose in my suffering.

"Do you ever wonder about this baby?" I said to her one night as she sat by my bed, fanning away the awful heat that clung to my skin like a sodden blanket.

"Wonder what?"

"If my sickness isn't some kind of punishment. A sign. That maybe this is really the Devil's child."

She laughed. "And if it is, when did you find time to fornicate with *him* that night?"

"I mean it, Erila. You—"

"Look. You know the worst thing that could happen to you? Your life could become peaceful and quiet and give you nothing to think about. You attract drama like flies to a dog's corpse. And unless I am much mistaken you always will. It's both the wonder and the sorrow of you. But as to the Devil's child...take it from me. If he wished to sire an heir in this city, there are a thousand candidates more deserving than you."

That week my sister came to visit. The news of my humiliation must have been common knowledge. "Oh, look at you! You look awful. Your face has gone quite scrawny. Still, you did always like getting attention." She was pregnant again and eating for two. But she hugged me hard enough for me to know that she was worried about me. "Poor thing," she said. "Never mind— before long you'll be sipping sweet wines and tasting roasted pigeon. Our cook has a recipe for the most delicious plum sauce."

I felt the saliva level rise in my mouth and wondered if, given my formidable aim these days, I might be able to vomit straight into her lap or just over her shoes.

"How is Illuminata?" I asked, to keep my mind off such sport.

"Oh, she thrives in the country."

"Don't you miss her?"

"I saw her at the villa during August. But she grows better away from the city than she would here in the heat and the dust. You have no idea how many children are succumbing to the weather. The streets are full of tiny coffins."

"Have you seen our brothers?"

"You don't know? Luca is a brigade commander now."

"What does that mean?"

She shrugged. "I have no idea. But he has three dozen Angels underneath him and he has even had an audience with the friar."

"I knew someone in the family would be honored eventually," I said. "And Tomaso?"

"Oh, Tomaso! You haven't heard?"

I shrugged. "I've been a little indisposed."

"He is ill."

"Not pregnant, I hope," I said sweetly.

"Oh, Alessandra!" and she laughed so much that her cheeks wobbled. I could live off that much fat for weeks, I thought. She gave a simpering little sigh. "Well, when I say ill, what I really mean is"—she lowered her voice to a dramatic whisper—"he has the boils."

"Oh, really!"

"Oh, really. You should see him. They're all over him. Ugh. He has locked himself in the house and refuses visitors."

For the first time in two months, I began to feel a little better.

"Well, where did he get those, I wonder?"

She dropped her eyes. "You know the rumor, don't you?"

"No," I said.

"About him."

"What is that?"

"I can't even bring myself to name it. Suffice it to say that there are those accused of the same thing who will lose their noses and the skins off their backs once their trials are complete. Can you believe that men could do such things?"

"Well," I said, "I suppose there must be sin for God to grant forgiveness."

"Our poor mother," she said. "Can you imagine the shame? She returns from months in the country nursing Father back to health to find her own son is ... well, all I can say is thank God there are some of our family walking in righteousness."

"Yes, indeed. Thank God."

"Aren't you glad you went the right way now?"

"With all my heart," I said softly. "When did you say she got back?"

I SENT ERILA TO ASK FOR MY MOTHER'S ATTENDANCE ON ME THAT same afternoon. Our feud had lasted long enough, and whatever it was she had known or not known I had need of her common sense now. The fact that she might bring news of the painter was, I swear, only something I thought about afterward.

I made an effort for her visit. Erila dressed me and I had her set two chairs in the sculpture gallery. The wind moved a draft through this great room and I thought she would appreciate the way the beauty of the stone remained so cool in the haze of the heat. I remembered the day we had sat in my bedroom at home, discussing my marriage. It had been hot then too, though nothing like now.

Erila showed her in and we stood and looked at each other. She had aged since our last meeting. That perfectly straight back had just the hint of a stoop in it, and though she was still a handsome woman it seemed to me at least that the light in her eyes had dimmed a little.

"How far into the pregnancy are you?" she said, and I could tell she was shocked by my appearance.

"I last bled in July."

"Eleven weeks. Hah! Have you tried mandrake and semilla?"

"Er, no. I think it is probably the only thing I have *not* tried."

"Send Erila out for some now. I will make up the drink myself. Why did you not send for me earlier?"

But I did not have the energy to start this now. "I . . . I did not want to worry you."

She was braver than I. "No. That is not the reason. You were so fierce with me. I didn't force you to marry him, you know."

I frowned.

"No, it has to be talked about. There will be no future if we do not. Tell me this. Even if I had known—and I did not—but even if I had, would that have stopped you? You were so determined to get free."

I had not thought of it before: how I might have reacted had I known. "I don't know," I said. "You really didn't know?"

"Oh, my child, of course I didn't."

"But you had seen him at court. And you reacted so strangely when I asked you about it. I—"

"Alessandra," she said, cutting me off firmly, "not everything is the way it sounds. I was very young. And despite my learning I was very ignorant. In all kinds of ways and about all manner of things."

Like myself, I thought. So she had not known after all. "So when did you find out?" I said quietly.

"About your brother?" She sighed. "I think I have both known and not known for a long time. About your husband? Three days ago. Tomaso believes he is dying. He is not, but when a man so pretty looks that ugly he mistakes it for something fatal. I think at last he has begun to understand the consequences of his actions. He is in a frenzy of pain and fear. At the beginning of this week he called in a confessor to gain absolution. Then he told me."

"Whom did he confess to?" I said anxiously, remembering Erila's stories about whispering priests.

"A friend of the family. We are safe. Or as safe as anyone is now."

We sat for a while, each of us taking in the other's revelations. I studied her tiredness. What had been my husband's memory of her? Beauty, wit, and learning. Must it always be a sin to be so confident? Must our Lord always see fit to have it knocked out of us?

"So, my child? We have come a long way since our last meeting. How is it?"

"Between him and me? As you see. We have made the marriage work."

"Yes, I do see. He spoke with me before I came to you. He is—" She stopped. "I don't know. He is—"

"A good man," I said. "I know. Strange, isn't it?"

I had wanted to talk to my mother like this for so long. To meet her woman to woman, as someone who had walked the same road before me, even if she had not passed through exactly the same places.

"And my father?"

"He is . . . he is a little better. He has learned to accept things. And that is a recovery in itself."

"Does *he* know about Tomaso?"

She shook her head.

"Well, Plautilla knows and she is outraged."

"Oh, dear Plautilla." And it was the first time I saw her smile. "She always did enjoy outrage, even as a child. At least this is for something worthwhile."

"And what of you, Mama? What do you think?"

She shook her head. "You know, Alessandra, these are such difficult times. I think God watches everything we do and judges us less by our success than by how hard we struggle when the path is rough. Do you pray as I told you? And go regularly to church?"

"Only when I am sure I will not throw up in it," I said, with a smile. "But yes, I pray."

I was not lying. I had prayed constantly over the last weeks as I had lain in bed with my stomach curdling, begging for an intercession that would leave my baby healthy and undamned, even if it could not do the same for me. There had been moments when my fear was so great I had not been able to tell what was the sickness of my body and what the sickness of my mind.

"Then you will be sustained, my child. Believe me, He hears everything that is said to Him, even when He appears not to listen."

Her words were like a temporary relief from fever. The God that ruled Florence now would have both me and the child eternally strung up by our entrails. The God I saw in my mother's eyes that afternoon had at least the capacity to distinguish gradations of guilt. I had missed her quiet shining intelligence more than I had dared let myself admit. "You know about the painter?" I said, after a while.

"Yes. Maria told me. Her words were that you were most responsible."

I laughed. "Me? Just imagine. How is he?" And for the first time in months I allowed myself to see him in front of me.

"Well, though he is still not garrulous he would seem recovered from whatever it was that ailed him."

I shrugged. "It was not so much. I think his loneliness and the burden of the work oppressed him."

"Hmm," she said, which was the sound she always made when I was a child and she hadn't yet decided whether to believe me.

"And the chapel?"

"The chapel? Oh, the chapel is wonderful, a beacon in our darkness. The Assumption on the ceiling is breathtaking. Our

Lady's face is most striking"—she paused—"for those who know the family well."

I looked down at the floor so she would not see the flush of pleasure rising in my cheeks. "Well, thankfully she is very high up. Anyway, who would recognize me now? You are not angry?"

"It is hard to be angry at beauty," she said simply. "She has such unexpected grace to her and, as you say, not many will read her as we do. Though your sister of course—"

"—will be outraged." We both smiled this time. "So. It is finished?"

"Not quite. Though he assures us it will be ready for the first mass."

"And when is that?"

"Luca is eager, Tomaso is captive for once, and Plautilla loves an event. If the mandrake and semilla work I think we could plan it for early next month. It will be good to have the family reunited again, don't you think?"

Thirty-six

T HOUGH IT WOULD BE NICE TO TELL YOU THAT MY mother's remedy had a miraculous effect on my constitution, the fact was that it worked no better than anything else. Or perhaps it simply took more time.

I was well into my fourth month and so thin that I looked more like a sufferer of famine than a woman rich with child, when, just as suddenly as it had come, the vomiting stopped. I woke up one morning and was already leaning over the bowl in readiness to spew up more of the lining of my empty stomach when I realized that the nausea had gone. My head was clear, my stomach juices quiet. I lay back against the pillow and put my hand over the swelling that as yet only I could see.

"Thank you," I said. "And welcome."

MY MOTHER HAD ASKED THAT WE COME THE DAY BEFORE SO ERILA could help with preparations and the family might spend a little time together. The summer was long over and with it had gone the scorching heat, but the drought remained. There was dirt and dust everywhere, clouds of it swirling up from wheels and horses' hooves, coating and choking passersby. Some of the people we passed looked almost as thin as I did. The stalls in the market were half empty, a testament to a failed harvest, the vegetables and fruit small and malformed. There was no sign of the snake man. The only people doing good business were the pawn merchants and the apothecaries. The boils had left their mark. Even those who were cured had the scars to show for it.

The house came out to greet us. Not the painter—but then he had always held himself apart—but Maria, Ludovica, and the rest of them. Everyone who greeted me was shocked by my appearance, though they tried, inadequately, not to show it. My mother kissed me on both cheeks and took me to the study where my father now spent all his time.

He was sitting at the table with a stack of account books in front of him and a pair of magnifying lenses on his nose. He didn't hear us come in and we stood for a moment watching him as he ran his fingers down each column, his lips moving silently as he counted, then made a flurry of notes in the margin. He looked more like one of the moneylenders on the streets than a prosperous merchant of the city. But then maybe he wasn't so prosperous anymore.

"Ah . . . Alessandra," he said when he saw me, my name coming out like a long wheeze from his chest. He stood up, and he was much smaller than I remembered, as if something at the center of him had caved in and the rest of his body curved inward to protect the hole.

We embraced, and our bones rattled together.

"Sit, sit, sit, my child. We have much to talk about."

But after we had exchanged pleasantries and he had congratulated me on my news and asked after my husband's welfare, it seemed there was little to say and his eyes began straying back to the columns of his books.

These ledgers, with their neatness and accuracy, had for many years been his pride and joy, the written evidence of our mount-

ing wealth. Now, as he looked, he seemed to keep finding mistakes, clicking his tongue angrily as he underlined them heavily,
scribbling further figures on the side.

My mother rescued me a little later.

"What is he doing?" I asked, as we tiptoed out.

"He is … he is seeing to business. As he always did," she replied
briskly. "So … now there is something else you should see."

And she took me into the chapel.

It was truly an amazing sight. Where there had been cold
stone in cold light now ran two sets of pews in fresh walnut, each
with polished carved heads at both ends. The altar was in place
with a delicate panel painting of the Nativity in the center, lit up
by a row of great candles in tall silver holders, their fiery glow
directing your eyes upward to the frescoes on the walls.

"Oh!"

My mother smiled, but as I walked toward the altar she let me
go alone, and a little later I heard the doors close behind her.
With the exception of a small piece of tarpaulin at the bottom
half of the left wall the frescoes were finished: complete, coherent, beautiful.

"Oh!" I said again.

Santa Caterina grew into her martyrdom now with gravitas
and serenity, her torture just a passing stage on her journey
toward the light, her face aglow with the same almost childish joy
that I remembered from that first Virgin on the wall of his room.

My father was portrayed to the left of the altar, my mother
opposite him on the other side. They were in profile, kneeling,
their dress somber, their gaze devout. For a man who had begun
life in a draper's shop it was a fitting elevation, but it was my
mother who caught the attention, even in profile, her eye so keen
and her posture alert.

My sister embodied the figure of the empress visiting the saint in
her cell, her wedding garments faithfully reproduced in such shining
color that she almost eclipsed the quiet beauty of the saint, while
Luca was to be found as one of her interlocutors, his bullish features

and stern gaze exuding a certain self-importance, though he would probably read it as authority. And Tomaso...well, Tomaso had got his wish. There he stood, cured of his present affliction for the purposes of posterity, strong and elegant as one of the court's most prominent scholars, a man whose dress sense was as vibrant as his mind. In generations to come, whichever family worshipped here, the young girls of the household would find their attention torn between piety and longing. How little would they know...

And me? Well, as my mother had intimated, I was in the heavens, so high that you would have to have youthful eyes and risk a crick in your neck to appreciate the depth of the likeness. But to really understand the power of the transformation, you would have to have seen what had been painted there before. The Devil was banished from his throne, all sign of cannibalism and terror lost in a shimmer of light. In his place now sat Our Lady: not so much a beauty as a substantial soul, with no sign of giraffe awkwardness, content at last with all that had been asked of her.

I stood with my head back, turning myself round and round to see how each wall reached up to the ceiling, until my head was giddy and the frescoes seemed to swim and swirl in front of my eyes as if the figures themselves were moving. There was a kind of joy in me the like of which I had not felt for so long.

And as I turned the next time he was standing there in front of me.

He was well dressed and well fed. If we lay together now, his flesh would take up more room than mine. My sickness had kept any longing at bay, but without it my fear was that my mind would be as giddy as my body.

"So? What do you think of it?" His Tuscan had less of an accent now.

"Oh, it is beautiful!" I could feel myself grinning, as if the happiness were overflowing and I could do nothing but let it pour out. "It is...it is Florentine." I paused. "And you...are well?"

He nodded, his eyes still fixed on mine as if there were a text he was intent on reading there.

"Not cold anymore?"

"No," he said softly. "Not cold anymore. But you—"

"I know," I said quickly. "It's all right.... I am better now." You must tell him, I thought. You must tell him. In case no one else has.

But I couldn't. Instead, as the words died away, we stood looking at each other, then kept on looking. If someone came in now they would surely know immediately. If someone came in... I remembered how many times I had had the same thought: his room that first time, the chapel at night, the garden... What had Erila once said to me? Innocence can spring more traps than knowledge. But in our innocence there had always been knowledge. I knew that now. I wanted to touch him so much it made my hands ache.

"So." My voice sounded strangely light, like the froth of egg whites when they are beaten into airy peaks. "Your chapel is done."

"No. Not yet. There is something still to be completed."

Now at last he put out his hand to me. As I took it my fingers slid over the thickened skin in his palm, but the scars were so rough that I couldn't be sure he would even feel my touch. He led me to the left wall, where he unhooked the remaining piece of tarpaulin. Underneath was a small blank space in the fresco, the outline of a woman sitting with her skirts full around her, her face turned to a window in which a white bird was framed looking back at her: Santa Caterina as a tender young woman. The screed plaster inside her absent image was still damp.

"Your mother told me you would be here this morning. The plasterer has just finished. She is yours."

"But... I cannot..."

My voice died away. I watched his smile grow. "You cannot what? Cannot paint a young girl who is about to defy her parents and the world in order to follow her own calling?" He picked up a brush and held it out. "In the sketches of your sister you made your father's cloth move like water. The wall is less forgiving than the page, but you of all people have no need to be afraid of it."

I stood staring at the space where Santa Caterina would be. My whole body was tingling. He was right. I knew her. Knew everything that she was feeling now: the collision of excitement and trepidation. In my mind I had painted her already.

"I have mixed ocher, skin tones, and two different reds. Tell me if there is any other shade you need."

I took the brush from his hand, and now it was impossible to know if my seasickness was about the danger of us or the challenge of her. The first stroke, and the sight of that iridescent color sliding off the brush onto the wall got me over my fear. I watched the way my wrist moved as it maneuvered the brush, the way the order and the action indelibly connected. Everything about it was so physical: the precision of each stroke, the texture of the paint as it collided with the plaster, how the two bonded and coalesced, the exhilaration as the image grew and rounded under your fingers... Oh, if I had been Fra Filippo I would never have wanted to be out of my cell.

For the longest time we did not talk. He worked next to me, preparing the paints and cleaning the brushes. And so Caterina grew into her garments, her sturdy peasant legs firm but unseen under the cloth. And her expression, when it came, spoke I hope of the courage it took to leave as well as the grace it gave her. Eventually my fingers grew numb with the tension of holding the brush. "I have to rest," I said, pulling away from the wall. And as I came up for air I felt my balance falter.

He grabbed my arm. "What is wrong with you? I knew it. You're ill."

"No," I said. "No. I am not...." I knew what I should say, but I couldn't get the words out.

We stood looking at each other again. I couldn't breathe. I had no idea what I was going to do next. We might never find ourselves alone again in our lives. We had done our courtship in this chapel, though neither of us had realized that was what it was.

"I don't—"

"I wanted—"

His voice was more urgent than mine.

"I wanted to see you. I didn't know ... I mean, when you didn't come I began to think ..."

His arms went around me, and his body was familiar to me as if all this time I had kept some living copy of it in my mind. And I felt desire—for I know now that that was what it was—flash up like a hot spring in my stomach.

The noise of the sacristy door opening flung us apart so fast that it was possible he might not have seen us. That he was in pain was obvious from the way he walked, though the feeling coming off him was more one of fury. No wonder. I was like Venus and Adonis rolled into one compared with him now. The boils had colonized his face. There were three of them, one on his left cheek, another on his chin, and the last in the middle of his forehead like the Cyclops' eye. They were fat and full of pus. He hobbled closer. Clearly he had them between his legs too, though they didn't seem to have affected his eyes. Well, we would know soon enough.

"Tomaso," I said, moving quickly toward him. "How are you? How is your illness?" And I swear there was not a shred of triumph in my voice, for surely suffering brings out the sympathy in all of us.

"Not as acceptable as yours." He looked at me steadily. "Though Plautilla was right, you do look like a scarecrow. We make a good pair now." He snorted "So. When is it due?"

"Er ... in the spring. April, May."

"So, an heir for Cristoforo, eh? Well done, you. I didn't think you had it in you."

I felt the painter stiffen at my side. I glanced at him. "You probably know," I said, in a voice that vibrated with jollity, "I am with child. But I have been ill with it, so it is yet to show."

"With child?" He stared at me. The mathematics were not hard, even for a monastery boy.

I stared back. If you love a man for his honesty, you cannot become angry when he shows it.

Tomaso stared at both of us.

"So, Tomaso, have you seen the chapel?" I said, turning to him with a fluidity that would have made my dancing teacher weep for joy. "Don't you think it is wonderful?"

"Mmm. Very nice." But he was still staring.

"Your likeness is most..."

"Flattering," he finished brusquely. "But then we had an understanding, the painter and I, didn't we? It is a wonder what secrets will do. I hear it was my sister who helped you through your...unfortunate illness. When was that? Early summer, wasn't it? How many months ago is that?"

"Speaking of secrets," I said sweetly, always the surest sign of vitriol between us, "Mother tells me you have been to confession." Come on, I thought. Leave him alone. You know you and I are the best players in this game. Anyone else gets knocked down too easily.

He scowled. "Yes... How good of her to keep you informed."

"Well, she knows how much I care for your spiritual well-being. Though it must have been a shock when you realized you weren't going to die after all."

"Yes. But I tell you, sister, it has its advantages." He closed his eyes as if savoring the moment. "As long as I am truly repentant, I am now saved. Which brings me great comfort, as you can imagine. Though I must say it makes me more intolerant toward other people's sins." And he stared again at the painter. "So tell me, how is Cristoforo?"

"He is fine. You haven't seen him?"

"No. But as you see I'm not fair company anymore."

I looked at him. I could detect the fear in his fury. How strange for a man to have been so loved and not have grown any tenderness as a result of it. "You know, Tomaso," I said, "I don't think your friendship was just about your beauty." And for a second I dropped my guard. "If it's any consolation, I do not see much of him either. He is busy these days with other matters."

"Yes, I'm sure he is." One could almost *touch* the open wound in his arrogance. I wondered for a moment if he was going to cry. "Well," he said briskly, "you and I will no doubt talk more another time. For now I have kept you occupied long enough." He gestured to the almost finished fresco. "Please. Go back to...whatever it was you were doing before I disturbed you."

We stood and watched him hobble away. When the boils burst, how much of his bitterness might drain away with their liquid? I wondered. No doubt that would depend on how disfiguring were the scars left behind. As to what he would do with his suspicions—well, worrying about that would simply make me weaker if and when it came to a fight.

I turned to the painter. How could he begin to understand what he had stumbled into? I didn't have the words, much less the stomach, to tell him.

"I should finish her skirt," I said harshly.

"No. I need—"

"Please...please, don't ask me anything. You are well, the chapel is finished, I am with child. There is much to be grateful for."

And this time it was I who ended the look. I picked up the brush and moved back to the wall.

"Alessandra!"

His voice stopped my hand. I don't think in all the time we had known each other that he had ever used my name. I turned.

"It cannot be left like this. You know it."

"No! What I know is that my brother is too dangerous to cross and we are both at his mercy. Don't you see? We must be strangers now. You are the painter; I am the married daughter. It is the only way we can save ourselves."

I turned back to the wall, only my brush was shaking too much to make the first stroke. I tightened my grip on it and willed my hand to be steady, steadier than my heart. His desire was all around me. All I had to do was turn back into it and let it envelop me. I put the brush to the wall and gave my longing to the paint.

After a while he joined me, and when my mother returned to the chapel to collect me, she found us painting side by side.

Though she did not say anything, that night she sent Erila to the servants' quarters and slept with me herself in my old bedroom, where she was so evidently restless that even I, who in the past had had so much courage for night walking, would not have dared to risk her half-open eye.

Thirty-seven

THE CONSECRATION WAS DONE BY THE BISHOP, WHO stayed for the shortest time, ate and drank liberally, and walked away with some splendid bolts of cloth and a silver communion chalice. Presumably he had somewhere to hide it all, since if the Angels got to hear of such gifts they would have had them out of his palace and on their carts before he could say Hail Mary.

The priest who took mass afterward was Tomaso's confessor. He had been a friend of my mother's family for a long time and had tutored me through my early catechism and heard my youngest confessions. God knows what sins I had embroidered for his delectation then. I had had an early penchant for drama and had sometimes wanted to appear guiltier than I really was because I thought my absolution might take up more of God's attention. Since I never quite got around to confessing to my confessions, there is an argument for saying I have been damned since childhood, but then the God that I grew up with had always been more benevolent than vengeful and I had been loved enough to believe he would continue that way. How many other families must there be in the city who now found themselves likewise wrong-footed by this new severity? Though watching the bishop pocket his rewards for doing what was, after all, God's work, it was easy to see how the battle lines had been drawn.

The service was simple: a short sermon on the grace and courage of Santa Caterina, the power of prayer, the richness of the frescoes, and the joy of the Word made paint, though the priest's ardor was mediated by the presence of Luca, who sat in the second pew like a lump of sourdough. My brother had grown fatter in the friar's service—I had heard a rumor that the threat of famine had seen a new wave of recruits to God's militia in the last few weeks—with an expanded sense of his own importance. Our conversation had been cordial, if banal, until I broached the subject of the pope's ban and the confusion it must bring to his followers, at which point Luca exploded with rage, claiming that Savonarola was the champion of the people, which meant only God had the right to exclude him from the pulpit, and he would preach again if and when he chose, regardless of any orders from Rome's wealthiest brothel keeper.

Indeed, my brother's rhetoric on the corruption of the established church was now so extreme and reasoned with such clear and fervent logic—in itself a tribute to the man who had taught him—that it seemed impossible for any compromise to be reached between the two sides. Yet if Savonarola did preach again, the pope could hardly countenance such a threat to his authority. Would he use force to crush it? Surely not. In which case would we end up with some kind of schism? While I could not bear the idea of a church that denounced art and beauty, did this really mean I approved of one that sold salvation and let its bishops and popes siphon off church wealth into the pockets of their illegitimate children? Yet schism was unthinkable. One of them would have to submit.

I glanced around at the rest of my family. My mother and father sat in the front pew, her straight back pulling him straighter. This was the moment he had dreamed about. While our wealth might be waning our heads were held high—apart, that is, from Tomaso, who sat alone, consumed by self-pity, even more self-conscious in his ugliness than he had been in his beauty. Next to him came Plautilla and Maurizio, sturdy and dull, and then my husband and me. An ordinary Florentine family. Ha! If you listened carefully you could hear the chorus of our sins and hypocrisies hissing up from our souls below.

The painter stood at the back, and I could feel his eyes upon me. We had spent the morning moving around each other like two tide pools in a river, drawn constantly close without ever seeming to merge. Tomaso watched us with hawk eyes but forgot us the instant Cristoforo appeared. The two of them met briefly in the courtyard over a groaning refreshment table, both of them as tense as racehorses, my mother and I pretending not to notice. They barely spoke to each other, and when we were called to the chapel Tomaso broke free and turned on his heel, a clear flounce to his movement. I chose not to catch my husband's eye, but I could not help noticing Luca's face as they walked passed him. I remember my mother's comment about Tomaso all that time ago: Blood is thicker than water. But was it thicker than belief?

"YOU WERE RIGHT ABOUT YOUR PAINTER." BACK HOME IN MY husband's house, we sat in his neglected garden courtyard watching the dusk fall, both of us a little nervous as to what to tell. "He has talent. Though given the atmosphere of the city he would do better to go to Rome or Venice to find his next commissions." He paused. "It's as well your spirit doesn't suffer from vertigo. How long did you sit for him?"

"A few afternoons," I said, "but it was a long time ago."

"Then I applaud him even more. He has caught both the child and the change in you. What happened to make such a man disfigure himself in so brutal a way?"

No, my husband does not miss much. "For a while he lost his belief," I said quietly.

"Ah, poor soul. And you helped him find it again? Well, you have saved something there, Alessandra. There is great sweetness to him. He's lucky the city has not corrupted him more." He paused. "There is something we must talk of now—if you do not know it already. The infection that Tomaso has…it is contagious."

"Are you telling me you are ill?" I felt my stomach turn with fear.

"No. I am telling you we both might be."

"In which case, where did *he* get it from?" I asked bluntly.

He laughed, though there was not much humor to it. "My dear, there would not be a lot of point in asking. I have been a fool for love when it comes to your brother, ever since I first set eyes on him in the back of a gambling haunt near the old bridge four years ago. He was fifteen years old then and brash as a young colt. It was perhaps unwise of me to expect that such an infatuation could ever be mutual."

"Well, I could have told you that," I said. "How long until we know for sure?"

He shrugged. "The disease is new to us all. The only hope is that people do not seem to die from it. Other than that, there are no rules and no medicines that apply. Tomaso has fallen fast, but it may just be that he contracted it early. No one knows."

I thought of the pimp hanging from Ponte Santa Trinità with his innards unraveling onto the ground, and how this had been punishment for, among other things, procuring for the French everything they desired. And it made me wonder again about the murderer. What force of rectitude must be inside him and what fury!

"But there is worse," he said softly. "Another contagion is arrived in the city."

I looked at him, and he dropped his eyes. "Oh, sweet Jesus, no. When?"

"A week, maybe longer. The first cases came to the morgue a few days ago. The authorities will try to keep it quiet for as long as they can, but it will out soon enough."

And though neither of us had said it, the word was already

loose in the air, sliding under doors, out between the window frames into the streets, into each and every house between here and the city walls, the fear of it more infectious than the disease itself. Either God was so impressed by Florentine piety that he had chosen to call the godly to him directly, or—well, the *or* did not bear thinking about.

Thirty-eight

THE PLAGUE ARRIVED AS IT ALWAYS DID, WITH NO RHYME or reason, no forewarning, and no hint of the level of damage it might cause or how long it would rage. It was like a fire that could destroy five houses or five thousand, depending on which way the wind blew. The city still bore the scars of the great purge of a century and a half before, when it had wiped out almost half the population. So many monks had died then, toppling like tenpins in their cells, that it had caused its own crisis of faith among those left behind, and the churches and convents were still littered with paintings from that time, all of them obsessed by the Last Judgment and the closeness of hell.

Yet surely Florence was different now. While the boils could be seen as a scourge worthy of sinners, even a public confession of fornication, the plague was another matter. If this was indeed God's punishment, what had we done to deserve it? It was a question Savonarola must answer.

THE NEWS OF HIS RETURN TO THE PULPIT TRAVELED AS FAST AS THE disease. I would have given anything to hear him preach, but while plague was indeed the great leveler, it had a proven fondness for those who were weak already. Had it just been me, I might have risked it for the sake of my insatiable curiosity, but I had to think for two now and in the end I compromised, accompanying Cristoforo in the carriage as far as the church to witness the throng, then going home while he went inside.

That the crowd was smaller was obvious to everyone. Of course there were good reasons for that—fear of contagion or the illness itself. It would be a reckless man who diagnosed waning influence from the attendance for one sermon. Once inside, my husband said, Savonarola's passion was undimmed, and no doubt all who heard him felt the fire of God in their bellies again. But on the streets, where his voice didn't reach, not all the people were ill. Some seemed just weary, their bellies suffering other pains, this time from hunger, so that after a while it might become hard to tell one ache from another.

The truth was that while the city still loved the friar and applauded his courage and her own closeness to God, she also wanted to be fed. Or at least be made to feel a little less miserable.

My husband's analysis on this topic was an elegant one. When the Medici had been in power, he said, because they had no more of a lifeline to God than anyone else (though a good deal more money), they had adopted a simple strategy to win the people. If they couldn't offer salvation they could at least offer spectacle, something to make even the poorest feel better, proud of their city and proud of its vision, even if that vision only extended as far as celebration. Not that such events were godless. Far from it; they were conceived in praise and gratitude to God. It was there in all of them—the jousting, the tournaments, and the parades— it was just that they wore a happy, noisy, even profligate face. And whatever might take place during the festivities, there was always the option of confession the day after. In this way for a brief period people forgot what they didn't have, and as long as things got better in the long run (or as long as they didn't get any worse), that seemed enough. Such was the color and confidence of their reign that people felt as if they had *lived* under the Medici, which was a different feeling from simply preparing to die.

Such secular celebrations, of course, were not within Savonarola's creed. There could be no carnivals or jousts in the New Jerusalem, and though he spoke passionately enough of joy when it came to God, his God was such a hard taskmaster that they were both becoming more associated with suffering. And while suffering cleanses, it can also get dreary after a time.

What better way to banish *dreary* then, than by a religious spectacle, an event that spoke of God but also served to light up one's everyday harsh existence? To make it—well, less *dreary*.

I MUST SAY THE BONFIRE OF THE VANITIES WAS AN INSPIRED IDEA. And the way Savonarola told it from the pulpit was irresistible: If Florence was suffering, it was because God had chosen her above all others and her journey had become a matter for His personal attention. As he, Savonarola, scourged and starved his body to make himself the perfect vessel for the Lord, so the city must show herself willing to make the sacrifices worthy of His great love. From the relinquishing of unnecessary wealth came exquisite blessing. What need did we have for such fripperies anyway? Cosmetics and perfumes, pagan texts, games, indecent art—all such objects and artifacts only distracted our attention and muddied our devotion to God. Give them up to the flames. Let our vanity and our resistance burn into nothing and disappear with the smoke. Into the space left would come grace. And while I am sure the friar himself never considered this, such a purging would also help ease the pain of the poor: for as well as bringing humility to those who had too much, for those with nothing, it offered the comfort that no one else would have it either.

Over the coming weeks, the vanities collected by the Angels rose up into a great eight-sided pyre in the middle of the Piazza della Signoria. Erila and I watched it grow with a mixture of awe and horror. You couldn't deny that the city felt alive again. The

building of it provided work for people who would otherwise
have grown weak from starvation. People had something to talk
about, a focus for gossip and excitement. Men and women went
through their wardrobes, children through their toys. Where
once we had flaunted ownership, now we explored the attractions
of sacrifice.

Of course, not everyone was enthusiastic to the same degree.
There were many people who, had they been left to their own
devices, might have chosen not to participate. This was where the
Angels came in, a clever move in itself because God's young
army had been somewhat underemployed of late, idle in a city
brought low by famine and illness. Some were more persuasive
than others. Savonarola had inspired certain young souls to great
rhetoric during his reign; there were a few whose words glittered
like the gold lacquer from Gabriel's mouth in the Annunciation.
I once saw one of them talk an elegant young woman into giving
up her concealed bangle and admitting to a hidden switch of
false hair. They had both parted shining from the encounter.

The Angels rolled carts through the streets, the leading one
carrying Donatello's sweet statue of the boy Jesus at its head.
They sang Laudate and hymns and visited each house or institution in turn, asking what they would like to give up. In some
places it became almost a new snobbery, as one household vied to
outdo another. In others the visits took on the edge of the Inquisition. The Angels had done their homework, seeking out the
richer families first to set a good example. If enough was given,
they thanked them and went on their way. If not, they invited
themselves in to look around. Of course the giving was voluntary,
but adolescent boys can be awfully clumsy when they are in a
hurry, and it only took a few tales of smashed Murano glass or
torn tapestries to bring out in many families a generosity born of
fear. Even when Florence had been invaded, our enemies had
behaved with more gentility, though it would have taken a brave
man to use the word *looting* in the Angels' presence.

The morning they came to our house I was sitting at an

upstairs window observing their progress down the street, their raucous singing—too many broken voices muddying the angelic ones—laid over the percussion of the cart wheels. The rules on indecent art were well known. There should be no images of naked men and women in houses where there were young girls. Since most houses had young women, even if they were servants, this could be more or less ruthlessly applied. By these standards my husband's sculpture gallery would be considered obscene. It was now behind locked doors, the key on his person, while in the courtyard a box of offerings was ready: some rich out-of-fashion clothing, some playing cards, various trinkets and fans, and a great ugly gilt mirror, which spoke more of bad taste than bad faith. I had been fearful that it wouldn't be enough (my pregnancy was making me more anxious than before), but Cristoforo was phlegmatic: While there were those in power who would almost certainly know about such collections as his, he argued, they would be careful whom they betrayed. Fortunes change quickly in a climate as volatile as the present one, he said, and clever politicians could smell dissent on a fair wind.

When they arrived at our house, we flung open the gates to them and Erila brought out a tray of refreshments while Filippo carried out the boxes.

There was a boy, maybe seventeen or eighteen, on the top of the cart, knee-deep in books and costumes, arranging the treasures to make room for new arrivals. I watched as he flung a wood panel painting of naked nymphs and satyrs to one side, the surface cracking and flaking as he manhandled it.

There were rumors that it wasn't only the patrons who were giving up their art but also the artists themselves, with Fra Bartolommeo and Sandro Botticelli leading the throng. Of course Botticelli was an old man now, more in need of the love of God than of any patron, though my husband hinted that if he had his eyes on paradise he would do better to confess to something other than sins of female flesh. For my part I couldn't help remembering Cristoforo's description of his Venus being born from the sea, and it made me glad that such paintings were locked away in the country. At least our cart's nymphs and satyrs would not be missed by history; the women's legs were entirely too short for their bodies and their flesh looked like dough before the oven.

"Hi, pretty lady. Have you anything for the flames? Any coral beads or feathered fans?"

He was a good-looking boy and had taken some trouble with his robe and haircut. In another Florence he could have been serenading me from below after a drunken night on the town. Especially since from his angle of vision there was no way he could know the size of my belly.

I shook my head, but I couldn't help smiling. Maybe it was nerves.

"What about those combs in your hair? Aren't those pearls I see on the edges?"

I felt the top of my head. Erila had braided me that morning, though with which headdress I couldn't remember. It would hardly have been ostentatious. Nevertheless I pulled them out. As I did so a section of my hair tumbled down my back. He watched it fall and grinned at me. His smile was infectious. Maybe even the Angels were getting tired of goodness. I threw the combs down to him and he caught them with a flourish.

Down below, his companions were discussing whether or not to go inside to look for more.

"Come on," he shouted, flashing me another fast smile. "If we waste time on every house we'll miss the flames." And as the cart rolled away, I swear I saw him slip the combs into his pocket.

By next morning the pyre was as big as a house. They lit the surrounding faggots at noon, and the moment could be heard all over the city, played in by a fanfare of trumpets and church bells and a swell of chanting from the great crowd gathered there. But not everyone's voice lifted up to heaven. While the piazza was full, there were some, like us, who came to watch the watchers as much as celebrate the deed.

As we stood there jostled by the throng, Erila and I saw things that made us despair. A few days before, a Venetian collector had sent a message to the Signoria, offering the fortune of 20,000 florins to save the art from the flames. His answer now came in the form of his own effigy, placed at the very top of the pyre. They had dressed him in the finest clothes, covered his head with a dozen switches of women's false hair, and placed firecrackers inside his stuffing. As the flames reached him, the crackers exploded and the effigy jiggled and yelped as the crowd roared and cheered. I later heard people swearing that they could smell singed hair, and such was the excitement and merriment that you felt it would be only a matter of time before it was human flesh we were roasting.

The chanting and prayers continued all day, led by the Dominicans and the Angels. But anyone with eyes could see there was one element of the church not represented. The Franciscans, who were feeling the cold winds of favoritism erode their traditional support among the poor, had begun to question Savonarola's great power. But they could not dent his triumph. The bonfire burned long into the night. For days to come the ashes of our luxuries rained gray snow over the city, coating our window ledges, dusting our clothes, and filling our nostrils with the sad smell of incinerated art.

And this time, when he heard, the pope excommunicated the friar.

Thirty-nine

WHEN THE DECREE REACHED HIM, SAVONAROLA TOOK HIS scourge and prayer book and locked himself in his cell in San Marco. He would do or say nothing until God had spoken to him directly. While few doubted his passion, now for the first time there were open mutterings about his judgment. Whatever his faults, the pope was still God's representative on earth, and without due respect for authority how could any state or government be safe?

While he prayed, the plague fed off the faithful. Even his own monastery was struck, the infection so rampant that many of the monks left. Meanwhile, those still committed to the New Jerusalem became even more intent, seeing enemies everywhere. The sodomites who had been arrested and imprisoned in the summer were now paraded through the streets and publicly flogged and mutilated in the main square. One of the men my husband had claimed acquaintance with, now named as Salvi Panizzi, was exposed as a continual and notorious offender and marked down for burning. But while his body might have been broken by the strappado and the rack, at the last minute the city proved nervous of such public shame and his punishment was commuted to a fine and life imprisonment in the insane asylum.

At Christmas, Savonarola gave his answer, returning defiantly to preach before a great crowd in the cathedral. His body was so thin he looked like a skeleton in robes, and his nose was as sharp as a death scythe. But his voice was cannon fire: force and flame. The pope's reply was swift. He sent ambassadors to the Signoria and demanded that they either imprison "this Son of Iniquity" or send him in chains to Rome. Disobedience would result in the whole city suffering his wrath. While the government procrastinated, Savonarola answered both of them at the same time. His words, spoken in the pulpit, slid through the city by a chain of whisperers: "Tell all those who seek to make themselves great and exalted that their seats are prepared for them—in hell. And tell them also that one of them has his seat in hell already."

Of the pope's reply to this, there is no record.

I NO LONGER REMEMBER THE EXACT CHRONOLOGY OF THE FOLLOW-ing months. There are times when sorrows and drama rain down with such force that you buckle under their weight for a while and cannot make out where you are.

What I do know is the plague hit our house early in the new year. The cook's younger daughter went down first. She was a thin little thing, no more than seven or eight years old, and though we did what we could she was dead within three days. Filippo was next. It went harder with him, and I felt such sorrow because he could neither hear our comfort nor tell us of his pain. He languished for ten days, growing weaker with each one. In the end he died in the night while no one was there. When Erila brought me the news next morning, I burst into tears.

That day my husband and I had our first proper argument. He wanted to send me out of the city, to the spa waters in the south or the hills to the east, where he said the air would be clearer. I was taking Erila's daily dose of aloe, myrrh, and saffron against the contagion and had grown stronger since the vomiting stopped, but I was still not yet my old self and for all my curiosity I think I might finally have been persuaded had not events overtaken us.

We were still locked in his room talking when the servant arrived from my parents' house.

The note was in my mother's hand:

Little Illuminata is dead from the fever. I would go to Plautilla but your father is ill and I fear contagion if I move from one house to the other. If you are well and feel fit to travel, your sister has need of you now. There is no one else I can ask. Take care for yourself and the precious young soul within you.

Plautilla had barely seen Illuminata since she dispatched her and the wet nurse to the country almost a year before. It would not be the first or last time that a child did not make it through the weaning, and my sister, who as far as I knew had spent her whole life more concerned with matters of surface than depth, already had another on the way. So I am ashamed to say that I was not prepared for what I found.

The sound of her grief met us as soon as we disembarked from the carriage. Her maidservant came running down the stairs to greet us, and both Erila and I could see the panic in her face. As we reached the top landing, the bedroom door opened and Maurizio emerged, almost haggard. The rise and fall of her wailing rolled like a storm wind after him.

"Thank the Lord you are come," he said. "It has been like this since the news came this morning. I can do nothing with her. She will not be comforted. I fear she will make herself ill and lose the baby."

Erila and I entered the room quietly.

Plautilla was sitting on the floor by the empty crib, now ready for the new baby, her hair unpinned and her dress half open at the top. Her belly was larger than mine and her face was bloated with tears. I could not remember a time in my life when I had seen her so lost and unkempt.

I sank myself down clumsily next to her, my skirts rising up around my protruding stomach, so that together we looked like two fat birds of plumage. But when I put out my hand to touch her, she veered away and her voice was shrill.

"Don't touch me! Don't touch me! I know he sent for you and I will not be comforted. I knew that woman would kill her. She had strange eyes. Maurizio must go to her house and bring back the body. I would not put it past her to palm us off with some scrawny corpse she has found in the village while she keeps Illuminata for her own. Oh, if only we had given more to the flames! I told him it was not enough, that God would punish us for our meanness."

"Oh, Plautilla, this is nothing to do with the vanities. This is the plague."

But she put her hands to her ears and shook her head violently. "No, no, I will not listen to you. Luca said you would try to sway me with your talk. You know nothing. Your head speaks and your soul suffers. I am surprised He has not brought you further down. Luca says it is only a matter of time. You should look to the baby when it comes out of you. If it is not healthy, there is no medicine that will save it."

I glanced at Erila. In loyalty to me she had never had much time for my sister, and I could feel her intolerance of this hysteria now. If it could not be stopped by reason, we would have to find some other way. I told her as much in my eyes. She nodded and moved silently out of the room.

"Plautilla, listen to me," I said, and though my voice was nowhere as loud as hers I made sure she could hear it. "If this is indeed His judgment, your grief is a vanity in itself. If you continue like this, you will bring on your own labor and have another death on your hands."

"Oh, you don't understand. You think that the way you see things is the way they are. You think you know everything. But you don't. You never did and you don't now!" And her cries grew wild again.

I let her sob some more, disturbed as much by the force of her passion against me as by her own pain.

"Look," I said more gently, as her thrashings subsided a little. "The one thing I do know is that you loved her. But you cannot blame yourself. You could have done nothing to save her."

"No, you are wrong—" She broke off. "Oh, I should never have hidden my pearls. I almost gave them—I did. But...but...they are so lovely. Luca says admitting our weaknesses will bring us closer to Him. But sometimes I don't know what He wants of us. I pray every night and I confess my sins, but I am not made of such stern stuff. They weren't even very fine pearls.... And I don't think that when I wear them I love God any less.... Are we not allowed to care for what we look like at all? Oh, I don't understand!"

But she had run out of rage and tears now, and this time when I put out my hand she did not pull away. I pushed a lock of damp hair back from her face. Her skin was glistening with sweat and tears, but she still looked—well, so comely.

"You are right, Plautilla. I don't know everything. I live too much in my head and not enough in my heart. I know that. But it seems to me that if God loves us He does not want us groveling. Or starving. Or even ugly simply for the sake of it. He wants us to come to Him, not to make it impossible to do so. Your selfishness did not kill Illuminata. She died of the plague. If it was God's will to take her, it was not to punish you but because He loved her so much. It is right that you grieve for her, but not that you destroy yourself in the process."

She was silent for a moment. "You really think so?"

"Yes, I think so. I think what has been happening to us here is mistaken. I think what it has done is to make us full of fear rather than love."

She shook her head. "I... I don't know. You were always so outspoken. If Luca were here, he would say—"

"How much do you see of Luca?"

She shrugged. "He comes this way with his boys. I don't think he feels welcome at home and... well, he was always nicer to me than you and Tomaso. I think we did not feel so stupid when we were together."

Her words cut deeper than years of her anger or scorn had ever done. How much damage had my arrogance done to my family?

"I am sorry, Plautilla," I said. "I have not been a good sister to you. But if you will let me, I will try and make it up to you from now on."

She leaned toward me and our stomachs met. I found myself imagining visions of Mary and Elizabeth: two women filled with child, their stomachs meeting as they stood together praising the mysterious ways of the Lord, a scene conjured up in a dozen wall paintings throughout the city. In a way I was right. The ways of the Lord *were* mysterious. And while there were no holy seeds in either Plautilla or Alessandra there was nevertheless a quiet revelation to be had from the love we had for each other.

So we rested together until Erila came back with a draft she had prepared. Plautilla took it from her, and we sat with her until she fell asleep.

Her face grew lovelier in repose.

"I do not believe that this is what God would want of us," I said, as we watched over her. "Pulling households and families apart. This man is destroying the city."

"Not anymore." Erila shook her head. "Now he is just destroying himself."

Forty

I T WAS WELL INTO EVENING BY THE TIME WE SET OFF FOR home. Maurizio pressed us to stay—I think he was somewhat frightened by the prospect of managing his changed wife—but both of us wanted to be in our own house and we declined politely.

The streets were different from the night we had driven the painter home. A slow drizzle was falling, and the cold made the dark seem more profound. But it wasn't just the season. The very atmosphere had shifted. In the last weeks since the excommunication an opposition was beginning to make itself felt. With the pope's might behind them, the Medici supporters were feeling strong enough to venture forth in public again, and groups of young men whose families stood to gain from a change of government had started appearing on the streets. There had even been the odd skirmish between them and the Angels. It was said it was they who had been responsible for the incident in the cathedral when someone had greased the pulpit with animal fat the night before Savonarola was due to speak. Then, during his sermon, a large chest had been dropped into the nave, smashing onto the stone floor and causing panic among the congregation. For once the forces of dissent had proved louder than his voice.

To get home from my sister's house we had to travel past the great stone frontage of the Medici Palace, now boarded up and ransacked, cross to the south of the Baptistery, and go west into the Via Porta Rossa. The road was empty, but halfway along I spotted the bulky figure of a Dominican friar sliding out from the darkness of one of the intersecting alleyways. His hood was down, his hands clasped inside his sleeves, and the dark brown of his robes made him blend in with the gloom. As we got closer he waved his arms to flag us down. We braced ourselves for an interrogation.

"Good evening to you, daughters of God."

We bowed our heads.

"You are late out on the streets, good sisters. I am sure you know such transgression is forbidden by our noble Savonarola. Are you alone?"

"As you see us, Father. But we are on an errand of mercy," said Erila quickly. "My mistress's sister lost her baby to the plague. We were bringing her comfort and prayer."

"In which case it is an ordinance sweetly broken," he murmured, his face still hidden by his hood. "And God has sent you on another errand of mercy now. There is a woman injured nearby. I found her in the doorway of a church. I need help to take her to a hospital."

"Of course," I said. "Will you ride with us and show us where?"

He shook his head. "The alley is too narrow for your wheels. Leave your carriage, and we will walk together and between us help her back."

We got down and tethered the horse. The street behind us was empty now and the alleyway he gestured toward pitch black. Such was the anxiety in us all now that even his cloth did not completely reassure me. I pushed away my fear. He moved ahead of us quickly, his hood low down, his robe slick with the rain. Not so long ago, the Dominicans walked the streets as if they owned them, yet now he seemed almost afraid of being seen. Most certainly, the tide was shifting.

From a street some way away I heard a cry. Surprise, or maybe pain. Then a gale of wild laughter. I glanced nervously at Erila. "How far is it, Father?" she said, as we crossed the Via delle Terme only to plunge back into another alley, farther into the dark.

"Here, my child, just here in Santi Apostoli. Can't you hear her cries?"

But I could hear nothing. The church's entrance loomed up to the left, its heavy doors closed fast. Sure enough, we could just make out a figure, half lost in the gloom: a woman slumped on the steps, her head low on her chest, as if she was too tired to get up.

Erila got to her before I did and crouched down. She put out a hand immediately to stop me from getting any closer.

"Father," she said quickly, "she is not ill, she is dead. There is blood all over her."

"Ah, no. Ah, me, she was moving when I left. I tried to stem the flow with my hands." He lifted up his arms, and as his sleeves fell back I could see the stains on them, even in the dark. He sank down beside her. "Poor child. Poor dear child. At least she is with God now."

With God perhaps. But it would have been a painful journey. Over Erila's shoulder I could make out the bloody mess of her chest. For the first time in many months I felt the saliva in my mouth rise up. Erila got to her feet quickly, and I could see that she too was shaken.

The friar glanced up at us both. "We must pray for her. Whatever her poor sad life, we will bring her to salvation with our songs and prayers."

He started to sing in a thick croaky voice. And suddenly there was something familiar about him: the dark cloak and the echo of a voice in another moment of darkness, one that had also made me sweat with fear. I took an involuntary step back. He broke off.

"Come, sisters." This time the tone was harsh. "Both of you, down on your knees."

But Erila now placed herself firmly between him and me. "I am sorry, Father. We cannot stay. My mistress is with child and she will catch a chill unless I get her home. These are not clement times for a pregnant woman to be on the streets."

He looked up at me as if he was seeing me properly for the first time. "With child? Is it a godly creation?" And as he spoke his hood fell back and now I caught sight of a pale spreading face like the moon's surface pitted with pockmarks. Pumice stone, I thought, a Dominican monk with a face like pumice stone who saw Florence as a sewer of evil. How long ago had Erila told me that story? Except I knew she was remembering it too.

"Indeed, most godly," she answered for me, as she pushed me farther away. "Godly and near to birth. We will send help from our house. We live right close by."

He stared at her, then dropped his head and turned his attention back to the body. He put a hand out over the woman's chest on the place where she was most bloody, and started to sing again.

We stumbled our way back to the cart. The dark was near impenetrable, and Erila kept my hand firmly in hers. Both of our palms were sticky with fear.

"What happened there?" I said breathlessly as we climbed back onto the carriage and whipped the horse into action.

"I don't know. But I tell you one thing. That woman had not been alive for some time. And he was reeking of her blood."

WE ARRIVED HOME TO FIND THE GATES TO THE HOUSE OPEN AND the groom and Cristoforo waiting in the courtyard.

"Thank God you are back. Where have you been?"

"I'm sorry," I said, as he helped me clamber down. "We were delayed in the streets. We—"

"I have men looking all over the city. You should not be out so late."

"I know. I am sorry," I said again. I put my hand out to him. He took it and held it tight, and I could feel anxiety like a fast tide washing over him. "But we are back now. Safe. Come, let us go in and sit together in the warm and I will tell you what we have seen tonight."

"There is no time for idle chat." Behind me the groom was unharnessing our horse. He waited until he was out of earshot. Erila was standing close by. I felt his hesitation and waved her away.

"What? What is it? Tell me."

"It is bad."

"Bad? What can be worse than death and possible murder?"

I am not sure he even heard me. "Tomaso is arrested."

"What! When?"

"He was taken this afternoon."

"But who—" I stopped. "Luca. Of course."

I stopped again, and in the light of the torches we stared at each other. It took me time to find the words.

"Surely it is just a warning," I whispered. "He is young. They probably mean to scare him." He said nothing. "It will be all right. Tomaso is not a fool. If he can't be strong he will be cunning."

He smiled sadly. "Alessandra, it is not a question of strength. Only a question of time." He paused. "I did not care for him enough these last few months." He said it so quietly I am not even sure if those were the words.

"This is not the moment for regret," I said urgently. "Maybe none of us have cared enough for one another. Maybe that's why all this has happened. But it is not the time to give up. You said so yourself. His is not the only voice in the city now. They wouldn't dare to come for you. Your name is too good and the tide is turning too fast among them. Come, let us go inside and talk further."

WE STAYED UP TOGETHER THAT EVENING, STARING INTO THE FLAMES as we had done during those few sweet weeks after our marriage before the acid of jealousy had leaked into me. He was the one who needed help now, and though I gave as much as I could it was not enough. Each time he fell silent I knew what he was thinking. How does it feel when you know that someone you love is in pain? When however much you close your ears you can still hear their screams? Though I could not honestly say I loved my brother, the thought of what might be happening to him now twisted my stomach. How much worse must it be for my husband, who had worshipped that perfect body as he held it in his arms? When the strappado was finished with it, it would be perfect no longer.

"Talk to me, Cristoforo. It will help to talk. Tell me. You must have thought about this moment. About what either of you would do if it came to this."

He shook his head. "Tomaso never bothered with the future. His talent was the present. He could make the moment so powerful that you might almost believe it was never going to end."

"So he will learn now. No one knows how he or she will behave until they are tested. He may surprise us both."

"He is afraid of pain."

"Which one of us is not?"

I had often wondered about the strappado. Maybe everybody does. Some days when you pass the Bargello prison in summer, when the heat has forced all the casements open, you can catch the echoes of pain rising up from inside. And you hurry past, reassured by the knowledge that it is no one you know or that they are criminals or sinners and either way there is nothing you can do. But you can still imagine.

Its purpose is to break your will by breaking your body. While there are a million other ways—pincers and fire and ropes and whips—wounds heal and scars grow over. But if it is used properly, there is no recovery from the strappado. Once your arms are tied rigid behind your back, they hoist you up and drop you again and again from a great height, and such is the pressure that it is only a matter of time before the sinews and the muscles crack and tear and your joints pop out of their sockets. Some believe it is fitting torture because it has echoes of the Crucifixion—the way Our Lord's arms would have been torn apart by the weight of His body hanging off the cross. The difference is that you do not die. Or not usually. Afterward, when they cut you down, it is said that you fall to the floor like a cloth doll. You sometimes see them, the survivors, in the streets years later: men with a kind of palsy shaking and rolling as they move, their limbs all aquiver and uneven. God has given man such fragility along with his beauty. The Bible tells us that before the Fall we felt no pain, and that our suffering is the fault of Eve's disobedience. It seems so hard to believe God would visit such a punishment for one single sin, however great. Surely pain is also there as a reminder of the transience and imperfection of our bodies as opposed to the radiance of our souls. Even so, it seems too cruel....

"Alessandra."

"I'm sorry?" My thoughts were lost in the flames and I had not heard his voice.

"You are tired. Why don't you go to bed? There is no point in both of us waiting."

I shook my head. "I will stay with you. Do you have any idea how long we have got?"

"No. One of the men they took in the summer...I saw him before his exile. He told me how it went with him. He said some of them gave names straight away, to avoid the pain. But confessions without torture are not considered reliable."

"So they confess twice," I said. "Before and after. I wonder if it is always the same names."

He shrugged. "We shall see."

I kept awake a little longer, but like Peter keeping watch over Christ's agony in the garden that last night, I found my eyes growing continually heavy. It had been such a long day and sometimes the child seems to have more power over when I wake and sleep than I do.

"Come."

I looked up and he was standing over me. I gave him my hand. He took me to my room and helped me onto the bed.

"Shall I call for Erila?"

"No, no, let her sleep. I will just lie here for a while."

And so I did.

The next thing I remember is the feel of him climbing onto the bed next to me, moving his body carefully nearer to mine until we lay side by side, like a stone couple in a chapel caught in sculpted death. He seemed at pains not to wake me, so I did not let him know that he had. After a while he stretched his arm across my belly until his palm cupped the heaviness of the child. I thought of Plautilla and the child she had lost, and of the friar and the woman's bloody stomach, and finally I thought of Our Lady, so calm and blessed about it all. And as I did so I felt the baby move.

"Ah," he said quietly. "He is getting ready for his entrance."

"Mmm," I said sleepily. "It is a good strong kick."

"I wonder what he will be like? With the right teachers he must surely have a mind like a new-minted florin."

"And an eye that can tell a new Greek statue from an ancient one." I could feel the warmth of his hand on my swollen stomach. "Still, I hope he may find it easier to love both God and art without confusion or fear. I would like to imagine that Florence could contain both in the future."

"Yes. I would like that too."

We fell silent. I put out my hand and gently laid it across his.

THEY CAME AT FIRST LIGHT, ROUSING THE HOUSE WITH THEIR pounding on the gates. In all such stories bad news comes with the dawn, as if the day itself cannot live with the dishonesty of false hope.

Though the noise woke me, my husband had been long up already. The baby was so big in me now and I was so tired that it took me a while to get myself off the bed and down the stairs. By the time I reached the courtyard, the main doors were already flung open and the messenger was there. Erila too was up, but then gossip slips through unseen cracks at times like this.

I had been expecting soldiers. Or even, God forbid, Luca and his brigade. But instead it was just a single old man.

"Mistress Alessandra!" It took me a moment to recognize him: Ludovica's husband, his age exacerbated by too much exertion.

"Andrea, what is it? What has happened?"

He looked so awful that it made me wonder what worse there could possibly be.

"My father?" I said. "Is it my father? He is dead?"

"No, no, your father is fine, mistress." He paused. "Your mother sent me. She said I am to tell you the soldiers came back to the house early this morning. And they took away the painter."

So Tomaso had fought pain with cunning after all.

Forty-one

THERE WAS NO MOVEMENT IN MY WOMB. I PUT MY HANDS over my stomach, prodding until I could make out the bony stretch of a leg and a buttock taut against my flesh. I prodded a little farther but there was no response. I tried not to panic. Sleep can resemble death sometimes, even when you are not yet born.

"Alessandra." Her voice stroked my eyes open. My faithful Erila was sitting next to me, her eyes fastened on mine. Behind her stood Cristoforo, his head caught in a halo of morning sun. I shifted my gaze back to Erila's eyes. Be careful, her look said. With every step you take now your life becomes more dangerous. And I cannot be there to help you.

I smiled at her. No wonder she could read palms and see patterns in the way sunflower seeds scattered themselves onto the ground. I wanted her to be next to me forever, so she could teach me such skills for handling life and I in turn could hand them on to my child. I understand, I told her silently. I will do my best.

"Hello." My voice sounded a long way away. "What happened?"

"You are fine. You passed out for a moment, that's all." My husband's voice was rich with relief.

"And the baby—"

"—is asleep, I am sure," interrupted Erila. "As you should be too. At such a time, any excess of emotion could damage both of you."

"I know that." I pulled myself up and took her hand quickly and briefly squeezed it tight. "Thank you, Erila. You can leave us now."

She nodded and moved away without another look. I watched her go, her unbound hair like a swarm of angry flies around her head.

"They did not take you." I smiled up at him. "The relief must have been too great for me." But even as I said it I could feel a wave of nausea rising up inside. I know it now, I thought. I know what you felt: that blind fear that comes from imagining what might be happening to someone you love, even now, as you think this very thought. I swallowed and tried again. "You know, Plautilla says that birth is as bad as the strappado. Still, I cannot believe that, because birth is about life and you would surely understand that when the pain came."

"Your sister knows nothing of such things," he said curtly.

"No. Cristoforo?" I heard my voice waver.

"I am listening."

"Cristoforo, I am so glad it is not you. So glad—" I broke off. "But you know this is Tomaso's hatred of me. He—" I stopped again, seeing Erila's eyes in front of me. "He could have spoken a dozen other names. He knows of my great love of art and how much I owe to the painter's encouragement." I found it hard to hold his eyes. "They will torture him too, won't they?"

He nodded. "If he has been named, yes. It is the law."

"But he knows nothing. And no one. So he will have no names to give them. But they will not listen to that. You know what will happen, Cristoforo. You know what they will do—they will continue and continue until he speaks, and in that way they will break the joints in his arms. And without his arms—"

"I know, Alessandra. I know." His voice was sharp. "I know very well what is happening here."

"I'm sorry." And despite my intended caution I was crying

openly now. "I'm sorry. I know it is not your fault." I started to pull myself off the couch. "I must go there."

He moved toward me. "Don't be stupid."

"No, no, I must go. I must tell them. If they don't believe me they can interrogate *me*. The law forbids the torture of pregnant women, so they will be forced to accept my word."

"Ah, this is total stupidity. They will never listen to you. You will only do more harm than good and embroil us all in their bloody guilt."

"Their guilt? But—"

"Listen to me—"

"It is not *their* guilt. It is—"

"God's blood, I have already sent—"

Our voices thrashed angrily around each other. I could imagine Erila standing outside in alarm, trying to make sense of the storm. I broke off. "What did you say?"

"I said—if you can find the calm to listen—that I have already sent to the prison."

"Sent who?"

"Someone they might listen to. You may think what you like of your brother, and in some ways I might think it too, but I would not have you believing that I would let an innocent man suffer in my place."

"Oh, you have not confessed?"

He laughed bitterly. "I am not that brave. But I have found a way into the ears of those who decide such things. You have slept through some momentous hours. History is running faster than the Arno in flood, and things are changing even as we speak."

"What do you mean?"

"I mean the monk's power is under real threat now."

"How?"

"Yesterday the leader of the Franciscan order openly attacked him, saying that he was not a prophet but a misguided lunatic and that the city risks damnation by following him. To prove it he challenged him to an ordeal by fire."

"What?"

"Both of them to walk together through flame to show whether Savonarola is really under the protection of God."

"Oh, sweet Mary! What is happening to us here? We are become barbarians."

"Indeed we are. But it is spectacle and in such times it substitutes well enough for thought. They are already building up the soaked timbers in the Piazza della Signoria."

"And if Savonarola wins?"

"Don't be naïve, Alessandra. Neither of them will win. It will simply encourage the mob. But he has lost already. This morning he announced that God's work was more important than such tests and nominated another friar in his place."

"Oh! But then he is exposed as both a fraud and a coward!"

"He would not see it like that, but it is the message the people will take. Most important, it means the Signoria need no longer side with him. They have been waiting for such an excuse ever since his excommunication."

"And so you think—"

"I think there is a chance that it will all topple now, yes. No one wants to be a follower of a leader doomed for destruction, however menial your position. At such times it is all too easy for the torturer to become the tortured. In the old days these crimes could be negotiated by influence and the size of your pocket. We must hope and pray that we might go that way again."

"So you will buy them out of prison?"

"It is possible, yes."

"Oh, God," and I was crying again now, no hope of stopping the tears. "Oh, God. We are living in madness here. What will become of us?"

"What will become of us?" He shook his head sadly. "We will do what we can, live the lives we have been given, and pray that Savonarola is wrong and that God in His eternal mercy can love sinners as well as saints."

Forty-two

THE DAY DRAGGED INTO EVENING, AND THE EVENING into night. Around midnight a message came for my husband. He left immediately. Outside, the city refused to sleep. It was like the old days to have so much activity so late at night. If you kept the window open you could hear the hubbub from the square.

For comfort, Erila and I went to my workshop. I kept thinking of that morning before my wedding when La Vacca had rung and my mother would not let me out to see what was happening. Just as she had witnessed the Pazzi violence with me in her womb, now I too was close to bloody business as my child came near to term. I tried to use paint to still my panic, but even the colors seemed thinner now and they did nothing to stop the thundering in my head.

Just after dawn the front gate opened and we heard his feet on the stone steps. Erila, who had fallen asleep, woke fast as a finger snap. As he came in I was up on my feet and would have gone to him if she hadn't stopped me with her warning glance. "Welcome home, husband," I said quietly. "How are you?"

"Your painter is released."

"Oh." And as my hand flew up to my mouth I felt Erila's eyes still me. "And . . . what of Tomaso?"

He was silent for a few seconds. "We could discover nothing of Tomaso. He is no longer in the prison. No one knows where he is."

"But . . . but wherever he is he will be safe. You will find him."

"We must hope that, yes."

But we both knew it was not a foregone conclusion. He would not be the first prisoner to disappear without trace from jail. Still, this was Tomaso. His story was surely too bold to end in the back of a cart with a makeshift shroud over him.

"What else?"

He shot a glance at Erila. She stood up, but I laid a hand on her arm. "Cristoforo, she knows everything that is between us. I would trust her with my life. At such a time I think she should hear the rest."

He stared at her for a moment as if seeing her for the first time. She bowed her head meekly. "So. What more do you want to know?" he said wearily.

"Did they—I mean . . . ?"

"We were lucky. The jailers were more interested in the day's news than the day's work. We found him before the worst had been done." I wanted to ask more but I didn't know how. "Don't worry, Alessandra. Your precious painter will still hold a brush."

"Thank you," I said.

"Perhaps you should wait before you thank me. You have not heard it all. While he is released, the charges still stand. As a for-eigner there is the punishment of banishment, with immediate effect. I have spoken with your mother and written a letter of introduction to some acquaintances in Rome. He will be safe there. If his talent is still in place, I think they will be able to use him. He is already dispatched."

Already dispatched. What had I thought, that there would be no price to be paid for his freedom? Already dispatched. The world seemed to shake for a few seconds and I could see how life could suddenly pull you through the cracks of destiny into despair, but I could not let that happen to me now. My husband was staring at me and there was, I thought, also a sadness to him that I had not seen before. I swallowed. "What more can you do about Tomaso?"

He shrugged. "We can keep looking. If he is in Florence, we will find him."

"Oh, I am sure you will."

He looked so tired. There was a flagon of wine on the table. I brought him a glass, sinking down as far as my stomach would let me to serve him. He took a long draft and put his head back against the chair. It seemed to me that his skin had grown yellow and loose with the night's worries, so that his face was now that of an old man. I put my hand on his. He stared at it but did not respond.

"And what of the city?" I said. "Does the ordeal still take place?"

He shook his head. "Ah, it becomes more farce at every turn. The Franciscan now says he will walk through the flames with no one but Savonarola. So another monk is substituted in *his* place too."

"In which case there is no point."

"None at all, short of proving that fire burns. They would do as well to walk across the Arno and judge by which one gets their feet wet."

"So why doesn't the Signoria put a stop to it?"

"Because the crowd is mad for it and to do so now would cause a riot. All they can do is try and limit the damage and bad-mouth the friars to whoever will listen. They are like rats on a sinking ship, eager to jump but afraid of the water. Still, they will have a privileged view from the windows when the flames start to lick."

There would have been a time when such news might have brought a frisson of excitement as well as terror, when I might have fantasized ways to escape the clutches of chaperones and lose myself into the crowd, to be a part of history. But not now. "I cannot bear that we are fallen so low. Will you go to watch?"

"Me? No. I have better things to do with my life than witness the humiliation of my city." He turned to Erila. "And what about you? From what I hear, you know more of what goes on in Florence than most of its government. Will you bear witness?"

She held his eye coolly. "I do not like the smell of burning flesh," she said quietly.

"Good for you. All we can hope for is that God agrees and somehow makes His own hand felt."

And so He did.

PERHAPS YOU DO NOT KNOW THE STORY. IN FLORENCE IT IS LEGEND now: how the mad monks disgraced themselves, squabbling and spatting until God threw a thunderbolt to bring the whole thing to a standstill.

If one is looking to diagnose sin, then pride would be the one that comes most easily to mind. And if one were to apportion blame, it is surely the Dominicans who must be spoken of first.

The ordeal was set for midafternoon that next day, the day before Palm Sunday. Under leaden skies, the Franciscans arrived on time, behaving according to their supporters with humility and worship. In contrast, their rivals, who had learned the power of theater from their leader, were outrageously late, finally entering the piazza in elaborate procession, carrying a great crucifix before them and swelled by the ranks of the faithful chanting the Laudate and singing psalms. And there, at the very back, came Savonarola himself, proud and defiant, holding aloft the consecrated host.

This was too much for the Franciscans, who demanded that it be removed immediately from his excommunicated hands. Things soured further when Savonarola's appointee, Fra Domenico, announced his intention to carry both the host and the crucifix with him into the flames. The Franciscan then refused to accompany him. Eventually, after much angry negotiation—during which time the corridor of fire was burning higher and hotter—

Fra Domenico agreed to leave the crucifix behind but insisted on keeping the host.

They were still bickering like children when God, understandably exasperated by their noise and arrogance, broke open the skies with a massive thunderstorm, dumping a torrent of water onto the flames and engulfing the square with smoke and confusion, so that as dusk fell the Signoria, relieved beyond measure that someone else had decided the matter in their stead, suspended the fiasco and ordered the crowds to go home.

That night Florence stewed in the poisonous juices of shame and disappointment.

Forty-three

"GET UP."

"What is it? What has happened?" Fear had me alert immediately.

"Shh. Quiet." Erila was leaning over me, ready for traveling. "Don't ask questions. Just get up and get dressed. Quickly. Make no noise at all."

I did as I was told, though the baby was so large now that even simple things took time.

She was waiting for me at the bottom of the stairs. It was the darkest part of the night. As I opened my mouth she laid her finger across it and pressed it to my lips. Then taking my hand she gave it a quick squeeze and guided me toward the back of the house, where she unlocked the tradesmen's door. We slid out onto the streets. The temperature was sharp, the leftovers of winter still in the air.

"Listen to me, Alessandra. We must walk, all right? Can you do that?"

"Not unless you tell me where we are going."

"No. I told you. No questions. It is better if you don't know. I mean it. Trust me. We don't have much time."

"Then at least tell me how far."

"It is a way. Porta di Giustizia."

The city gate of the gallows? I started to speak, but she was already off into the darkness.

We were not the only ones. The city, crazy after the anticlimax of the day, was alive with gangs of men in search of sport. We kept our heads well covered and took the side streets, where the night was thickest. Two or three times Erila stopped suddenly, holding me back and listening, and once I am sure I heard something or someone behind us. She walked back a few steps to check, peering into the darkness, then plunged onward, pulling me faster. We passed remnants of the day's barricades but avoided the piazza, crossing to the north near my father's house, then cutting back down behind Santa Croce until we joined the Via de' Malcontenti, that sad, somber street down which condemned prisoners are made to walk, attended by friars in black.

The baby was awake and fidgeting, though there was less room for its movements now. I felt an elbow or maybe a knee slide thickly under the surface of my stomach. "Erila, stop. Please. I cannot go so fast."

She was impatient. "You must. They will not wait for us."

Behind us the bells of Santa Croce rang the beginning of the 3 A.M. watch. The streets gave way to more open country here, the plots and gardens of Santa Croce monastery to either side, ahead the gate with the great walls of the city running thick around it. I remember Tomaso telling me how in summer such places made good sporting ground for those who wanted to play. I had imagined young women with coquettish smiles, but he was no doubt talking of other things. But the mood was for another kind of transgression now, and the scrub ground leading up to the gate was deserted.

"Dear God, I hope we are not too late," Erila murmured. She pushed me back into the shadows of a large tree. "Don't move from here," she ordered. "I will be back."

She disappeared into the gloom, and I leaned back against the trunk. I was panting from the exertion and my legs were shaking. I thought I heard something moving to my left and turned quickly, but there was nothing there. At the gate there would be soldiers: 3 A.M. would mark the changing of their watch. Why had the hour been so important?

"Erila?" I whispered after a while.

The silence now was profound and the open darkness more scary than the streets. I felt a short sharp pain in the bottom of my womb, but whether it was fear or baby it was hard to know. From the dark under the wall I saw a figure emerging, Erila, half walking, half running. When she reached me she grabbed me by the hand.

"Alessandra. We must go back. Right now. I know you're tired, but we must move quickly."

"But—"

"But nothing. I will tell you, I promise, but not now. Now please just walk." And there was a terror in her voice I had never heard before that stopped my protests. She held me by the hand, and when I became breathless she supported me under the elbow. We moved from scrubland back into city streets. Her eyes were everywhere, trying to read the darkness. When we reached the Piazza Santa Croce I halted, the great brick façade of the church looming over us.

"I have to stop or I will be ill," I said, my voice shaky with exhaustion.

She nodded, her eyes still darting every which way. The piazza was a gray lake under shafts of broken moonlight, the single rose window of the great church looking down on us like the Cyclops' eye.

"So, tell me."

"Later. I will—"

"No. Tell me now. I don't move until you do."

"Oh, sweet Jesus, there is no time for this!"

"Then we stay here."

She knew I meant it. "All right. Tonight, after you had fallen asleep, I was sitting in my room when your husband came to the servants' quarters. He spoke with his man. I heard everything they said. He told him that he must take a pass to the Porta di Giustizia tonight. He said it was urgent; there was a man, a painter, who was leaving at three A.M. and he would need the document to be allowed through." She closed her eyes up tight. "I swear to you that was what he said. That's why I brought you. I thought——"

"You thought I could meet him. So where was he?"

"He wasn't there. Neither he nor the servant. No one was there."

"So it is the wrong gate. We must go——"

"No. No, listen to me. I know what I heard." She paused. "I think now that I was meant to hear it."

"What do you mean?"

She glanced around. "I think your husband——"

"No...oh, God, no! Cristoforo doesn't know. How could he know? It's impossible. No one knows but you and me."

"And you don't believe your brother didn't guess?" she said angrily. "That day when he came upon you in the chapel?"

"I think he suspected, but there was no time when he could have told Cristoforo. I watched them every minute they were together. He didn't tell him. I know. And they haven't seen each other since because Tomaso is still missing." She stared at me, then dropped her eyes to her feet. "Isn't he?" As I said it I felt panic like vomit rise up in my throat. "Oh, sweet Jesus. If you are right...if it was a trap——"

"Look, I don't think anything anymore. All I know is that unless we get home we will be discovered for certain."

I could feel the fear in her. She was not used to being wrong, my Erila, and this was not the time to falter. "Listen to me," I said fiercely. "I am glad you did it. Glad. Do you understand? Don't worry." It was my turn now to reassure her. "I am well. Let us go now."

We walked rapidly, retracing our steps so that the darkness clothed us both for most of the journey. If we were being followed, surely we would have known. The baby was still now, though the exertion had taken its toll and I could feel a slow grinding ache at the bottom of my womb. All around us we could hear shouting. To the south of the cathedral we came across a phalanx of youths, armed and raucous, heading toward the cathedral square. Erila pulled me fast back into the shadows as they passed. With the dawn would come Palm Sunday Mass in the cathedral, and while Savonarola himself could not preach, one of his disciples was due to take the pulpit. In a city where gambling would soon be back on the streets, I would not have taken a wager on his getting as far as the sermon.

As we moved back into the street I felt a stabbing deep in the lower half of my back and I let out a fast breath of pain. Erila turned and I saw my own panic reflected in her eyes. "It's all right. It's all right," I said, trying to laugh but not managing the right sound. "It's just cramp."

"Dear God," I heard her mutter.

I took her hand and squeezed it hard. "I told you, I am fine. We have made a pact, this baby and I. It will not be born into a city ruled by Savonarola. And he is not gone yet. Come. We are not far now, though maybe we could walk a little slower."

THE HOUSE WAS IN SILENT DARKNESS. WE SLIPPED IN THROUGH THE servants' door and up the stairs. My husband's door was closed. I was so weary I could barely undress myself. Erila helped me, then laid herself down in her clothes on a pallet by the door. I know she was worried about the pains. She took some drops from her mother's medicine pouch and gave them to me. Before I fell asleep I put my hands over my belly, but where once the hillock had been riding high, almost up to my rib cage, now the baby had moved down in my womb, its body pressing heavily on my bladder. By the calculations on the calendar it was not due for three weeks yet, by which time both wet nurse and midwife would be installed.

"Be patient, little one," I whispered. "It's only a short wait now. We will have both city and home ready for you."

And the baby, in obedience to our pledge, let me sleep.

Forty-four

WHEN I WOKE, ERILA WAS GONE AND THE HOUSE WAS QUIET. I felt heavy with sleep. Her potion had done me well. I lay for a moment trying to work out the time of day from the light around me. It must be afternoon already and everyone at siesta. The grinding in my stomach was back, as if someone was raking the bottom of my womb with a scrubbing brush.

I got myself to the door and called out for her. No answer. I pulled on a robe and made my way slowly downstairs. The kitchens and servants' quarters were all empty. Close to the pantry was a small storeroom where they kept the sacks of flour and hung the cured meats. As I passed by it I heard a humming noise. Inside, the cook's elder daughter was sitting on the floor with a mound of what looked like raisins in front of her, counting them off into small piles, then popping one in her mouth. Sturdier than her sister, she had survived the plague but her mind was less developed than her body and there was a certain vacancy about her. By her age I was reciting Dante and Greek verbs, though such skills were of little use now.

"Tancia?" I made her jump. She covered the raisins hastily with her skirts. "Where is your father?"

"My father?...He is gone to fight the war."

"What war?"

"The war against the monk," she said, and she made it sound like great sport.

"What about the other servants?"

She shrugged. We had only ever spoken a few words, she and I, and she seemed frightened of me now. With my hair undone and my huge belly I must have been a wild sight. "Answer me. Is there nobody here?"

"The master said everyone could go," she said loudly. "But I was not allowed."

"And did my slave go too?"

She looked at me blankly.

"The black woman," I said impatiently. "Erila. Did she go too?"

"I don't know."

And as she said it, the first rush of pain hit me: a belt of metal around my lower abdomen, squeezing so tightly it felt like my insides might burst out onto the floor. "Aah!" It so knocked the breath out of me that I had to hold the side of the door to steady myself. The spasm lasted maybe ten or fifteen seconds, then released. Not now. Oh, God, please not now. I am not ready.

As I came up for air she was staring at my stomach. "The baby is big, mistress."

"Yes. Yes, it is. Tancia, listen to me." I made my words clear and slow. "I need you to do something for me. I need you to take a note across the city to my mother's house near Piazza Sant' Ambrogio. Do you understand?"

She stared at me, then gave a little laugh. "I cannot, mistress. I don't know where it is, and the master said the others could go to see the war but I had to stay here."

I closed my eyes and took a deep breath. Please God, if I am to go into labor, at least give me Erila. Don't leave me alone in the house with a halfwit girl. It couldn't be happening. It couldn't. It was too early. I was just exhausted and scared. I would go back to bed and sleep again. When I woke the house would be alive again and I would be fine.

I climbed the stairs carefully. As I reached the first floor I heard a noise, the scrape of a chair or a shutter banging on its hinges? It was coming from Cristoforo's gallery. I walked carefully along the corridor, my hands cupped under my belly for support, and pushed open the door.

Inside, an early spring sun was sending a wash of golden light across the tiles and over the statues. The body of the discus thrower glowed in its warmth.

"Good morning, wife."

It was my turn to be shaken now. I turned to find him sitting at the other end of the room, a book on his lap, the statue of Bacchus, in drunken languor, half falling off his plinth behind him.

"Cristoforo. You scared me! What is happening? Where is everyone?"

"They are gone to witness history. As you were once so eager to do. The mob broke up the service at the cathedral this morning. The Dominicans fled back to San Marco and are besieged there now in their monastery."

"Dear God. And Savonarola?"

"Is inside. There is a warrant for his arrest from the Signoria. It is only a matter of time."

So it was indeed ending now. I felt the grinding in my womb again. This baby, it would seem, had a head for politics. Surely it was my husband's child after all.

"And Erila? Is she gone to watch too?"

"Erila? Don't tell me your trusted Erila has left you. I thought she was always by your side—wherever you go." He paused. I realized too late what the words meant. "You slept late, Alessandra? You must have been up in the night. What could have prompted that?"

"I . . . I am tired, Cristoforo, and I think the baby's coming may be sooner than we thought."

"In which case you should go back to bed."

There was no mistaking it now, the blank cold politeness. When had it first appeared? Had he been this different when he came back with the news of the painter's release? Had I been so relieved that despite Erila's warnings I had not paid enough attention to his manner?

"Is there news of Tomaso?" I said.

"What makes you ask?"

"I . . . I was just praying that he was found."

He looked away from me at the statues. If the discus thrower had not been so concentrated on his work, one might almost have thought he was listening. "You know it is said that great artists can only tell the truth in their work. Do you agree with that, Alessandra?"

"I—I don't know. I suppose so, yes."

"And would you say that a baby is God's work of art?"

"Surely."

"In which case might it not be possible to detect a lie in a baby?"

I could feel my skin going cold and clammy. "I don't know what you mean," I said, and I heard the slight waver in my voice.

"No?" he paused. "Your brother is safe."

"Oh! Thank God for that. How is he?"

"He is . . . changed. I think that would be the right word."

"Did they . . ."

"Did they what? Wring the truth out of him? It is always so hard to tell with Tomaso. Sometimes he lies more credibly than he tells the truth. About all manner of things."

I swallowed. "Perhaps it is best to remember that before you believe everything he says," I said softly.

"Perhaps. Or it could be that his facility with such things runs in the Cecchi family."

I stared at him. "I have never lied to you, Cristoforo."

"Really?" He held my look. "Am I the father of your child?"

I took a breath. There was no going back now. "I don't know."

He held my eye for a moment, then put down his book and got to his feet. "Well, thank you at least for your honesty."

"Cristoforo—it's not what you think."

"I think nothing," he said coldly. "Our bargain was a child. The conditions, as I recall, were more about discretion than fidelity. The fault was with the marriage. I should have learned from your mother's past. Now you must excuse me. I have business to attend to."

"What do you mean, my mother's past?" But he was already up and moving toward the door. "No. Don't go, Cristoforo, please. This is not the truth either." I stopped. What could I say to him? What words could possibly tell of the fondness as well as the hardship. "You must know that we have felt—" From deep inside I felt the belt start to tighten again, faster this time. I would need all my breath for the pain now. "Ah...the baby...please, I beg you stay...just until Erila returns. I can't do it alone."

He looked at me. Maybe he simply saw another lie. Or maybe my body, which had been so distasteful to him even when it was intact, now offered only the prospect of woman's gore and blood.

"I will send someone," he said, and turned on his heel and walked out.

As the door closed behind him the pain roared in, a ring of steel muscle biting into pulp. I thought of the snake in the garden, whispering into Eve's ear; then, after she had succumbed, I imagined it curling itself around her abdomen and squeezing and squeezing until a misshapen fetus slithered out of her. And thus were sin and agony born together. This time it bent me double and I had to brace myself against Bacchus' stone flesh until the spasm passed. It was longer, deeper. I counted twenty, then thirty. Only at thirty-five did it start to dull and subside. If the baby was keeping to his side of the bargain, Savonarola must surely be taken already.

Of course I had heard stories of labor. What pregnant woman

after Eve has not? I knew that it starts with a series of increasing waves of rhythmic pain, as the entrance to the womb stretches open to allow the baby out, but that if I used my breath and held my nerve I might find a way to ride them, assuming they did not last forever. Then would come the turn, when the baby's head began to force itself through, at which point all one could do was push and pray that God had given you a body that would not rip into pieces, as had happened to my aunt and my mother before me.

But I would not think of them now. First I had to get to my room. I was halfway across the landing when the next contraction hit. I was ready for it this time. I grabbed hold of the stone balustrade and tried to count my way through it, my breath forced out of me in a series of low moans. The pain rose, peaked, held, then started to ebb away. You can do this, I thought. You can do this. Still, my cries must have been louder than I realized because below me I spotted Tancia in the corner of the courtyard, staring up at me, eyes wide with fright.

"Tancia, I—"

I never finished the sentence. As I got myself upright I suddenly felt the most terrible urge to urinate. I tried desperately to hold on to my bowels, but the pressure was too great. We both heard the crack—like the snap of a whip against a wall—as something in me opened and suddenly the stone floor beneath me was awash with bloody water. There seemed gallons of it; gushing out of me, pouring like a waterfall down my legs and across the landing till it dripped down into the courtyard below. Tancia gave a shriek of panic and disappeared.

How I got myself back to my room I don't recall. The next wave was so fierce it brought tears to my eyes. It had me on my knees, my hands on the edge of the bed. The pain was everywhere, in my loins, in my back, in my head. It and I were one, fused, blocking out thought, blocking out everything. This time the peak lasted forever. I tried to breathe but each gasp came out sharp and shallow, and by the time the steel mouth started to relax its grip I could hear myself crying with fear.

I sat upright and forced myself to start thinking. Once in my life I had seen the sea, a beach near Pisa where my father's cloth ships came in to dock. I must have been very young because all I remember is an infinite horizon and the sound of the waves, and how each wave had a life of its own, a muscle rippling and flexing, rising from the belly of the ocean till it flipped over and crashed down into foaming surf that drained away over the whispering sands. My father told me that day how as a young man he had once been in a shipwreck near the coast and how, as he swam for dear life to shore, he had learned to use the waves, lifting himself on top of each and moving with it, but how when he missed one it tumbled him under, making him swallow water until he feared he would drown.

I knew now that I too was swimming for my life. Only in this sea the waves were pain, each one fiercer than the last, and that my only hope was to ride them in to shore or I too would go under and drown. As the next wave grew, far out to sea, I closed my eyes and imagined myself growing and rising with it. . . .

"Alessandra."

The voice came from somewhere a long, long way off. But I could not listen to it now or I would be sucked under the water.

"Hold on, child. Get down on all fours." Closer now, louder, commanding. "Down. It will help."

I took a risk and listened. As my hands hit the floor I felt her palms push down low into my back, a deep firm pressure. The wave was peaking, cresting. "Breathe," the voice said. "Breathe: in . . . out . . . that's it; good girl. And again: in . . . out . . ."

I heard a low moan, which must have been my own voice as the white surf hurtled toward the beach and then slowly broke and ebbed away. And as I looked up at her I saw the fear and pride mixed in her eyes and knew I was going to be all right. My mother was come.

I fell half against her. "I—"

"Don't waste your energy. How long between the contractions?"

I shook my head. "Four, five minutes maybe, but they are coming quicker."

She held me as best she could as she pulled pillows off the bed and laid them on the floor so I could rest against them. "Listen to me," she said quietly. "Erila is gone for the midwife, but she and the rest of the city are on the streets. They will follow, but this bit you must do yourself. Is there no one else in the house?"

"Tancia, the cook's daughter."

"I will get her."

"No! Don't leave me!"

But she was gone already, out on the landing, her voice huge and commanding as a church bell. While the girl might ignore me, she would not ignore my mother. As she came back the pain hit again. This time she was with me from the start, using her hands as a power force on the bottom of my back to massage and spread the steel band as it squeezed into me.

"Alessandra, listen to me," she ordered. "You must find a way to absorb the pain. Think of Our Lord's agony on the cross. Be with Him, and Christ will help you bear it."

But I had sinned too much for Christ to help me now. This was my punishment, and it would go on forever. "I can't."

"Yes, you can." Her voice was almost angry now. "Concentrate. See the marriage chest in front of you. Find a face or a figure there and keep focused on it as you breathe. Come, child, use that great mind of yours to hook into the pain. Now breathe."

When I fell back onto the pillows afterward I saw Tancia at the door, eyes wide with horror. As my mother barked instructions to her I felt a sudden fury even stronger than my fear, and I heard my voice start to yelp and curse, as if I was somehow possessed. Both of them broke off and stared at me. I think Tancia would have run again if my mother hadn't slammed the door first.

"Do you want to push? Is that what you feel?"

"I don't know, I don't know," I snapped. "What happens next? How do I do this?"

Amid my terror she surprised me, her face breaking into a

smile. "The same way you made the baby. Just do what your body tells you. God and nature will do the rest."

And then, suddenly, it changed. Out of my exhaustion rose the most overwhelming need to push, to force it out of me. I tried to pull myself up but I couldn't make it.

"Ooh, it's coming, I can feel it."

She grabbed me by the arm. "Get up. It will hurt more on the floor. Get over here, girl. Hold your mistress up. Hook your elbows under her armpits. Go on. That's it. Support her back upright against you. Come on, brace yourself, take her weight. Lift her. Now."

Tancia might be stupid but she was strong. I hung from her arms, my whole body shaking, my skirts hooked over my shoulders, my legs spread wide, my belly huge beneath me while my mother crouched at my feet. When the need came now I pushed, and I held the push till there was no more breath, until I felt my face go purple and my eyes water with the strain, and it seemed like the whole of my anus and sex was tearing apart.

"And again. Push! The head is there. I can see it. It's ready to come."

But I couldn't do it. Just as suddenly, the urge left me and I fell back limp and shaking against Tancia's arms, a woman cut down from the rack, every limb quivering like water with pain and fear. I could feel the tears running down my face and the mucus dribbling from my nose, and I would have sobbed if I hadn't been too frightened of the energy it would have taken. There was no time to recover before it came again, this terrible need to expunge, expel, to shit this baby out of me. Except I couldn't do it. With each push I felt myself about to explode. Something was terribly wrong. The head was deformed, so large it would never come out. The sin of its conception was now visited upon its birth and we would hang here forever, baby and I, in perpetual torment as it tried to tear its way out of my body.

"I can't . . . I can't." I could hear the panic in my voice. "I am too small. This is God's punishment for my sins."

My mother's voice was firm, as it had been all through my life, guiding, cajoling. "What? You think God has time for your sins? Even now Savonarola is under torture for heresy and treachery. His screams can be heard in the square. What are your faults to compare to his? Keep your breath for the baby. Here it comes. Now push, push down for all your life. Come on!"

Again I pushed.

"Yes, yes, again! It's there. It's nearly out." I felt myself stretch to breaking point, but still I would not give.

"I can't," I whimpered, as I gasped for breath. "I'm scared. I'm so scared."

This time she didn't shout at me but knelt up and took my face in her hands and stroked the wetness away. And while her hand was gentle her voice was urgent. "Listen to me, Alessandra. You have the greatest spirit I have ever seen in a girl, and you haven't come this far to die on the floor of your bedroom. Just one more push. One more and it will be over. I will help you. Just listen to me and do everything I say. Is it coming again? Yes? Take a deep breath. The biggest breath of your life. Yes, that's it. Good. Now hold it. Now push, push. Hold. Push! And again. *Push!*"

"Aaaah!" And as my voice howled around the room I heard another sound, the rip of my own flesh as the inside of me tore open to let the head through.

"Yes. Yes!" I didn't need her voice to tell me. Out it came. I could feel it, a huge fast slithering power and a sense of release like nothing I had ever known before. "Oh, it is here. It is come. Oh! Oh, look at it, look at it!"

And as Tancia and I fell to the floor I saw at my feet a shining little goblin, crunched and hunched and covered in shit and blood and slime. "It's a girl," my mother said, in a hushed voice. "A beautiful, beautiful little girl."

She picked up the gluey little body and turned it upside down by the feet, and it choked as if its nose and lungs were filled with water until she slapped it hard on the rump, and then out came this angry vibrating little yell, a first instant protest against the insanity and outrage of the world it had entered.

And because there was no knife or scissors, she used her teeth to bite sharply into the cord, severing it that way. Then she laid her on my stomach, only I was shaking so much that I could barely hold her and Tancia had to catch her as she slid down toward the floor. But then I had her and as my mother massaged my stomach to push out the afterbirth, I lay on the floor, this warm, slimy, creased little animal clasped in my arms.

So it was that my daughter was born. After they had washed and wrapped her tight in swaddling cloth, because there was no wet nurse to feed her they brought her to me again and we watched in a kind of awe as she rooted her way like a blind worm to my breast, her gums fixing onto my nipple with such unexpected force that it made me yelp, her tiny jaws sucking and sucking until I felt the sweet pain of the milk starting to flow. And only then, after her demands had been met and she had fallen off the breast like a full tick blown up with fresh blood, did she deign to sleep and let me sleep too.

Forty-five

OVER THE NEXT FEW DAYS I FELL IN LOVE: DEEPLY, profoundly, irrevocably. And if my husband had seen her too I have no doubt she would have won him also, with the miracle of her fingernails, the gravity of her unblinking gaze, and the glow from the palpable spark of divinity within her.

As my world shrank into the pupils of her eyes, history was being made outside. My mother had been right about our joint agony. While my insides had been squeezed and stretched by the force of new life, Savonarola was hearing the sound of his own screams as his sinews snapped under the weight of the strappado. His reign over the New Jerusalem had ended that morning with the storming of San Marco. Though his loyal monks had fought more like soldiers—there was much talk of the mad strength of one Father Brunetto Datto, a giant of a Dominican with skin like pumice stone who wielded a knife with particular wild pleasure—in the end they were overcome, and the mob had broken in and found Savonarola bowed in prayer on the steps of the altar. From there he was taken in chains to the fortress tower of the Palazzo della Signoria, where the great Cosimo de' Medici had been held sixty years before on the same charge of treason against the state. But while Cosimo had had the means to charm and bribe his jailers, there was to be no such relief for Friar Girolamo.

He was subjected first to the strappado and then the rack. With each broken bit of body he pleaded guilty to another charge: false prophesy, heresy, treason, anything they wanted to hear just so long as they would stop the pain. At which point they had cut him down and taken him to his cell. But with the pain gone he recanted, crying out that it was torture and not the truth that had broken him and calling on God to bring him again to the light. Yet with the first ratchet of the rack he confessed again, and this time they went on until he had not the voice, let alone the courage, to deny again.

Thus was Florence freed from the tyranny of the man who had set out to bring her to God, only in the end to find that God had deserted him. But though I had good reason to hate him I could only feel pity. At my bedside, Erila laughed at my compassion and told me how birth was notorious for softening a woman's brain. And so two days passed and there was still no word from my husband.

On the morning of the third day I woke to a shining sun and the sight of Erila and my mother in urgent conversation at my door. "What is it?" I said from the bed. They turned, exchanging fast glances. My mother came forward till she was standing close.

"My dear child ... there is news. You must be brave."

"Cristoforo." Because, of course, all this time I had been expecting something. "It is Cristoforo, isn't it?"

She came to me and took my hand in hers as she told me, her eyes reading the journey of my feelings. It was a story of our time: how the city had been in the grip of bloodlust in the hours following the storming of San Marco, with old scores to be settled, old enemies hunted down. But not all the violence had been just, and a number of other bodies had been found, including one in the alley of La Bocca near the old bridge, a notorious place where the flesh of both men and women was traded under cover of night. And how there, in the light of a new morning, under the mess of stab wounds someone had recognized the cut of fine cloth and the nobility of a good face.

I sat rock-still like one of his statues, my flesh grown cold at her words.

"You must be brave, Alessandra," my mother said again, and her voice reminded me of the times when I was a child and she was teaching me how to speak to God as if He were my father as well as my Lord. "Such things are His will and it is not for us to question them." She held me tight for a moment, and when she was satisfied that I had not broken apart with the shock she said softly, "My dear, your husband has no other family. If you are strong enough, it is asked that you come and claim the body."

IF LABOR SOFTENS FEELINGS IT ALSO UNRAVELS MEMORY, MAKING some moments stand forever and others fade almost as they happen.

Though a wet nurse had been found, we took the baby because I could not bear to be separated from her. The servants, I remember, were standing by the door as we left, eyes down, their future torn apart by the news. On our way we stopped at the Baptistery. With my husband gone there had been no one to register the birth and it was the law that it must be done within sixty hours. A white bean for a girl, black for a boy. Under the golden cupola where the life of Our Lord unfolded in dense gleaming mosaics, the birth box rattled with new life.

Outside, the streets were filthy with the debris of rioting: sticks and boulders and bits of clothing clogging the gutters and all of it lit by a dazzling sun. But though the weather was joyful the mood was somber. We were a godly state no more, and no one quite understood how much rejoicing we should take from that.

The plague had taken so many victims they had had to set up a temporary morgue across the river, commandeering a set of rooms in the hospital of Santo Spírito. As we were guided through the labyrinth at the back of the church, I thought of my painter and his nights spent recording the ways in which violence dissected the human body. I clutched the baby closer and walked as a child myself again, in the footsteps of my mother, with my maidservant close behind.

The official at the door was a rough man, his breath rancid with stale beer. He had a makeshift ledger in which were written columns of numbers and in some cases names. The writing was crude. My mother did the talking, telling our story in the same way she moved through the world, with grace and clarity. People listened to my mother. When she was finished he shuffled himself out of his chair and walked with us into the room.

It was as one might imagine a battlefield after the army has moved on. There were rows of bodies lying on the floor, wrapped in winds of grubby linen. There was so much blood on some of them it made one fear they might still have been alive, dumped here to leak away the remains of life into their makeshift shrouds.

My husband's corpse was on a pallet near the end of the room. At another moment in history one might have hoped for more ceremony for the more noble names, but Florence was hemorrhaging death now and any space would have to do.

We stood at the feet. He looked up at me. "You ready?"

I gave the baby to my mother. She smiled at me. "Don't be shocked, my child," she said. "There is a greater power at work here than both of us."

He leaned down and pulled back the shroud. I closed my eyes and then opened them again—onto the bloodied face of a middle-aged man I had never seen before in my life.

By my side Erila let out a broken howl. "Oh, master, oh, master, who can have done this to you?" As I turned she flung herself into my arms, clutching at me and howling. "Oh, my poor lady, don't look, don't look, it is too awful. What will become of us now?"

I tried to shake her off, but she clung like a leech. "Are you mad?" I whispered in horror. "This isn't Cristoforo!" But her wailing continued. I stared helplessly at my mother, who came immediately to join us. The man was watching keenly now. No doubt he had seen the way grief takes enough women to be ready for anything.

My mother glanced down at the body, then up at me. Her look was keen. "Oh, my dear, dear daughter," she said loudly. "I know what you must feel. How hard it is to understand how God could allow such a thing, to take away the man you loved for no reason. Grieve for him, grieve for your Cristoforo, and let him rest. He is gone to a better place."

As I stood there, my mouth open with dumb shock, my new soft womanliness came forward to help me and I started to weep; fat fast tears which once started were a law unto themselves. And all this commotion now woke the baby and she started to yell too, and so we stood there, a vision of female grief unleashed, and the man took his pen and marked a large cross beside my husband's name.

BACK IN THE UNCOMFORTABLE, UNCOMFORTING RECEIVING ROOM, Erila—whose tears had dried immediately once we left the building—brought us spiced wine and insisted that I take a potion from her pouch, before hugging me and then leaving us, closing the door firmly behind her. The baby lay in my arms blinking up at me as I faced my mother.

"So," I said numbly. "Where is he?"

"Gone."

"Gone where?"

"Into the country. With Tomaso. The morning of your labor he came to get me and told me what had passed between you. Once it was decided, he arranged for a body to be found with a note written in his hand so it would lead the authorities to us for identification. I am sorry for the distress it caused you. I didn't tell you because I feared in your softened state you might not be able to hold with the pretense." She sounded as matter-of-fact as a statesman whose job it is to take on grave questions and make sense of them for the rest of the frightened population.

But I did not have her serenity. "I ... I don't understand. Why? Was it so important if the baby wasn't his? Because——"

"Because it might have been? Don't worry, Alessandra. I know it all. I am not here to judge you. There is another court for that, and in that court I suspect you and I might find ourselves standing together some day." She sighed. "It was not to do with the baby. He felt ... well, I should not speak for him. He asked once it was revealed that I give you this. Though I think it would be wise if you destroyed it after."

And from out of her bodice she drew a letter. I took it with shaking hands. The baby whimpered in my arms. I hushed her back into quiet and cracked the seal.

His hand was so elegant. Such a contrast to the violent scrawl in the Santo Spírito record book. It gave me pleasure just to look at it. Pleasure and recognition.

My dear Alessandra,

By the time you read this we will be gone. And you, God willing, will be delivered of a healthy child. Tomaso is in need of me. The damage done to him is terrible, and with his beauty gone and his body broken his need is even greater. I cannot rid myself of the accusation that my lust in some way created him, and so it is my duty now to tend the pain I have caused. My duty. And yes, still my desire. If you and I stayed together I would feel that pain for the rest of my life and would be an embittered companion for you and the child.

With me dead a different future is now possible for you. With no other family to call upon my assets, a will has been drawn up which allows enough money to Tomaso to secure a life of modest comfort for us and which bequeaths the rest of my estate to you. As such it is uncommon and there may be those who question it, but it is legal and binding and it will be honored. The future is for you to decide. You are young enough to marry again. You may choose to return to your family or even, if you have the stomach for it, to live alone. I do not doubt your courage for an instant. Though I believe your mother has thoughts on this which you should listen to.

I ask you to forgive me my harsh words to you in the gallery. Despite our arrangement I found myself more drawn to you than I had realized and your betrayal cut me deep, just as mine cut you in similar ways. I want you to know that I felt as much for you as it was possible for me to do, and that I always will.

The key enclosed with this letter opens the manuscript cupboard in my study. You will be surprised by its contents. I am aware that some might label it theft, but since we both know it could otherwise have become war booty or worse—fuel for the fire—I would prefer to see it in your hands than any others I can think of. You understood this great new art of ours as well as any man I ever knew. Your father would have been proud of you.

I remain your loving husband,
Cristoforo Langella

I closed my hand tight over the key and read the letter a second time. And then a third. After a while my mother had to take it from me because my tears were turning the ink into rivulets of black wash, and such was its content that it would not do to obscure its meaning now. Erila was right. A woman's brain is reduced to milksop by birth. In such a state we will love anyone, even those who have deserted or betrayed us. Now it seemed I must bring up my daughter with no husband and not even her blood grandfather to care for her. *Your father would have been proud of you.* How easily the world can be turned upside down by a few well-chosen words.

Finally, when I looked up into my mother's eyes she met my gaze directly. He would never have written such a thing if he had not spoken to her first, surely?

"You know what it says?" I asked, when I had the wit to talk.

"Those things that directly concern your future and my past we spoke of before he wrote it. The rest will be private to you."

And still she did not look away. Throughout my life she had radiated a quiet calm intelligence, which she had used to still the storms of rebellion and questioning that she found in me. It had never occurred to me that she might have suffered from such storms herself, or that her acceptance of God's will and belief in His infinite mercy had any history of conflict within it. But I know now that it is not easy for daughters to think of their mothers as separate beings with lives and desires that are not subservient to their own. And just as I have since forgiven my own daughter that failure so I am sure my mother had forgiven me. To give her her due, that day she did not evade my questions or lie to me in any way. I think after so long there may even have been a relief in the telling of it.

"So," I said at last. "The inscription by Lorenzo de' Medici in the book of *Discourses* that he gave my husband was dated 1477, the year of my conception. But you were not at court then, surely? Your brother's star was already high enough to have you married off to a good husband. Isn't that the story we were always told?"

"Yes," she said quietly. "I was already married. And as we are talking of such things, you should know it was not an unhappy union, however it may sound to you now. It had already brought me three healthy children whom God in His great grace spared from illness or early death. I was blessed indeed. But what you say about that year, Alessandra, is not the whole truth. While I had been at court before, I also returned then briefly. Though not in any public sense."

She fell silent. I waited. Even the air seemed still around us.

"My brother had such grand friends," she said at last, and her smile was wry. "The court was filled with men of such depth and cleverness. For a girl who had been taught to think and speak her mind it was heaven before Judgment Day. And while the Platonic notion did not allow for us women to join in their deliberations, they were *Florentine* Platonists and thus of course even the greatest of them could be beguiled by beauty when it came with an equal talent for learning. Which, like you, I had. Though, like you, it was both my glory and my burden.

"My brother, who understood the dangers within such perfect purity, had made it his business to see that I was married off to avoid further risk. But even he did not have the power to prevent my being called back.

"Lorenzo and his court spent the early summer of 1477 at his villa at Careggi. I was one of a few invited visitors.... It was a long time ago." She stopped again, and for a moment I thought she might not go on, that she had indeed trained herself to forget it. She took a breath. "There was music, talk, art, and nature—the gardens alone were an earthly paradise. The beauty of the body was as much a subject for discussion as the beauty of the mind. Both were seen as stepping-stones on the road to God's love. I was not brought up to be coquettish. I was as serious and in some ways as innocent as you. But like you I was impressed by intelligence and study and art. And while I had resisted it once, by that summer I had been in love for too many years to know how to stop."

I saw again her tears over the body of Lorenzo in the chapel of San Marco so long ago. What had been Tomaso's words in my ear that day? That despite his ugliness, his love poetry could ignite the coldest of hearts. I sighed, looking down at the radiantly tranquil little face in my arms. It was hard to know how blunt the nose might be as she grew older, or how sharp the chin. No doubt that would also depend on her own father. Whoever he was. "Well, at least I know why I am ugly," I said quietly.

"Oh, Alessandra, you are not ugly. You have such beauty you almost turned the head of a sodomite."

And of course I was entranced by the way the word held as much pleasure in its transgression for her as it had done for me. So we sat together for a while in that faded unfashionable room, the afternoon silence broken only by my daughter's fast sweet breathing, in the peace of the knowledge that there were no more secrets left to tell.

"So," I said eventually. "What happens now?"

She sat for a moment. "You know the choice as well as I."

"I will not marry again," I said firmly. "A second marriage would disenfranchise the child, and I will not do that."

"That is true," she said calmly.

"And I cannot come home. I must have my own life now. So I suppose that I must set up house alone."

"Alessandra, I think that would be most unwise. Our city is cruel to widows. Both you and the child would find yourselves outcasts, lonely and spurned."

"We would still have you."

"Not forever."

The thought was cold frost to me. "Then what can I do?"

"There is one alternative we have not discussed." Her voice was steady. "To marry yourself to God."

"Marry myself to God? Me? A widow with a paintbrush, a black slave, and a child. Which convent, pray, Mama, do you think would ever take us?"

I watched as a sly slow smile crept over her face.

"Why, the one you always dreamed about, of course, Alessandra."

Forty-six

WE LEFT THE CITY—THIS WIDOW WITH HER PAINTBRUSH, black servant, and child—on 10 May in the year of Our Lord 1498.

Ours was not the only farewell that day. In the great square of the Signoria another pyre had been built over the last few weeks: Savonarola and his two faithful Dominicans were to be garroted and burned. Finally Florence was to get her smell of roasting human flesh.

My Erila had been keen to stand witness, if only to complete the history of it all, but I forbade it. The world was so bright and new for my daughter that I did not want even the scent of suffering near her. We rode out, passing rivers of people moving toward the square, but there was little sense of carnival to them. Though he had been hated, he had also been loved, and in the violence unleashed after his arrest I think many had begun to regret the passing of the New Jerusalem, even if it had shone brighter in intention than reality.

Still, his enemies had stood firm against him. In the days leading up to the trial, further rumors of perfidy passed through the city like acrid smoke in the wind. In particular a story circulated out from the jail that his most faithful accomplice, Father Brunetto Datto, the monk who had fought with such bloodlust in the final battle and who was to die with him that day at the stake, had been found to be mad with piety and that during his torture he had confessed to all manner of sins: the skewering of a young girl found on the streets after dark and the taste of her flesh between his teeth, the harvesting of genitals of prostitutes and their clients in the church of Santo Spírito, even the buggery of a young sodomite on the thrust of his own sword. But the real terror came not from the confessions but from the glee with which he admitted them, boasting of the ways that God had used him as a divine messenger to bring back sinners to the true path. Until at last his torturers had become disgusted, stuffed a rag into his open mouth, and threatened to set fire to it unless he stopped his blasphemies.

The day Erila brought these stories back to me was the first and only time I have seen her undermined by gossip. As she sat on the edge of the bed, the baby lying next to her staring up with solemn eyes, she told of how Father Datto, before they finally silenced him, had given directions as to where they could find one final body: that of a young prostitute with her breasts sliced off, left to rot in the crypt of Santi Apostoli.

So it was I remembered the dark voice that had chased me from the loggia the night before my marriage, and the great bear of a friar waving us down in the street with his bloodied hands, and I began to understand that while I might sometimes have felt excluded from God's grace, I had in fact been mightily protected. And in its way that knowledge brought me back into a more tender relationship with Our Lord.

However, that afternoon in my bedroom with Erila we did not dwell on such things. Instead, together we set about packing up the marriage chest for a second time, filling it with drawings and books and, best of all, the thick unbound manuscript recovered from my husband's closet and hidden carefully away in a mound of colorful shifts and velvet cloths.

Not long before we left, we visited my family in the old house in Sant' Ambrogio. Luca, whose Angel face was still bruised from the glorious final skirmishes of his army days, was sullen and displaced (not so different, in fact, from earlier times), but he managed to wish me well before he slouched off to his room. Plautilla, now huge with child, cried until her husband reprimanded her so sternly that it shocked her into silence. And my father... well, my father gave me a bolt of his favorite scarlet cloth to make up into dresses in my new home. I kissed him and wished him well and did nothing to disabuse him of his ignorance, and then he took my mother's hand and let her lead him back to his ledgers. The last I saw of them was as they went together into his study, her clean, clear gaze disappearing behind the closing door.

So that May day we rode out of the city with my husband's groom and two of his slaves as guide and carriers, spurred on by the promise of their freedom at the end of the journey. The morning was warm and sunny, the air hazy with the threat of greater heat.

We had made our way out through the Porta di Giustizia and were leaving the city precincts when we heard a great crack of thunder. It was the sound of gunpowder igniting the fire in the square, which meant that the hangman had done his work and the trio of monks had been garroted ready for the flames. We crossed ourselves and said a prayer for those now brought to God, calling upon His mercy for all sinners, dead and alive.

And as we made the slow climb out of the valley floor into the hills beyond, we could see from miles away the pillar of smoke, rising up from the sea of rooftops and dispersing into the balmy spring air.

PART IV

Forty-seven

M Y SECOND MARRIAGE——THE MARRIAGE OF SISTER LU-
crezia to God——though legally bigamous, proved
much more successful than my first.

What can I tell you of this place?

When we first came here it was indeed heaven on
earth. The convent of Santa Vitella is set in deep Tuscan countryside far to the east of Florence, the rolling wooded
hills graduating into gentler vines and olive slopes, and views to
make you understand God as the first and finest artist of all.
Inside its fortress walls at that time was a thriving community:
two cloisters (the larger with its arches decorated by Luca Della
Robbia, thirty-two blue-and-white ceramic heads of saints, each
one subtly, marvelously different from the last); generous gardens, practical as well as glorious since they provided most of our
food; and the refectory and the chapel, small when I arrived but
to grow bigger and more gracious in the years to come. And all of
it run by women. A republic built if not on virtue then on female
creativity.

There were, you see, so many of us: the women who did not fit
in. The women who loved life as much as they loved God yet

found themselves removed from it, incarcerated within convent walls. The new prosperity of the cities had bred us (the larger the dowries, the fewer the families who could afford them), and the new freedom of learning had encouraged us. But the world was not ready for us, so many of us ended up in places like Santa Vitella. And while we would not be considered wealthy, our dowries, when added together, were ample enough to fund our freedom. In the end it was simple mathematics: the numbers started to overwhelm the rules. Erila and I were lucky. We came well after that moment had been reached.

Each one of us arrived already formed. Some came with memories of the gowns we had worn, or the books we had read, or the young men we had kissed or at least yearned to. Behind closed doors, though we honored God and prayed to Him often, our imaginations moved in a hundred different ways. Of course some were more superficial than others. There were those who turned their cells into would-be beauty parlors, using their free time to twitter over their toilette or refashion their habits to show a little coiffured hair or a glimpse of ankle. Their greatest pleasures were to hear the sound of their own voices raised in the chapel choir and to cultivate the art of entertainment, and though the walls were high and the gates were locked, on certain nights you could still hear their laughter mingled with deeper male voices echoing round the cloisters.

But not all our sins were of the flesh. There was the woman from Verona who was so passionate about words that she sat all day writing plays, stories shining with morality and martyrdom with a hint of unrequited love and romance in between. We put them on inside the convent, the better seamstresses making the costumes and the more exhibitionist of us playing all the parts (male as well as female). Then there was the nun from Padua, whose love of learning had been even greater than mine and who had spent years defying her parents and refusing to marry. When at last they realized her devotion couldn't be beaten out of her, they brought her studies to us. Unlike her parents, we took great care of her. Her cell became our library and her mind one of our greatest treasures. During the early years after my arrival I spent many evenings debating God and Plato and the journey of humanity to divinity with her, and there were times when she made me think more deeply than my childhood tutors. She was our very own scholar and, as Plautilla grew, she—together with me—became her teacher.

PLAUTILLA...

For the first month my daughter had no name. But when the news came from Florence that my sister had died giving birth to a strapping son, first I wept and then I christened my child. So in this way I managed to keep memories of my family around me.

Of course she was the darling of the nunnery. Everyone loved her. For the first few years she wandered round like a wild child, petted and spoiled. But as soon as she was of age we began her education, a process fit for a Renaissance princess. By the time she was twelve she knew how to read and write in three languages, embroider, play music, act, and of course pray. Inevitably, she grew up with a certain adult gravity because of the dearth of other children, but she wore it well and as soon as the facility between her eye and her hand began to show, I took my old copy of Cennini from my dowry chest, sharpened a fat pebble of black chalk, and prepared a boxwood panel with ground bone and spittle ready for her to scratch her first attempts at silverpoint. And because there was no one to make her self-conscious about her talent, she took to it instantly, so that long before I spotted her father's gray-green cat stare I knew whose child she was.

Erila also flourished. The job of conversa, a post designed specifically for slaves, was traditionally a menial one—serving the servers of God—but since ours was not a traditional nunnery I paid for her release and she soon created another role for herself; doing errands, moving gossip, and running a postal service for the nuns between the convent and the local town (with which we had a lively trade of forbidden luxuries) in a way that earned her a tidy fortune. Before long she was feared and adored in equal proportions, and thus she became a free woman at last—though by then she was so essential to the sisters and so much a family to Plautilla and me that she chose to stay with us as a way of enjoying it.

As for me—well, the winter after we arrived, our convent began building work on a new chapel and with it came the commission of my life. The Reverend Mother was a shrewd woman who, had she not fallen for the charms of a rich married neighbor, might have risen to run a noble family in Milan. In some ways she ran a more satisfying one here. Mindful of mixing our transgressions with our achievements, she managed the finances of the convent with more acumen than the Medici bankers and soon had enough to endow a new chapel. The bishop, who was less charming and more venial than she was—the skinny arm of Savonarola had never reached this far into the country—visited two or three times a year. In return for our superior hospitality (the refined pleasures of the palate were one of many unorthodox ways we celebrated God), Bishop Salvetti brought artistic gossip from the big cities and gave his blessing to the new plans, which, because she had a talent for architecture, were largely of the Reverend Mother's own making. But while she could see the light and space of classical proportions in her mind, the walls when they were finally finished were bare.

And so at last I got my chapel to paint.

The summer before I started, I sat in my cell working on the designs as Plautilla made flower chains in the orchards surrounded by a group of giggling young novices who saw her as their greatest plaything. My subjects would be the life of John the Baptist and the Virgin Mary. With only my memories and no master to help me, I used Botticelli's illustrations as my teacher, studying the way his liquid pen animated a thousand different human figures in heaven and hell with barely a dozen strokes each, creating complex stories of despair and joy.

The painting of the frescoes took a small lifetime. Plautilla was almost seven when I started. At first there had been little I could teach her because I knew so little myself: A lifetime of books and the skirts of Santa Caterina hardly made an expert. But Erila used her connections and in the city of Verona found a young man recently graduated from his master's studio who was, she deemed, dedicated and discreet enough to spend his days in the company of worldly nuns without being either overwhelmed or corrupted. So he taught and we learned. And by the time he left twenty months later the scaffolding was built, I could apply my own screed plaster to the walls, and Plautilla could grind and mix many of the pigments. It was only a matter of time until she began to add touches of her own.

As the chapel grew crowded with saints and sinners, the bishop's visits spurred me on with talk of outside genius. He came often from Rome, and though he could tell me nothing of my painter, he had much to say about that city's greatness and how it had overtaken Florence in matters of art. He talked of how much of that brilliance came from the hands of a belligerent young Florentine, an artist so intense in his own connection with God that even the pope could not command him. His most recent work, commissioned by his native city, was a giant sculpture of David hewn from a single block of flawed marble, so majestic and so virile in its humanity that the poor beleaguered Florentines did not know quite what to do with it. They had to take down arches and destroy houses to move it from the workshop to the Piazza della Signoria. It stood now, he said, at the entrance to the Palazzo, David's readiness to smite Goliath a constant reminder to all those who would threaten the city's Republic. And while its proportions dazzled the eye of all who saw it, my bishop said there were others who spoke equally warmly of a much earlier work executed when he was still a teenager: a life-size white cedar crucifix in the church of Santo Spírito where the body of Jesus was so young and so perfect it brought tears to the eyes of all who saw it.

Now, after many years, I finally learned the name of Michelangelo Buonarroti, and I wondered at the way fate had taken both my painter and his nemesis to the same city. But though such stories whetted my curiosity, I did not dwell on them. Though the poets might tell you differently, it is not possible to hold on to passion when there is nothing to keep it alive. Or maybe it was proof of God's further mercy to me that since Plautilla's birth he had released me from the grip of longing for that which I could not have. And so, like color in the sun, my memories of the painter faded.

In their place grew a certain pleasure from ritual and order. My days were simple: rising at dawn for prayer, then spending the first hours applying the screed plaster to the area of wall I would work on that day. A break for morning food—in summer, cold meats with fried zucchini flowers and vegetable jams; in winter, cured hams and spiced pies and broth—then filling in the paint before the plaster dried or the sunlight fell below the window, making the light too dim for my brush. Where once I had yearned for the world outside, now my vision was reduced to the transformation of a damp square of plaster into a set of shapes and colors that could only be understood once the whole was completed.

Thus, after so many years, Alessandra Cecchi finally learned the virtue of patience, and each twilight as she put aside the brushes and walked back across the cloisters to her cell, I think you could say that she was content.

And this feeling lasted for many years, until the spring of 1512.

Forty-eight

THE CHAPEL WAS ALMOST HALF FINISHED WHEN LATE ONE afternoon word came to me that I had a visitor.

Given the liberality of our institution, visitors were not uncommon, though less so for me. My mother had come every other year since my arrival and stayed for a few weeks to savor the growing of her granddaughter. But recently her eyesight had grown dim and she was needed full time to companion my father, who had become something of a recluse as well as an invalid. Her latest news had arrived by letter through a courier only a few months before. Luca had finally been married off to an ox of a girl who was pushing out sons as if she were equipping an army, while Maurizio, who after my sister's death had taken a wife with more dowry and less breeding, was widowed again. Of Tomaso and Cristoforo there was nothing. It was as if they had disappeared into the air. Sometimes I imagined them somewhere in an elegant villa on the edge of a town, living like two survivors of a brutal war, tending each other's needs and spirits until one of them died. And through all these years I heard nothing to disabuse me of this fantasy.

So to my visitor.

I asked that he—for it was a he—be shown into the reading room, which housed our small but proud collection of books and manuscripts, both secular and divine, and said that I would come when I had cleaned my brushes and my hands. I had forgotten that Plautilla was already there at the writing desk, busy on the illustrations for a newly copied Psalter, so when I opened the door quietly I saw them before they saw me, sitting together at the desk bathed in a honeyed light of late-afternoon sun.

"You see now? It makes a finer line that way," he said, handing her back the pen.

She stared down for a moment. "Who did you say you were?"

"An old friend of your mother's. You do much illustrating of the word of God?"

She shrugged. Though she had developed a comfortable enough level of conversation with our young chapel artist, she was shy of men—no doubt as I had been at her age so many years before.

"I ask because you have a lively pen. I wonder that the sheer force of it might not detract from the words."

I heard my daughter click her tongue in that gesture of quiet frustration she had learned from Erila. "Oh, I don't see how you can believe that. The more glorious the image, the closer it brings the supplicant to Christ. Write in one place the name of Our Lord, put a figure representing Him opposite, and which one stimulates more devotion?"

"I don't know. Is it a wise question?"

"Yes indeed! The man who said it is a wise painter. Perhaps you do not know him; his work is quite modern. His name is Leonardo da Vinci."

And he laughed. "Leonardo? Never heard of him. And how do you know what this Leonardo says?"

She looked at him seriously. "We are not as isolated as we may look here. And some news is more important than other. Where did you say you came from?"

"He comes from Rome," I said, walking across the darkened room into their sunlight. "Via Florence and a monastery at the edge of the sea where the winter wind is so cold it freezes your eyelashes and turns the breath in your nostrils to ice."

He turned and we looked at each other. I would have known him immediately, with or without the fashionable cloth. He was a good deal sturdier, the coltishness of youth long gone, and he was handsome; one could really see that now. Although that may also have come from the fact that he knew it. Confidence is a dangerous thing: too little and you are lost, too much and you are guilty of the other sins that grow from it.

As for me? What did he see in the nun who stood before him, her working habit stained with paint, her face aglow with the sweat that comes from concentration? My stature had not altered. I was still ungainly, still halfway to a giraffe, though he had always been tall enough to make me forget my height. For the rest—well, though there were forbidden mirrors in our convent then, I had long since stopped looking in them. There had been a certain pleasure in leaving behind the primping and crimping that comes with desire. Over the years the beauticians of the cloisters had occasionally cajoled me into trading skills, and I had conjured up half a dozen decorative devotional scenes in their cells in exchange for a better-cut habit and softer skin. But it had never been my intention to woo anyone. My fingers did the work of a man, both with the brush and sometimes in my own bush, as Erila was so poetically wont to put it. As a result I had grown from a girl into a woman without noticing it.

"Mama?"

"Plautilla?"

She was staring at us both. The room now held two sets of cat's eyes. It made me giddy to look into both of them. I touched her lightly on the head. "Why don't you finish up, child? The light is beautiful outside. Go and record God's hand in nature for a while."

"Oh, but I am tired."

"Then lie in the sun and let its rays lighten your hair."

"Really! May I?"

Wary lest I change my mind, she packed up quickly and left. And in her going I saw again her aunt, unplaiting the same rich chestnut hair and gathering up her belongings as she sped out of the room to leave my mother and me to talk the harsh business of marriage in the silence left behind. It was so long ago it felt almost new-minted in my mind.

We stood in silence for a while, half a lifetime in the space between us.

"She has a strong stroke," he said at last. "You have taught her well."

"It did not take teaching. She was born with a true eye and a steady hand."

"Like her mother?"

"More like her father, I think, though I doubt his first teachers would know him now from his fast dressing."

He moved his cloak aside to expose its vermilion lining. "You don't approve?"

I shrugged. "I saw better dyes in my father's warehouse. But that was a long time ago, when artists bothered more about the color of their paints than their own cloth."

He smiled a little, as if the sharpness of my tongue pleased him. The cloak fell shut.

"How did you find us?"

"It wasn't easy. I wrote to your father many times but he never replied. Three years ago I went to your house in Florence, but no one was there and the servants were strangers and would tell me nothing. Then this winter I spent an evening in the company of a bishop who boasted that there was a nun in one of his convents who was painting her own chapel with help from her natural daughter."

"I see. Well, I am glad that Rome has afforded you such drinking companions, though I had better hopes for the painter I once knew than to be reduced to the likes of Bishop Salvetti. Still, if the wine flowed well enough, you probably don't even remember his name."

"Actually I do. But I remember more how his story made me feel," he said evenly, treating my tart tongue for what it was, a hasty defense against feeling. "I have been looking for you both for so long, Alessandra."

I felt a flush go through me. Erila was right: It does not do for women to stop thinking about men. It leaves them vulnerable to the moment when they return.

I shook my head. "It was all a lifetime ago. I wager we are much changed now."

"You do not look changed," he said gently. "Your fingers are as stained as they always were."

I curled them up beside me as I had done so often when I was a child. "Your tongue is more honeyed, though." And my voice was still stern. "Where did your shyness go, I wonder?"

"My shyness?" He was silent for a moment. "Some of it went in my journey to hell those weeks in the chapel. And some of it was shocked out of me in the Bargello prison. The rest I keep locked inside. Rome is not a city for the shy or the unsure, though you would do better than to judge me by appearances. When I was a young man I met a girl who had both rich costumes and a sharp tongue. Yet her soul proved larger than many who wore more holy cloth."

The forcefulness in his voice touched a chord of memory. I felt something twist inside me, but it was all so long ago I could no longer be sure what was pleasure and what was fear.

The door opened and a fresh-faced young nun put her head in. She was recently arrived from Venice, where her parents had had trouble keeping her in the house of a night, and she was still something of a thorn in our sides. She saw us together and giggled. As she swooped out, still grinning, he said, "Does your convent have somewhere we could be alone?"

With the door closed, my cell which up till then had been big enough to contain my whole life, was suddenly too small. Above my bed was a full-sized study of the birth of the Virgin, the baby's delicious plumpness taken from a hundred sketches of our daughter. I watched his face break into a smile.

"Is she in your chapel?"

I shrugged. "It is only a sketch."

"Still, they are alive. Like the woman and baby in Ghirlandaio's *Birth of the Virgin*. I saw the chapel again when I was in Florence last. Sometimes I think I have seen nothing painted that surpasses it."

"Really?" I said. "That's not what our bishop tells us. He is forever extolling the new fashions of Rome."

He shook his head. "I am not sure you would like the art of Rome so much now. It is grown a little...fleshy."

"Man as important as God," I said, thinking back to my late-night conversations with our learned nun.

"In some hands, yes."

"And in yours?"

He moved away from me to the window. Outside, a group of younger sisters were crossing the cloister for Vespers, their laughter entwined with the sound of the bells. "It is hard sometimes to swim against a tide." He turned and looked at me. "Perhaps you should know that I am come wearing my best clothes."

We stood watching each other. There was so much to say. But I was finding it hard to breathe. It was as if someone had lit a fire in the room and it was taking up all the air between us.

"And you should know..." I faltered. "You should know that I am given to God now," I said firmly, "and that He has granted me forgiveness for my sins."

He looked directly at me, and his cat's eyes were serious now. "I know that. I too have made my peace with God, Alessandra. But in that peace there is not a day that has gone by when I have not thought of you."

He took a step toward me. I shook my head against the words. I had grown so quiet in my self-sufficiency. It was too painful to let it go.

"I have a child. And a chapel to paint," I said fiercely. "I have no time for such things now."

But even as I said it the old Alessandra was back in me. I could sense her stirring, desire like a dragon's head lifting from slumber, sniffing the air, feeling in its belly a great rush of fire and power. He sensed it too. We were so close, I could feel his breath around me. His smell was sweeter than I remembered, despite the grime of the road. In another lifetime I had been the bold one to his fear. Now it was his turn. He took my hand and knitted my fingers through his own. Between the two of us our stained flesh made up a palette of color. We had always been bound to each other through the power of longing, even when we understood nothing of desire. I made one last try.

"I am scared," I said, the words spilling out without my approval. "I have lived so differently these last years, and I am scared now."

"I know that. You forget I have been scared too in my time." He pulled me toward him and kissed me gently, pulling at my bottom lip with his own, sliding his tongue inside, calling me out to play. And the taste of him was so warm and I remembered it so well, even though we had been almost children then.... He broke off. "But I am not scared now." And his smile lit up both our faces. "And I cannot tell you how long I have waited for this moment, Alessandra Cecchi."

He undressed me slowly, placing the layers of my habit carefully to one side and studying me anew with each garment gone, until at last my shift was removed and I stood naked in front of him. I had been most frightened of my hair, which had once been my only glory and which could no longer fall like a river of black lava down my back. But when the wimple was off its unruly shortness sprang up like tough grass, and he moved his hand across it, ruffling and playing with it as if it was an attribute of great joy and beauty.

I have heard it said that some men like the idea of taking nuns. Of course, it is the grossest of crimes because it is adultery against God. I suppose for that reason alone one can see how those who live for sensation would find it most potent, which is why they usually have to be mad on war or drink before they can do it. But he was neither. He was mad on tenderness.

He put his hands between my legs, tracing up the line of my inner thigh, sliding his finger into the crack of me, playing with the swollen folds of skin he found there, his eyes bold as his touch, locked into mine, studying me all the time. Then he kissed me again, and as he broke away he said my name over and over. And all the time he seemed to be at such ease that it made me laugh and I wondered again how someone once so gauche should have become so confident. "Since when did you become so sure about such things?"

"Since you sent me away," he said softly, kissing me again, closing my eyelids with his lips. "Stop thinking now," he whispered in my ear. "For once, still that vibrant spinning mind of yours."

He lay down with me and he parted my sex with his fingers again, carefully, acutely, his eyes holding mine the whole time, and when he had found my rawness he used his fingertips to catch at the edge of it to orchestrate the pressure and so begin the sweet-sour rise in me. That afternoon he showed me things I had never imagined: specialties of sex, delicacies of desire. Most of all I remember the feel of his tongue on me, like the clean edge of a cat's tongue, firm rasping little flicks, lapping up the milk. Each time I groaned he lifted his head to check that I was with him, his eyes bright as if laughter were no more than a breath away.

I have heard it said that in heaven even the substance of matter is changed by the light of God, so that you can look through solid things to see what lies beyond. As the light turned to dusk in my cell that night, I think I could for that moment see through his body to the very soul of him. Though Erila would no doubt claim a more musical experience, one where after many years I finally heard the sweetness of the top string on the lute.

· · ·

BECAUSE OF HIS TALENT WITH A BRUSH, THE REVEREND MOTHER gave him leave to stay awhile. By night he taught me the art of the body and by day he helped with the chapel. Where there were mistakes, he did what he could to rectify them; where I had settled for adequacy without fire (and there were many examples of it), he added the spark of his brush to bring it more alive. I know he saw its shortcomings, but he did not dwell on them.

When he wasn't with me he was with Plautilla, and under his charge she blossomed. I watched as his knowledge lit up her curiosity, growing them closer together both in art and conversation.

And the longer they spent in each other's company, the more sure I was about what I had to do.

Even without him it would only have been a matter of time before she left me. I had always known that. Not in the most lenient of orders would she have been allowed to stay indefinitely without taking the veil, and I could never allow that. Her future was too big to be contained by convent walls and there was nothing more that I could teach her. She was almost fourteen, the age when young talent must find a master if it is to flourish. If Uccello could train his own daughter in his workshop, then so could he now, and if there was ever a city that could bend the rules to include the errant talent of a female hand, surely Rome at this moment was it. The rest would be up to her.

It was arranged that they would leave before the worst of the summer's heat came in. Of course when I told her, she could see only the loss and the terror, and at first she refused to go. I was gentle with her, mindful of how my mother's chastisements had never achieved anything but to make me more stubborn. When my reason did not work I told her a story: of a young woman who had wanted to paint so much that it had led her into transgressions of such magnitude that her greatest wish in life was now to give to her daughter what she could not have herself. And having listened, at last she agreed to leave me. She was, I realize in retrospect, a more obedient child than I had ever been. But it would not do now to dwell on the ways that my rebellion had defined my life.

In her chest, along with my hopes and dreams, I also packed the manuscript swaddled in velvet cloth. I had no need of it now and it deserved better than the damp marriage chest of an aging nun. Before I wrapped it away for the last time he sat with it open in front of him. I watched his fingers read the penned lines with awe, and I knew he would take as good care of it as I, and in that way it would find its way forward into history.

Forty-nine

THE NIGHT BEFORE THEY LEFT WE LAY TOGETHER ON MY hard bed, our bodies sticking and sucking in the summer heat. The exhaustion of our fed desire had left us languid and sleepy. He dipped his fingers into a bowl of water and traced a cool wet line from my hand up one arm across my chest and down the other, resting gently for a moment on the thin white scar that decorated my wrist and inner arm.

"Tell me again," he said quietly.

"You have heard it a dozen times already." I shrugged. "The blade slipped and—"

"—and you used the blood to paint your body." He smiled. "And where did you paint, here?" He touched my shoulder. "Then here?" running his finger down across my breasts. "And then here?" and his finger moved over my stomach toward my sex.

"No! Even I did not have so much wildness."

"I don't believe that," he said. "Still, it would have looked fine enough—the scarlet against your chestnut skin. Though there are other colors that would suit as well."

I smiled and let his hand lie where it had reached. Tomorrow I would put on my habit, go back to my chapel, and become a nun again. Tomorrow.

"If you knew how many times I have painted your body in my imagination…"

"And once in reality—on a chapel ceiling."

He shook his head. "You were never the right model for the Madonna. Your eyes were always too bold. Why do you think I was scared of you for so long? You have always been Eve. Though I wouldn't rate the serpent's chances against your mind."

"I think that might depend on whose face it carried," I said.

"Ah, you still do not think of the snake as a woman? You still defy Masolino in that."

I shrugged. "I think," I said, and smiled as he mouthed the next words along with me, "I think there is no scriptural evidence for such a rendering. Though I have yet to see a painter brave enough to challenge it."

So it was that the serpent joined us in our bed on that last night. And though I know that what we did was a blasphemy, I cannot wish it undone: the way its wild green and silver body grew under his brush, curling over my breasts, then plunging down deep across my stomach before disappearing into my hair where, just as the thickest encased it, he placed the lightest out-line of his own face in the tangle. And as he worked, I remembered moments of desolation as well as pleasure, and the body of the mountebank with the slow lust of his muscles rippling under his shining skin.

Next morning I rose from the bed, concealed the glorious painting that was now my body under my habit, and said goodbye to my lover and our child.

I SPENT SO MUCH ENERGY CONVINCING PLAUTILLA THAT SHE MUST go, I had forgotten to store up enough to console myself. The days after they rode out the sadness flowed in like disease, wrap-ping me in a cold fever of desolation, and the farther the miles unwound between us the more it felt as if my insides were unraveling off a spit onto the floor.

I had once accused my lover of the sin of despair. Now it seemed I would succumb to it myself. My chapel remained untouched, the life of the Virgin barely begun. At night I lay on my bed, tracing the memory of desire in the folds of the snake's body. But the summer flared up like fire and with the heat came night sweats and dust and dirt, and before long the shining colors started to bleed and fade like my father's rich fabrics left out in the sun. And so my spirit faded with them.

The Reverend Mother humored my pain for a while and then became impatient with the delay. In the end it was Erila who saved me, though to begin with I feared she too had deserted me. Florence was a long journey from Loro Ciufenna and the dyers of Santa Croce were a closed guild unto themselves, so that even when she found them in the back streets by the river, their makeshift workshops bright with needles and stolen colors, they were loath to give their secrets to a stranger. But no one could resist Erila for long. Of the mountebank, she told me later, there was no trace.

She arrived back one evening when the light was at its most sublime, unpacking the small leather case and laying the contents out on the floor by my pallet: medicaments, ointments, cloths, needles and scrapers, and the collection of tiny bottles. The color in each little vial was muted and muddy, the density of ink rather than paint. It was only once the skin was punctured and the dye leaked pinpoint by pinpoint into the wound that its vibrancy was released. Oh, but then the shades were amazing, raw and new like the first brushstrokes of God in the Garden of Eden, and at the sight of them mingling with the sting of my blood something of the old flame flickered up in me. That first night we worked by candlelight, and by the time the dawn came in there was half an inch of serpent's tail on my shoulder restored to its former greatness and my body was exhausted from the pleasure to be had from bearing the pain.

As the days went by we got faster and I became more resilient. The snake under our fingers grew more seductive as we learned better how to wield the needle and judge how many tiny wounds it took to bring alive each flicker of its muscle. As it rolled and curled its lascivious way over my breasts and my belly, I could see it well enough to take over the needle myself. So it happened that the moment when I reached the fading contours of my lover's face I was alone, and there was a sweet catharsis to be had in the cruelty of the needle as I added the dart of a serpent's tongue sliding from his mouth toward my sex.

In this way I got back my appetite for living and returned to my chapel walls.

THE YEARS THAT FOLLOWED WERE TUMULTUOUS. THAT NEXT SPRING my father died, propped in his study chair, his abacus and ledgers in front of him. Luca took over the house and my mother retreated to a convent inside the city, where she took a vow of silence. Her last letter wished God's grace upon me and urged me to confess my sins as she had confessed hers.

Meanwhile, in her beloved Florence the battered Republic took back the Medicis after decades of exile. But Giovanni de' Medici, now Pope Leo X, was a pale shadow of his learned father. My fat greasy half-brother—for that, amazingly, was who he was—had been forged in the flames of sycophancy and squandered wealth. Under his pontificate, Rome grew as flabby as his body. Even her art became corpulent. The letters from my painter told of a young woman artist whose brush would soon be as fine as any man's, but of a city stewing in its own decadence; of banquets that went on for days and patrons so rich they threw their silver plate into the Tiber after each course (though it was rumored that they later sent servants to dredge it up again).

The next year my painter and my daughter left Rome bound for France. In the past he had received invitations from both Paris and London, cities where the new learning was still in its infancy and where there would be better chances for patronage for those who stood by the old ways. So they left with their brushes and the manuscript. I charted their course on a map my learned nun procured for me from a cartographer in Milan. Their ship landed in Marseille, from where they traveled to Paris. But the invitation promised there did not lead to rewarding work and in the end they were forced to sell some of *The Divine Comedy* to keep themselves alive. In this way they moved through Europe, but their letters told of a growing aggression toward the established church and what some considered to be its idolatrous art, and finally they crossed to England, where the young king, schooled in the Renaissance, was eager for artists to make his court great. For the first years they sent me stories of a rain-soaked people with a harsh language and harsher manners. And of course I couldn't help but think of his monastery and wonder that life had led him back into a gray palette once more. But then the letters stopped coming and I have not heard from them for some years now.

I had little enough time to mourn. Soon after the chapel was completed, the church came down upon us. Our creativity had become too monstrous even for these louche times. It had always been a matter of time until the whispers reached the wrong ears. When our bishop died the man appointed in his place was cut from sterner cloth, and in his wake came church inspectors who smelled the Devil everywhere: in the cut of our habits, the perfumed cloth in our cells, and most of all in the books on our shelves. Only my chapel survived their scrutiny because by then the humanity of such art had become almost ordinary. My chapel and my body. But that was a matter between God and myself.

Those of us who had been through it before took it quietly. We knew better than to fight. The few who did resist were crushed and transferred. In some ways it was not so terrible. Our playwright and most of our seamstresses and beauticians went, but the scholar remained, though her library was purged. A new Reverend Mother was brought in from outside, pure and upright with a more censorious God in her backbone. With the chapel finished, I developed a healthy voice for Vespers and hid my eccentricities behind my prayer book. As long as I was acquiescent I was too old to be a threat. Of course I lost my painting materials. They left me my pens, though, and so it was that I started this history of my life, which for a while staved off the loneliness and boredom of the new order.

My greatest loss was Erila. Of course there was no room for her wayward commercial spirit in this strict new world. To have stayed she would have had to become the menial she had always rejected, and anyway she had already forged a life outside. With help from me and her own savings, she set herself up in an apothecary shop in the town nearby. Such a quiet place had never seen such a wildwoman, and of course there were those who thought she was a witch, though ironically more of a white one than black. But it didn't take long before they came to depend on her remedies and advice as much as the nuns had done. And so she achieved a respectability of sorts. We laugh about it on the occasions she is allowed to visit: how life provides the most bizarre of endings to one's story.

I FINISHED THIS MANUSCRIPT TWO MONTHS AGO, AND IT WAS THEN I decided what I must do. It is not so much that I am in pain—by now the memories are as dim as my eyesight—it is more that the years roll out in front of me like thin pastry and I cannot bear the idea of this rigid foreverness and long slow slide into decrepitude. Having decided, it was of course to Erila I went for help, one last time. The tumor was her idea. She had seen a number of them, evil things that rose out from the skin in a manner both gross and mysterious. Women especially were prone to them around their breasts. They grew as much on the inside as on the surface, eating deep into the vital organs of the body until the sufferers drowned in the agony of their own decay. There was no treatment, and even so-called physicians were frightened of them. Once afflicted, sufferers were known to hide themselves away from society like wounded animals, howling their pain in the darkness, awaiting their own death.

The pig's bladder was inspired and easy, a matter of a visit to the kitchen while the others were at prayer. Erila helped me fill it and fix it to my chest and gave me drafts and ointments to make me vomit or raise my body temperature for times when I needed the illness to be more overt to keep them away. And in the end it is she who will bring me the poison when I need it, extracted from the roots of one of the medicinal plants she tends in her garden. It will cause me pain, she says, and she cannot guarantee its swiftness, but of the outcome there is no doubt. The only remaining question is what they do with my body afterward. Our convent has yet another new Reverend Mother now, the last remaining survivor from the old days: our scholar, who over the years has managed to find genuine vocation in her solitude. I cannot tell her everything, of course, though I have asked for her indulgence in leaving my body and the habit intact. It is not my intention to embarrass her rule. I like and respect her too much to do that. Because she knows this and has some memory of my past misdemeanors, she inquired no further, only agreed.

YOU ARE WONDERING ABOUT MY DEATH, YES? ABOUT THE SIN OF suicide and the final impossibility of God's forgiveness.

I have thought much about it.

Before the manuscript left my hands I studied those crowded circles of hell. Suicide is indeed a grave sin, in some ways the gravest. But I find it almost comforting how Dante portrays it. The appropriate punishment for the appropriate sin: for those who would choose to leave the world before their appointed moment, hell has them bound back into it forever. The souls of the suicides are rooted deep into the earth, woven into the structures of trees, their blasted branches and trunks acting as live food for all manner of harpies and birds of prey. In the middle of the canto, Dante tells of how a pack of hounds in pursuit of sinners comes bounding in through the wood and, in their flight, rips to shreds a small tree whose soul cries out plaintively to have his leaves collected and returned to him.

Hunted by dogs. I have hated the Onesti legend for so long, maybe I was always bound to share its heroine's fate. But it will not all be pain. I have memorized Dante's geography of hell well. The wood of the suicides is near to the burning ground of the sodomites. Sometimes they rush in, beating down the flames that ignite constantly all over their scarred bodies, and, as Dante would have it, on occasion there is time for them to stop and converse a little with other damned souls about art and literature and the sins for which we are all condemned. I would like that.

I have made my goodbyes. One afternoon I took off my wimple and lay in the garden with my face in the sun, near to the fig tree that we had planted soon after our arrival and by whose growth we had measured Plautilla's own. I did not even bother to move when the young nun found me there and ran twittering back to the house with news of my "transgression." What do they know of me anyway? It was all so long ago and old nuns are so invisible. They shuffle and smile with watery eyes and mumble over their porridge and their prayers, all of which I have learned to do admirably. They have no idea who I am. Most of them don't even know it was my fingers that were responsible for the images that shine off the walls as they sing in the chapel.

So now I sit in my cell waiting for Erila, who comes tonight to deliver me the draft and say her goodbyes. It is to her I will entrust this document. She is no longer anyone's slave and she must do with the rest of her life as she sees fit. All I have asked is that she dispatch it to the last address I have for my daughter and the painter, in an area of London near the Kings Court called Cheapside. Still, we both know my father would never let a document or contract of any worth out of his hands unless he had either a copy or proof that his agent was there to receive it, and even then he might take out insurance against its safe arrival. Recently Erila has talked of travel with a kind of hunger that comes only to those who were born in a place other than that in which they will die. If anyone can find my daughter, she will. I can do no more.

The night is coming in, a blanket of heat and humidity. Once Erila is gone I will swallow the draft quickly. In accordance with my mother's wishes I have prepared my confession and the priest is called for. Let us hope he has a strong stomach and a silent tongue.

THERE IS ONE THING I HAVE FORGOTTEN: MY CHAPEL.

It took so long—in some ways it was my life's work—and yet I have said so little of it.

The lives of the Virgin and John the Baptist. The same subjects as Domenico Ghirlandaio's Capella Maggiore of Santa Maria Novella, which my mother and I had seen together when I was just ten years old. It was my first taste of history, and just as it remained the greatest Florentine memory for my painter, so it is also mine. Because while there may be better artists and greater achievements, Ghirlandaio's frescoes tell you as much about the glory and the humanity of our great city as they do the life of any saint, and in my opinion it is that which makes them so affecting and so true.

So in the spirit of that truth which was once so central to our new learning, I will not hide this fact now.

My chapel is sadly mediocre. Should future connoisseurs of the new art come upon it they will glance at it for a moment and then pass on, noting it as an attempt by an inferior artist in a superior age. Yes, it has a feel for color (that passion I never lost), and there are times when my father's cloth moves like water, and the occasional face speaks of character as well as paint. But the compositions are clumsy and many of the figures, for all of my care, remain staid and lacking in life. If kindness and honesty were to be held in mutual regard, one might say it was the work of an older artist without training who did her best and deserves to be remembered as much for her enthusiasm as for her achievement.

If that sounds like a statement of failure from an old woman at the end of her life, you must believe me when I tell you it is absolutely not. Because if you were to put it with all the others—all the wedding panels and birth trays and marriage chests and frescoes and altarpieces and panel paintings that were produced during those heady days when we brought man into contact with God in a way he had never been before—then you would see it for what it is: a single voice lost inside a great chorus of others.

And, such was the sound that the chorus made together, that to have been a part of it at all was enough for me.

MICHELANGELO'S WHITE CEDAR CRUCIFIX WAS LOST FOR MANY YEARS after Napoleon's invasion of Italy. It was rediscovered in the 1960s, reattributed, recently restored, and now hangs in the sacristy of Santo Spírito church on the south side of the river. When he was a very young man, Michelangelo also worked as an assistant to Domenico Ghirlandaio on the frescoes for the Capella Maggiore in Santa Maria Novella.

Botticelli's illustrations for Dante's *Divine Comedy* disappeared from Italy soon after they were painted, only to turn up in various parts of Europe centuries later. In 1501 his name appeared in one of the church's denunciation boxes, and he was brought before the Night Police on the charge of sodomy. There is dispute among scholars as to whether the charge was slander or truth.

The Night Police operated throughout the fifteenth century and beyond, policing sodomy and other forms of indecent fornication in Florence. With the exception of the Savonarola years, 1494 to 1498, their control was much lighter than in many other cities.

In the early sixteenth century, as dowries rose and the number of unmarried women increased, certain convents in northern Italy were found to be operating with particularly lax rules on behavior. The Church investigated, and the offending convents were either cleansed or closed down.

ACKNOWLEDGMENTS

THIS BOOK IS BUILT ON A SCAFFOLD OF HISTORY CONSTRUCTED from a number of contemporary sources, eminent scholars, and art historians. The facts are theirs; any mistakes are entirely my own.

I could not have written it without the love, intellectual encouragement, and support of Sue Woodman, who has given me more than she will ever know (though I daresay she suspects). Berenice Goodwin, a great art teacher and a good friend, read the manuscript at an early critical stage and was inspirational, both in saving me from my worst mistakes and substantially enriching my understanding of the period. My deep thanks go to Jaki Authur, Gillian Slovo, Eileen Quinn, Peter Busby, and Mohit Bakaya, each of whom in their unique way fed my spirit during difficult times. For their assistance in Florence, thanks to Isabella Planner, Carla Corri, and Pietro Bernabei. Also, thanks to Kate Lowe, who helped me firsthand with her scholarship. And finally to my agent, Clare Alexander, who had infinite patience and clarity of criticism, and to Lennie Goodings, my longtime editor and friend, who was the best midwife one could have on a book which, in keeping with its title, had a colorful labor. For your tenacity and vision, Lennie, I remain in your debt.

For those wanting to read more about this extraordinary period, I offer the following short bibliography:

Leon Alberti. *On Painting.* Penguin Classics.

Francis Ames-Lewis. *Drawing in Early Renaissance Italy.* Yale University Press.

Ugo Baldassarri, ed. *Images of Quattrocento Florence.* Yale University Press.

Michael Baxendale. *Painting and Experience in 15th Century Italy.* Oxford University Press.

Elizabeth Birbari. *Dress in Italian Painting.* John Murray.

Anthony Blunt. *Artistic Theory in Italy 1450–1600.* Oxford University Press.

Eve Borsook. *Companion Guide to Florence.* Companion Guides.

Cennino Cennini. *The Craftsman's Handbook (Il Libro dell'Arte).* Dover Publications.

Christopher Hibbert. *The Rise and Fall of the House of Medici.* Penguin Books.

Graham Hughes. *Renaissance Cassoni.* Art Books International.

Lisa Jardine. *Worldly Goods.* Macmillan.

Luca Landucci, trans. Jervis A. Rosen. *A Florentine Diary from 1450 to 1516.* Ayer Company Publications.

Jean Lucas-Dubreton. *Daily Life in Florence in the Time of the Medici.* Macmillan.

Michael Rocke. *Forbidden Friendships: Homosexuality and Male Culture in Renaissance Florence.* Oxford University Press.

Paola Tinagli. *Women in Italian Renaissance Art.* Manchester University Press.

Giorgio Vasari, trans. George Bull. *Lives of the Artists.* Penguin Classics.

Martin Wackernagel. *The Work of the Florentine Renaissance Artist.* Princeton University Press.

Evelyn Welch. *Art and Society in Italy 1350–1500.* Oxford University Press.

Christine Klapisch Zuber. *Women, Family, and Ritual in Renaissance Florence*. University of Chicago Press.

For permission to quote from Cantos I and XIII of Mark Musa's translation of Dante's *The Divine Comedy, 1: Inferno*, published by Penguin Books, I would like to thank the Indiana University Press. For permission to quote from Canto XXXIII of Dorothy L. Sayers and Barbara Reynolds's translation of *The Divine Comedy, 3: Paradise*, also published by Penguin Books, I would like to thank David Higham Associates.

THE
BIRTH
OF
VENUS

SARAH
DUNANT

A Reader's Guide

1. Alessandra has the will and the talent to be a painter. However, she does not have the training or the social opportunity she needs. How well does *The Birth of Venus* explain why there are no women's names in the great roll call of artistic geniuses of the Renaissance?

2. The image of the serpent with a human head is a motif that runs through the novel in many different forms. What are its guises, and how does its meaning shift as the novel progresses?

3. In their own ways, both Alessandra and her mother subvert and rebel against the world they live in. Which one of them do you think is the happiest or most fulfilled?

4. Erila is a slave with no rights or apparent power, so it is ironic that she is the only character in the novel who seems to have any real freedom. How is it that she is able to walk an independent path when those around her are trapped by their circumstances?

5. Lorenzo the Great dies early on in the novel, yet his spirit and that of his family inhabit the book both politically and culturally. What does the book convey about him and the impact that the Medicis had on Florence?

6. Alessandra's entire world is circumscribed by her belief in God. Yet at the time in which she is writing, there seem to exist two different versions of God; which one predominates depends on whether the believer is a follower of the Renaissance or of Savonarola. What does Alessandra see as the difference between the two versions, and how fairly do you think she judges them?

7. To what extent is Savonarola the villain of the novel?

8. To what degree is this a novel about a city as much as a character?

9. The novel contains many different kinds of love: intellectual, spiritual, sexual, maternal. Which moves you most and why?

10. Alessandra and her brother Tomaso are at odds with each other from the beginning of the novel. To what extent should we trust Alessandra's judgment of him, given that they are in competition for the same man?

11. How much sympathy do you have for Cristoforo as a character, and what image of homosexual life in Florence do you derive from his thoughts and actions?

12. Alessandra's marriage, though painful in some ways, is in other ways quite fulfilling, given the confines of the time. In an era when women were seen as fundamentally inferior, do you think it would have been possible for them to have an equal relationship sexually and intellectually with men?

13. In the fifteenth century, *melancholy* was the only word in use to describe the psychological state of depression, and there was no treatment for the condition. How different would suffering from depression have been in a time when all meaning was seen to emanate from God? And why does the painter fall into such a state?

14. The convent described at the end of the novel is based on real records and real places. If you were a woman in fifteenth-century Florence, would you have preferred to live outside or inside its walls?

Afterword

The heroine of *The Birth of Venus*, Alessandra Cecchi, was born of my imagination. But everything in the book about the time she lived through is historically accurate. The last decade of the fifteenth century in Italy was an astonishing period: one of great beauty and great brutality, where creativity was often financed by corruption.

Nowhere were those contradictions more evident than in the city of Rome. And Rome in the 1490s is where my most recent novel, *Blood and Beauty*, is set. It also has a remarkable young woman at its center. Born at exactly the same time as Alessandra, she too was smart, well educated, and torn between obedience and rebellion. She too had an extraordinary life, especially as a teenager. But that is where the similarities end, because the heroine of *Blood and Beauty* actually existed, and was the most famous and most maligned woman in Renaissance history. Her name: Lucrezia Borgia. Murder, incest, and sexual rapaciousness—Lucrezia has been accused of them all. But the truth, as ever, is more complex and challenging than centuries of historical gossip.

The illegitimate daughter of Spanish cardinal Rodrigo

Borgia, Lucrezia was just thirteen years old when her father became Pope Alexander VI, in 1492. Charismatic, clever, and corrupt, with a huge appetite for life and power, Rodrigo used his children as tools in his attempt to build a new dynasty. Lucrezia was the perfect marriage pawn. By the time she was twenty she had been married three times. The first union was annulled for nonconsummation (though her husband claimed he had known his wife "an infinity of times"), the second ended in the brutal murder of a man she genuinely loved, and the third took her into one of Italy's oldest and most prestigious families, as Duchess of Ferrara.

The drama and heartbreak of her life, along with her determination to free herself from the clutches of her passionate, violent brother Cesare and her adoring but suffocating father, make for one of the great stories of the Renaissance.

To give you a taste of this extraordinary family, what follows is the opening of *Blood and Beauty*, when Rodrigo Borgia, sixty-one years old and vibrating with ambition and energy, manipulates his way into becoming the most powerful man in Christendom.

You may not feel like reading it straightaway. I know that when I finish a book that works for me (as I hope *The Birth of Venus* might have worked for you), I need space to let its feelings and atmosphere fade a little. But maybe in a few days, when you start to miss this most rich and glorious period in Italian history, you'll want to take a journey inside the Vatican, into one of the greatest chapels ever built (though you will have to imagine it when it was new, before Michelangelo got his hands on it), to experience life inside the Roman conclave of cardinals. *Blood and Beauty* awaits. I trust you won't be disappointed.

—Sarah Dunant

Read on for an excerpt from

Blood & Beauty

by

Sarah Dunant

Chapter 1

August 11, 1492

DAWN IS A PALE BRUISE RISING IN THE NIGHT SKY WHEN, from inside the palace, a window is flung open and a face appears, its features distorted by the firelight thrown up from the torches beneath. In the piazza below, the soldiers garrisoned to keep the peace have fallen asleep. But they wake fast enough as the voice rings out:

"WE HAVE A POPE!"

Inside, the air is sour with the sweat of old flesh. Rome in August is a city of swelter and death. For five days, twenty-three men have been incarcerated within a great Vatican chapel that feels more like a barracks. Each is a figure of status and wealth, accustomed to eating off a silver plate with a dozen servants to answer his every call. Yet here there are no scribes to write letters and no cooks to prepare banquets. Here, with only a single manservant to dress them, these men eat frugal meals posted through a wooden hatch that snaps shut when the last one is delivered. Daylight slides in from small windows high up in the structure, while at night a host of candles flicker under the barrel-vaulted ceiling of a painted sky and stars, as vast, it seems, as the firmament. They live constantly in each other's company, allowed out only for the formal business of voting or to relieve themselves, and even in the latrines the work continues: negotiation and persuasion over the trickle of aging men's urine. Finally, when they are too tired to talk, or need to ask guidance from God, they are free to retire to their cells: a set of makeshift compartments constructed around the edges of the chapel and comprised of a chair, a table and a raised pallet for sleeping; the austerity a reminder, no doubt, of the tribulations of aspiring saints.

Except these days saints are in short supply, particularly inside the Roman conclave of cardinals.

The doors had been bolted on the morning of August 6. Ten days earlier, after years of chronic infirmity, Pope Innocent VIII had finally given in to the exhaustion of trying to stay alive. Inside their rooms in the Vatican palace, his son and daughter had waited patiently to be called to his bedside, but his final moments had been reserved for spatting cardinals and doctors. His body was still warm when the stories started wafting like sewer smells through the streets. The wolf pack of ambassadors and diplomats took in great lungfuls, then dispatched their own versions of events in the saddlebags of fast horses across the land: stories of how His Holiness's corpse lay shriveled, despite an empty flagon of blood drained from the veins of Roman street boys on the orders of a Jewish doctor, who had vowed it would save his life; how those same bloodless boys were already feeding the fishes in the Tiber as the doctor fled the city. Meanwhile, across the papal bedclothes, the Pope's favorite, the choleric Cardinal della Rovere, was so busy trading insults with the Vice-Chancellor, Cardinal Rodrigo Borgia, that neither of them actually noticed that His Holiness had stopped breathing. Possibly Innocent had died to get away from the noise, for they had been arguing for years.

Of course, in such a web of gossip each man must choose what he wants to believe; and different rulers enjoy their news, like their meat, more or less well spiced. While few will question the cat claws of the cardinals, others might wonder about the blood, since it is well known around town that His Holiness's only sustenance for weeks had been milk from a wet-nurse installed in an antechamber and paid by the cup. Ah, what a way to go to heaven: drunk on the taste of mother's milk.

As for the conclave that follows, well, the only safe prediction is that prediction is impossible: that and the fact that God's next vicar on earth will be decided as much by bribery and influence as by any saintly qualifications for the job.

AT THE END OF THE THIRD DAY, AS THE EXHAUSTEd CARDINALS retire to their cells, Rodrigo Borgia, Papal Vice-Chancellor and Spanish Cardinal of Valencia, is sitting appreciating the view. Above the richly painted drapery on the walls of the chapel (new cardinals have been known to try to draw the curtains) is a scene from the life of Moses: Jethro's daughters young and fresh, the swirl of their hair and the color of their robes singing out even in candlelight. The Sistine Chapel boasts sixteen such frescoes— scenes of the life of Christ and Moses—and those with enough influence may choose their cell by its place in the cycle. Lest anyone should mistake his ambition, Cardinal della Rovere is currently sitting under the image of Christ giving St. Peter the keys of the Church, while his main rival, Ascanio Sforza, has had to settle for Moses clutching the tablets of stone (though with a brother who runs the bully state of Milan, some would say that the Sforza cardinal has more on his side than just the Commandments).

Publicly, Rodrigo Borgia has always been more modest in his aspirations. He has held the post of vice-chancellor through the reign of five different pontiffs—a diplomatic feat in itself—and along with a string of benefices it has turned him into one of the richest and most influential churchmen in Rome. But there is one thing he has not been able to turn to his advantage: his Spanish blood. And so the papal throne itself has eluded him. Until now, perhaps; because after two public scrutinies there is deadlock between the main contenders, which makes his own modest handful of votes a good deal more potent.

He murmurs a short prayer to the Virgin Mother, reaches for his cardinal's hat, and pads his way down the marble corridor between the makeshift cells until he finds the one he is looking for.

Inside, somewhat drained by the temperature and the politicking, sits a young man with a small Bacchus stomach and a pasty face. At seventeen, Giovanni de' Medici is the youngest cardinal ever to be appointed to the Sacred College, and he has yet to decide where to put his loyalty.

"Vice-Chancellor!" The youth leaps up. The truth is one can only wrestle with Church matters for so long and his mind has wandered to the creamy breasts of a girl who shared his bed in Pisa when he was studying there. There had been something about her—her laugh, the smell of her skin?—so that when he feels in need of solace it is her body that he rubs himself against in his mind. "Forgive me, I did not hear you."

"On the contrary—it is I who should be forgiven. I disturb you at prayer!"

"No . . . Not exactly." He offers him the one chair, but the Borgia cardinal brushes it away with a wave of the hand, settling his broad rump on the pallet bed instead.

"This will do well enough for me," he says jovially, slapping his fist on the mattress.

The young Medici stares at him. While everyone else is wilting under the relentless heat, it is remarkable how this big man remains so sprightly. The candlelight picks out a broad forehead under a thatch of tonsured white hair, a large hooked nose and full lips over a thick neck. You would not, could not, call Rodrigo Borgia handsome; he is grown too old and stout for that. Yet once you have looked at him you do not easily look away, for there is an energy in those sharp dark eyes younger than his years.

"After living through the election of four popes I have grown

almost fond of the—what shall we call it?—'challenges' of conclave life." The voice, like the body, is impressive, deep and full,
the remnants of a Spanish accent in the guttural trim on certain
words. "But I still remember my first time. I was not much older
than you. It was August then too—alas, such a bad month for the
health of our holy fathers. Our prison was not so splendid then,
of course. The mosquitoes ate us alive and the bed made my
bones ache. Still, I survived." He laughs, a big sound, with no
sense of self-consciousness or artifice. "Though of course I did
not have such a remarkable father to guide me. Lorenzo de'
Medici would be proud to see you take your place in the conclave, Giovanni. I am sincerely sorry for his death. It was a loss
not just for Florence but for all of Italy."

The young man bows his head. *Beware, my son. These days Rome
is a den of iniquity, the very focus of all that is evil.* Under his robes he
holds a letter from his father: advice on entering the snake pit of
Church politics from a man who had the talent to skate on thin
ice and make it look as if he was dancing. *Few men are to be trusted.
Keep your own counsel until you are established.* Since his father's
death only a few months before, the young cardinal has learned
its contents by heart, though he sorely wishes now that the words
were less general and more particular.

"So tell me, Giovanni"—Rodrigo Borgia drops his voice in an
exaggerated manner, as if to anticipate the secrets they are about
to share—"how are you holding up through this, this
labyrinthine process?"

"I am praying to God to find the right man to lead us."

"Well said! I am sure your father railed against the venality of
the Church and warned against false friends who would take you
with them into corruption."

*This current College of Cardinals is poor in men of worth and you
would do well to be guarded and reserved with them.* The young man
lifts an involuntary hand to his chest, to check the letter is concealed. *Beware of seducers and bad counselors, evil men who will drag
you down, counting upon your youth to make you easy prey.* Surely not

even the Vice-Chancellor's hawk eyes are able to read secrets through two layers of cloth?

Outside, a shout pierces the air, followed by the shot of an arquebus: new weapons for new times. The young man darts his head up toward the high, darkened window.

"Don't fret. It's only common mayhem."

"Oh . . . no, I am not worried."

The stories are well known: how in the interregnum between popes Rome becomes instantly ungovernable, old scores settled by knife-thrusts in dark alleys, new ones hatched under cover of an exuberant general thuggery that careers between theft, brawling and murder. But the worst is reserved for the men who have been too favored, for they have the most to lose.

"You should have been here when the last della Rovere pope, Sixtus IV, died—though not even Lorenzo de' Medici could have made his son a cardinal at the age of nine, eh?" Rodrigo laughs. "His nephew was so hated that the mob stripped his house faster than a plague of locusts. By the time the conclave ended only the walls and the railings remained." He shakes his head, unable to conceal his delight at the memory. "Still, you must feel at home sitting here under the work of your father's protégés." He lifts his eyes to the fresco on the back wall of the cell: a group of willowy figures so graceful that they seem to be still moving under the painter's brush. "This is by that Botticelli fellow, yes?"

"Sandro Botticelli, yes." The style is as familiar to the young Florentine as the Lord's Prayer.

"Such a talented man! It is wonderful how much . . . how much flesh he gets into the spirit. I have always thought that Pope Sixtus was exceedingly lucky to get him, considering that three years before he had launched a conspiracy to kill his patron, your own father, and wipe out the whole Medici family. Fortunately you are too young to remember the outrage."

But not so young that he could ever be allowed to forget. The only thing bloodier than the attack had been the retribution.

"Luckily, he survived and prospered. Despite the della Rovere family," Rodrigo adds, smiling.

"My father spoke highly of your keen mind, Vice-Chancellor. I know I shall learn a lot from you."

"Ah! You already have his wit and diplomacy, I see." And the smile dissolves into laughter. The candle on the table flutters in the wind of his breath and his generous features dance in the light. The younger man feels a bead of sweat moving down from his hair and wipes it away with his hand. His fingers come away grimy. In contrast, the Borgia cardinal remains splendidly unaffected by the heat.

"Well, you must forgive me if I show a certain fatherly affection. I too have a son of your age who needs counsel as he climbs the ladder of the Church. Ah—but of course, you know this. The two of you studied together in Pisa. Cesare spoke often of you as a good friend. And an outstanding student of rhetoric and law."

"As I would speak of him."

In public. Not in private. No. In private, the cocky young Borgia was too closeted by his Spanish entourage to be a friend to anyone. Which is just as well, since whatever money he put on his back (and there was always a sack of it; when he came to dine you could barely see the cloth for the jewels sewn onto it) a Borgia bastard could never be the social equal of a legitimate Medici. He was clever, though, so fast on his feet that in public disputation he could cut to the quick, pulling arguments like multicolored threads from his brain until black seemed to turn into white and wrong became just another shade of gray. Even the praise of his tutors seemed to bore him: he lived more in the taverns than the study halls. But then he was hardly alone in that fault.

The young Medici is glad of the shadows around them. He would not like such thoughts to be exposed to daylight. If the emblem on the Borgia crest is that of the bull, everyone knows it is the cunning of the fox that runs in the family.

"Well, I admire your dedication and pursuit of goodness,

Cardinal." Rodrigo Borgia leans over and puts his hand gently on his knee. "It will loom large in God's grace." He pauses. "But not, I fear, in the annals of men. The sad truth is that the times in which we live are deeply corrupt, and without a pope who can withstand the appetites of the wolves prowling around him, neither he nor Italy will survive."

While the back of his hand lies thick as a slab of meat, his fingers are surprisingly elegant, tapered and well manicured, and for a second the younger man finds himself thinking of the woman who graces the Vice-Chancellor's bed these days. A flesh-and-blood Venus she is said to be: milk-skinned, golden-haired and young enough to be his granddaughter. The gossip is tinged with disgust that such sweetness should couple with such decay, but there is envy there too; how easily beauty snaps onto the magnet of power, whatever a man's looks.

"Vice-Chancellor." He takes a breath. "If you are here to canvass my vote . . ."

"Me? No, no, no. I am but a lamb in this powerful flock. Like you, I have no other wish but to serve God and our holy mother the Church." And now the older man's eyes sparkle. They say that while Giuliano della Rovere has a temper fit to roast flesh, it is the Borgia smile that is more to be feared. "No. If I put myself forward at all it is only because, having seen such things before, I fear that a deadlock could push us into hands less capable even than my own."

Giovanni stares at him, wondering at the power of a man who can lie so barefacedly and still give the impression that his heart is in his voice. Is this then his secret? In these last few days he has had occasion to watch him at work; to notice how tirelessly he weaves in and out of the knots of other men, how he is first to help the elder ones to their cells, or to find the need to relieve himself when negotiations stick and new incentives are called for. A few times the younger man has walked into the latrines and found the conversation fall silent at his entrance. And almost always the Vice-Chancellor will be there himself, nodding and beaming over his large stomach with his tool held loosely in his hand, as if it was the most natural pose on earth for God's cardinals to adopt in each other's presence.

Inside the cell, the air feels as thick as soup. "Sweet Mary and the saints. If we are not careful we will boil alive as slowly as Saint Cyrinus." Rodrigo fans his face theatrically and digs inside his robes, holding out a glass vial with an intricate silver top. "Can I offer you relief?"

"No, no thank you."

He digs a finger inside and anoints himself liberally. As the young man catches the tang of jasmine, he remembers how he has detected remnants of it—and a few other scents—around the public spaces over the last few days. Does each camp, like a pack of dogs, identify itself by its smell?

The cardinal is making a business of putting the bottle back in his robes while he stands up to take his leave. Then, suddenly, he seems to change his mind.

"Giovanni, it seems to me you are too much your father's son not to recognize what is happening here. So I shall tell you something I have not made public." And he bends his large frame to get closer to the young man's face. "Don't be alarmed. Take it as a tribute to your family that I share it: a lesson as to how influence moves when the air grows as thick as stinking cheese. Della Rovere cannot win this election, however it may look now."

"How do you know that?" the young man says quickly, the surprise—and perhaps the flattery—overcoming the reticence he had vowed to hold.

"I know it because, as well as being able to count, I have looked inside men's hearts here." He smiles, but there is less mirth in him now. "In the next public scrutiny the della Rovere camp will pick up more votes, which will put him ahead of Sforza, though not enough to secure victory outright. When that happens Ascanio Sforza, who would not make a bad pope, though he would favor Milan too much for Florence—and you—to ever stomach him, will start to panic. And he will be right to do so.

Because a papacy controlled by della Rovere will be one that favors whoever pays it the most. And the money that he is using to buy his way there now is not even his own. You know where it comes from? France! Imagine. An Italian cardinal bought by France. You have heard the rumor, I am sure. Gross slander, you think, perhaps? Except that in this city slander is usually less foul than the truth." He gives an exaggerated sigh. "It would be disastrous of course: a foreign power sitting in the papal chamber. So, to sink his rival, Ascanio Sforza will turn to me."

He stops as if to let the words sink in.

"Because at that point I will be the only one who can stop the water from rushing downhill in that direction."

"Turn to you? But—" *I say it again, my son: until you become accustomed, you would do well to make use of your ears rather than your tongue.* "But I thought . . ." He trails off.

"You thought what? That a Borrjja pope would be a foreigner too," he says, resurrecting the hawking guttural of his name. "A man who would advance only his family and be more loyal to Spain than to Italy." For a moment there is a flash of undisguised anger in his eyes. "Tell me—would a Medici pope care less about the Holy Mother Church because he loves his family and comes from Florence?"

"Cardinal Borgia, it was not my intention—"

"To offend me? No! And neither did you. Powerful families must speak openly to one another. I would expect no less."

He smiles, only too aware that the comparison between the two could be read as offense the other way.

"Yes, I am a Borgia. When I embrace my children we speak in our native tongue. But I defy anyone to say I am less Italian than those who would now put their noses into the French coffers. If the papal crown is up for sale—and as God is my witness I did not start such a process—then at least let us keep the sale inside this room." He sighs again and claps him on the shoulder. "Ah! I fear I have said too much. See! You have pulled the truth from me. Your father's blood runs deep in your veins. Such a politician he was! Always with one finger held up wet to the wind so that when he felt it changing he could move the sails to keep his ship of state on course."

The young Medici does not answer. He is too impressed by the show. The politics of charm. Having grown up with a father who could turn vinegar to honey when it suited him, he knows better than most how it works; but this mix of geniality, cunning and theatrics is new even to him.

"You are tired. Get some rest. Whatever happens it will not be settled until tomorrow at least. You know, I think my Cesare would look almost as fine as you inside scarlet robes." And the last smile is the brightest of all, possibly because there is no dissembling. "I can see you both standing together, tall and strong as cypress trees. Imagine what a fire such youth and energy would light under this deadwood of old men." And he lets out a gale of laughter. "Ah, the foolish pride of men who love their sons better than themselves."

After he has gone the young man sits examining all that he has heard, but while he should be considering the next public scrutiny, he cannot get the image of Cesare Borgia in scarlet out of his mind. He sees him inside a tight knot of men, striding through the streets of Pisa as if every closed door will open to him before he has to knock, and even then he might not choose to go in. God knows the government of the Church is full of men who have only a passing acquaintance with humility, but however contemptuous or lazy (and he is too much his father's son not to know his own failings), in public at least they make an effort to do what is expected of them. But never Cesare Borgia.

Well, whatever the Borgia arrogance, his father's ambitions will fail him. He might be laden with Church benefices, but he will rise so far and no further. Canon law, which they have wasted years of their lives studying, is marvelously clear on this: though there are riches to be had for those born on the other side of the blanket, no bastard—even a papal one—can enter the Sacred College of Cardinals.

Outside, people are gathering in readiness for supper. He hears Rodrigo Borgia's laughter ringing out from somewhere in the main body of the room where the more public canvassing takes place. If the della Rovere camp is to gain votes before losing, then someone must be canvassing for him now, in order to make victory seem secure.

From under his robes he pulls out his father's letter, the paper limp with a sweat that comes from more than the heat of the room. For the first time since he has set foot in the conclave, when he gets to his knees the prayers come from the heart.

Chapter 2

NEXT MORNING, THE THIRD SCRUTINY OF THE CONCLAVE takes place in the formal antechamber off the great chapel.

The count shows the della Rovere faction pulling ahead by a small but appreciable margin. Della Rovere sits stony-faced, too good a politician to give anything away, but Ascanio Sforza, who wears both pleasure and pain on his sleeve, registers his alarm immediately. He glances nervously in the direction of the Vice-Chancellor, but the Borgia cardinal keeps his eyes down as if in prayer.

Outside, the camps disperse in their different directions. Borgia takes his leave to visit the latrine. Sforza watches him go, moving nervously from one foot to another, as if his own bladder is about to burst. The doors have barely closed when he follows. When he comes out a few moments later he is ashen. His brother may rule over a swath of northern Italy, but it is a different kind of muscle needed here. He disappears into the throng. After a while a few of his most powerful supporters also feel the call of nature. Finally, Borgia himself emerges. For once he is not smiling. It is the countenance of a man who seems resigned to the process of defeat. Except of course such a pose would be exactly what was called for if the losers were turning the tables on the winners before they knew it was happening.

Despite the locked doors, by the time darkness falls the news has slipped like smoke out of the Vatican palace and is gossip at the city's richest dinner tables, so that all the great families, the Colonna, the Orsini and the Gaetani (each with their own interested cardinals in the fight), go to bed that night with the name of the della Rovere family rolling around their mouths, the winners dreaming of the spoils in their sleep.

Meanwhile, halfway between the Ponte Sant' Angelo and the Campo de' Fiori, darkness provides cover for another kind of business. The Borgia palace is known throughout Rome as a triumphant marriage of taste and money. It is not only the house of an immensely wealthy cardinal, but also the office of the vice-chancellorship, raising revenues for the papacy and a profitable accounting business in itself. Before the final scrutiny takes place, those who are paid to watch for such things claim they spot the stable doors at the side of the palace opening to let out a pack of animals. First comes a fast horse—a Turkish purebred, no less—carrying a cloaked rider. Following are six mules. The horse has already reached the northern city gate while the mules still plod their way up one of Rome's seven hills. But then silver makes a heavy load, even for beasts of burden. Eight bags of it, they say, each one packed long before, for so much money can never have been counted in one night. Its destination? The palace of Cardinal Ascanio Sforza. If defeat is bitter then there are ways to sweeten the taste it leaves behind.

Inside the conclave, the gold-painted stars in the Sistine Chapel ceiling look down on a night of high activity. Old and young, venal and saintly are all kept awake by the chatter of men. So much horse-trading is taking place that it is a wonder men do not come with abacuses under their robes, so they can work out the profit margins on the offered benefices faster. Once the tide starts to turn the trickle soon becomes a flood. Plates of food are left untouched. The wine is drained and there are calls for more to be passed through the hatch. Johannes Burchard, the German Master of Papal Ceremonies and a man of exquisite precision, notes each request and the time of it down in his book. What he himself thinks remains a secret between him and his diary.

It is the stillest, deadest time of night when the cardinals take their places in a formal circle in their great, carved wooden chairs under canopies, each one embroidered with the crests of their individual benefices. The air is a mix of stale body odor, dust and heavy perfumes. Most of them are ragged with tiredness, but there is no mistaking the underlying excitement in the room. To be part of history is a heady business, especially if you can make a profit from it yourself.

The vote is taken in silence.

Now as the result is announced the room erupts into a loud "AAAAH" in which it is not easy to distinguish fury from triumph. All eyes turn toward the Borgia cardinal.

Tradition calls for only a single word. *"Volo."* "I want." But instead this big man, fine-schooled in politics and subterfuge, leaps up from his seat, brandishing both his fists high in the air, a prizefighter with his greatest opponent at his feet.

"Yes! Yes. I am the Pope . . ." And he lets out a great guffaw of childish delight.

"I AM THE POPE."

"HABEMUS PAPAM!" "WE HAVE A POPE!"

At the palace window the figure pauses, gulping in the fresh night air. Now another figure joins him, arms outstretched with tightly closed fists, like a street magician about to deliver a trick. The hands unclench and a storm of paper scraps is released. They flutter down in the breaking light, a few catching on the dying embers of the torches and flaring up like drunken fireflies. Such a piece of theater has never been seen in the history of a conclave and the people below jump and fight each other to catch them before they land. Those who can read screw up their eyes to decipher the words scribbled there. Others hear it from the voice.

". . . Rodrigo Borgia, Cardinal of Valencia, is elected Pope Alexander VI."

"Bor-g-i-a! Bor-g-i-a!"

The crowd goes wild at the name, the square fuller by the second as the news brings people running from the warren of steamy streets on either side of the Ponte Sant' Angelo, the old stone bridge that crosses the Tiber. After such a wait, they would probably cheer the devil himself. Yet this is more than fickle love. The established families of Rome may moan about tainted foreign blood and a language that sounds like hacking up phlegm, but those with nothing to lose warm to a man who opens his purse and palace at the drop of a feast day. And Rodrigo Borgia has been spending his way into Roman hearts for a long time.

"BOR-G-I-A!"

Unlike many rich men, he always makes it clear how much he enjoys the giving. No discarded basement hangings or halfhearted generosity from this vice-chancellor. Oh no: when a foreign dignitary tours the city or the Church parades its latest relics, it's always the streets outside the Borgia palace that are strewn with the freshest flowers, always his windows that unfurl the biggest, brightest tapestries, his fountain that turns water into wine faster and longer, his entertainments that tickle the most jaded palates with firework displays that light the night sky into the dawn.

"BOR-G-I-A!"

It was barely six months ago when Rome celebrated the fall of Moorish Granada to the armies of Christendom. A triumph for his native Spain as well as for the Church, and he had opened his palace and turned his courtyard into a bullring, with such a frenzy of the sport that one of the bulls, goaded into madness, had run amok in the crowd, spearing half a dozen spectators on its horns. In swift retaliation it had been skewered by the young Cesare, his church garments discarded in favor of full matador finery. How he brought the raging bull to its knees and then severed its throat with a single knife-thrust was all anyone could talk about for days. That and the money paid out to the families of the two men who later died of their wounds. The purse of a wealthy old man and the athletic prowess of his strutting son. Generosity and virility entwined. What better advertisement could there be for the reign of a new pope?

THE RUNNERS ARE ALREADY SPREADING INTO THE CITY. AT THE Ponte Sant' Angelo moored boatmen slip their oars into the water and cut a rapid line toward the island and Ponte Sisto, broadcasting the news as they go. Others cross the river then span east into the thoroughfare of the bankers, the ground-floor trading houses still boarded up against random violence, or south into the busiest part of the city, where rich and poor live separated by alleyways or open sewers, all huddled inside the great protective curve of the Tiber.

"ALLESSANDEER."

In a second-story bedroom in a palace on Monte Giordano, a young woman wakes to the sound of men, wasted on gossip and booze, careering their way down the street. She flips over in the bed to where her companion lies sleeping, one shapely arm flung across the sheet, thick eyelashes laid on downy pale cheeks with lips like peach flesh, open and pouting.

"Giulia . . . ?"

"Hummm?"

They are not usual sleeping companions, these two young beauties, but with the nerves of the house all a-jangle, they have been allowed to keep each other company, listening for the shouts of the mob and teasing each other with stories of chivalry and violence. Two nights before, a man had been running through the streets howling, begging for his life, a gang at his heels. He had thrown himself against the great doors, hammering to be let in, but the bolts had remained in place as his screams turned to gargles of blood and the girls had had to put their heads under the pillows to shut out the death rattle. Come the dawn, Lucrezia had watched as a band of friars in black robes picked up the body from the gutter and placed it on a cart to be taken, along with the rest of the morning harvest of death, to the city morgue. In the convent she used to dream sometimes about the wonders of such work: seeing herself swathed in white, a young St. Clare aglow with poverty and humility, eyes to the ground, as the howling mob parted to greet her saintliness.

"G . . . IA . . . HABEMUS BORGIA."

"Giulia! Wake up. Can you hear them?"

She has never liked sleeping alone. Even as a small child, when her mother or the servant had left her and the darkness started to curdle her insides, she would steel herself to brave the black soup of the room as far as her brother's bed, creeping in beside him. And he, who when awake would rather fight than talk, would put his arms around her and stroke her hair until their warmness mingled and she fell asleep. In the convent she had asked to share the dormitory rather than the privilege of a single cell that was owed to her. By the time she came out, Cesare was long gone and her aunt impatient with what she called such nonsense.

"And what will you do when you are married and sent off to Spain? You cannot have your brother with you then."

No, but the handsome husband they had promised her would surely guard her instead, and when he was out at war or business she would keep a group of ladies around her, so they might all sleep together.

"AALESSANDER. VALEEEENCIA. BOOORGIA . . . YEAAAH."

"Wake up, Giulia!" She is upright in bed now, pulling off the anointed night gloves that she must wear to keep her hands white. "Can you hear what they are shouting? Listen."

"BORGIA, ALEXANDER."

"Aaaah." And now they are both shouting and scrambling, clambering over each other to get from the bed to the window, the nets slipping off their heads and fat ropes of hair escaping and tumbling down their backs. They can barely breathe with excitement. Lucrezia is pushing at the shutter locks, though it is strictly forbidden to open them. The great bolts jump free and the wooden boards snap apart, flooding the room with the light of a white dawn. They dart their heads quickly to look down on to the street, then pull back as one of the men below spots them and starts yelling. They slam the shutters again, convulsed with laughter and nerves.

"Lucrezia! Giulia!" The voice of Lucrezia's aunt has the reach of a hunting trumpet.

She is standing at the bottom of the great curved stone staircase, hands on stout hips, plump face flushed and small dark eyes shining under black eyebrows which grow thicker and closer together the more she plucks them: aunt, widow, mother, mother-in-law and cousin, Adriana da Mila, Spanish by birth, Roman by marriage but first, last and always a Borgia.

"Don't open the shutters. You will cause a riot."

Later, she will bore the world and its wife with the story of how she herself learned the news. How she had been woken in the dead of night, "so black I could not see my hand in front of my face," by what felt like the stabbing of a dozen needles in her mouth. Such a vicious tooth pain that it was all she could do to pull herself out of bed and make her way to the great stone staircase in search of the bottle of clove wine. She had been halfway down when her taper had gone out. "As suddenly as if someone had put a snuffer cap over it."

It was then that it had happened: something or someone had passed by her in a great wind. And though she should have been in terror for her life, for the city was full of burglars and brigands, instead she had felt warmth and wonder filling her whole being, and she had known, *known*—as certainly as if they had stopped and whispered it in my ear," that her cousin, Vice-Chancellor and Cardinal of Valencia, was chosen as God's vicar on earth. The pain had disappeared as fast as it had come and she had fallen on her knees on the stone steps then and there to give thanks to God.

As the city stirred she had dispatched a hasty letter and woken the servants. Theirs would soon be one of the most important houses in Rome and they must be ready for a deluge of visitors and feasts. She had been about to rouse her charges when she heard the girls' voices and the crack of the shutter frame.

"If you are so awake, you had better come down here."

Her command is met by a tumble of laughter and voices, as the two young women throw themselves out of their room, across the landing and on to the stairs.

A stranger seeing them now might well think they are sisters, for though the elder is clearly the star—her adult beauty too arresting to brook comparison, while the younger is still closed in the bud—there is a camaraderie and intimacy between them which speaks more of family than friendship. "Borgia! Valencia! That's what they're calling. Is it true, Aunt?"

Lucrezia takes the last flight so fast that she can barely stop herself from colliding into her aunt at the bottom. As a child it was always her way to greet her father thus, launching herself into his arms from the steps, while he would pretend to stagger as he caught her. "It is him, yes? He has won?"

"Yes, by the grace of God, your father is elected Pope. Alexander VI. But that is no reason to parade around the house like a half-dressed courtesan with no manners. Where are your gloves? And what of your prayers? You should be on your knees thanking Our Lord Jesus Christ for the honor He brings upon the family."

But all this only meets with more laughter, and Adriana, who even in stately middle age still has something of the child in her, is won over. She hugs this young woman fiercely to her, then holds her at arm's length, pushing back the shock of chestnut hair, not so full nor so golden as Giulia's, but wonder enough in a city of raven-haired beauty.

"Oh, look at you. The daughter of a pope." And now there are tears in her laughter. Dear God, she thinks, how fast it has gone. Surely it cannot be so many years? The child had been not yet six when she had arrived to live with her. What bloody murder she had screamed at being taken from her mother. "Oh, enough now, Lucrezia." She had tried her best to soothe her. "You will see her still. But this is to be your home now. It is a noble palace and you will grow up here as a member of the great family to which you belong."

But the soothing had only made her sob louder. The only comfort she would take was from Cesare. How she worshipped her brother. For weeks she would not let him out of her sight, following him around, calling his name like a bleating lamb until he would have to stop to pick her up and carry her with him, though he was barely big enough himself to stand the weight. And when Juan mocked her for her weakness, he would punch and wrestle him until the younger one ran scream-ing to whoever would listen. And then the baby Jofré would join in, until the house was like a mad place and she had no idea how to calm them.

"Ah, we Borgias always cry as hard as we laugh." It did not help that Rodrigo always indulged them so, allowing everyone to yell and climb all over him the minute he walked in. "It is our nature to feel each slight and compliment more deeply than these insipid Romans," he would say, besotted by whatever incident or story of misbehavior had just been recounted. "They will settle soon enough. Meanwhile look at her, Adriana. Feast your eyes on that perfect nose, those cheeks plump as orchard plums. Vannozza's beauty is there already. Her mother's looks and her father's temperament. What a woman she will become."

And how nearly she is there, Adriana thinks as she stares at Lucrezia now. Fourteen next birthday and already her name is on a betrothal contract to a Spanish nobleman with estates in Valencia. Her eyes will shine as brightly as any of the gold in her dowry. But then they are all handsome, these bastard children of Rodrigo Borgia. How merciful of God to so readily forgive the carnal appetites of a servant he has singled out for greatness. Had she been a more envious woman, Adriana might feel some

resentment; she who despite Borgia blood and an Orsini marriage had only managed to squeeze out one scrawny, cockeyed
boy before her miserable, miserly husband died in apoplexy.

Life had been infinitely richer since his death. No widow's cell
in a convent for her. Instead, her beloved cardinal cousin Rodrigo
had made her guardian of his four children, and the status had
brought her a pleasure as deep as the responsibility she felt on
their behalf. Family. The greatest loyalty after God in the world.
For these eight years she has given it everything: no lengths she
has not gone to to elevate their name, nothing she would not do
for her handsome, manly cousin. Nothing, indeed, that she has
not done already.

"And good morning and congratulations to you, Daughter-in-
Law."

She turns now to the oh-so-lovely creature who stands nest-
ripe and willowy on the top step, and for a second her beauty
takes her breath away. It had been the same three years before,
when Giulia's marriage to her son had been first suggested by the
cardinal, a man who could make even an act of procurement—
for that was what it was—an elegant proposal.

"Giulia Farnese is her name: a magnificent girl, sweet, unaffected. Not a fabulously rich family, but you may trust me that
that will change soon enough. After their marriage, young Orsino
will want for nothing. Not now, nor ever again. He will be a rich
man with an estate in the country to rival any of his father's family, and the freedom to do with it as he wants. As his mother—and
in many ways the mother of all our family—he will, I know, listen to you. What do you say, Adriana?"

And he had sat back smiling, hands clasped over spreading
stomach. What she had said had been easy. What she had felt, she
had buried too deep to allow access. As for the feelings of the girl
herself, well, they had not been discussed. Not then and never
since that day. At the time of the wedding the girl had not been
much older than Lucrezia is now, but with a more lovely—and
perhaps more knowing—head on her shoulders. In a city of men

sworn to celibacy, beauty such as hers is its own power broker, and with the promise of the papacy there is already talk of a cardinal's hat for one of her brothers. Family. The greatest loyalty after God.

"You slept well, Giulia?"

"Until the noise, well enough." The young woman's voice, sweet though it is, is nowhere near as melodious as her body. She pulls back the long strands of hair that have slipped around her face, while the rest falls down her back, a sheet of gold reaching almost to her knees. That hair, along with the scandalous smoke of her marriage, is the stuff of the latest Roman gossip: Mary Magdalene and Venus fusing into the same woman in a cardinal's boudoir. It is said that the Vice-Chancellor moves his intercessional painting of the Virgin into the hall on those nights, lest the blessed Mary should be offended by what she might see. "When should I be ready? When will I be called for?"

"Oh, I am sure His Holiness will be busy with great business for some days. We must not expect a visit soon. Use the time to be at your toilet, sweeten your breath and choose carefully from your wardrobe. I do not need to tell you, Giulia, the wondrous favor that is now bestowed upon us all. And perhaps most upon you. To be the mistress of a pope is to be in the eye of all the world."

PHOTO: © CHARLIE HOPKINSON

SARAH DUNANT is the author of the international
bestsellers *Sacred Hearts* and *In the Company of
the Courtesan*, which have received major acclaim
on both sides of the Atlantic. Her earlier novels
include three Hannah Wolfe crime thrillers, as well
as *Snowstorms in a Hot Climate, Transgressions,* and
Mapping the Edge. She has two daughters and lives
in London and Florence.

www.sarahdunant.com
Facebook.com/SarahDunantAuthor